Scan

?50

*This is a stu...
that s... you away
and keeps you captivated until
the last page is turned . . .*

**He would marry her and possess her
in every way possible.**

The Duke of Kylemore knows her as Soraya, London's most celebrated courtesan. Men fight duels to spend an hour in her company. And only he comes close to taming her. Flying in the face of society, he decides to make her his bride; then, she vanishes, seemingly into thin air.

Dire circumstances have forced Verity Ashton to barter her innocence and change her name for the sake of her family. But Kylemore destroys her plans for a respectable life when he discovers her safe haven. He kidnaps her, sweeping her away to his hunting lodge in Scotland, where he vows to bend her to his will.

There he seduces her anew. Verity spends night after night with him in his bed . . . and though she still dreams of escape and independence, she knows she can never flee the unexpected, unwelcome love for the proud, powerful lover who claims her both body and soul.

By Anna Campbell

CLAIMING THE COURTESAN

ANNA CAMPBELL

CLAIMING The COURTESAN

An Avon Romantic Treasure

AVON BOOKS
An Imprint of HarperCollinsPublishers

AVON BOOKS
An Imprint of HarperCollins*Publishers*
10 East 53rd Street
New York, New York 10022-5299

Copyright © 2007 by Anna Campbell
ISBN: 978-0-06-123491-0
ISBN-10: 0-06-123491-5
www.avonromance.com

First Avon Books paperback printing: April 2007

Avon Trademark Reg. U.S. Pat. Off. and in Other Countries, Marca Registrada, Hecho en U.S.A.
HarperCollins® is a registered trademark of HarperCollins Publishers.

Printed in the U.S.A.

10 9 8 7 6 5 4 3 2 1

Acknowledgments

As this is a first book, I have a lot of people to acknowledge. First, I'd like to thank everyone at Avon Books who steered *Claiming the Courtesan* on its journey from manuscript to book. I'd particularly like to thank my wonderful editor there, Lucia Macro. Heartfelt thanks to the Art Department for my gorgeous cover. I'd also like to thank my agent, Julie Culver of Folio Literary Management, who supported this project from the moment she read it. My gratitude also goes to the marvelous writers I've met through Romance Writers of Australia and Romance Writers of America. I offer a special thank you to the members of my writing group, Turramurra Romance Writers in Sydney.

Finally, I dedicate this book to three remarkable women—my beloved mother, Dagmar; my oldest and dearest friend, Jill Turner; and my critique partner extraordinaire, Ann See.

Chapter 1

London, 1825

Justin Kinmurrie, Duke of Kylemore, looked across the tumble of stained sheets to where his mistress lay in apparent exhaustion. His Grace suspected the exhaustion was feigned, but he had been too well pleasured to take issue with the hint of artifice.

He paused in tying his neckcloth to admire her supine body, naked, creamy and glowing in the afternoon light. The long legs. The delicately rounded hips. The slightly concave stomach. The magnificent breasts cushioning the pigeon's blood ruby pendant he'd given her two eventful hours ago to mark the end of their first year together.

For a long and delightful moment, his attention lingered on those lush white mounds with their rosy crests. Then his eyes traveled up to her face, pale and pure as any painted Madonna's.

Even after all this time, the contrast of the harlot's body

and the saint's face sent a very masculine thrill through him.

She was beautiful.

She was the most notorious woman in London.

And she belonged to him, as much a part of his prestige as his perfect tailoring, his famous stables or his rich estates. He permitted himself a slight smile as he returned to dressing in front of the large gilt mirror.

"Shall I call Ben Ahbood to assist Your Grace?" Her extraordinary eyes, light gray and clear as water, were, as usual, expressionless in her gorgeous mask of a face. He sometimes wondered if this lay at the heart of her fascination—her innate detachment despite her skills as a lover.

No, it was more than that.

It was the promise that for the right touch, the right word, the right *man,* worlds of heat and feeling and meaning waited behind that serene gaze. The duke, for all his current well-being, had never deceived himself that he'd breached this formidable reserve. And after a year as her protector, he was beginning to understand he never would.

Did she guess how intriguing her distance made her? He would be surprised if she didn't. Emotional containment in no way meant she wasn't as clever as a glen full of vixens.

"My lord?"

He shook his head. "No. I can manage." In truth, her huge mute manservant, widely rumored to be a eunuch, made him uncomfortable, although he'd submit to keelhauling before he confessed to that shaming fact.

She stretched her supple body, the body that both maddened him and gave him more pleasure than he'd ever imagined. Kylemore recognized the return of arousal. By the glint in her eyes, so did she, damn her knowing soul.

"It is not so late." One slender hand slid up to toy with the ruby. The movement drew his attention—as, he realized, she was perfectly aware—to the round, full breasts he found so alluring.

"I am not at leisure this afternoon, madam."

"That's a shame," she said neutrally, rising to scoop a blue peignoir from the floor. Kylemore deliberately ignored her naked back and the way her buttocks tightened as she bent.

Or ignored the sight as much as any red-blooded man could.

It had always been this way between them, from the moment he'd met her cool assessing gaze across a crowded salon six years ago. She'd been another man's mistress then. And she'd had another keeper since, in spite of Kylemore's efforts to capture her interest. She had only consented to their present arrangement after the exchange of a small fortune and contracts detailed enough to keep a coven of lawyers in a flutter for a month.

But if he'd believed that finally possessing this woman would end their subtle battle for dominion, he was to be sadly disappointed. If anything, the game between them was more intense than ever.

And while the world might consider the advantages his, he knew his mistress had equally puissant weapons of her own. Her beauty. Her detachment. And most of all, the fact that he'd wanted her six years ago and, curse her, he wanted her still.

With unwilling regret, Kylemore watched her veil her lithe curves with the peignoir. Not that the diaphanous silk did much to conceal the glories beneath.

She flicked her black waist-length hair away from her face and came to stand behind him. Their eyes met in the mirror, where he took such a lamentably long time to dress.

"I can't persuade you to change your mind?" She twined her arms around him and pressed her warmth to his back, filling his head with the scents of recently satisfied woman and the sensual ambergris perfume she favored. He closed his eyes as her deft fingers fiddled with the fastening of his trousers, then slipped inside to stroke his stiffening cock.

The speed and vigor of his response made him brush her hand away. A man at the mercy of his appetites was no more than a brute animal. "Next time."

She didn't show any chagrin, Devil take her. She merely shrugged, wandered across to lean against the carved bedpost and watched as he repaired her predations on his clothing. He pulled on his coat and turned.

"I thank Your Grace for your continuing kindness." She stepped toward him and kissed him on the mouth.

They rarely kissed, and a kiss as a gesture of affection was an unprecedented event.

But that's what this felt like to Kylemore. She wasn't trying to seduce him. After a year, he would recognize seduction. And he'd already given her the extravagant pendant. Even greedy as she was, she couldn't hope to coax another maharajah's bauble from his pocket.

No, he could only assume she'd kissed him because she'd wanted to.

That revolutionary idea had just taken hold when she drew away. The soft pink lips that had clung so sweetly to his—and sweet was the only word he could bring to mind—curled into a faint smile. "Good day to you, Your Grace."

He snatched at her hand and, still lost in the memory of her kiss—which was absurd, given the debaucheries they had indulged in all afternoon—raised her slender fingers to his lips with the reverence due to a princess.

When he lifted his head, he caught a bewilderment that matched his own in her silver eyes. "Good day to you too, madam."

He released her and strode from the room, down the stairs and out of the villa he'd bought her a year ago. But no matter how far he went, he couldn't quite banish the memory of her mouth on his in a kiss that was almost . . . *innocent*.

His infamous, dangerous, enigmatic Soraya. And he was no closer to understanding her now than he'd been six years ago.

She heard the duke's determined footsteps take him out of the neat little house. He always moved as if he knew exactly where he was going. It was one of the first things she'd noticed about him.

But for a moment, when she'd kissed him, he had looked young and unsure, not like the chilly, self-possessed Duke of Kylemore at all. Thoughtfully, she went behind a gaudy—and remarkably lewd—Chinese screen and replaced the aqua peignoir with a plain cotton wrap. There was a knock on the door just as she emerged.

"Come in," she said, absently collecting discarded garments from the floor. The house had a full domestic staff, all on the duke's retainer, but old habits died hard.

A hulking figure in striped Eastern robes entered and observed her out of perceptive dark brown eyes.

"I've got those lasses downstairs heating water for your bath, Verity," he said in the thick Yorkshire accent she had tried and failed to eradicate.

"Thank you." Verity Ashton, familiar to the world as the incomparable Soraya, looked around the wreck of the bedroom. "I can hardly believe my time as Soraya is over at last."

The man sighed and tugged off his flowing headdress. Immediately, the inscrutable Ben Ahbood, mute Arabian guardian to London's most scandalous demimondaine, became Benjamin Ashton, North Country farm lad and as unassailably English as pork pies or the white cliffs of Dover. "Did you say owt to his nibs?"

Verity ignored the hint of hostility toward the duke. Her

younger brother hadn't approved of any of her protectors, but for some reason, he reserved particular opprobrium for Kylemore. An antipathy she suspected the duke shared, if he could bring himself to admit feeling anything for so lowly a creature as a fallen woman's manservant.

"No, you and I agreed it's better just to disappear."

Ben made a disapproving sound deep in his throat. "But now you're feeling bad about it. I don't know how a soft-hearted widgeon like you survives in this cutthroat world." He took a tray from the dresser and began methodically stacking scattered plates and glassware. The disordered room, she knew, offended his sturdy yeoman's mind.

In his four years with her, Ben had never really reconciled himself to her profession. If he hadn't been a mere child of ten when she'd launched her present career, he would have stopped her, she knew. But then, if he hadn't been so young, if her sister hadn't been even younger, perhaps she'd have had some choice in the matter.

"I think . . . I think the duke is an unhappy man," she said softly, dismissing the old memories. She rarely dwelt on the past, but today was an ending, so inevitably she contemplated Soraya's beginnings.

Ben cast her an unimpressed glance. "As unhappy as a great fortune and a pretty face and all a man can want could be. He's nobbut spoilt, that's all. He won't like losing his toy. But all that lovely brass will soon buy him another. Don't fret yourself over yon high-toned bastard."

"Not saying good-bye seems shabby. We don't have to sneak away. When I became the duke's mistress, he knew the arrangement was only for a year. He signed a contract that said so."

"He was so mad with lust back then, he would have signed away his soul if you'd asked. And smiled as he did it. Take my word, lass—a written agreement means nowt to a sodding duke. When he got you, he'd wanted you for five long years. He meant to have you, never mind the price."

She bent her head, studying the fine Turkish carpet beneath her feet. It was, in fact, the only genuine Middle Eastern item in the room.

"I suppose so."

Not for the first time, she wished she'd never kissed the duke. Any demirep worth her hire knew that was asking for trouble.

"You're eight and twenty, Verity. You'll soon be too long in the tooth for this lark. Then see if high and mighty Kylemore thinks twice before changing you in for a fresher bit of muslin."

Verity laughed briefly. "What an old crone you make me sound!"

Her brother smiled back. "Oh, I don't reckon you're ready for the knacker's yet. But you've planned this a long time. Don't let misplaced pity change your mind."

"You're right." The duke had always been a means to an end, her chance to leave this unnatural life behind forever. He'd soon recover from whatever damage her departure inflicted on his pride. "Soraya is no more."

Ben's smile widened. "That's grand, lass. Aye, and I don't mind telling you summat else—I'll be right glad to see the back of Ben bloody Ahbood, the sultan's favorite eunuch, as well!"

An hour after leaving his mistress, the Duke of Kylemore stood in his large library, embroiled in a quarrel with his mother.

This was in no sense an exceptional occurrence. Kylemore and the duchess shared a difficult relationship at the best of times—and the best of times were fleeting and rare. But today's clash was even more bitter than usual.

"You will marry, Justin! You owe it to your name and your family. You owe it to me. You owe it to the title." This wasn't a new conflict, but his mother had taken it up with particular vehemence this afternoon. She stood opposite him, tall and slender, and blindly set on her wishes prevailing.

"There are times I believe the world would be a better place if the title sank into permanent oblivion," Kylemore said wearily, leaning one elbow on the carved marble mantelpiece and staring down into the unlit grate.

"Justin! What would your dear departed father say if he could hear you?"

"My father was too addicted to drink, opium and the viler sins of the flesh to care."

"How dare you say that?"

"Because it's true." Kylemore looked up. With a sense of inevitability, he watched his mother shake out a scrap of lace to dab at her eyes.

"What in heaven's name did I do to deserve a son who is so unfeeling?"

"I don't believe that's a line of argument you wish to pursue, madam," he said icily.

His mother could produce crocodile tears at will. The sight of her clutching a handkerchief evinced only ennui.

"Letitia would make you the perfect wife, Justin."

Kylemore suppressed a shudder. "She'd make you the perfect spy, you mean." His mother had pushed her ward, Lady Letitia Wade, at him for years. But recently, her efforts had become increasingly desperate, perhaps because she saw any hold she had over her son dwindling away to nothing.

Margaret, Duchess of Kylemore, cared for one thing only—power. In its pursuit, she'd seduced half the government, lied, connived and manipulated. Without a shred of compunction, she destroyed anyone and anything that hindered her own selfish ends. He'd seen her in action often enough.

But her days of influence faded, and she knew it. Planting the whey-faced Letitia, always utterly her creature, into her son's household was something of a last stand.

The duchess's delicate chin took on a stubborn line. "People are talking. If you don't make it right, the poor child's reputation will be beyond redemption."

"If there is gossip, it has only one source. And that is you." Kylemore took a step closer. "I will never take that sheep-featured little sneak to my bed. If tongues are wagging about her sleeping under my roof, perfectly well chaperoned, I might point out, that can easily be remedied. The dowerhouse is ready for occupancy."

His mother's yelp of outrage held no artifice. "Leave Town? In the middle of the season? You must be mad. Everyone will condemn you for cruelty and neglect if you compel me to this monstrous act."

Kylemore had had enough. He perhaps hadn't hated his mother for his full twenty-seven years, but, God, he felt as if he had. And the ideal revenge lay so close to hand. The moment had arrived to show the duchess how truly monstrous he could be.

He permitted himself a cold smile. "I think not. The world will consider my actions perfectly reasonable in a newly married man."

Of course, his mother didn't immediately understand. Her fine-boned face, with its deep blue eyes and black, winged brows—a face whose twin he saw and loathed every time he passed a mirror—cleared with relief. "Oh, Justin! You were bamming me. Lud, I should have guessed. Letitia will be in a transport. She's always held a *tendre* for you."

Kylemore had no difficulty keeping his smile in place. "I doubt it." The duchess's ward was terrified of him, he knew. That the chit contemplated him as a husband without running screaming to the nearest nunnery spoke volumes for

Margaret's sway over her. "But I'm afraid you mistake me, Mother."

The duchess was an astute woman, although vanity and self-interest sometimes clouded her judgment. "Don't do anything rash to spite me, Justin. Remember the Kinmurrie honor," she said, abruptly somber.

"Oh, the Kinmurrie honor is uppermost in my mind, dear Mother." He saw her flinch at the savage edge he lent the endearment. "I intend to bring home a bride to do that honor proud."

"Justin . . ." She reached out to touch him, but he moved out of her reach. He was pleased to note she was seriously frightened now.

"I don't expect a long betrothal, Mother. My wife will wish to take up her duties as soon as possible. Given the situation, you and Letitia should make arrangements for an early removal." He bowed briefly in her direction. "Your servant." He stalked out of the library, his mind hard with a determination as bright as a diamond.

Verity was in the kitchen when the maid found her. "Beg pardon, miss, but His Grace is in the drawing room asking for you."

"What?" She spun around too quickly and knocked the pottery candlestick she was packing to the flagstones.

"Oh, miss!" Elsie fluttered around her, wringing her hands at the shattered mess on the floor. "Oh, miss, don't move or you'll cut yourself."

"It's all right, Elsie." Although, in fact, Verity had been rather fond of the sturdy brown candlestick. "Did you say the Duke of Kylemore was here?"

"Yes, miss. I'll get a broom and sweep up the pieces."

The terrified pounding of Verity's heart blocked out the maid's fussing. Why was Kylemore here? He called on her with almost military regularity on Mondays, Tuesdays and Thursdays. He arrived, he took his pleasure, he departed. Occasionally, he sent a carriage to bring her into Town for the theater or a party. But having left Kensington, he never, ever returned on the same day.

Was it a coincidence this was the very evening she meant to disappear from his life? He must have found out. But how? She'd been so discreet, so careful.

Her hands shook as she pulled off her grubby apron and stepped over Elsie, who was dealing with the remains of the candlestick. Verity hardly did the legendary Soraya justice in her plain gray muslin, but antagonizing the duke by making him wait seemed unwise. If he'd discovered her plans, she needed every shred of goodwill she could garner.

Although she sailed into his presence with her head high, her heart raced. Her intentions weren't strictly illegal, but strict definitions of legality became irrelevant if one's enemy was a powerful man. And a duke was about as powerful as a man could be.

"Your Grace? What an . . . unexpected pleasure."

Slowly, he turned from contemplating the empty spaces on the walls. The picture dealer had left in the last hour with the unremarkable artworks Kylemore had deemed suitable for his mistress's abode.

Verity rushed in before he could speak. "I shall order tea. Or would Your Grace prefer to . . . go upstairs?" The bluntness was unworthy of the great Soraya, but she was badly rattled.

The duke's puzzled gaze settled on her with much the same expression he had worn facing the blank walls. "You look . . . different."

Verity could imagine she did. Soraya never appeared before her protector in less than her best—unless she wore nothing at all.

Kylemore considered the depleted room. "What is happening here?"

Verity gave Soraya's laugh—low, husky, endlessly suggestive. "Your Grace has caught me in a domestic moment. We are cleaning the house." With studied elegance, she subsided onto a chaise longue and gestured for the duke to be seated.

"We? I don't expect my mistress to play the household drudge. If you require more staff, you need only ask." He sat opposite her, all black-haired, hawk-nosed magnificence. His gentian-blue eyes surveyed her critically.

She shrugged. "I like to see my standards are met, Your Grace. The house is, after all, mine." She hoped he'd recall the reminder after she'd gone.

"You have a smudge on your cheek."

Unbelievably, she colored. She, who had traded her chastity for a livelihood at the age of fifteen. Today, it seemed, was to be full of singularities.

The kiss. The duke's second visit. And now a blush.

Perhaps the time had really come for the great Soraya to retire.

"I have displeased you with my appearance," she said evenly. "I shall go and change into a gown more appropriate to receive Your Grace." She started to rise.

"No, I am discourteous. I apologize."

Astonishment sent Verity back onto the chair.

Unprecedented indeed! She couldn't have just heard her proud, difficult lover say he was sorry.

The duke's expression was unreadable. "You could never be less than breathtaking."

"Thank you," she said, although his remark hadn't entirely sounded like a compliment.

"You will make a most spectacular duchess."

If she hadn't known better, she would have guessed he'd

spent the day in his cups. Her fear had subsided enough for her to find Kylemore's odd humor irritating.

"It is Your Grace's pleasure to joke, I see."

Kylemore's eyes glittered with a hard light. "I am far from joking, madam." His deep voice took on its customary tone of command. "I am here to inform you we will marry as soon as I have obtained a special license."

Shock forced a genuine laugh from her. "Now I know you really are mocking me." She stood, meaning to serve him a glass of wine, but he reached out and caught her wrist, forestalling her.

"This is a strange answer to my proposal."

"I haven't heard a proposal," she said before she could stop herself.

"I want you to be my wife."

She stared down into his face, noticing the muscle that jerked in his cheek. Strong emotion gripped him, she realized. Not only that; he was, it appeared, serious about this crackbrained idea.

"Your Grace, flattered as I am by your interest, you must see what you suggest is impossible." When his jaw took on a stubborn line, she continued in a harder voice. "Even if the world, your name and your family countenanced such a mésalliance, I am afraid my own pride would deny you."

"Pride?" He spoke as if the word were inconceivable in connection with a fallen creature such as herself. "This is a preferment beyond your wildest dreams."

"My dreams are surprisingly humble."

Beneath a growing sense of unreality, Verity was angry. Only an overbearing bully could expect her to be grateful for this lunatic offer. She was canny enough to see that he was hatching some scheme, although she couldn't fathom his purpose.

A more conceited woman would ascribe the duke's offer

to a sudden surfeit of passion. But Verity knew better. He was plotting something to his own advantage. And she had no intention of becoming entangled in whatever he was up to.

Her, a duchess? The idea was comical in its unreality.

She kept her voice cool. "Pray release me. Your tender wooing is likely to leave a bracelet of bruises." Not precisely true. His hold was firm without actually hurting her.

"I'll let you go when you answer me."

"I thought I had." Necessity meant she'd devoted most of her life to catering to self-centered men. Now she'd reached her limit. "But as Your Grace insists, here is my reply. I have submitted to becoming your mistress, my lord. No power on earth could compel me to become your wife."

Perhaps if he'd phrased his ridiculous suggestion less arrogantly, she might have tempered her refusal. Or perhaps with escape so close, she couldn't contain her natural frankness, hidden so long in the pretense of being Soraya.

Furious color bloomed along his cheekbones. "You respond hastily, madam, and with a disdain I cannot believe I deserve. I have come to lift you from the gutter into an honorable state of matrimony."

"At least I am free in the gutter."

He surged to his feet and glared down at her. Even their most extreme moments of passion had never held so much genuine emotion. "You speak very lightly of gutters. You forget I could destroy you with a word."

The duke loomed over her, tall, powerful, his lean muscled body radiating strength. But Verity refused to cower before him. Verity, not Soraya. Somewhere in this encounter, Soraya had vanished forever.

"Very pretty, sir. I almost find myself charmed into accepting your suit."

Verity thought he might strike her, he who had never lifted a hand in anger to her before. She braced herself. She'd endured violence in the past. She could endure it again.

But unbelievably, he mastered his rage. He unclasped her arm with an ironic gesture. "There is no purpose continuing now. You are overset and not thinking clearly."

Verity forbore to point out that he'd hardly been a paragon of tranquility himself. He had at last released her, he spoke of going, and after this afternoon, she never intended to see him again.

Speaking normally was an effort. "As Your Grace wishes." *Just go,* her heart cried. *Just go and leave me in peace.*

Secretly she had always liked the Duke of Kylemore, sensing the lonely battle he fought to maintain his facade of perfection. But his startling, woefully unsuitable proposal of marriage and his behavior in the last few minutes made her remember the old rumors of insanity running through the Kinmurrie line.

His high color indicated he was still far from calm. "I shall return for your answer tomorrow. In the meantime, spare some consideration for the Duchess of Kylemore's jewels. They make today's ruby look like a fairground trinket."

So you believe me to be no more than a grasping jade, Verity thought resentfully. She didn't blunt her sarcasm. "I assure you, my mind will dwell on nothing but diamonds and emeralds."

That didn't please him, she could see. "Tomorrow at four, madam. I await your consent." No gentle kiss on the hand now. Apparently his mistress merited a courtesy his prospective bride did not.

Kylemore ignored her bobbed curtsey and stalked toward the door. "As you should know by now, I always get what I want. And do not doubt I want this marriage." He sent a frosty nod in her direction, the picture of aristocratic male omnipotence, and left.

But when Kylemore rode up to the pretty little villa the next day, it was silent and empty. The notorious Soraya, his chosen weapon against his hated family, was gone.

Chapter 2

Kylemore entered the house and in a matter of moments ascertained it was not only uninhabited but also looted of everything of value.

Had his marriage proposal frightened his mistress into precipitate flight? He wouldn't have said Soraya was a woman who scared easily. Yesterday, she'd seemed outraged rather than terrified.

Perhaps his parting threat had sent her scurrying for whatever bolthole currently sheltered her beguiling hide. But he doubted it.

From long habit, he kept a tight rein on his temper. Pointless to vent his fury now. No, far better to conserve it for when he caught up with the deceitful trull.

And he would catch up with her.

He paused in the parlor. He should have realized what was afoot yesterday when so much had been missing from the house.

Cleaning indeed! He'd wager the rapacious piece had

never in her life encountered the sharp end of a scrubbing brush. Although to be fair, she'd been dressed for it. He had a sudden piercing vision of her sitting before him in that remarkably shabby frock.

Beautiful, of course, and damned fetching as always. But tall, straight and disdainful, as though she already were the duchess he planned to make her. And subtly, not the same person as the compliant courtesan he'd farewelled in the early afternoon.

When she'd sent him on his way with a kiss, damn her duplicitous soul to hell.

The Judas kiss.

He remembered her air of suppressed panic when he'd proposed. No, she'd plotted her betrayal long before he'd asked her to marry him. The house's forlorn abandonment reeked of a carefully executed departure.

He started to go upstairs when he heard a muffled thud from the back of the dwelling.

So he wasn't alone after all. With triumphant eagerness, he flung open the door from the parlor and found himself in a totally unfamiliar hallway. His heart pounded with an expectation that included a shaming dose of relief.

He strode down the shadowy corridor, his boot heels ringing on the flags. The kitchens had been cleared like the rest of the house. But here, all was not pristine. His eyes fell on a few scattered crumbs along the sink.

"Come out. I know you're here." His voice echoed in the empty room. "This is childish."

He began to bang open doors, coldly amused to think of the magnificent Soraya reduced to cowering in a cupboard.

But when he hurled wide the pantry door, he discovered instead a small servant girl, nearly catatonic with dread and clutching the remains of a bun.

"Jesus!" he cursed. "For God's sake, what are you doing? Come out at once!"

The girl whimpered, and to his horror, her eyes filled with tears.

"Stop that!" he snapped. "Where is your mistress?" *And mine,* he thought grimly.

She merely shook her head and pressed further away from him.

Kylemore took a deep breath. Terrifying the girl would render her useless as a source of information.

But beneath his impatience lingered a memory of just how it felt to be alone and defenseless and scared for your life. He bundled the unwelcome recollection back into the dark corner of his soul, where it lurked with other events he had no desire to revisit—ever.

"Come, child. I mean you no harm." He moved back from the door as if to prove his good intentions.

The maid didn't budge, but at least she spoke. "Please, sir! Please, Your Grace, don't hurt me. Mr. Ben turned us all off last night but I didn't have nowhere to go so I hid down here. Please don't hurt me."

"I have no intention of hurting you," he said with asperity, then immediately regretted it as she huddled into the wall once more. He deliberately gentled his tone. "You have my word. Come out where I can see you."

He stepped away as the girl emerged reluctantly. "I know you, don't I?"

Her curtsey was unsteady. "Yes, Your Grace. Elsie. I let you in yesterday. I didn't mean no mischief by staying. Mr. Ben said we was all to go to Your Grace's town house tomorrow for our wages. The buyers don't take over until next week. I didn't mean no harm, sir."

Kylemore spoke as kindly as he was able, given the tempest

raging inside him. "I'm sure you didn't, Elsie. This will remain our secret if you agree to answer my questions. Our secret and I'll give you a gold sovereign for your help."

Elsie's eyes rounded at the offer, although she still trembled. He assumed tête-à-têtes with the nobility were outside her ken.

"Yes, sir. Th-thank you, sir." She bobbed into another curtsey.

"First of all, where is your mistress?"

Elsie shook her head. "I don't know, Your Grace. She and Mr. Ben went off in a hired carriage last night. I was the only one left behind, but I didn't hear their direction. They was both dressed for traveling, though." Elsie, when not fearing for her life or virtue, was clearly far from stupid.

"Did they take all the household things with them?"

"No, sir. Only a few boxes in the carriage. Everything else was sold, even Miss Soraya's clothes. Which was odd. She still needs to dress herself, don't she?" Elsie relaxed into her story. "There's been blokes in and out of the house all week carting away pictures and furniture and stuff."

"And you believe the house has been sold as well?"

"Oh, it has, sir. A nabob's moving in. I caught a peek at him last week—all brown and burnt he is, sir. Quite nasty. Why, Mr. Ben, he said . . ."

Suddenly Kylemore realized just what had niggled at him earlier. "Mr. Ben? You mean Ben Ahbood, the servant? He spoke?" he asked sharply.

Elsie's confidence faltered and she looked at Kylemore with renewed nervousness. "Of course, sir."

"And he has spoken this whole time?" A horrible suspicion grew in his mind. A suspicion that the mystery of Soraya's disappearance wasn't such a mystery after all but the oldest story in the world.

Elsie clearly thought his questions were insane. "Yes, sir. How else could he tell us what to be getting on with?"

"And how did this Mr. Ben sound?" he asked in a dangerous tone.

"How do you mean, sir?"

He curbed his impatience before he panicked her into her cupboard again. "Did he speak as I do? As you do? Did he sound foreign?"

She frowned. "I don't know about foreign. He didn't sound like me—or you either, sir."

Given that Kylemore spoke with the clipped accents of the upper classes and Elsie had a decided Cockney twang, he couldn't say that narrowed the field much.

"And he and . . . and Miss Soraya." He nearly choked on the name. His mistress was lucky she wasn't here now or he might have choked her instead. "Did they seem close, friendly?"

"Oh, yes, sir!" Elsie said with enthusiasm.

Then she must have perceived his hostile reaction to that information, because she went on. "Not in any untoward way, sir. Just friendly. Affectionate, like. Please don't get the wrong idea about Miss Soraya, sir. She was always awful good to us staff, whatever else she was, begging your pardon. Why, she gave all of us a month's wages extra and good references afore she left. Even though she said she was sure Your Grace would see us right anyway, considering we was really working for you."

Kylemore was in no mood to listen to praises of his absconded paramour. But Elsie had clearly been fond of Soraya, and apart from further encomiums on the jade's character, he could discover little else from the girl. Eventually he sent her on her way with the promised sovereign and instructions to see his butler at Kylemore House about work in the kitchens there.

Then he furiously combed every inch of the villa, although he already knew the crafty bitch he'd kept in such high style would have made sure nothing here could help him trace her. She hadn't even left him so much as a mug to smash, and by the time he'd finished his mad search, he dearly needed to smash something. Preferably Ben Ahbood's smug face.

All the time, his mind circled the problem of Soraya and just how much of a fool she'd made of him in their dizzyingly expensive year together.

Ben Ahbood was not mute after all. If he was not mute, it was highly unlikely he was a eunuch either. And no man could know Soraya without wanting her.

So had she played Kylemore false with her manservant?

They had been living together, Devil take them. Only a soup-brained nitwit could imagine their relationship was innocent.

The idea of that hulking brute grunting over Soraya's pale naked beauty became too much. Cursing, Kylemore burst out of the house into the garden. He breathed deeply and struggled to order the anarchy hurtling through his head.

He was Cold Kylemore, famous for his self-control. No damned twopenny whore and her fancy man could disrupt his sangfroid.

Where the hell could she have gone? Why in the name of all that was holy had she left him? Had she really abandoned him for another lover?

Casting around desperately for clues to her disappearance, the duke thought back to what he knew of the woman who had shared his bed this past year. Surprisingly little, he realized.

Now, futilely, he wished he'd taken the time to find out more. But he had been so lost to his physical passion that he'd never paused to explore more than her body.

He turned sightlessly back toward the house that had witnessed some of the few happy hours of his adult life. With evening closing in, it loomed before him. Dark. Lost. Forsaken.

If that treacherous slut thought she had left the Duke of Kylemore similarly bereft, she'd learned nothing during their liaison.

And if she imagined she had eluded him with her lies and her midnight flit, she was wrong about that as well.

"Damn her," he whispered into the encroaching night. "Damn her to hell." He could no longer bear to be here, where Soraya had been and now so abruptly was not.

The empty house seemed to mock him as he mounted his horse. Ignoring the animal's snort of protest, he wheeled around and galloped for London in a furious clatter of hooves.

He rode hard. He rode blindly. He rode without a care for the fine horseflesh between his thighs. And all the time, his mind beat out a rhythm of the chase.

Soraya, Soraya, Soraya.

Only when he was back in Town did necessity force him to ease his breakneck pace. When his horse nearly trampled a woman crossing the street, he took a deep breath and hauled on the reins.

He shook his head to clear it and looked around at the twilit city. How strange that life should continue normally for other people when his own world had changed so irrevocably in the space of an afternoon. Around him, shopkeepers closed up, children played with hoops and tops and dolls, families took the late spring air. All perfectly usual. All things he'd seen ten thousand times before.

His attention focused on a pair of sweethearts poring over a shop window. A tall young man and a pretty blonde girl.

How he hated them. How he wanted them dead.

And he wanted them to scream as they died.

A woman in a stylish bonnet moved past them, a small woman with a trim waist and a fashionable air. A woman who moved with a peculiar grace.

His breath caught in his throat.

He flung himself from the saddle. In this crowd, he had a better chance of catching her on foot. And by heaven, he meant to catch her.

The woman turned the corner out of sight.

Soraya had underestimated him indeed if she'd thought he wouldn't find her so close to home.

Without a thought for his horse, he set off at a run. He treated the people in the street as so many inanimate obstacles, hurling them out of the way without excuse or apology, not pausing when he recklessly knocked a child's hoop flying or sent a puppy skittering out of his path. Only one thing mattered—that the traitorous strumpet didn't escape him.

As he rounded the corner, he slipped and almost fell. When he steadied himself against the rough brickwork, the jade was ahead of him, looking for all the world as if she was enjoying a pleasant evening's stroll.

Oh, she would pay for what she'd done to him. She would pay with everything she had to give. And then he would demand more. And she didn't even know her short-lived bid for freedom had ended.

How delightful. How he would laugh when he saw her face.

His lips curved in a wolfish smile as he contemplated his inevitable triumph over the presumptuous baggage.

He dived forward and grabbed her, not caring how his fingers bit into that slender shoulder. The woman gasped and turned.

But he already knew.

"I beg your pardon?" she snapped in outrage.

Kylemore's hand dropped away as an awful weight settled

on his heart. This was not Soraya. Soraya was too clever to risk discovery after what he now recognized as all her planning.

"I was mistaken, madam. My apologies. I thought you were someone else."

"Keep your hands to yourself, sir, until you are sure of whom you are accosting!" She was an attractive piece, past first youth, but with a nice sensual mouth and flashing dark eyes. Once, he might have taken the time to soothe her temper and discover whether that shapely figure was a product of corsetry alone.

Kylemore made his excuses again, but in truth, he'd already forgotten the woman. He flicked her from his mind with no more thought than he'd give a speck of lint on his coat. Less thought, in fact. His tailoring was always high on his list of priorities.

He headed back to where he'd leaped so precipitately from the saddle. God knew if his horse would still be there.

But some public-minded citizen had tied it to a hitching post outside an inn. At least he wouldn't have to walk all the way to Mayfair—although in his present frame of mind, it might be safer if he did.

He mounted and rode on, but his attention was focused far from the capital's busy streets.

Where could Soraya be? He had known her six years. Something over that time must hint at her whereabouts.

With a pang he didn't want to examine, he recalled his first sight of her. Like lightning from a clear summer sky, she had just arrived in London from Paris. Her protector then had been Sir Eldreth Morse, a rich and aging baronet who had held some embassy position in the French capital. Sir Eldreth was a bachelor with a passion for beautiful things. And by far the most beautiful thing in his famous collection was his young mistress, the incomparable Soraya.

Kylemore, frankly curious to view this creature who had set the men of the ton on their collective ear, had met her at Morse's town house shortly afterward. He'd been unprepared for his reaction, although the level of the furor should have warned him.

Because, of course, London had seen beautiful women before.

But Soraya was . . . more.

One look at her across Sir Eldreth's drawing room and Kylemore had known the same urge to possess and conquer that had raised his reaving ancestors from minor Highland lairds to dukes of the realm.

But the cool-eyed beauty's lack of interest in him had been insultingly plain. Nothing he did or said, no material inducement he dangled before her exquisite nose could separate her from her elderly lover.

That season, every man in the beau monde seemed to scheme to steal her away. Until it finally became obvious she was, astonishingly, perfectly content to remain loyal to her keeper.

And that was when her real notoriety started.

Three young men, all bright hopes of their generation, shot themselves for love of her. There were duels, several killing matters, even though the survivors must have known their victory brought them no closer to obtaining what they so desperately desired.

Within months of her arrival, Sir Eldreth Morse's mistress was the most hated and most idolized and most scandalous woman in England.

Kylemore observed the chaos with increasing frustration. Surely he could do something to make her his. But all his power, all his fortune, all his attractions couldn't shift her from her damned inexplicable devotion to the portly baronet.

Secretly, he sent investigators to France to ferret out what they could about her. But she'd been both as famous, as faithful and as elusive in Paris as she was in London.

Of course, rumors abounded, but all proved infuriatingly difficult to substantiate. Some said Sir Eldreth had rescued her from a Turkish harem—or a harem in Egypt or Syria or Persia. Unlikely heroics for the notably sedentary baronet, although the evidence of the girl's name indicated some exotic origin.

If her name really was Soraya, which Kylemore had always doubted.

Other people believed she was a laundress Morse had picked up in the alleyways around Les Halles. Or she was a former child prostitute who had seen her chance with the rich English milord and taken it.

Kylemore always treated these tales—and even more outlandish stories he heard over the years—with skepticism. His own guess about her, if she was indeed French, was she came from a respectable family that had fallen foul of the Revolution or Bonaparte. He'd lay money that breeding lurked somewhere in her background. Her effortless self-possession outdid any fine lady he knew.

Perhaps she was English. She spoke the language as well as he did.

"Watch it, yer lordship!"

The shout wrenched Kylemore back to the present. A thickset countryman clutched at his horse's bridle, clearly trying to save himself from being knocked down.

The famous Kinmurrie glare cowed the fellow, although Kylemore knew the bumpkin was only guilty of wandering unwittingly into his path. He forced himself to concentrate on reaching Grosvenor Square without causing damage either to himself, his mount or London's traffic.

* * *

The moment Kylemore slammed into his town house, his mother appeared at the top of the staircase. Since their argument yesterday, he had deliberately avoided her. He wondered with distant amusement just how long she'd been hovering above, waiting for him to come back. He hoped it was hours.

"Justin, I must speak with you."

He stripped off his gloves and handed them to the attendant footman. "Not now, madam."

She marched down the steps with elegant determination. "What plans are you making? What is this ridiculous talk of an engagement?"

"I shall inform you of developments." He turned toward his library.

His mother forgot her self-importance to go so far as to hurry after him. "That's not good enough! And you cannot really expect me to leave London!"

He whirled on her as he reached the door. "I have spoken, madam. And as head of this family, I expect to be obeyed. You and your ward will be gone from this house by week's end."

"Justin, this is cruel. This is . . ."

He didn't know what she read in his face, but his expression must have been daunting enough to convince her that retreat was the wisest course. And the duchess was a woman who quailed at nothing.

"As you wish," she said in a subdued tone he'd never heard from her before.

"Yes, as I wish," he said savagely, knowing that nothing, in fact, was as he wished.

He strode into his library without a backward glance. Soraya didn't know what she'd unleashed in her lover by deserting him. But she would find out. And she would be sorry.

Kylemore poured himself a brandy and downed it in a single gulp. He was usually a man of abstemious habits. His father's pathetic example had always stood as a warning against the dangers of self-indulgence. But now he refilled his glass and collapsed in a chair in front of the fire. He had agreed to meet his cronies at his club, but he was in no mood to act the civilized gentleman tonight.

The liquor's warmth couldn't melt the chill inside him. What was Soraya doing now? Had she left him for another protector? Was his humiliation already public knowledge? Did the world snigger tonight at the thought of Kylemore's mistress fleecing some other rich blockhead?

How his rivals would gloat at his rejection. How they would fawn over the fortunate fellow who was now Soraya's keeper.

He swore and flung the empty glass into the fire.

Had she taken another lover? Or had her favors become her brawny manservant's exclusive prerogative? The thought aroused another burst of sick anger. Just when had Ben Ahbood become an inseparable part of Soraya's mystique?

Kylemore couldn't remember the first time he'd noticed the brute. He'd certainly been with Soraya after Sir Eldreth's death three years ago, when the male half of the beau monde had predictably gone mad trying to secure her interest. Two other dukes had been in the running, as well as an Italian prince and one of the tsar's cousins, not to mention a parcel of fellows holding lesser titles.

In the six months Soraya took to consider her next step, there were more duels between especially excitable supplicants. Although thankfully, this time, the self-destructive element among society's sprigs controlled their inclinations to end it all.

Kylemore had been sure of himself—and of her—and had remained above the vulgar displays of masculine competitiveness that kept London buzzing that season. He'd always known at some bone-deep level she would be his. And she'd known that too. She put up a great show of indifference, but some link, some invisible thread tugged her inexorably toward him.

So he stood apart from the fray and waited for her inevitable choice. Only to watch Soraya do the utterly unanticipated.

From her clamoring legion of admirers, she chose James Mallory. Not a whiff of a title. A mere Mr., a shy young man recently back from India. Of good but unremarkable family. And rich. At least there she'd lived up to Kylemore's expectations.

If his inconvenient fascination for the chit had allowed, Kylemore would have given up the game then and there. She'd had her shot at greatness and instead given herself to a commonplace milksop with no social polish, however deep his pockets were.

Although to be fair, James Mallory had cut quite a dash after Soraya singled him out as her lover. He'd soon developed enough town bronze to snare one of the season's prettiest heiresses. To whom, then, amazingly, he showed every sign of fidelity.

Which meant Soraya was back seeking a protector.

Not that she gave any indication her sudden freedom was unwelcome. And by this stage, Ben Ahbood, or whatever the bastard's name really was, had been very much in evidence.

Of course, she had neither explained nor excused. The legendary Soraya's factotum was a mute Arabian Samson. If the world disapproved, she shrugged her straight, slender shoulders and proceeded just as she pleased.

This time, Kylemore left nothing to chance. No gentlemanly hanging back, no self-confident hesitation in expressing his interest. The morning Mallory's engagement to Lady Sarah Coote was announced, Kylemore presented his card at Soraya's house. He'd waited five years. He had no intention of waiting one moment longer.

Soraya appeared neither delighted, dismayed nor disconcerted to find a duke in her parlor at an hour more suitable for breakfast than for callers. Instead, she listened calmly and, Devil take her, had said she would think about what he proposed. Her protector hadn't been in evidence, although Kylemore would have happily faced him down if he had.

But, Kylemore remembered with a churning in his belly, Ben Ahbood had admitted him to the house, then sent him on his way. And the lout's manner toward him had done no honor to his dignity as a duke.

Soraya's response had come a week later, couched in a swathe of legalities. Kylemore's original offer had been extravagant. She requested he increase it to a king's ransom, including clear title to all property and goods he gave her.

And, he remembered now with another unpleasant twinge, after a year, if either party were dissatisfied, the arrangement ceased forthwith.

Oh, she'd been clever, his grasping, cunning mistress. Clever and faithless. And he'd been guilty of fatal complacency.

She'd been overtly true to her two previous keepers. He should know—he had cast every lure to coax her away. But perhaps she'd duped everyone and her real allegiance was to the blackguard who lived hugger-mugger with her.

Her subtle hints about Ben Ahbood's sexual incapability had been a masterstroke. Kylemore had always admired Soraya, but her audacity now took his breath away.

His excellent brain—like his looks, inherited from his despised mother—clicked back into working order. Coldly, calmly, he vowed to track down the cozening trollop and her lover.

The blood of generations of ruthless men ran in his veins. Soraya had no idea what she'd started when she played the Duke of Kylemore for a fool. He smiled in cold anticipation of the day she discovered the mistake she'd made in betraying Justin Kinmurrie.

A late summer storm had stirred the North Sea off Whitby Sands into fury. Verity flung the veil back from her black bonnet and stared out into the windswept world around her. The beach was almost deserted, and no one would notice the widow Symonds hold her face up to the cold gale or smile out at the restless ocean.

She'd been in Whitby for three months and still could hardly believe that the transition to her new life had been so easy.

The scandalous Soraya had left London with her manservant. Several days later, the respectable widow Mrs. Charles Symonds had taken a house in this Yorkshire fishing town with her brother, Benjamin Ashton.

I'm free, I'm free, her heart chanted in time with the gray water lashing the shore.

I'm free. I'm independent. My life is my own at last.

I'm free, but becoming uncomfortably damp, her more practical self pointed out as spray flew up to darken her black bombazine. She chuckled and moved back from the edge.

The townspeople, all good sturdy Yorkshire folk, had been mildly curious about her arrival with her brother but had soon accepted them. Verity Symonds was still in deep mourning for the young husband she'd lost to a fever six months ago. The young husband who had left his relict perfectly well provided for, by all appearances.

Mr. Benjamin Ashton, too, seemed a good enough chap, clearly from local stock, as he, unlike his sister, hadn't lost his accent. In fact, it was soon bruited about that Mr. Ashton sought a suitable property where he could establish a sheep farm.

As she climbed the steps to her house at the top of the

ridge, Verity considered whether she'd stay in Whitby. She loved the sea and the old town and the brooding ruins of the ancient abbey on the hill. The place was far from the eyes of society and conveniently close to the moors, where her brother had always wanted to settle.

Ben had hated London. She found it an immense satisfaction to witness his transparent happiness at resuming his true identity. At last, he followed his own ambitions after playing her silent bodyguard for so long. Helping him fulfill his dreams was the very least she owed him.

Not for the first time, she wished she could remove her sister from the school near Winchester where she'd boarded since she was five years old. How wonderful to reunite the entire Ashton family. But the risk was too great that Soraya's notoriety would taint Maria's future.

Wherever Verity went, Soraya would always cast a shadow. That sobering thought accompanied her up the last of the steep rise to her lodgings.

She let herself into the house and paused in the confined hallway to remove her bonnet and gloves. Her brother's voice was raised in anger somewhere at the back.

This was strange enough to make her hurry toward the sound. But as she neared the kitchen, it was the second voice she heard—soft but clear, and as cutting as a saber through flesh—that made her stop.

The Duke of Kylemore had found her.

Chapter 3

How long did Verity stand in that dim corridor while her foolish sense of security leached away to nothing? Later, common sense told her it must only have been seconds. Dread held her immobile. She had a prescience of doom as relentless as those pounding waves upon the beach, where she'd been so stupidly sure of herself.

When awareness returned, she was halfway back to the door. If she ran far enough and fast enough, surely Kylemore wouldn't follow. Britain held a thousand places to hide. Or she could go abroad. He'd never trace her in America. Or New South Wales. Or wildest Borneo, if it came to that.

With shaking hands, she reached out for her bonnet, then realized just what she was doing. She couldn't flee with merely the clothes she stood up in and the few coins in her reticule. The sound of a crash, probably a chair smashing on the flagstones in the kitchen, made up her mind for her.

The duke had no legal claim on her. She'd held her own against him as Soraya. Verity Ashton was no lesser creature. She took a deep breath, turned and headed toward the kitchen.

The duke pinned Ben to one wall, his cane across her brother's throat. The sight of her lover after so long made Verity's breath hitch with fear as she paused in the doorway.

"Come on, you lying bastard. Hit me! You know you want to," Kylemore taunted in a low, jeering voice. "Hit me, for Christ's sake."

"You'd like that, wouldn't you?" Ben, thank God, kept his fists by his sides. "But magistrates don't encourage the lower orders to beat up the bloody nobility. I won't hang for the sake of your sodding pretty face, Your Grace." This last with utter contempt.

A jerk of the stick against Ben's Adam's apple made him gag. "If you don't hang for that, Lord knows, you'll hang for something else."

"Stop it," Verity said firmly. Her apparent calmness hid trembling terror. "For pity's sake, there's no need for this!"

Neither looked at her.

The duke continued, still in that same soft, teasingly threatening tone. "How does it feel to know she gave it all to me for so long? To know you begged for another man's leavings? Did you listen at the door to hear every sweet little moan and sigh she made as I did exactly what I wanted to her?"

"I said stop it!" Verity insisted more sharply. The duke had discovered most of their secrets—how else had he found them? And he was clearly mistaken, and fuming, about her relationship with her former manservant.

Ben's smile was scornful. "You're nowt to her but a nice fat fortune. Every moan and sigh meant gold. Gold for her and gold for me. So, my lord, still feel so bloody high and mighty?"

Verity glanced across to where her maid-of-all-work

watched from the corner with a mixture of avidity and horror. Whatever else resulted from this afternoon, her chances of remaining in Whitby as a respectable widow had just disintegrated. But before she worried about that, she somehow had to stop her lover from murdering her brother.

Kylemore smiled back at Ben with a distinctly vulpine curve to his lips. "Perhaps it was you she gulled. While your filthy hands defiled that perfect white flesh, she lay there wishing for a real man."

Ben's face twisted with revulsion. "You? A real man? You're nowt but spleen and vanity tricked out in fancy rags. When the lass wanted a real man, she knew where to turn."

Dear heaven, if she didn't do something quickly, there would be bloodshed. The scent of impending violence rose another notch. While Ben might outweigh the duke, Kylemore's lean body was lithe and strong, as she was intimately aware.

"Listen, you idiots!" With unsteady hands, she grabbed a large blue-and-white platter from the dresser near the door.

"I'll kill you." Unbelievably, Kylemore's voice didn't rise, although Ben, she saw, struggled to contain his thirst to fight back. She knew if her brother made the slightest retaliation, the duke would set out with utter mercilessness to destroy him. That cane concealed a sword. He'd shown her the mechanism one afternoon in Kensington.

"Then who will hang, Your Grace?" Ben asked snidely.

This had gone more than far enough. "You're both acting like schoolboys!" She lifted the platter and deliberately dashed it against the flagstones.

The sound of smashing crockery echoed in the suddenly silent room.

Her gesture finally captured their attention. The duke turned toward her, his blue eyes blind with anger. Ben, too, looked in her direction, although the duke's stick kept him trapped. She realized that through all their squabbling over her, neither had actually known she'd been in the room with them.

She drew herself up and spoke with all the authority the woman who had once been the great Soraya could muster. "Benjamin Ashton, stop baiting him. We're in enough trouble." She turned to the duke. "And you, Your Grace, let him go."

Kylemore's lip lifted in a sneer. "Pleading for your lover, madam?"

She resisted an urge to hurl more crockery. "He's not my lover." Then, momentarily forgetting the respect due to his exalted rank, she spat, "He's my brother, you damned fool."

"Your brother." Strangely, Kylemore didn't even consider questioning the truth of her assertion.

He stared at the woman he'd at last found, then around the stark little kitchen. He hadn't noticed much about it when he'd stormed in to find the abhorred Ben Ahbood showing every sign of being at home. All he'd wanted then had been to kill. The incongruity of this adequate, but hardly luxurious, house as a setting for his jewel of a Soraya hadn't registered.

But it registered now as he took in the details of his surroundings.

"Yes, my brother." She moved forward and righted the chair he'd knocked over when he'd lunged at his rival.

Except his rival was apparently no rival at all. He'd tormented himself night and day over a chimera.

"Let him go. Your quarrel is with me," Soraya said. In spite of all the hatred he'd expended on her since her disappearance, that husky voice fell on his tortured, lonely soul like rain on parched earth.

He lowered his stick, and Ben Ahbood—Ben Ashton, he

supposed—slumped gasping against the wall. The hostile black eyes, familiar now as they had been in the Arabian manservant, focused on him.

"Get out," the younger man rasped.

"Oh, be quiet, Ben," Soraya said wearily. She looked across at the maid. "Marjorie, please clean up this mess." She turned on her heel. "If Your Grace would follow me? Ben, stay here. I wish to speak to the duke alone."

Kylemore almost laughed. She did a damn fine job of turning a drama of Shakespearean proportions into a domestic comedy. He even found himself following that straight, black-clad back down the hallway and into a neat parlor. Discovering his exotic mistress ensconced in bourgeois—and apparently chaste—respectability was the last thing he'd pictured.

She turned to face him, her chin up. He could have told her she was wasting her time trying to blend in with her lackluster environment. No one—no man, in particular—would ever believe she was born for anything but sin.

The howling beast that had taken up residence in his heart since she'd gone quietened as she leveled her cool gray eyes on him. "I owe you an apology, Your Grace."

That was the very least she owed him, the unscrupulous baggage. He'd prefer her on her knees, begging forgiveness. But that wasn't Soraya's style, as he should have known.

She went on in the same dispassionate voice. "I wanted to tell you it was over, but my brother insisted you'd make trouble and I allowed him to persuade me against my better judgment."

Her brother had been right, Kylemore thought grimly. "Rich protectors are deuced thin on the ground in this back-water, I'd have thought."

A spark of annoyance lit her eyes. "That is of no conse-quence, Your Grace. I don't seek a rich protector. I have retired. My life will be one of blameless propriety and good works from now on."

He did laugh out loud at that. He couldn't help himself. "What a charmingly nonsensical notion, my dear Soraya." He paused. "Except you call yourself Verity Symonds, don't you? Am I permitted to know your real name after our long and . . . *close* acquaintance?"

She looked uncomfortable, although he couldn't tell if it was at the implication of deception or his reference to their liaison. "It's Verity Ashton. And I don't see why my ideas are nonsensical. Although your stoush in the kitchen has destroyed any future I might have had in Whitby. I can't imagine Marjorie keeping her mouth shut about a duke brawling with Mrs. Symonds's brother."

"I found you once, I can find you again," he said evenly.

She looked unconcerned at his threat, blast her. "Why would you bother? A man like you has no trouble getting someone to warm his bed. There's nothing special about me."

Amazingly, she wasn't being coy or eliciting flattery—she'd always been remarkably free of the usual female wiles. But surely she knew she was a woman beyond the common calling. She was the incomparable Soraya, whatever damned name she chose to call herself now.

With difficulty, he kept his voice neutral. "So after the deal of trouble I expended to find you, I'm to go on my way without a murmur of protest?"

"You were angry. You thought I'd deceived you. Now you realize that isn't the case. I haven't taken another lover and have no intention of doing so." She moved forward to the door, clearly trying to end the interview. "So you see, there's nothing here for Your Grace. Soraya no longer exists. Verity Ashton and her brother can be of no interest to you. You've satisfied your curiosity about what became of your mistress."

"Yes," he said, although, of course, he lied. His curiosity, if anything, was more consuming than ever. "This new life will pall. You weren't born for obscurity."

"After my years of public notoriety, obscurity will be a blessing," she said. He could see that she was sincere, deluded creature that she was. "I don't expect you to understand."

"Oh, I understand," he said. "More than you can know."

Hadn't he wasted his childhood yearning to be just an ordinary boy from an ordinary family? But maturity had brought the knowledge that some burdens were never to be laid down, no matter how unwilling, how unfit, how resentful the bearer.

His spectacular mistress still needed to learn this lesson.

"I believe we have nothing more to say to each other. You were a generous and kind lover, Your Grace. Please don't make me remember you otherwise." The presumptuous slut even had the gall to smile at him when she opened the door, as if dismissing an inconvenient caller. "Good day."

He bent his head in a show of acknowledgment, although in reality he did it to hide a surge of ferocious need. "At least do me the courtesy of accompanying me to my carriage."

With predatory avidity from under his lashes, he saw her glance nervously around the room, as if seeking an excuse to refuse. She wasn't quite as self-possessed as she wished to appear, but her compulsion to speed him on his way superseded sensible caution. "As you wish."

With false decorum, he presented his arm. After a tiny, telling hesitation, she took it. The light, irritatingly reluctant contact burned. Her touch had the same effect on him it always had. If anything, his hunger had only become fiercer after so long without feasting on its desire.

Soon, he soothed his rioting appetites. *Soon all you want will be yours.*

As they moved out into the mean little hall, her scent surrounded him. Fleetingly, it disoriented him. It made her Soraya and not Soraya.

His worldly mistress had always floated in a cloud of musk and ambergris. The woman at his side smelled of violet soap. Although far from unpleasant, it was vaguely unsettling, as though he'd somehow set his revenge on the wrong target. But beneath the fresh scent of flowers lingered the haunting essence of the woman he craved so endlessly.

Her brother waited outside the parlor. He clearly, and rightly, suspected Kylemore's intentions. *A canny laddie, Benjamin Ashton,* Kylemore admitted to himself.

"His Grace is leaving," Soraya—Verity—said.

Ashton looked unimpressed. "Just like that?"

"I've found out what I wanted." Kylemore looked around the poor dwelling with unconcealed derision. Good God, Soraya belonged in a palace, not in this hovel.

"You won't be coming back, then," the young man said flatly. It wasn't a question.

"No," Kylemore said and meant it.

"I'll just see His Grace to his conveyance." She looked troubled. He couldn't blame her. The atmosphere of loathing and mistrust was thicker than the impenetrable sea fogs that regularly swept in along the Kylemore coast.

"I'll come with you," the fellow said.

Silently, they left the house and climbed the short distance to the peak of the hill. Kylemore had left his carriage near the abbey, not wanting to risk either his fine vehicle or expensive horseflesh on the precipitous streets.

"Well, here we are," Verity said.

He found it damned hard getting used to her new name.

But whatever she called herself, nothing changed the fact that she was his. He glanced down at her perfect face and read the relief there. She must have expected the worst when she'd found him in her kitchen. Now she'd congratulate herself on bringing events to such a favorable conclusion.

Favorable to her anyway, the manipulative jade.

Kylemore nodded to his two brawny footmen before he shifted his hold on her arm so that she couldn't escape. "You can't think I'll let our association end this way, my dear. Or has changing your name chased away all your wits indeed?"

She tried to pull free. "It ends this way because I say it does, Your Grace," she said sharply.

He smiled, admiring her nerve. Unluckily for her, nerve would do her no good where he meant to take her. "I'm afraid the wishes of a self-serving demirep are of no consequence."

He was delighted to see her assurance evaporate as she registered his implacable tone. Frantically, she looked past him to her brother. "Ben, do something!"

Kylemore snapped out a command in Gaelic, and the stalwart Ben Ahbood found himself restrained by two even more stalwart Highlanders, brought precisely for this purpose.

"Let her go, you bastard!" Ashton shouted. "I'll bloody kill you for this!"

The girl tugged and wriggled to break free, but her strength was no match for his. "Don't hurt him! None of this is his fault."

Kylemore tightened his grip and focused a blazing glare on her distraught features. "No, it's yours. And you will pay. Now, if you stop fighting me and get into the carriage, I promise your brother won't be harmed."

"Don't do it, Verity lass!" A few feet away, Ashton made a creditable job of defending himself, even against such odds.

Kylemore inclined his head toward the coachman, who

hadn't left his perch. "Pray turn your attention to my man, madam. I'm sure you'll agree cooperation is preferable."

The gray eyes darted upward and widened as she observed the gun the driver pointed directly at her captive brother. Immediately, she stilled in Kylemore's hold.

"I will come," she said calmly. All trace of emotion left her voice. "You can let Ben go."

"Not just yet," he said, preparing to hand her into the carriage and not even pretending to conceal his exultation. He'd caught her, and this time, nothing in heaven or on earth would stop him keeping her. He spoke in rapid Gaelic over his shoulder. "Hold him in the abbey until nightfall. On a stormy day like this, there shouldn't be many people about to wonder what you're doing. Knock him out if you have to."

"Verity, don't go with him!" Ashton struggled uselessly to shake off his captors and lunge to his sister's aid.

The sister merely shook her head and gave him a sad smile. "I'll be all right, Ben."

"Get in," Kylemore growled, refusing to be moved by her courage. She'd brought this disaster on herself when she'd betrayed him. Anything he did to her was more than deserved.

She cast a disdainful glance up at the leveled pistol and then at the duke. "As Your Grace desires." She made no attempt to hide the irony in her words.

Kylemore followed her inside and slammed the door after him. The shades were drawn, but even in the gloom, he saw that the gaze she turned on him was stony. The formidable control, so familiar after a year together, was back in place. She meant to freeze him into letting her go.

Too late, my lady, he thought with a bleak spurt of humor. *I've been frozen all my life. This particular demon is only at home in snow and ice.* He heard the coachman shout to the horses and Ashton's blasphemous protest as the coach rolled into motion. The scheme had proceeded with perfect smoothness. But then, his plans usually did.

Kylemore scooped up several lengths of cord from the bench beside him. "Put out your hands."

"I will not be bound."

God, what a woman she was. Most females would be caterwauling to the skies by now, but his mistress sounded as though she attended afternoon tea, not her own abduction. He knelt before her, balancing himself against the coach's swaying. "I've tied you up before. You enjoyed it."

Of course, the cheap jibe didn't rattle her. He hadn't imagined it would. She merely settled her rain-clear gaze on him. "I consented to those games, Your Grace. An important difference."

"Not to me." He let a superior smile curl his lip. In truth, he felt rather superior. Having gotten what he wanted, he'd happily fling back his head and shout his victory aloud. "Put out your hands."

She shrugged and did as he bid. "I suppose if I don't, you'll order your thug of a driver to shoot me."

He tightened the knots. "I could gag you as well, you know." Negligently, he flipped her skirts up to her knees. "I find myself less than beguiled by your wardrobe, madam."

With displeasure, he surveyed her thick cotton stockings and sturdy halfboots. Practical, but far from alluring. The Soraya he knew had worn only silk next to her skin.

Silk. Or him.

"I wasn't out to beguile," she snapped as he tied her ankles together.

He pulled down her skirts and returned to his seat with an urgency he hoped she didn't note. This woman was in many ways a stranger, but she still exercised the same heady tug on his desires, damn her. But he had some control, Devil take it. He wouldn't throw her on her back and tup her the minute he had her in his power, no matter how his starving senses screamed for him to do just that.

A silence fell as he fought and won against his unruly passions. He resented this effortless hold she had over him. He always had. But nothing in six years had broken him of his addiction to this one exquisite woman. He craved her the way his father had craved opium. Would his particular obsession prove just as fatal as his sire's?

Broodingly, he stared across at her, taking in her shuttered expression and the way she gracefully braced herself against the lurching motion, even constrained as she was. She clearly meant to deny him tears, protests, tantrums. Perhaps she saved them for a more telling moment.

But when, a long while later, she did speak, she used the same unruffled voice as before. "Just what do you want of me, Kylemore?"

He settled back against the squabs with a faint smile. "Nothing too onerous for a woman of your talents." He let his smile broaden as intoxicating satisfaction flooded through him, headier than the strongest liquor. "You've given me three months of misery and trouble, madam. Now it's only fair you recompense my efforts with sensual pleasure."

Chapter 4

"**K**idnapping is a capital offense," Verity said steadily. *Never let him see you're frightened,* her mind chanted in time with the creaking carriage. *Never let him know you're weak.*

Kylemore remained unconcerned, damn him. "No magistrate will lift a finger to save a common whore from supplying what her patron has paid for. Especially if her patron is one of the greatest men in the kingdom."

His insulting description of her shouldn't rankle. She *had* sold her favors for money. All the same, his dismissive words hurt. Daunting to realize quite how much they hurt.

She fought to conceal her unwelcome reaction. The ruthless autocrat sitting opposite wanted her to play the hysterical female, weeping and begging for mercy, but she'd promised herself the day she'd left London that she'd never be this man's—any man's—puppet again. The Duke of Kylemore didn't yet realize that compliant Soraya, with her silken sensuality, was gone forever. Instead, she'd become a creature of iron and ice who would submit to no man's demands.

She'd cried, alone and afraid and grieving, when her parents had died. She'd raged and wept when necessity had compelled her to become an old man's mistress. Tears hadn't helped on those occasions. They wouldn't help now. Instead, she must be cunning and observant. She must think and plan and wait. In this alone she was like Kylemore: Control was her refuge and her weapon.

Circumstances had forced her to learn to interpret men. This particular specimen might be more opaque than most, but she could tell the duke was stubbornly set on this reckless course, even though heaven knew no good could come of it.

She moistened a dry throat. "My brother will have the law on you."

"The same brother who pimped for you in London?"

She'd defend Ben even if she'd never stoop to defend herself. "That's not true. He protected me."

The monster had the nerve to smile at her again. The curve of that beautifully shaped mouth conveyed a mixture of condescension and disdain. "You hardly need protecting from the man who has been your acknowledged lover for the past year. No, my dear Soraya, you deceive yourself to expect rescue from that quarter."

"Don't call me that!" In their hated bonds, her hands curled into fists. She took a deep breath to quell her stormy reaction. *Never let him see. Never let him see,* she repeated silently. She spoke more calmly. "My name is Verity Ashton."

"As you wish," he said without any great interest. "But don't imagine anything else has changed, because it hasn't."

The smile developed a tinge of smugness. Because of course, he had seen. He was an astute man with an uncanny ability to read her. From the start, he'd known that beneath her composure, she was scared and bewildered and furious.

None of which meant she must admit defeat. She straightened her spine, sent him a glare of virulent, but unfortunately impotent, hatred and turned her head away.

They covered several miles in increasingly oppressive silence. She tried to concentrate on her physical woes. But while the cords constraining her were tight, the silk didn't chafe anything except her pride. It was more uncomfortable trying to balance against the vehicle's motion, but even that eventually became automatic.

The duke studied her with unwavering intensity. She endured his inspection as the coach swayed along the road, stealing her away from Whitby and her shattered dreams of contentment. With every second, the tension between them wound tighter and tighter. A tension heavy with her fear and his unrelenting purpose. And something else she didn't want to acknowledge. The sexual awareness that always quivered between them was almost tangible in the dimly lit carriage.

Verity had no illusions about her ultimate punishment.

He wanted her. He'd take her. He was angry enough to hurt her. Nor had she missed the significance of those few moments when he'd knelt at her feet. The catch in his breath. The swiftly hidden tremor in those elegant hands as he'd bound her.

He was still in thrall to his lust. Of course he was. Why launch himself on this lunatic path otherwise?

His need was a weakness the great Soraya would have immediately exploited. But until she had no other choice, Verity refused to descend to cheap harlot's tricks, however many spiteful names Kylemore cared to call her.

The duke was strong and ruthless. Any thin veneer of decorum that existed between them in London had disintegrated to nothing. She sensed he'd been pushed so close to the edge that he'd do anything. Anything.

But he wouldn't prevail, she told herself bravely.

And wished to heaven she believed it.

"I didn't betray you," she said, as much out of a need to break the screaming silence as out of any great wish to communicate with him.

His eyes in the gloomy interior didn't even flicker. "Yes, you did."

"Our contract was for a year. Everything you gave me was legally mine. You know about Ben now. I was never unfaithful."

"Fortuitous for you—and him—you weren't." The duke spoke with an indolence she didn't trust as he stretched out his legs in the well between the two benches. If one disregarded the banked fires under those lazily lowered eyelids, he was the picture of relaxed control. "You speak of quibbles. Inessentials. In your heart, you know you betrayed me when you left. In your heart, you knew I'd seek reparation."

The problem was she *had* known. Because of this knowledge, she'd fallen in with Ben's scheme to disappear into the night with him as though they'd been a pair of housebreakers. She'd spoken no promises to Kylemore, but every time they'd made love, every time he'd produced an empress's jewel to adorn her, she'd committed herself to stay. Legally, she'd been free to go. On a personal level, she'd deceived, then abandoned, him.

Unspoken guilt had nagged at her ever since she'd left. But she realized now she'd been wise to flee him and his obsessive desire. What had been unwise was allowing him to find her again.

"If I admit that's true and beg your forgiveness, will you let me go?" she asked without any expectation he'd agree.

He laughed softly, and the deep sound sent a chill of apprehension along her spine. "No, that's too easy, madam. Although I vow you'll do both before I'm finished with you."

Unhappily, she was sure she would too. She spoke quickly

before the thought lodged in her mind and chipped away at what little courage she had left. "How did you find me?"

"With more difficulty than I anticipated, I must say. I compliment you on your cleverness."

It didn't sound like a compliment. She shivered although it wasn't cold inside the closed carriage.

He went on. "At first, I tried all the obvious places. But if you'd taken a new lover, everyone concerned was damned discreet about it. My inquiries turned up no information about your whereabouts at all."

"That must have been—"

"Humiliating? Yes, it was." He cast her a level look from under his sharply marked brows. "I've already said you have a great deal to make up for."

"I owe you nothing," she said with a staunchness even she found unconvincing.

He ignored her interjection. "In the meantime, my agents searched across the country, concentrating on the fashionable towns. It never occurred to me you didn't plan to continue your profession."

"Why?" she asked sourly. "You believed I was so madly in love with my manservant that I absconded with him."

The annoying smile, which had come and gone ever since he'd seized her, reappeared. "What I understood to be your affair with Ben Ahbood hadn't prevented you trying to bleed me dry. Why would it stop you hooking your claws into some other gullible source of income?"

"You don't think very highly of me, do you?" she asked through stiff lips.

"On the contrary, my dear. I have the greatest respect for your business acumen," he said dryly. He folded his arms, his fathomless dark blue stare still probing her every secret. "Your only truly foolish act was to refuse my offer of marriage and run away. You must know you couldn't find a more generous provider."

Inwardly, she recoiled at the contempt in his drawling voice. Oh, he wanted her, all right, but he despised himself for it. And he'd make her pay for his weakness.

"I only had one thing to sell. You can't blame me for getting the best price I could," she said.

"No. And you can't blame me for getting value for my money." Clearly feeling he'd stemmed any insubordination in the lower orders, he proceeded with his explanation. "I started to think about wills and legacies. Sir Eldreth was a rich man and a bachelor. Likely he made provision for you. Especially considering your touching display of loyalty. And I remembered you waited six months before taking your next lover. It argued an independent income of some kind."

"Perhaps it argued discrimination," she retorted, bitterly resenting this cold accounting of her life.

"Not when Mallory was your next choice. The man's a nonentity."

"He was always kind to me," she returned just as sharply.

Unimpressed eyebrows arched over Kylemore's deep blue eyes. "A woman like you needs more than kindness. We both know it." He reached across to lift the blind on a gray world.

The light was unforgiving on his handsome face, revealing marks of tiredness and strain. He looked as if he'd tormented himself close to madness since she'd disappeared. She found the idea more terrifying than flattering to her vanity.

He let the flap fall, enveloping them in twilight once more. "It's raining again. We shall have a wet journey north."

"North?" she asked, although it hardly mattered where he took her. Her eventual fate at his hands would be the same in London as it would be in Outer Mongolia.

"Yes. We visit one of my properties in the Highlands. It's

the only place I'm sure we won't be disturbed. It's the only place I can rely on the staff not to spread word of your presence." This time, his smile held only gloating anticipation. "My revenge is a purely private concern."

A weaker woman would have started screaming then. But Verity clung with difficulty to her self-possession. He was determined to intimidate her, that much was obvious.

The pity of it was he succeeded.

He paused, as if waiting for her reaction. When she denied him a response, he looked a little chagrined.

You'll face more such disappointments, she told him silently with the first satisfaction she'd experienced since this nightmare started. *Get used to it.*

He made a dismissive gesture with one pale, elegant hand, as if wordlessly denying her capacity to affect him. "Where was I? Ah, yes. Sir Eldreth's will. I got hold of it and noted a large annuity to a Miss Verity Matilda Ashton. Inquiries on his estates and amongst his cronies revealed Miss Ashton was neither a relative nor a family retainer. In fact, nobody knew who she was. By the way, Matilda doesn't do you justice. It's hard enough seeing you as Verity—particularly given truth isn't exactly your strongpoint. But Matilda!"

"It was my mother's name," Verity said, trying not to let his needling scratch at her control.

"Ah." He released a derisive puff of breath. "I hope she was a worthier citizen than her daughter has turned out to be."

"She was."

Thank God that gentle, devout woman had died before she saw what Verity had become. Her mother believed everlasting hellfire awaited a harlot at the end of her path. Verity had no intention of confiding that morsel to the overbearing tyrant opposite her.

"It was then a minor matter to arrange for certain less

scrupulous contacts to break into Sir Eldreth's solicitor's office and steal Miss Ashton's direction. You enjoy the delightful result of my enterprise."

How she hated his smooth, superior voice, with its hard consonants and clear vowels. The coward who skulked in her soul whispered she could never succeed against someone with a voice like that.

Courage, Verity, she told herself, fisting her bound hands in her lap. *He hasn't won yet. Although he undoubtedly will if you convince yourself he's invincible.*

"You'll soon tire of rape and compulsion." Baiting him was risky, but she had to establish some power of her own in this cruelly unequal contest.

"You mistake me, madam," he retorted smoothly. "My desire is for a partnership in the fullest sense of the word."

In spite of all her fear, she gave a scornful crack of laughter. "If wishes were horses, beggars would ride."

His intense expression didn't lighten. "I think you'll find we're all beggars when it comes to desire."

At last, he offered her some advantage, and she was desperate enough to take it. "I was a whore, Your Grace. Whores tup for money, not for pleasure. You confuse me with some fine lady who chooses where she lies down. I spread my legs for men because they pay me to do it. In your case, they pay me a fortune."

Even in the poor light, she saw he whitened under her taunts. "More than that lay between us and you know it."

It was her turn to sound superior now. "I'm glad Your Grace thought so. I'd fear my skills failed if you hadn't."

Yes! This was what she must do. Fight him. Insult him. Make him scramble to keep up. Soon, he'd weary of her acid tongue and her obstinacy. He wanted exciting, compliant Soraya, not her pigheaded facsimile, Verity.

He must have guessed her intention. "Making me angry won't convince me to release you. Although it might make me less . . . careful."

Anger surged up, clean and powerful as the waves she'd watched on the seafront that afternoon. "I don't want your care! I don't want anything from you. I despise you."

Strangely, her outburst only made him calmer. "Have a thought for your safety, madam. Where we're going, I could do away with you and not one soul would utter a word of protest."

She shrugged sullenly. "So kill me. Kill me now and save yourself the inconvenience of a long journey. Threats won't change the way I feel."

As she should have expected, the challenge didn't dent his self-assurance. "Perhaps not. But I'd hate to end this particular drama just when it's getting interesting."

Balancing himself against the lurching with an ease she resented, he crossed the carriage to share her bench. Verity cringed into the corner before she could stop herself. The seat was narrow, and while he wasn't a heavyset man, he had plenty of lean strength to fill the available room. His legs lay alongside hers, and their heat seeped through her thick black skirts.

But she was a fighter. She'd had to be.

"So you've decided to murder me after all." She hoped her statement was mere bravado.

He turned his dark head and regarded her steadily. She suspected he understood how unnerving she found his brooding concentration upon her.

"No, not yet." His lips quirked with frosty amusement. "Although you might wish I had before I'm finished."

She inched further into the padded leather on the side of the coach, but it made no difference to how the duke dominated the space. The bumping carriage constantly moved him against her, creating suggestive friction. Each brush of his arm or his thigh seared her with unwelcome reminders of pleasure.

"What are you going to do?" she asked in a voice she struggled to keep steady. Curse him for tying her up. Her bound hands were helpless to push him further away.

"Don't you like surprises?" he asked softly. For all their talk of murder and his earlier attack on Ben, she sensed no violence in him now.

"No, I don't," she snapped, light-headed with a nauseating mixture of nerves and anger. Just what was he playing at?

"How sad," he murmured. "That is something we should remedy." He raised one long-fingered hand and trailed it down the side of her face to cup her chin.

Every second of that mocking caress burned. She tried and failed to wrench away. "I won't lift my skirts for you in a moving carriage."

His touch was gentle but inexorable. "You'll lift your skirts when and where I say. You gave up any right to command me when you ran off."

"I'll fight you." She prayed it was true.

"I count on it." He leaned forward to rub his cheek against her face. His shadow beard prickled faintly against her skin. His warm, musky scent, familiar from a hundred afternoons in Kensington, enveloped her.

She stiffened, rejecting the false tenderness as much as the threat of force. "Stop it!" she grated out.

Kylemore laughed softly. "Shh," he breathed into her ear as he nuzzled at her throat.

I can bear this, she swore to herself. *I can bear this.*

"Verity." He nibbled his way to her shoulder, brushing aside her dress's high neckline. "Verity, you're as delicious as Soraya ever was."

"I hope I make you choke." She was horrified to hear a

husky edge to her defiance. He laughed again, the short huffs of breath warm across her collarbone.

"That's my girl." He turned her more fully toward him and concentrated on a sensitive nerve between her neck and her shoulder. Twelve months of intimacy had taught him that attention to that particular spot drove her insane with pleasure.

Because of course they both knew her insults were empty. She bit back a moan. The Duke of Kylemore was a skillful lover who had always drawn a response from her. A genuine response, not the tired ruses of a doxy placating her rich keeper. She'd enjoyed his lovemaking, had even found it exciting if she'd ever permitted herself that much feeling when they'd been together.

It was just a healthy young woman's natural response to a vigorous lover, she'd always told herself.

Her first vigorous lover.

With more effort than she wanted to acknowledge, she distanced herself from what he was doing to her now. In London, sex had taken place in a strange atmosphere of trust. Since her desertion, he no longer trusted her. And she certainly didn't trust the madman who'd snatched her from the public road and tried to kill her brother. The memory helped stifle any response to his touch.

Eventually, the duke sat back and studied her with an expression of displeasure on his spoiled, handsome face.

Good, she thought.

"You can't escape me, even in your mind. There's no point wishing yourself somewhere else," he said in a tone completely different from the seductive purr of a few seconds ago.

"Unfortunately, you make it impossible for me to go anywhere, Your Grace." She raised her tied hands in an ironic gesture. "I find myself less than enraptured with your hospitality."

His aristocratic annoyance melted as he gave a snort of laughter. "Do you, by God?"

"Untie me," she said, suddenly finding her bonds unbearable. "I can't jump from a moving carriage."

"You could scratch my eyes out."

"My ambitions relate to damaging other parts of you entirely," she said with relish, although she wasn't sure she was capable of doing him any real harm. In Whitby, she could have turned his coachman's pistol on him and shot without hesitation. But now this forced intimacy gnawed at her resolution to make him suffer for what he'd done.

Perhaps he knew that.

She straightened. What sort of mouse was she to let a few halfhearted caresses from a cast-off lover soften her? A cast-off lover determined to assert what he saw as his rights.

Well, she decided who had rights over her. And she denied the Duke of Kylemore the ownership he claimed.

"You're doing it again," he said softly.

She blinked. "What?"

"Letting your mind wander."

She shrugged with a forced show of indifference. "If only I could help it. But nothing here holds my attention."

Chapter 5

The moment Verity spoke, she recognized her mistake.

She'd meant the challenge to slash and wound. Instead it had emerged as a sexual invitation. And of course, Kylemore didn't fling away in the offended sulk she'd set out to provoke.

A wolfishly delighted smile lit his face. "I'll just have to try a bit harder, then, won't I?"

She closed her eyes and tried not to hear the emphasis he placed on "harder." "Don't do this," she whispered. "Please."

He gave a soft laugh. "Begging for mercy already, Soraya? I thought you'd last longer against me than this."

"I'm not Soraya," she said, the little defiance all she could invoke.

Because he was right. She'd do anything, including sacrificing her pride, to avoid the slow seduction she knew he intended.

"Yes, you are." He curled his hand around her head,

spearing his fingers through her decorous widow's braids and angling her face up toward his.

She braced herself for assault. But the duke was too subtle for that. With tantalizing slowness, he brushed his mouth across hers. It couldn't even be called a kiss. Not really. It was like an extension of his gentle nuzzling before. Except now he touched her lips. And he'd kissed her so rarely and never with quite this concentrated purpose.

She tried to pull away, but the hand on the back of her head was implacable. This time when he glanced his mouth across hers, he lingered a second longer, moved his lips into a ghost of a kiss, over before she knew it had begun.

She gave a whimper that held no desire, only fear. "Please stop."

He raised his other hand and smoothed a few tendrils of hair away from her forehead. "Why? I'm only kissing you. After everything we've done with each other, this can hardly signify, can it?"

But of course, he knew it did. She could see that knowledge in his gentian eyes. Knowledge and no real tenderness, although his touch lied and told a different story. He was set on dominating her, and luck or perception meant he'd lighted on the one strategy that would vanquish her.

She could fight force, but her life had been devoid of tenderness since she was fifteen. Even its false likeness had the power to open a rift in her heart.

Somewhere, though, she found the will to resist. "All right. Take me," she said flatly. She glanced sideways. "If you untie my legs and bring me onto your lap, we should manage something to take the edge off you. At least enough to stop you plaguing me for the moment." It was deliberately crude, but she was frantic to shatter the tremulous desire hovering between them.

He gave another of those soft laughs that made the hairs

on her arms rise. "Perhaps later, madam. Right now I'm quite content with the innocent joys of kissing."

"But I don't like to be kissed," she said helplessly.

He stroked his fingers across her cheek until he held her head in both hands. "You kissed me when you left me, if you recall."

"A mistake," she said unsteadily.

She'd known that even at the time. How she wished she'd let him go on his way that afternoon. How she wished she'd followed her instincts and never taken the Duke of Kylemore as her lover at all.

Ever since she'd met him, a voice inside her had insisted he and only he could break through the protective shell that was Soraya. But calamitously, she'd ignored the shrill warning from her instincts. As his mistress, she'd endured a year armoring herself against the empathy she'd always felt for him. An empathy that was absurd. A Cyprian and a duke of the realm could have nothing in common.

Before her capitulation, he'd pursued, she'd resisted. Every lure he cast her way was a move in the game. Part of her had relished the contest. Even her final play was a challenge— she'd deliberately demanded an impossible fortune for her compliance, an amount no sane man would pay for a woman.

But no Kinmurrie was ever completely sane.

The duke had called her on her bid. She'd found herself unexpectedly having to pay her gambling debts. She'd assured herself she could survive a year, a little year, with him and emerge with her detachment intact. And she'd almost succeeded.

Almost.

And the disaster that little word *almost* promised sat beside her now, plotting to destroy her.

Well, she wasn't finished yet. The Duke of Kylemore needed to learn that. This time when his lips met hers, Verity remained as unrelenting as rock. She closed her eyes and deliberately enumerated all her reasons to hate this man.

His arrogance.

His selfishness.

The way he ripped her away from the life she'd planned for so long and had finally gained the chance to achieve.

The hands in her hair began to move in soothing circles, finding and loosening each knot of tension. And all the time, he kept nipping and nibbling and sucking at her lips.

She hated him.

Her captive hands clenched as she fought to remain unmoved.

He was unmistakably aroused, in spite of her lack of encouragement. Any moment, he'd fling up her skirts and force himself into her. She almost wished he would so she'd have no choice but to loathe him.

At least rape would end this torture that hovered so close to drugging pleasure. She tried to summon disgust. But in truth, he was heartbreakingly gentle.

He knew gentleness was his greatest weapon, damn him.

And he smelled wonderful. Clean, strong, healthy male, free of the cloying toilet waters so many of his sex used. He smelled of the outdoors. For one lost moment, she yearned toward that alluring scent before she remembered she was made of stone and stone didn't yearn.

But he, so attuned to her, so close to her in this confined space, noticed her momentary weakening. "I can do this all the way to Scotland, you know," he murmured against her mouth.

"I'm not a toy," she retorted.

"You're what I say you are. That's the price of betrayal." A few deft movements and her hair cascaded around her shoulders. He ran his fingers through the tumbled mass, straightening the kinks. "That's better. Now you look like my mistress.

Although I own to finding the seduction of the virtuous widow rather piquant. We must save it for another occasion."

His easy confidence rankled, as she was sure he meant it to. "I'm not your mistress any more. I told you—Soraya has gone forever."

The relentlessly combing hands paused, then resumed. She tried to tell herself the stroking didn't disturb her, but each movement was a promise of delight.

Lying promises, she reminded herself.

"Soraya is just hidden, that's all." His certainty made her want to hit him.

"You'll get tired of this." She hoped she was right.

"Perhaps. But do you really doubt whose will is stronger?" His hands slid around to rest on her shoulders.

If he shifted those hands an inch, they could be around her throat. He'd already threatened her with violence. She struggled to awaken her fear as a barrier against him, but it was impossible when his touch conveyed only tender possession.

Tender possession?

Curse her, but she was a fool.

He connived endlessly at her destruction while she sat gulling herself into thinking he had some regard for her. She deserved to be in this fix if she allowed herself to credit such sentimental drivel.

Verity heard Kylemore sigh. "I'll make a deal with you, Miss Ashton."

She lifted her chin. "I already know you don't keep to your bargains, Your Grace."

At least when he talked to her, he wasn't kissing her. Even though his deep voice slid along her veins like warm honey and the motion of the speeding carriage rubbed his body against hers in a ceaseless, erotic rhythm.

"Well, this is my offer. Kiss me properly and you are safe from my attentions until we reach my hunting box."

"'Properly' means what exactly?" she asked with suspicion.

He laughed. "That's familiar—you barricading yourself behind legal definitions. Their protection is spurious, as you should know by now."

Devil take his confidence. "If I cooperate, will you untie me?" She had nothing to haggle with. They both knew she was totally in his power.

"It depends how genuinely you cooperate."

As he sat back, she took a deep breath. And unwillingly inhaled his essence. He seemed to have permeated the very fabric of the carriage. She wondered despairingly if he'd similarly permeated her life. Would she ever be free of him, even when this ordeal was over?

As surely it had to be over one day.

His fine-boned face indicated his irritation with her havering. "I needn't offer you anything. You're my prisoner. You have no say in what I do to you."

The bastard was right. This time, hating him was no effort at all. "So I let you kiss me, and in return, you maul me no further until we reach our destination?"

Another curl of his lip. "If you participate fully in the kiss, I swear not to toss you on your back and plow you with the thoroughness you deserve."

She swallowed nervously. "That's not what I said."

"No, but that's the proposition on the table. Take it or leave it." He folded his arms and waited for her decision with ill-concealed impatience.

Her inevitable decision. One kiss in exchange for a breathing space? A breathing space in which surely she'd find some chance to escape. She had no alternative but to agree.

Verity met his eyes in the shadowy interior. "All right."

"Good."

She waited for him to take her in his arms, but he didn't

move from his relaxed pose against the shiny dark leather of the upholstery. Although she told herself she should be grateful for any reprieve, however short, his lack of action quickly began to irk her.

"I'm ready," she said sharply.

Those supercilious eyebrows rose. "I believe the arrangement was you were to kiss me."

Would this humiliation never end?

No, it's just started, a bleak voice inside her whispered. "Damn you," she said in a low, hard tone. "Damn you to hell."

"Too late, I'm afraid." He gave her a wintry smile. "Are you reneging? To think a mere kiss defeated the great Soraya."

She'd used her mouth on his whole body. She'd taken him in her mouth and brought him to climax. But she'd never given a lover's kiss to him. Or any man.

It was an unwelcome and melancholy reflection.

He leaned against the padded side of the carriage, angled toward her. It was a simple matter to wriggle closer and balance herself with her bound hands on his thighs. The long muscles in his legs stirred under her fingers. He wasn't as composed as he wanted to appear. That insight gave her the impetus to continue.

She could do this. She could do this.

For God's sake, it was only a kiss. She was the notorious Soraya. Surely she could kiss a man and survive the experience.

Tentatively, she pressed her mouth against his. He tasted familiar. He should. They'd been lovers for a year. He remained impassive as she rubbed her lips across his, testing taste and texture. His lips were firm beneath hers, firm and smooth. And utterly unresponsive.

Clearly, he meant to make her work for her reprieve.

Of course he did. She had to remember this was about revenge and nothing else. The bargain for her kiss was just a twisted plan concocted in the tortuous labyrinth of his mind.

Well, if she could become London's greatest courtesan from her unlikely beginnings, she could certainly kiss a man into forgetting his coldhearted agenda.

Verity took a deep breath, trying to ignore his damned evocative scent, and used her imagination. She began to copy the way he'd kissed her earlier, coaxing him into joining her. The muscles of his legs hardened beneath her hands. She didn't look down to check if anything else was hardening.

But still he didn't kiss her back.

"What's the matter, Your Grace?" she taunted softly against his skin. "This was your idea, if you recall."

"You're yet to engage my interest sufficiently," he said in a negligent tone.

His answer would have infuriated her if she hadn't heard the unsteadiness in his voice. Making her service him was apparently to be part of her penance. Service him without engaging his participation, it seemed.

Except he was far from unmoved. She briefly considered bringing her hands further up his thighs to confirm that.

Soraya wouldn't have hesitated. Verity was more cautious. This was meant to be just a kiss, after all. She didn't want to end up flat on her back while the duke "plowed" her, to borrow his regrettably graphic terminology.

She returned to her task with renewed determination. And still he didn't surrender.

"I know you're trying to teach me a lesson," she panted against his cheek.

He didn't bother to deny it. "And are you learning anything?"

"I'm learning you're not the only one who is as stubborn as a mule."

She could tell he laughed against his will, and she fought not to find that sudden glimpse of his humanity disarming. "You know, Verity or Soraya or whoever you are at this moment, sometimes your gall takes my breath away."

In spite of everything, she smiled. "I hope not just my gall does that, Your Grace."

He started to reply, but she slammed her mouth against his and began to use her tongue in an open-mouthed, passionate kiss. This time Kylemore answered her with desire. Not because he wanted to, Verity knew, but because he had no other choice.

That was her last rational thought for a long time as the kiss swept her up in a conflagration of dark pleasure she'd never known before. It was hot in this firestorm, hot and dangerous, but she hurled herself into the blaze without a thought to her own protection. His arms lashed around her as he dragged her across his lap.

Shamingly, Kylemore was the one who eventually pulled back.

He lifted himself slightly away from her. She lay on the bench. Somewhere in that tempestuous kiss, he'd brought her beneath him. A few moments more and he'd have been inside her. The weight of him, hard and hot against her belly, even through her skirts, indicated that was still a possibility.

Even this wasn't enough to return her to reality. Without a squeak of protest, she lay beneath him lost in delight.

"If I don't stop now, I won't," Kylemore said tautly. His expression was strained. The arms he supported himself upon imprisoned her in a cage she could summon no great eagerness to escape. "Unless that's what you want."

"Want?" she repeated stupidly, blinking up at him. Her mouth felt swollen and her heart pounded as though she'd run from him instead of surrendered mindlessly to his importunity.

"Shall I take this embrace to its natural conclusion?" Briefly, he was the courtly lover she'd known in London.

She sucked in a shaky breath to steady her rioting responses. The creaking of the coach was loud in her ears as she scrambled to gather her scattered thoughts and, even more importantly, her scattered defenses. Fleetingly, she remembered the duke describing his kiss as innocent. It had been about as innocent as Lucifer overseeing an orgy in hell.

"Madam?" he asked, then very deliberately pressed his erection into her stomach.

The crude gesture brought her back to herself as nothing else could have. All the lovely bonelessness drained away from her body as she stiffened in unspoken rejection.

"No," she managed to croak out. Then, on a note of desperately sought recklessness, "but I believe my sterling efforts have earned the end of my bondage."

He looked at her strangely. "I untied your hands while you kissed me."

"What?" she asked uncertainly, then realized it was true. Worse, her arms encircled him and she caressed his back.

She was only a breath away from drawing him down for more of those devastating kisses. She vaguely remembered him tugging at her hands during their tempestuous embrace. He must have released her then.

A different heat clawed its way up her face. Of all the humiliations her abduction involved, she'd hated those bonds the most. Yet she'd been so lost in the whirlwind of his kiss that she hadn't even noticed she was no longer constrained.

"Get off me," she snarled, snatching her hands away from him.

He didn't budge. She should have known he wouldn't respond to an order. "I've never had sex in a carriage before," he said thoughtfully.

Neither had she, but she refused to admit it. "I prefer a bed."

A slow smile crossed his face as the vehicle's movements evocatively jostled her against him. For a moment, he looked almost approachable. "Does that mean you've reconciled yourself to returning to me?"

Oh, curse her for blurting out these suggestive comments. Soraya would never be so easy to catch out. Verity was badly rattled and likely to plunge herself deeper into trouble with every word.

In overdue self-protection, she spoke ironically, just as Soraya would have. "Do I have any option, Your Grace?"

That couldn't be disappointment in his eyes, could it? The fleeting expression vanished when he rolled off her and returned to his own seat. "No, you don't," he said.

She sat up shakily, at last able to brace herself against the swaying vehicle, and began to straighten her clothing. Surprisingly, apart from a few buttons undone at her collar, everything was in place. She left her hair loose. Without pins or hairbrush, it was impossible to bring it into anything approaching order.

He leaned forward to raise the blinds. After the gloomy intimacy, even the brightness of the rainy evening jarred her. She narrowed her eyes and looked across at the duke.

He was a study in rumpled elegance. How could such a hell spawn be so beautiful? When she'd first seen him six years ago, he was twenty-one, just emerging from youth. She'd thought him the most perfect creature God ever created. But even then, that eerie self-possession had already settled over his narrow, intelligent face. With a despairing honesty, she admitted that maturity merely added to his attractions.

She watched him struggle to regain his usual unruffled manner. But his color was high, and his mouth was full and softer than usual.

The world that called him Cold Kylemore had no real understanding of him. An inferno of passion blazed beneath the duke's nonchalance. She could only guess at the effort required to keep that bottomless pit of emotion secret.

Except it was no longer a secret—at least to her. He was angry, he was bitter, he was hurt, although she knew he'd face torture before he admitted to the last. He was also as randy as a hare in spring. It surprised her he'd kept his promise and not taken her. She knew him well enough to read some of his restlessness as unsatisfied lust.

When she'd left him, she had thought he'd find another mistress quickly and, if not forget Soraya, at least do his best to ignore the rejection. The duke had a strong sexual drive. She'd always assumed that on the days he didn't ride out to Kensington, he relieved his itch with other women. Someone like him would always attract feminine notice. She'd never duped herself into believing him faithful to her alone.

But the man sitting opposite, who had gone back to staring at her, blast him, was almost feverish with desire. She could smell the lust on him. The unbelievable idea gained credence in her mind that he hadn't had a woman in a long time. Perhaps even since she'd run away.

It was absurd. It couldn't be true.

Although she thought, leaning down to untie her feet, that might explain what had driven him to this rash abduction.

So why wasn't he pumping three months of frustration into her right now? She couldn't make him keep his bargain not to touch her. And he'd have her soon enough anyway.

None of this made sense. Just as that furious kiss made no sense if he meant to leave her alone for the moment. Which, amazingly, it seemed he did.

"What was that all about?" she asked a long time later.

To his credit, he didn't pretend to misunderstand the question. "The kiss? You said it yourself. It was to teach you a lesson." He used the cold, cutting voice again, and despite herself, she shivered.

"That you can touch me whenever you feel like it?" She injected a challenge into her voice. "I already knew that."

He smiled slightly. "Yes. But now you know when I touch you, you're not immune. And that thought will eat at you like acid."

He was right, damn him. For the first time in this long, disheartening day, she was truly terrified.

Chapter 6

Kissing her had been an almighty mistake.

Kylemore settled back against the squabs and strove to preserve his appearance of detachment. All the while, an unrelenting battle raged against his most fundamental urges. His muscles clenched to the point of pain as he stopped himself lunging for her and finishing what he'd started. The promise he'd made her didn't matter a damn. But his own ability to master his animal passions did.

She'd been delicious in his arms, the fulfillment of every lonely dream that had tormented him over the last three months.

She'd been too delicious. If he took her now, where was his victory? He'd be irrevocably back in her thrall and she'd know it, the clever little cat. He had snatched her from her brother's clutches to demonstrate his power over her, not to become her adoring slave once more.

Yet again, she confounded his most carefully laid plans. One kiss from the reluctant Verity Ashton, with her teasing, deceptively innocent violet perfume, and he was right back where he'd been with Soraya. Yearning. Longing. Needy.

Hell.

She'd brought him to his knees without even trying, damn her. He strove to keep the extent of his turmoil from his expression. Then he realized he needn't worry whether his troubled emotions showed.

Soraya—Verity—wasn't looking at him but staring out of the window at the darkening landscape. The fading light revealed she was frantic with misery and fear.

He beat back the twinge of pity that swam up through the murky ocean of lust inside him. She was in this predicament through her own fault. If he'd cowed her into submission within hours of setting out, well and good. The baggage deserved to stew in her iniquity. Perhaps the kiss hadn't been an unalloyed disaster after all.

He shifted to relieve his discomfort. Hell, he had to have her. Desire threatened to scorch his resolution to ashes. Three months of agonizing abstinence howled at him to take her. Especially when for several heated moments, she'd wanted the act as much as he had.

Well, perhaps not quite.

He shifted again and tried to calm the tempest in his blood by telling himself he'd have her soon enough.

But he didn't want her later.

He wanted her now.

He'd set out to prove the advantages were now his. What he'd actually proven was that he was as vulnerable to her as he'd ever been, confound her. Humiliatingly quickly, the kiss had changed from an act of domination to something else entirely, something he didn't want to think about.

The irony was that the whole devastating encounter had in the end been remarkably chaste. They had kissed. That was all. He'd hardly even touched her perfect body. The body whose every curve and line was imprinted on his memory. With a stifled groan, he shifted again.

He'd sworn he wouldn't take her until they reached Scotland. The delay was designed to extend her torture so that by the time he actually bedded her, she'd already suffered days of apprehension and self-recrimination.

So why did it seem the only victim stretched out on the rack right now was His Grace, the Duke of Kylemore?

The kiss had been extraordinary.

Bewitching. Intoxicating. Overwhelming.

Puzzling.

He'd almost say she hadn't quite known how to go about the business at first. Which was ridiculous. Soraya's clever, skilled mouth had already tasted every inch of him. His arousal tightened another excruciating notch as he remembered some of the things she'd done to him.

Good God, at this rate, he'd be a gibbering wreck before they even crossed the border.

He darted an angry glance at Soraya.

Verity. Miss Ashton.

She was close enough to fuck and she might as well have been in Timbuctoo. He couldn't risk touching her again. His self-control had barely survived the last hour.

It was going to be a very long journey.

When the carriage rolled into the village of Hinton Stacey several hours later, night had fallen. Kylemore's prisoner was still silent. But then, his mistress had never been the most garrulous of women. He told himself he didn't care—he hadn't abducted her for her conversation.

"Put out your hands." He reached for the cords. He hadn't tied her up after that scorching kiss, although he'd meant to.

Her face was a pale glimmer in the gloom as she turned toward him. "No."

So that's the way of it, he thought, with a regret he refused to examine. Apparently, she'd devoted the hours since he'd kissed her to rebuilding her defenses.

What had he expected? That one embrace would turn her into a quivering mass of acquiescence? His gaze dropped to the betrayingly unhappy line of her lips. He'd give up his last hope of heaven to taste that mouth again, which was odd, given that kissing her had never been a particular obsession when she'd been his willing lover.

"I'm afraid the word *no* lost its power between us when you ran away." With a roughness born more of his anger with himself than with her, he reached out to grab her hands.

"I will not be bound!" she cried, sliding across the leather seat to avoid him.

The idea of scuffling with her was too undignified to be borne. Or at least that's what he told himself. He certainly wasn't afraid of his own reactions to her in a struggle.

"If I have to hurt you, I will," he said, far from sure it was true.

She treated the threat with the respect it deserved. "Oh, charming."

My God, but she was brave. All his life, courage was the quality he'd admired most. It was startling to realize at this moment that a lowly strumpet demonstrated more nerve than any man he knew.

He injected a reasonable tone into his voice, recognizing bluster would never succeed—or not without him harming her indeed. And his much-vaunted ruthlessness recoiled utterly at the idea.

A great villain he proved in this drama.

"There is a hot meal, a bath and a necessary awaiting us, madam. I'm sure you are as eager to step out of this coach as

I. I am perfectly willing to leave you here under guard while I go inside. But I warn you—we travel the rest of the night and we do not stop. For any reason."

He sensed she was digesting this information. Eventually, she spoke in a small voice. "I hate to be tied up."

The conscience he wished he'd left in London with his extravagant town house and dissolute companions pricked him yet again. He fought to bundle it back into the recesses of his black heart before it troubled him further.

"Give me your word you won't try to escape and you may go free." Strangely, he believed she'd keep any promise she made, in spite of how she'd tricked and used him.

"I can't do that," she said sadly.

"Then put out your hands. I have no wish to coerce you into submission, but I will if I have to."

"Very well."

She waited in trembling stillness while he tied her hands and ankles. For all her defiant talk, she was frightened. This time, his conscience didn't merely prick, it kicked.

"Don't you want to gag me as well?" Her jeering tone did nothing to hide her misery.

He kept his voice cold. "If you keep sniping at me, I may. So be careful."

He sat back, wrestling the compulsion to silence her not with a gag but with his mouth on hers. When he knelt at her feet, her teasing scent had swirled around him once more, a sly invitation to take her into his arms and kiss her again. Then move from kissing to full satisfaction.

The carriage lamps outside shed enough light for him to see her brows contract with bewilderment. Kylemore understood her confusion at the seeming concession. But she'd soon find out that no help for a wayward mistress waited where they went tonight.

*   *   *

Verity continued to sit in quivering silence after Kylemore tied her up. From his comments, she guessed they now headed for an inn. A disreputable inn where abducted women created no stir—not exactly unusual on any road north to Gretna Green.

But when the carriage turned off the road, it rolled between gateposts carved with the Kinmurrie golden eagle. It was too dark to see much; the rain had stopped, but the sky remained cloudy. The carriage lamps illuminated thick bushes growing along the edge of the drive. To a woman teetering on the edge of panic, the sight was far from reassuring.

They pulled up before a large country house, and a man rushed forward to open the carriage door. "Welcome, Your Grace. *Madame*. I trust your journey hasn't been too onerous."

The man had a distinct Scottish brogue. Surely they couldn't be north of the border yet. Kylemore's horses were fast, but they would need to fly to manage that feat.

"It's had its moments," Kylemore said with an irritating huff of laughter as he stepped out.

A blush rose in her cheeks at the deliberate reminder of how she'd succumbed to him. That melting, manipulative kiss had violated her inner self in a way sex never had. And worse, she suspected her tormentor knew it.

The man continued, "Everything is prepared as you requested."

"Thank you, Fergus." Kylemore turned to reach back into the coach and scoop Verity into his arms.

He accomplished the awkward maneuver without difficulty. She wanted to despise him as nothing more than a hulking bully. But unfortunately, his physical dexterity, impressive as it was, paled in comparison to his mental agility. If she had to make an enemy, she thought on a grim spurt of humor, she'd at least chosen one worthy of the name.

Under the impassive gaze of the middle-aged servant, Kylemore hitched her more securely against him. Four torches lit the smooth turning circle before the house, so she saw the Scotsman glance at her bonds, then look away with no change in expression.

There would be no rescue from that direction. No wonder Kylemore hadn't gagged her. She could scream herself hoarse and Fergus would just level another impersonal stare upon her.

The duke's arms were warm and secure around her and reminded her unbearably of how he'd held her when he'd kissed her. Although she knew it would do no real good, Verity stiffened to make it difficult for him to carry her.

"Stop it," he said sharply, shifting his hold. Curse him, he didn't sound remotely breathless as he climbed the wide stairs up to the house's main door.

"I don't care if you drop me," she said defiantly. Fresh air and escape from the carriage, with its pervasive memories of how they'd kissed, combined to reawaken her spirit.

"Brave words. But I doubt you'd appreciate being bruised on the cold hard marble." The firmness of his chest pressed into her side as he tightened his grip.

This close, he felt large, ruthless and powerful. But he smelled like passion and pleasure and peace. Devil take him for kissing her. She began to struggle. Not that her trussed state allowed much leeway for movement.

"If you don't behave, I'll haul you over my shoulder."

"Your Grace's humble servant would never seek such an honor," she said acidly.

"Right." His loud exhalation indicated endless masculine irritation. "Remember, you asked for this."

He balanced her upon her bound feet on the top landing and bent to take her over his shoulder. It was exactly how a farm laborer lifted a sack of wheat. The sudden image from her childhood held her immobile for the moment Kylemore took to settle her as a helpless burden. Her unbound hair flopped around her face in a tangled black curtain. She fisted her dangling hands and made an ineffectual attempt to pummel him into letting her go.

"I didn't ask for this," she choked against his superfine coat. She felt the powerful muscles of his back flexing through the material as he moved.

"Too late," he said, striding toward the door that his minion held open.

Kylemore was so tall that the floor loomed a very long way off indeed. She gulped with a combination of terror and outrage. Not that she thought he'd let her fall. His plans to hurt her didn't include smashing her on the ground.

They were in a candlelit hall now. Elegant black and white tiling replaced the marble landing. Unfortunately, it looked equally hard, and the geometric pattern made her dizzy as she crossed it flung across the duke's shoulder.

"Welcome, Your Grace."

Verity's tumbling mane of hair prevented her from seeing the woman who greeted them.

"Good evening, Mary," the duke said as urbanely as if he'd been at a ball in Mayfair and not lugging a captive about in God knew what obscure corner of the kingdom.

Verity grunted and wriggled to clear her vision, but it was useless. She was humiliated knowing that her rump stuck up in the air and her calves and ankles were exposed. She tried to kick the duke, but his arm remained secure across her thighs.

"The rose room has been readied," the woman, another Scot, said. Both servants sounded absurdly calm, considering that their master carted around a bound and clearly unwilling woman. Perhaps they were used to assisting His Grace with abductions.

"Excellent. We shall bathe. Then supper, I think."

"Very good, Your Grace." Verity heard the servant move away as the duke started up yet more steps. She tried again to kick him to relieve some of her frustration.

He retaliated quickly with a slap across her bottom.

"Ow!" She wriggled in protest, although her skirts and petticoats meant he hadn't actually hurt her. No, the blow had only stung her pride.

"Be still," he growled and began to take the stairs at what from her precarious viewpoint seemed a reckless pace.

By the time he placed her on her feet in a luxurious bedroom, she felt disoriented and a little sick. But that didn't stop her from fighting.

"You really are a savage, aren't you?" she said bitterly. She shook her head to try and clear her hair from her eyes.

"Just remember it," he said, unfazed by the insult. "Here." Impatiently, he reached out and smoothed back her hair, then smiled wryly as she glared at him. "Why don't you sit down? There's a bed just behind you. Your bath shouldn't be long."

"I'd rather stand." She was almost out of her wits with the need to thwart him any way she could.

He shrugged, unimpressed. "As you wish."

Then unbelievably, he turned to go. She'd expected him to stay and continue to torment her. "I shall join you for supper."

The moment she was alone, she subsided onto the bed. As, she suspected—damn him—he'd known she would.

Verity carefully studied the room for a way to escape. This was the first time she'd been alone since her abduction. She had to use the opportunity. Not that she could do much right now, bound as she was. But the duke had mentioned a bath and a meal. Surely he wouldn't keep her tied up then.

Unless he meant to wash and feed her himself.

She gave a shiver, not, much as she hated to admit it,

entirely of disgust, at the idea of those large capable hands soaping her naked body.

The villa in Kensington had boasted the most modern of bathrooms. She and Kylemore had explored the room's sensual potential on a number of occasions. The breath caught in her throat as she remembered the sensation of her wet and naked flesh sliding against his while warm water had lapped around them.

But that had been Soraya. Now she was Verity. And Verity's stern soul had no truck with such decadent pleasures.

To distract her from memories that threatened to prove a disastrous weakness—a weakness she was determined to conquer or die trying—she returned to inspecting the room. It was large and comfortable, with a delicate, rose-patterned wallpaper. Mahogany furniture. An elaborately carved mantel over a grate. Brocade curtains covering two sets of windows.

All disappointingly normal, at least for the rich. Her childhood self would have been speechless with wonder at the thick patterned carpet and silk hangings on the bed, but the woman she had become recognized her surroundings as nothing exceptional, a room for the daughter of the house perhaps.

She should be grateful Kylemore hadn't dumped her in the cellar. It had been a distinct possibility. He was determined to humiliate her, after all.

Perhaps he'd chosen this bedroom with a more specific purpose. Perhaps he meant to relieve his itch for her on this pretty pink coverlet before they traveled on. He'd said he wouldn't touch her, but she didn't trust his word. Especially when every gesture proclaimed his hunger for her.

She shivered in her bonds, terrified of what he'd do to her, terrified she'd respond as mindlessly as she had to that dazzling kiss. Then what hope did she have of prevailing against him?

He meant the memory of that kiss to taunt and torment her, and, God help her, it did. When he'd abducted her, she'd have laughed if anyone had suggested the duke retained any sexual power over her. Now she knew just how easily he could have her on her back, and the knowledge filled her with roiling dread.

The stout door that Kylemore had locked behind him— she had already considered and dismissed that particular avenue of escape—opened. Fergus and a brawny young man hauled in a tub. A woman, whom she assumed was the Mary who'd welcomed them downstairs, followed, carrying soaps and a pile of towels.

The gaping door behind them beckoned, but tied as she was, there was no point even trying to run.

Yet.

She watched silently as the three servants, one of whom was clearly Fergus's son, if his sandy complexion and square jaw were any indication, filled the tub. The room brimmed pleasantly with scent, as if the wallpaper indeed bloomed with masses of pink rosebuds. The sweet perfume lent a jarring air of innocence to her ordeal.

She waited for Kylemore to reappear, but when the door finally closed, only Mary remained. As the woman came toward her, Verity reflected that with her kind blue eyes and untidy graying hair, she made an unlikely criminal accomplice.

Gently, she untied the cords from around Verity's wrists. "I'm Mary Macleish, Fergus's wife and the housekeeper here. Allow me to help you, *madame*," she said in a soft Scots burr.

She addressed Verity with the same French title Fergus had

used upon their arrival. It suited an absconded mistress as well as anything else, Verity supposed. The word's English equivalent, *my lady,* was laughably inappropriate.

As she knelt to release Verity's ankles, something in the woman's carefully controlled features indicated censure. Knowing her chance to make an ally could end any second with Kylemore's arrival, Verity mustered the courage to speak.

"The duke has abducted me. I'm here against my will. Please, you must help me to get away," she said urgently in a low voice.

She doubted the duke would descend to listening at keyholes. But who knew? She'd never have imagined him driven to kidnapping either.

The woman's busy hands paused, then she resumed removing Verity's shoes and stockings. "My family and I owe everything to His Grace. I'm sorry for your plight, *madame,* but I cannot credit the duke truly means you harm." Mary stood up. She kept her eyes downcast, as if she couldn't bear to witness Verity's suffering because if she did, she'd have to do something about it. "I'll help you out of your gown."

"But he does mean me harm. He's said so. You've seen how he treats me." Verity looked helplessly into that impassive face. Frantically, she leaned forward and grabbed Mary's wrist with her newly unbound hands. "Please, I beg of you. Help me! For God's sake, you have to help me."

"There's no need to take the Lord's name in vain," Mary said with more disapproval than Kylemore's unorthodox arrival downstairs had aroused in her. "I told you I can never go against the duke."

Verity could see that as far as the servant was concerned, nothing more remained to be said. But she couldn't give up, not when this might be her only moment away from her jailer. Emotion made her voice shake. "He tied me up. He stole me away from my family. He's threatening to rape me. Surely, you as another woman . . ."

Mary's eyes flickered nervously to the side, as if Kylemore might appear out of the air and send her packing without a reference. "I won't hear anything against him, *madame*. His Grace saved my whole family from poverty and starvation. There isn't a Macleish in this house who wouldn't die for him." This time when she looked at Verity, her eyes held genuine sympathy. "I am very sorry you've come to this pass, but I cannot aid you. Now, please stand up and I'll assist you with your bath."

"If you don't help me escape, you're as guilty as your master," Verity said caustically, although she already knew she was wasting her time. The woman was blindly devoted to Kylemore, and nothing could suborn her loyalty.

A difficult flush reddened Mary's face. "That is as may be, *madame*. But I . . . I cannae help ye. I dinna ken what else tae tell ye." In her growing distress, her Scots brogue thickened. "Please, dinna ask me tae gae against His Grace."

Angry frustration rose to choke Verity. With a disgust aimed more at the woman's employer than Mary herself, she knocked the woman's hand aside from the buttons that fastened the front of the black dress.

She was on her own. Again.

"Leave me," she said flatly.

Mary looked troubled. "His Grace told me to attend you."

"Then attend me by granting me privacy," Verity snapped.

The woman bowed her head in reluctant acknowledgment. "Very well. But I'll stay by the door in case you need me."

In case I turn into a puff of smoke and drift through the keyhole, Verity thought bitterly. Mary left with her shoulders bowed in regret, but that didn't keep her from locking the door securely behind her.

Verity dealt with her most immediate needs, then flung

the curtains back from the windows. Opening them, she peered out. Enough light reflected from the room behind to allow her to assess her chances of getting out this way.

Not great, she decided bleakly.

She was two floors up, and no convenient trees grew close to the house. If she jumped, she'd break her neck. Which offered one solution to her difficulties, she supposed.

She leaned out further, searching for a drainpipe or balcony or ledge, but the building held faithful to the purity of its Palladian origins and was starkly unadorned with meaningless decoration. Verity wondered if she had time to tie the bed hangings together into a rope before another parade of Macleishes marched through the doorway.

"Don't even think about it." The duke strolled into the square of light below her window and lifted a cigar to his lips.

"I was just . . ." she began nervously. The last thing she wanted was for him to invade her precious privacy because he suspected her plans.

He laughed softly and exhaled a cloud of smoke. The smell of fine tobacco rose up to her, blending evocatively with the freshness of the damp garden. "I know exactly what you were just. Go and have your bath. I won't risk losing you so early in the game. That would be poor sport indeed."

He sounded as if he relished watching her fight against the net he twisted around her. Loathing surged up in her so strongly that she would have shot him then and there if she'd had a pistol.

"I am pleased I amuse Your Grace so mightily." Her voice dripped sarcasm.

"Oh, so am I," he said lightly. "And to think the entertainment has only just begun."

Childishly, her only response was to slam the window shut.

* * *

When Kylemore let himself into the rose room, he found his mistress once more garbed as the virtuous widow. The black dress was buttoned tight to the neck. She'd tortured her silky hair into a severe knot. A forbidding expression darkened her silver eyes. Clearly, she wished him to believe she was armored against his wiles.

Unluckily for her, he hadn't even started to exercise his wiles.

Of all the reactions he'd expected during this mad escapade—anger, hatred, satisfaction—he hadn't expected this mad joy. Yet the sight of Soraya sitting before the crackling fire, rebellious and ready to snarl at him over every concession, cheered him as nothing else had in months.

He was indeed as lunatic as his forebears.

He took the seat opposite her at the table and poured them both some claret. From a dresser nearby, an array of covered dishes sent out teasing and tempting smells. But of course, nothing teased and tempted like the beautiful woman scowling at him over the damask tablecloth as if she wanted to kill him.

She probably did, he thought with a mental shrug.

"Should I remove that knife from your reach?" he asked lazily, lounging back and bringing his glass to his lips.

She looked down with surprise, and he saw that she hadn't considered her cutlery's potential as weapons. Not for the first time, he suspected she was a gentle creature at heart. Or at least gentler than she wanted the world to realize.

Gentle? Ha! This was the woman who had used and betrayed him without a moment's hesitation. She could hold her own in a pit of vipers. He mustn't let her beauty gull him into believing her anything but a grasping jade.

Although, God knew, she was beautiful, even in the unbecoming gown and with that unflattering hairstyle. Its starkness merely emphasized the perfect oval of her face, the wide clarity of her remarkable eyes and the soft fullness of her mouth.

Her mouth . . .

He looked away before the thought of kissing that mouth overpowered him. Yet again, he reminded himself that he hadn't stolen her away to fall back into her clutches. He'd stolen her away to show her she couldn't make a fool of the Duke of Kylemore without paying the price for her treason.

He rose to his feet, partly to keep himself from reaching for her. "Shall I serve you? Mary is an excellent cook."

Surprisingly, that damned succulent mouth quirked with sardonic humor. "The condemned prisoner ate a hearty meal?"

He began to fill her plate. "You're welcome to face your fate on an empty stomach, if you prefer."

"No," she said steadily. "I'd rather keep my strength up."

He laughed softly. He wanted her to keep her strength up, too, but for a completely different purpose. He slid a crowded plate in front of her and returned to serve himself.

True to her word, she ate everything placed before her. He noticed, though, she drank sparingly. Clearly, she was determined to keep her wits unclouded by alcohol. He could have told her she wasted her time plotting escape. Having caught her, he meant to keep her.

"The gown didn't meet with your approval?" He indicated a rich ruby garment spread across the bed. He'd sent it up with Mary for his mistress to wear after her bath.

It was a dress exactly right for Soraya—stylish, flamboyant, subtly exotic. He'd chosen it with great pleasure from the modiste who regularly supplied his mistress's wardrobe. He'd had even greater pleasure imagining slowly stripping it away to reveal Soraya's delectable body.

"No, I'd rather wear my own clothing." She didn't even glance toward the extravagant garment.

Strangely, he had to agree that the dress was inappropriate for the woman who sat with such hard-won composure across from him. It was a whore's dress, although admittedly a woefully expensive whore's dress. While his companion's determined lack of artfulness could have almost convinced him she was indeed the chaste widow.

But of course, he knew better. The recollection of those long afternoons of sin in Kensington contradicted any image of propriety she strove to convey now.

Once more, the troubling idea snagged in his mind that she wasn't the same woman she'd been then. And for the first time, he thought of her as Verity before he thought of her as Soraya.

"You'll find yourself well and truly sick of those black rags before we're done," he said now. "And what's the use of this small defiance? It does nothing to change the outcome."

She shook her head and didn't answer him, although he imagined he understood. Each compromise was another step on the road to final defeat. Little did she know she was already inexorably on that road.

Or perhaps she did know.

He rose to his feet and noticed her quickly suppressed recoil. Some devil made him move behind her and place his hands on her shoulders. As if she screamed it at him, he felt her urge to jerk away.

"You promised you wouldn't touch me," she said sharply.

"An offer I've decided was a mistake," he said gently. He curled his fingers over her slender bones, testing her fragility and her strength.

"I won't let you do this!" she cried out. Twisting from his hold, she dove awkwardly for the fire irons. It was the first ungraceful action he'd ever seen her make. "I'll kill you before

I let you take me again," she panted, raising the poker. Her exquisite face was white with tension.

Without shifting from where he stood behind her empty chair, he laughed dismissively. "Don't be a fool, Verity. What are you going to do? Beat my brains out?"

"If I have to," she said. Her perfect breasts heaved under their covering of black bombazine, and strands of hair from the severe hairstyle broke free to brush her cheeks.

Her defiance wasn't a surprise. After all, he'd taunted her into fighting him since the abduction. "You know I can get that poker away from you in the blink of an eye."

"You can try," she said unsteadily.

"Put it down. You achieve nothing except my displeasure." He stepped toward her and extended his hand in a gesture of command. His voice became harder as he continued. "And considering you're completely at my mercy, that might be unwise. So far, I've been remarkably restrained in my actions. Things could go much, much worse."

"You don't frighten me."

"Well, I should," he murmured, beginning to circle her.

The poker remained uplifted, and he couldn't doubt she meant to use it. He supposed he should be nervous facing this furious Valkyrie brandishing an iron club, but instead he felt more alive than he had in three long months.

"I should never have trusted you," she said, edging around to keep him in view.

"Don't pretend you ever did," he said softly and with unexpectedly genuine regret.

His response must have puzzled her, because she frowned and for a moment forgot to watch his eyes. Smoothly, he ducked around her. With ease, he avoided the poker she aimed a little too late at his head. Grasping her arms from behind, he tugged her back against him.

"Let me go, you foul cur!"

He ignored her insult. He wished he could ignore how warm she was. This close, he couldn't help but notice how she trembled. Fear lurked very close beneath the surface of her resistance. But then, he'd immediately understood that.

"Drop it, Verity."

She struggled in his grip. "No, you bastard!"

"Tut, tut, language." His grip slid down to her wrist and tightened just short of pain. "Give it to me or I *will* hurt you."

Something in his voice must have convinced her, because with a despairing exhalation, she dropped her makeshift weapon. It thudded on the carpet at their feet.

He turned her so she faced him. "This is absurd," he said mildly. "Anyone would think you were a frightened virgin. And you must know I'm the last man in creation to fall for that act. For a year, I've had you each way from Sunday. What secrets can your body possibly hold for me now?"

Her eyes were desolate with defeat above the sullen line of her mouth. "I am no longer your mistress," she said dully.

He flung her away with an exclamation of disgust. "If we didn't have to travel on, I'd demonstrate how untrue that is."

She frowned in obvious confusion. "Travel on?" she asked after a fraught pause.

"Yes. I told you in the carriage we headed north without delay." He spoke over his shoulder as he headed out of the room. "I'll be back in half an hour. Use your reprieve to decide cooperation is the safest way to proceed."

Chapter 7

The depressing awareness of failure and the more galling knowledge that she'd behaved like a silly little fool accompanied Verity as Kylemore escorted her to the carriage half an hour later.

Tall, brooding, ominously quiet, he stalked beside her as they left the rose room and descended the stairs. She had no idea what he was thinking behind his mask of aristocratic hauteur. After her attack on him, she supposed he must be fuming. One large hand circled her arm with an implacable hold that told her he had no intention of letting her go until he'd wreaked his cruel revenge to his satisfaction.

Just what had she expected her theatrics with the poker to achieve? A woman's fury would never cow the duke. She'd been so afraid that he'd meant to rut over her on that brocade-covered bed that fear had disordered her reason.

If she brought herself to murder him, she'd hang—which would put a more permanent end to her long-term plans than anything Kylemore devised. If she injured him, she'd only make him angrier than he already was. The grim acceptance seeped into her heart that until he tired of her, nothing short of death could end this persecution.

From the beginning, she'd fatally misread the truth of how he felt about her. In London, she'd assumed he'd wanted her because winning the notorious Soraya complemented his prestige. A year's intimate contact with the duke had taught her that he rated his standing in the world highly indeed.

But now she looked back and considered in a different light altogether his six years of pursuit and the fortune he'd paid to gain her. The light of the Duke of Kylemore's obsession.

For her.

She'd heard rumors about madness in the Kinmurries from her earliest days in the capital. She'd always discounted the talk as overblown gossip. Until now.

She shivered, more frightened than she'd ever been in her life. Worse, he was perceptive enough to note her terror and use it against her.

Once they were outside the manor, she saw why he hadn't tied her up again. Macleishes surrounded her. Their set expressions indicated they wouldn't hesitate to act should she show the slightest sign of mutiny.

But her chastening humiliation in the rose room meant rebellious impulses had temporarily deserted her. Pitting herself against Kylemore's physical strength had been a mistake. She still cringed at how easily he'd disarmed her.

Two more Macleish sons traveled on with the duke. With no great interest, she watched them climb up next to the driver. One set of jailers was much the same as another. The only jailer who really mattered was the lean, powerful man pressed so close to her side.

Kylemore bundled her into the coach without a word. He followed her inside, sat opposite her, knocked sharply on the roof, and they were away. He didn't release his proprietary clasp on her arm until they picked up speed.

How she wished she'd controlled her temper at the house. Now he was more careful than ever to stop her eluding him.

It was a long time before Verity finally asked the question that had puzzled her since their arrival at the manor. "Have we already reached Scotland?"

He roused himself from his abstraction. He hadn't spoken since they'd started north again, what felt like hours ago. She expected him to sound hostile or angry, given that she'd just tried to smash his skull, but he spoke with his usual urbane calmness.

"No. We're still in Yorkshire. Why?"

"The Macleishes."

"They're caretakers at Hinton Stacey. I only open the house a few weeks a year during the shooting. Otherwise, the Macleishes run it for me."

"They seem remarkably devoted to you," she said sourly. Mary Macleish's automatic and sincere praise of the duke had shocked and bewildered her. The woman had described someone Verity didn't recognize.

By the light of the carriage lamps outside, she saw his cynical smile flicker. "They know which side their bread is buttered on."

But Verity thought it was more than that. The Macleishes treated the duke like a hero. Did he conceal a better man within than he let the world see? And would that better man relent in his quest for retribution against his mistress?

Unfortunately, she doubted it.

He reached out and took her hands. "We both need to sleep." He laced her hands together and tied one end of the cord to his own wrist.

She was too tired and discouraged to protest. What good

would it achieve anyway? He'd do what he wanted with her. That was the unvarnished reality of being his captive.

After four days on the road, Verity viewed her short stay at Hinton Stacey with a nostalgia she'd never have believed possible. She had no more steaming, perfumed baths, no more freshly cooked meals served on fine china that gleamed in the candlelight. And as for the large bed that had terrified her into attacking her abductor, it was laughably removed from the sleeping arrangements she endured on that endless journey.

They traveled night and day. She grew to hate the rattling, constantly moving carriage almost as intensely as she hated Kylemore.

Kylemore, who didn't touch her but who wanted to so much that every moment between them was as sharp and cutting as a new knife. Kylemore, with his iron nerves and his nonchalance and his eternal surveillance. Even when she relieved herself in some isolated thicket, he and his henchmen patrolled the area within earshot.

It was mortifying. It was infuriating. It was clearly meant to break her spirit.

Verity Ashton's spirit was harder to break than most. She refused to succumb to weakness or fatigue or anxiety. Hating Kylemore with every shred of her being gave her the strength to endure.

Enough of Soraya remained for her to consider subverting one of the Macleishes. The youngest boy, who she guessed was about sixteen, cast shyly admiring glances in her direction when he thought nobody noticed.

But the part of her that remembered working as a servant revolted at the prospect of destroying someone's livelihood for her own purposes. The Macleishes were abetting a crime, but they were only the Devil's helpers. The blame lay with their master. Such a greenling didn't deserve to face destitution for his loyalty to an evil employer.

She'd hoped some rustic Lancelot might turn up to rescue her when they changed horses, but Kylemore held his hand over her mouth every time they stopped. And he always sent someone ahead to make arrangements so the changes happened smoothly and with notable speed.

On the fourth night, they camped in an abandoned crofter's cottage instead of going on. Verity was so sick of the rattling, cramped conveyance that she didn't question this change in their wearisome routine.

They'd crossed the border the day before, and with every mile, the roads worsened. Today, the carriage had lurched and bumped so violently that she was surprised none of her teeth had shaken loose.

As darkness closed in, she sat on the carriage rugs, which the Macleishes had spread for her comfort upon the sod floor. She watched silently as they prepared the evening meal. Oatcakes and salt herring yet again.

Verity, you're getting soft, she told herself. *There was a point in your life when oatcakes and herring would have seemed a feast.* But self-castigation didn't keep her from thinking that she'd sell her soul for a hot bath and a meal she ate with a knife and fork.

At least the roof was whole and she was, mercifully, dry. The temperature had dropped, and a sullen rain fell outside. The dank wind through the unsealed windows was a bleak reminder of how far north they'd penetrated. It might be August, but she was cold.

Wondering where Kylemore was, she shifted closer to the fire. He'd never left her alone and untied before. She didn't waste what remained of her energy in making escape plans.

Even if she managed to evade the Macleishes, where could she go in this depopulated wasteland? What a brutal place this Scotland of Kylemore's was.

She heard voices and the sound of horses outside. The duke strode in, his dark hair sleeked back from his high fore-head and his manner as purposeful as ever. She eyed him resentfully. Even after coming in out of the rain, he didn't look as if he'd been dragged through a muddy hedge.

Oh, no. His Grace had taken advantage of his lackeys' valeting skills. His Grace's linen was white and pristine.

His Grace made her want to scream.

"Andy and Angus have arrived." He addressed the Macleishes. "We'll sleep here tonight. You can take the coach down to Kylemore Castle tomorrow."

More travel plans. She lost interest. She didn't know where they were. She didn't know where they went. Even if she did, her opinion was of no importance.

Kylemore brought over her meal and sat next to her, stretching his long booted legs toward the fire. She'd become inured to his silence. Leaving Whitby, his humor had been to mock and berate. But since she'd threatened him with the poker, he'd hardly said a word to her. The longer they traveled, the further he withdrew into himself.

She didn't fool herself into thinking that the lack of com-munication indicated he no longer hungered for her. He hungered, all right. He just didn't do anything about it. And the delay was gradually sending her mad.

Why didn't he just take her? What did he wait for? Cer-tainly not her consent. If he preferred privacy, it would be easy enough to send the Macleishes ahead while he took his pleasure.

When they'd left Hinton Stacey, she'd been sure he'd meant to use her without delay. That passionate kiss, regretted more than she could say, had made any protest she voiced moot. But aside from binding and unbinding her, he'd barely touched her.

She was free now, but she knew that he'd tie her up before they slept. She'd reached such a pitch of exhaustion that she could no longer muster even a murmur of objection.

She bent her head and began to eat, although she hardly tasted the humble fare. She was so tired that she wanted to lie down and never move again. Every bone and muscle ached. Perhaps a bed on the ground would provide more rest than sitting up in the coach, but she doubted it. Her abused flesh felt every bump and hollow in the floor beneath the rugs.

Two newcomers joined them around the fire—clearly, the Andy and Angus Kylemore had mentioned.

Then she recognized the overgrown thugs who had assisted so efficiently at her abduction. Her dinner tumbled to the ground as she surged upward on legs that trembled after so long in the carriage.

"What have you done with my brother?" she cried shrilly. "Tell me what you've done to Ben."

"Hold your peace, woman!" Kylemore leaped to his feet and was behind her in an instant. He slid his arms around her waist before she could launch herself upon the two men.

As if a puny creature like her could damage those man mountains. Although she'd dearly love to. Her boiling rage made a mockery of her earlier apathy.

"Let me go!" she snarled, fighting against the duke's imprisoning hands.

"There's no use shouting at them. They don't have the English."

Kylemore addressed the men in what she guessed was Gaelic. One of them replied readily enough, while keeping an uncertain eye on Verity.

"Your brother is fine." Kylemore's deep voice rumbled

close to her ear. She tried to ignore the clean, male scent of him. He still smelled like the outdoors, although now it was an outdoors washed clean by the freshness of rain. "They released him in the abbey and have followed us ever since."

Verity gave up her futile struggle. Bitter experience told her he'd only let her go when he was ready.

"They just left Ben there no worse for the encounter?" she asked, not bothering to hide her mistrust.

Another exchange in Gaelic before Kylemore answered her, still, damn him, without moving away. His breath brushed against her cheek and made the blood surge hot beneath her skin. "Apparently."

"I don't believe you," Verity said coldly, stifling her disquieting sensual awareness. "Ben would come after me."

More Gaelic. An infuriating burst of masculine laughter. Even the younger Macleishes joined in. Kylemore's grin was a flash of brilliant white as he released her and stepped in front of her, elegant, handsome, impervious.

How she hated him.

"I'm sure he would have if he'd had a stitch of clothing to cover himself with," he said.

Anger surged up as strongly as it had when he'd snatched her from her brother's care in Whitby.

"You, sir, are a member of a barbarous race," she said with contempt. "All of you disgrace the name of men."

The duke's smile froze on his face. "At least none of us is a thief or a liar, madam," he said in the frigid voice that always sliced her to the quick. It was a voice he'd never used when he'd spoken to Soraya. Not until the day she'd rejected his marriage proposal.

She raised her chin and cast him a disdainful glance. "I was an honest whore. A pity neither you nor your men can lay claim to so much virtue as that."

Proudly, she returned to her corner. Curling her legs under

her, she stared sightlessly ahead and tried not to watch the Scots' triumphant hilarity. She blinked away the first tears she'd shed since this ordeal had started.

Poor Ben. He didn't know if she was alive or dead. Her heart grieved for her brother's humiliation and his anguish when he failed to find her. It hadn't missed her notice that Kylemore used mainly side roads. Nor that now they were in the wilderness, anyone would find it impossible to pursue them.

Her brother was resourceful and clever. He'd find her, if anyone could. As it had so many times since she'd left Whitby, that frail hope beat back her dangerous weakness.

Her jailers caroused late around the campfire, drinking some disgusting spirit the new arrivals had brought with them. Verity sat on the rugs in the shadows, but she didn't fool herself that the men's seeming distraction put freedom within reach. Every time she so much as shifted, Kylemore's cold blue stare settled on her.

The duke didn't join in the revelry, although she was surprised at his level of familiarity with his henchmen. He'd never been a model of sociability, but she knew him enough to recognize the strong bond he shared with these men. She couldn't imagine a group of English servants behaving with such ease in the presence of their aristocratic master.

Eventually, Kylemore left his companions and came across to where she waited. In the uncertain golden light, his expression was unreadable. Whatever liquor he'd imbibed had made no inroads on his uncanny control. She suppressed a shiver that had nothing to do with the cold air and everything to do with what he might want from her.

Was he still angry over her insult? Did he mean to punish her? She'd long ago accepted that none of the Macleishes would interfere if the duke chastised her physically. In

London, he'd never mistreated her. Here beyond the reaches of civilization, who knew what he'd do if she tested his temper far enough? He might kill her. Sometimes on this endless journey, she wished he would.

He knelt before her in a pose that conveyed nothing of supplication. "Give me your hands."

His voice brooked no argument. Wordlessly and with a scorn she wanted him to see, she obeyed. She did her best to hide her fear, as she had since he'd reappeared to fracture her quest for chaste anonymity. A pity she knew her false bravado didn't fool him in the slightest.

He bound her, then tied the end of the cord around his own wrist. The pattern was familiar after the nights in the carriage, when both had grabbed what sleep they could sitting opposite one another. But tonight, of course, was different. For the first time, they hadn't traveled through the night.

Although she thought it unlikely he'd ravish her in full view of his men, she couldn't stop herself from hissing, "Remember your promise."

His face remained impassive. "Don't worry. You're safe enough for now."

Sometimes she wondered if she imagined his tamped blaze of desire, but on this occasion she had no doubts at all. Lust all but smoked from his lean form.

Strange to consider that while he'd always been in many ways a puzzle to her, she'd never had any difficulty assessing his precise level of sexual arousal. When she'd seen him across Sir Eldreth's crowded drawing room, she'd known immediately that he'd wanted her. She'd known that even before she'd known who he was.

She wished to heaven she'd never found out who he was.

The duke lay down. For as long as she could, Verity sat up, but eventually exhaustion made her stretch out next to him. He grunted wearily and tugged one of the rugs up to keep them from the chill. She waited for him to haul her into his arms, but he lay separate from her and stared up into the rough rafters of the roof. The men across the room gradually settled. All was quiet apart from the rain pattering on the roof when Kylemore spoke.

"Don't pin your hopes on your brother rescuing you."

Verity didn't answer but moved as far away from him as the length of the ties allowed. Unfortunately, it wasn't far enough to forget he was there.

Verity woke to a delicious feeling of heat and comfort. It was dark, but something told her night was almost over. To confirm that impression, the first morning bird called from the trees outside the cottage.

Kylemore's powerful arms twined around her, and he slept heavy and still beside her. His scent and heat surrounded her like a sensual miasma. Under the blanket that covered them to the waist, he'd flung one long leg across hers in an unmistakable claim of ownership.

It was too much for her to bear. Choking with outrage, she struggled frantically to put some distance between them.

He groaned as he half woke. "Jesus, woman! What is it?"

"Let me go!" she said in a fierce whisper, punching him wildly in her attempt to free herself.

He sat up and rapidly worked at the cord that tangled them together. "Damn it, Verity. Settle down," he snapped.

Thank God he no longer clutched her as if they were lashed together in a rough sea. She took her first full breath since she'd woken.

"Tie me to something else," she said, still with a trace of her earlier hysteria. "I don't want to sleep with you."

"You're being absurd," he said in a bored voice, fiddling with the knotted cord.

"Is everything all right over there, Your Grace?" One of

the Macleish boys lifted his head and rubbed bleary eyes in the light of the dying fire.

"Nothing I can't handle." Then a short burst of Gaelic that made the other man laugh sleepily.

Verity had no trouble interpreting their masculine amusement at her foolishness. She wished every male on earth to Hades at that moment. With the hottest spot reserved for the fiend at her side.

Eventually, Kylemore straightened the ties. With a long-suffering sigh, he lay down once more. She was thankful to notice he kept a space between them this time.

"Don't touch me again!" she said vehemently, lying on her back and staring blindly up into the shadows in the roof.

"As you wish, madam," he said wearily. He rolled away and went back to sleep with annoying speed.

Verity listened to Kylemore's even breathing, while her heart pounded with dread and self-doubt. How could she snuggle up to him with the trust of a child? She hated him. She feared him. And if she'd learned anything, it was that she had to be constantly on her guard. This time, her blistering contempt focused solely on her own ruinous weakness rather than on the obliviously slumbering rake beside her.

Chapter 8

The rain stopped before dawn, and the day promised to set fair. Verity stood next to the duke in the unreliable sunshine and watched the detested coach rattle away down the hill.

"Is this our final destination?" she asked incredulously. "I imagined something more fitting to Your Grace's consequence."

She'd left—under his escort, of course—to wash in a stream that ran behind the ruin. Now she found their transport abandoning them. Doubtfully, she glanced at the tumbledown cottage. It was whole but hardly luxurious.

"The coach can go no further in these hills. Now we take the ponies." He gestured with one elegant hand toward a previously unnoticed string of horses tied under a tree.

This was the most information she'd managed to coax out of him in days. "But didn't you say we go to Kylemore Castle?"

"No. I said the Macleishes did. My home isn't nearly private enough for what I intend." His voice bit, as if he realized he'd briefly treated her as a fellow human being and now regretted it. He strode over to where Angus and Andy, apparently all that remained of their escort, waited.

She stumbled after him, risking another withering setdown. "That's very well, except for one thing."

He turned to her. Ill-concealed impatience shadowed his fine-boned, intelligent face. "I've already told you—what you wish is of no consequence."

She gritted her teeth. "But it is of very great consequence that I don't ride."

The blank look of genuine amazement that chased his annoyance away would have made her laugh in other circumstances. Obviously, the thought had never occurred to this scion of the aristocracy that the entire world wasn't flung on horseback before it could walk. But Verity had never ridden. She was frightened of horses, a legacy of a childhood accident when one of her father's draft team had trampled her.

"You'll pick it up soon enough," he said flatly after a pause. He left her and headed toward the ponies as though his pronouncement solved the issue. When she didn't immediately follow, he stopped and turned his head. "Come on."

"No," she said sullenly.

Nothing on earth—dangerous noblemen with uncertain tempers included—was coaxing her any closer to those snorting, murderous beasts.

He sighed with irritation and stalked back in her direction. "We can't stay here. You must see that. The coach has gone. The ponies are the only way we can proceed."

"Then I'll walk."

He cast a speaking look at her slight figure. "You'd collapse halfway up the first hill."

"Then leave me here to starve," she snapped. "That should be plenty of revenge for you."

"Not nearly." He spoke lightly, although she had no doubt he meant what he said.

"I'm not riding."

His jaw firmed in a way she'd have found daunting if she hadn't already been so daunted by the prospect of getting on a horse. "Yes, you are."

She sidled away but not quickly enough. He caught her wrist and tugged her closer. "You're not going anywhere."

Without releasing her, he bent and scooped her into his arms. He hadn't carried her since they'd left Hinton Stacey. For a moment, surprise and unwelcome memories of how he'd kissed her in the carriage held her quiescent.

Then she started to wriggle. "Put me down!"

He laughed, damn him. "Behave or I'll throw you over my shoulder again. We haven't time for this nonsense. If the weather breaks, you'll think our journey until now paradise in comparison."

"I don't ride!" she protested.

"You do now." He paused and gave her a searching look. "You're shaking like a leaf."

She thought she caught fleeting concern in his eyes. Then she dismissed the impression as the kind of wishful thinking she'd abandoned with her chastity so many years ago. Anger with herself added extra edge to her retort. "Of course I'm shaking, you great oaf."

He laughed again, the heartless bully, confirming that his brief moment of compassion had never existed. "You're giving Angus and Andy great entertainment. They're convinced all Sassenach women are mad."

"I don't care," she muttered.

She was shivering violently by the time Kylemore stopped in front of the lead pony, an evil-looking dun. In spite of everything, she shrank against her tormentor.

"Please, Your Grace, put me down." Not even the most sympathetic ear would hear anything except a mewling plea in her words.

Of course he didn't relent. He'd snatched her from her home to torture her, after all.

She braced herself for mockery, but instead he spoke with a quiet steadiness that penetrated her dread as surely as a knife through soft butter. "I didn't think you were afraid of anything, Verity."

I'm afraid of you, she admitted despairingly in her heart, then gasped as he dumped her unceremoniously in the side-saddle. Only with the greatest effort did she keep herself from screaming. She froze into trembling stiffness.

The horse wasn't large, but she felt a dizzyingly long way from the ground. She sucked in a deep breath to control her roiling nausea and clutched at the saddle for balance.

"Angus!" Kylemore shouted to the nearest giant as the horse showed every sign of bolting under its awkward burden.

The giant grabbed the reins and spoke soothingly to the heaving demon beneath her. Kylemore placed his gloved hands on either side of her. His looming nearness melted the icy paralysis that held her motionless, and she tried to slide off.

"Stop that," he said softly, leaning in to keep her in the saddle. "You'll frighten the horses."

His effrontery penetrated even her all-pervasive panic. How she loathed him. Terror and hatred fought for dominance in her quaking soul. If only she'd wrenched the pistol from his grasp in Whitby and put a bullet through his black heart. She whipped her head up to glare at him.

"*I'll* frighten the horses?" she repeated in outrage.

"Yes. They're simple creatures. Hysterical women unnerve them." Firmly, he hooked her feet into the stirrups and adjusted the length. He placed one hand on the small of her back to hold her upright. She tried and failed to ignore the warm support. "You're as stiff as a board. Relax."

"That's easy for you to say," she said resentfully while remaining as still as she possibly could.

How was she to cling on when the cursed beast moved? She would fall and its churning hooves would smash her to pieces. She closed her eyes and swallowed another surge of nausea.

Kylemore sighed and gently began to stroke her. Every nerve in her body focused on the circles his hand made on her back. Despite the shudders of fear that wracked her frame, she adopted a more natural pose.

"I can't take you up with me," he said gently. "My pony will barely hold my weight as it is. And the going is too rough and uneven for us to ride Tannasg."

She felt what little color she had left in her cheeks drain away. Opening her eyes, she looked across to Tannasg, the duke's huge gray gelding tethered nearby, who seemed to loom at least ten times larger than the denizen of hell beneath her.

He must have read her expression. "Exactly. Now, be brave. We're going on with the ponies." With his free hand, he loosened her fingers from where they hooked into the front of the saddle and placed them in the animal's coarse mane. The pony shifted restively under her.

Kylemore whispered Gaelic reassurances to the horse. Verity was mortified to hear exactly the same tone he'd used to convince her to stay in the saddle. She was even more mortified when the animal proved just as pliant as she under his persuasion.

"I can't do this," she said unevenly.

"Yes, you can. I'll lead you. You'll be quite safe. Just hold on and pray if it makes you feel better."

"Nothing will make me feel better," she said with a trace of sulkiness.

He reached out to touch her cheek. "Take heart, Verity. You've never lacked courage before."

The uncomplicated friendliness of the gesture astonished her so much that it took a few moments to comprehend something even more amazing. He'd just complimented her on something that had nothing to do with Soraya's sultry beauty and everything to do with Verity's sturdier qualities.

And he no longer seemed to think of her as Soraya first and Verity second. That deep voice had spoken her name without hesitation.

By the time she'd come to terms with that startling realization, their small caravan had lurched into motion, and she trailed meekly in Kylemore's wake.

Beauty bit sharper than any blade. No matter how Kylemore tried, he couldn't stop it slicing deep into his heart, making mockery of the armor he'd built up over years of absence.

From the broad back of his pony, he looked at the Highlands in late summer glory and tried to keep shrieking memories of terror and misery at bay. But they overwhelmed his ramshackle defenses and possessed his soul. He closed his eyes in unspoken anguish.

He hadn't been this far north since he was seven years old. He'd forgotten the clear air, the endless rows of mountains fading to blue, the wide skies, the red of the rowan berries, the purple of the heather, the soft music of running water. He'd forgotten this ineffable beauty woven like a rich gilt thread through the wretchedness of his childhood.

Beauty.

The one weakness he'd never conquered until he'd encountered Soraya and fallen victim to even greater weakness.

Although originally, of course, her beauty was what had drawn him toward her and his own destruction. He'd glimpsed her, exquisite, perfect, proud, across Sir Eldreth's drawing room and known he must possess her and keep her as his forever.

What he discovered now only deepened his insatiable fascination. Strange to admit he'd learned more about her during these days of arduous travel than he ever had when she'd played his cooperative paramour.

He'd come to realize Soraya was in many ways a falsehood. Soraya was at ease with her gorgeous body and with sexual pleasure. Soraya was a creature addicted to luxury who would recoil in fastidious horror at the privations of this journey. Soraya was endlessly compliant to a lover's demands. Asked for one word to define his mistress, he'd have chosen *sybarite*.

Verity, on the other hand, was made of sterner stuff.

Verity guarded her chastity like a miser guarded his treasure. Nothing of the seductress softened that intransigent soul. Every time Kylemore touched her, she looked like she wanted to cry. Or bite and scratch at him like a wild cat. Soraya had certainly bitten and scratched upon occasion, but only as part of her repertoire of love games.

Verity had endured the journey without complaint. When he'd set out on this trek, a childish streak in him had relished the idea of his mistress whining and caviling at the hardship. Her weakness would somehow justify how he treated her. But against his better judgment, with every day that passed, his grudging respect for the woman he'd abducted grew. It was damned inconvenient, but he could do nothing about it.

She took everything he threw at her and still came back fighting. He even found a grim amusement in realizing that she'd come closest to breaking not because of anything he'd done but at the prospect of riding a horse.

He didn't want to respect her. He wanted to foster the rage that had sent him on this reckless quest. He wanted to hate her as he'd hated her in London, even while he couldn't forget how he wanted her with every breath.

Broodingly, he surveyed the starkly magnificent scenery that surrounded him. There was a truth in this landscape that pulverized self-serving deceptions about how far he'd come from the sniveling craven he'd once been. He'd never intended to return to the site of his shameful agony and fear.

Yet again, it was bleakly apparent that what he wanted didn't count. He just hoped to hell his ruthlessness endured. Perhaps he could fight his childhood recollections. But could he hold out against the woman who trailed after him, her flawless face ashen as she clung to her ungainly pony?

That night, they stopped at another deserted cottage. Verity noted there was no shortage of abandoned buildings to shelter the traveler. Plenty of buildings but no inhabitants. They hadn't encountered another soul all day. Even accounting for the duke's desire for secrecy, this seemed peculiar.

The countryside became wilder with every mile. Yorkshire, where she'd grown up, was more rugged than the south, but these dramatic Scottish hills and cliffs and lochs were outside her experience. She quashed a superstitious notion that Kylemore conveyed her beyond the reach of human help.

One thing, however, she was sure of—Ben couldn't trace her here. Kylemore's confident assertion that her brother would never find her was fully justified, damn him. The confusing maze of ridges and valleys meant nobody had a hope of tracking their party.

Her horse still made her nervous, although she'd managed to control it after a fashion. During her long day in the saddle, she'd decided the beast's principal role was as a four-legged instrument of torture. She groaned and shifted her sore rump, trying to find a more forgiving position on the ground. There was a rug under her, but it didn't help much.

Kylemore crossed the room and dropped to his haunches before her. If she hadn't hated him already, she'd hate him now. How could the rigors of travel not affect him? It was unnatural. He didn't look tired or worn, although something told her his mind was troubled.

Not that she was naïve enough to imagine he fretted over what he did to her. No, something else disturbed his vaunted sangfroid. She banished any curiosity with a mental shrug. He was welcome to keep his secrets.

"Sore?" he asked softly. On the few occasions she'd seen his expression that day, she'd remarked its grimness. But right now, if she hadn't known better, she'd believe he was genuinely concerned for her comfort.

She dismissed that fatuous conclusion and sent him a fulminating glare. "You'd love me to admit that, wouldn't you?"

A faint smile flickered across his face. "Behave yourself or I won't do my magic and make you feel better."

She surveyed him sourly. "How are you going to accomplish that? Shoot me?"

"If all else fails, I'll keep that in mind." He turned his head and spoke in Gaelic. The two giants rose from the corner, where they sat talking in low tones, and left the cottage to the duke and his captive.

The time had come. Finally after all the fraught waiting, he meant to reassert his rights of possession over her body. She was too worn out to summon anything more than a dull anger. She told herself she'd survive this as she'd survived so much else. After hours on that wretched horse, she already ached so badly that she probably wouldn't even feel him pounding into her.

But beneath the tiredness and meaningless bravado, her heart keened in misery.

"Lie back."

"This won't help," she said tonelessly, obeying him.

What was the point of fighting? This moment had been inevitable from the beginning, and for all her hard-held defiance, she didn't want him to hurt her.

He laughed briefly. "Miss Ashton, you have a nasty, suspicious mind." For once, she didn't sense any hostility. The change only heightened her fear. When he was kind, he was at his most dangerous.

He began to unlace her half boots. She couldn't rouse the will to flinch away. He'd easily catch her if she tried to run on legs stiff after a day's unaccustomed riding.

His hands were cool on her bare legs. She'd rinsed her stockings, and they currently adorned a discreet hawthorn bush outside. She tensed. Perhaps she wasn't quite as inured to her fate as she'd thought.

"Relax," he murmured. "Or I might forget my good intentions."

"As if you have any," she muttered. "As if you have ever had . . . Ohhh!"

Whatever she meant to say faded in a long sigh of pleasure as those adept fingers began to mold the muscles in her calves.

"That's enough," she eventually forced herself to insist, although she thought that if he stopped touching her, she'd weep.

"In a minute," he said, and she couldn't summon further demurrals.

"Roll over," he said after a blissful interval.

With no thought to protest, she turned onto her stomach and lay still as he raised her skirts to reveal her legs to the evening air. For a long time, the firelit cottage was silent except for the crackle of the flames and the sound of his hands working her flesh.

She'd floated off into a world of weary pleasure when she felt him reach beneath her to release the front of her dress. As his fingers brushed across her breasts, her instincts prodded her into hazy wariness.

"What are you doing?" she asked huskily.

He tugged her dress down, uncovering her shoulders—and effectively trapping her arms. "I'm sure your back is as sore as the rest of you," he said neutrally.

Actually, her rump had taken the worst punishment during the hours on that iron-backed succubus. But despite her current state of exhausted stupidity, she knew better than to invite him to touch her buttocks. Even allowing him to rub her back was asking for trouble.

"You should . . ."

He began to knead her tight shoulders. She took a moment to remember what she meant to say. "You should stop now. I feel much better."

Those fiendishly competent fingers didn't pause. She tried to tell herself she wasn't glad.

"You've got another day of riding tomorrow, Verity."

"Oh."

She supposed she'd known that. Of course this poor ruin was only another temporary camp. But her befuddled mind hadn't actually gone so far as to register that more horseback-based misery awaited her so soon. She closed her eyes and let the duke's healing hands continue.

What was the use resisting him? He always won in the end.

She'd drifted away into a sleepy daze when she felt him arrange her dress into respectability. Then a breath of air before a blanket settled over her.

"Sleep, Verity," he said softly.

She snuggled into the warmth, luxuriating in the glorious

looseness of her limbs. She was too lethargic to be surprised at his care.

"Thank you," she whispered, but he'd already gone.

Only in the morning did she realize this was the first night during their endless purgatory of a journey that he hadn't tied her up.

Late the next afternoon, they paused on a cliff. The duke turned back toward Verity.

"That's where we're heading." His deep voice sounded even bleaker than usual.

Perhaps the journey was finally taking its toll on even his patience. Today, she'd seen little trace of last night's Good Samaritan, with his undemanding kindness and gentle hands.

She was just as tired and ill-humored as she'd been yesterday after a day in the saddle. It was impossible to arouse any interest in where they stopped tonight. She swore to herself that she'd never, after this, take life's more prosaic comforts for granted. Warm water. Clean clothes. A hot meal eaten at a table. She'd savor each of these humble luxuries and send thanks to her Maker for providing them.

That is, if she ever had the chance to enjoy such pleasures again.

Without urging, her pony ambled up to stand beside Kylemore's. Verity looked over the edge into a valley like so many she'd already seen. Woods. A clear stream winding into a large, shining loch. No sign of people.

Then she realized this valley wasn't exactly the same as every other. This valley contained a substantial house with a cluster of other buildings around it. A house, moreover, in good repair. A house that was even inhabited, if the smoke coming from the chimney was any indication.

She waited for Kylemore to say something else, but he

merely guided his pony onto the path down the ridge. Her mount, tied to his saddle, followed.

Their small and rather odd caravan—a nobleman, a whore, two giants, a string of pack ponies and a thoroughbred worth as much as a small estate—made its way downward. The duke's promise to leave her alone finished when they reached the house, clearly the hunting box he'd mentioned back in Whitby an eon ago.

The grueling journey was over. Now her real punishment began.

Chapter 9

Kylemore reined in on the rough patch of grass before the house. Strangely, everything was exactly how he remembered. After so many years away, his memory should have played tricks, but each detail matched his starkest recollections.

The child hidden inside him longed to run away screaming. The self-contained nobleman he'd since become kept his seat on his inelegant mount and waited for Angus to announce their arrival. He didn't look at Verity—perhaps because those perceptive gray eyes would see too much if he did.

"Your Grace!" Hamish Macleish opened the door and rushed out. "Your Grace, I didnae ken ye would arrive today."

Unlike the house, Hamish had changed. When they had last met, Hamish had been a vigorous man in the prime of life. He was still tall and straight, but his hair was white, and twenty harsh winters had weathered his face into crags and lines.

"Your Grace, come away in with ye out of the evening air. Your lady will like a bonny fire and a cup of tea, I'm sure."

"I'm sure," Kylemore said, dismounting and turning back toward Verity.

Actually, her expression indicated that *his lady* might prefer a dash of hemlock in that tea. He needn't have worried about her divining his secrets from his demeanor. She looked too petrified to contemplate anything except the fate awaiting her in this house.

He'd wanted to crush Soraya's pride. Now he found little satisfaction in her terrified silence.

"I'll at least get you inside before I have my wicked way with you," he sniped under his breath, hoping irritation might melt the frozen dread from her face. But his hands were gentle as he lifted her from the saddle.

She hardly seemed to hear him, but she trembled under his hold while she found her balance.

He frowned. What was the matter with the chit, for God's sake? He knew she was afraid—he'd set out to make her so. But it wasn't as if he planned to do anything to her he hadn't done before. Or did she imagine he really intended her harm? If he'd wanted to murder her, it would have been considerably more convenient to do it back in Yorkshire.

Anger with Verity—anger part of him recognized wasn't her fault at all—carried him over the threshold as he hauled her inside. There was indeed a good fire in the parlor, as Hamish had promised, and the ugly, old-fashioned furniture stood exactly where it had when he'd been a boy. Twenty years had passed, and the house's layout was imprinted on his mind as if his torments here had occurred only yesterday.

He released Verity and moved forward to stand beside a bulky carved oak armchair, where the servants had often restrained his father with thick leather straps. It was the only chair in the house sturdy enough to hold the sixth duke when his madness was upon him. With a shuddering breath, Kylemore banished the horrific image of his father drooling and screaming and tearing at his bonds with long-fingered hands identical to his own.

When Kylemore had left as a bawling seven-year-old, he'd sworn nothing on earth would make him return to this place. He hadn't counted on his passion for the conniving demirep who hovered hesitantly on the rug before the grate.

Although it was hard to see the avaricious harpy of his accusations in the pale, frightened girl before him. Hard to see the great Soraya.

Her unbecoming black dress was worn, dirty and bedraggled. Her beautiful hair, despite her valiant efforts on the road, badly needed a maid's attention. She looked tired, scared, defeated.

Hell, there had to be something wrong with him. He still thought her the most beautiful creature he'd ever seen. Nothing he'd done to her had diminished her loveliness.

Hamish followed them in. "Shall I serve tea, Your Grace?"

Kylemore glanced at Verity. She looked ready to collapse. He'd wanted to vanquish her, but the prospect of her prostrate at his feet through sheer exhaustion didn't seem much of a victory.

"No. Trays in our rooms, Hamish. Perhaps bring *madame* tea while her bath is prepared."

Hamish bowed. "As Your Grace wishes."

As he left, Kylemore tried not to remember that the last time they'd met, Hamish had called him Justin—not Your Grace. Then, he'd been proud to call Hamish his friend. The intervening years had altered that closeness as well.

Verity was so still that she could have been planted there. He sighed and crossed the room to lift her in his arms. Unless he helped her, he doubted she'd make it upstairs to the first real bed she'd seen in days. Another twinge of conscience, familiar after days on the road, joined the noxious mix of feelings inside him.

When she stiffened, rejecting his touch, his uncertain temper snapped. His nerves were on edge—they had been for days—and her stubborn resistance provided his turbulent emotions with a focus.

"For Christ's sake, woman! You're safe until you've washed at least," he growled down into her wan features.

Wan no longer. A difficult color rose in her cheeks. The unworthy jibe would sting the proud Soraya. He beat back an unwelcome wave of protectiveness; he'd brought her here to punish her, not to become her nursemaid, blast her.

Despite this, his hold was tender as he strode out of the parlor, across the hall and up the stairs. He told himself he only imagined she was lighter than she'd been at Hinton Stacey. But he was guiltily aware that she'd eaten very little in the last week. She seemed terrifyingly fragile, nothing but birdlike bones and perfect white skin.

Then he met her fierce silver eyes.

"I haven't surrendered," she said steadily.

He read the defiance in her as sharply as if she'd carved it on his flesh with a needle. He should have known better than to think he'd conquer her so swiftly. That stalwart soul wouldn't bow just because she was weary and afraid. Renewed relish for the contest between them swamped his brief uncertainty.

Two maids were in the bedroom filling a bath and laying out soaps and towels. They curtseyed and greeted him in the musical Gaelic he still thought of as his heart's language.

He placed Verity on her feet in the center of the room. Everything was prepared as he'd ordered. Of course it was. He was the Duke of Kylemore, he thought with no satisfaction whatsoever.

"I shall see you in the morning," he said abruptly.

She blinked at him with dazed surprise. She must have expected him to jump on her before she'd had a chance to take off her shoes. Devil take her, after all this time in her company, he was certainly randy enough for it.

But not ready in the ways that mattered. Too many elements conspired to crack his usual control. The house. His memories. His need for her. Her vulnerability, in spite of her gallant efforts to keep fighting.

No, he'd be wiser seeking what rest he could well away from her and her drawn face and her fiery eyes.

He paused in the doorway. "Burn that black dress when *madame* has taken it off," he said in Gaelic to the maids.

The next morning, Verity stirred as one of the maids brought her a cup of chocolate. Whatever else the duke intended for her, starvation mustn't feature in his plans. Last night's tray had been crammed with delicacies she hadn't seen since leaving Kensington. He'd even sent up a bottle of fine claret.

Kylemore had been true to his surprising farewell. She'd bathed, eaten and, astonishingly, slept in peace.

Sitting up, she responded to what she assumed was a greeting from the maid, another Scot who didn't, it appeared, speak any English. Gingerly, she shifted on the mattress to test if yesterday's saddle-induced discomfort still persisted.

A little, she decided. But a night in a bed had worked wonders. Perhaps His Grace should go back to making her sleep on the ground. She felt much readier to tackle him today.

The maid opened the heavy curtains, which had been drawn since Verity had entered the room yesterday. In the space of a breath, all her well-being evaporated.

The windows were barred.

* * *

Verity thought she'd be confined, but no one stopped her when she left her room. With Angus and Andy dogging her heels, she began to explore her prison. The main house was more a sprawling farmhouse than anything else, like an over-grown version of the home she'd grown up in. The interior was dark and oppressive and decorated almost solely with hunting trophies. The heads of long-dead deer lined the walls, and sad examples of the taxidermist's art crowded together in large display cases to stare out at her with lifeless glass eyes.

Going outside was a relief. As she glanced around the un-kempt grounds with a frown, she rubbed her wrists. The memory of her bindings still chafed, even if the silk cords had left no mark.

After endless days of traveling, she found it strange to spend a whole day in one place. The air was brisk for sum-mer, and she huddled into the teal merino dress the maids had produced for her that morning. Although she knew her pervasive chill had nothing to do with the weather and ev-erything to do with rampant apprehension.

The area immediately around the house had been coaxed into a straggling lawn. Fields lay behind the barn. The rest of the valley was mainly forest, although patches of heather and bracken grew in clearings high on the hillsides. A path led down to a loch. Farm buildings and a couple of cottages where the servants must live completed the settlement. She supposed the scene was beautiful, in its forbidding way.

She soon understood why her jailers permitted her so much freedom. Unless she took chances on the road over the mountains or she was an exceptionally fine swimmer, escape was impossible. And she couldn't ask for aid, because apart from the man who'd greeted them yesterday, none of the valley's residents spoke English.

At first, Verity was relieved the duke left her alone. Main-taining her courage was easier when she didn't have to endure that searching indigo stare. But as the interminable day dragged on, she almost wished he'd appear. Anything to end this awful hiatus, when every minute seemed to stretch across an hour.

Then she'd remember how he'd kissed her in the carriage and fear would flare again. Somehow in that kiss, he'd bypassed her will and her intellect and her hatred. He'd discovered the real woman hidden beneath Soraya's tricks and seductions. The real woman Verity had never allowed to breathe free in all her years as a courtesan.

What was she to do? How was she to protect herself from Kylemore? Worse, how was she to stifle her own response?

Since her abduction, she'd desperately tried to resurrect Soraya. She so needed the other woman's self-possession and knowing superiority. But the worldly demimondaine stubbornly refused to emerge from the land of shades.

Instead, all she found within herself was Verity's cowering heart. Verity wasn't strong enough to withstand the Duke of Kylemore. He'd subjugate her totally and leave her with nothing after this was over.

He hadn't gone to this trouble for the sake of a quick tumble. He hadn't even gone to this trouble to reclaim what he'd shared with Soraya. No, he meant to destroy her. They both knew it.

Eventually the pervasive gloom of her thoughts forced her back to the equally gloomy house. There must be some way she could avoid her fate. Her inevitable, long-promised fate. But nothing sprang to mind, and there was no one to help her. She was as isolated from human assistance as if she were on the moon. Kylemore knew exactly what he was doing when he'd brought his mistress to this isolated hunting box.

Kylemore silently admitted he'd had no idea what he was doing when he brought his mistress to his childhood home.

He already suspected that keeping Verity here was a mistake. She only made him vulnerable, just as this place made him vulnerable. And if ever he needed to hold fast to ruthlessness, it was now.

He flung himself off his mount's back in the shadowy stables and cursed at length. Hamish had followed him inside out of the twilight, and he reached for Tannasg's reins.

"Taking the Lord's name in vain never did much tae help a situation, laddie," he said in a soft, reproving burr. The lanterns were already lit, and they cast a soft glow over his stern expression.

They had been riding all day. After that appalling journey, any sane man would welcome the chance to stay in one place. But then, Kylemore had never considered himself a sane man. Nor would anyone else if they knew the facts behind this latest disaster, the abduction of his unwilling paramour.

At least the hours in the saddle today had achieved one positive outcome—Hamish Macleish no longer *Your Graced* him to death. Kylemore hadn't expected them to regain their old closeness. But the day together had revived some of their earlier ease in each other's company. Not to mention that it distanced him from both the house's agonizing memories and his troublesome mistress.

Soraya. Verity. The woman he yearned for with every breath.

The woman who, as far as Hamish's conversation was concerned, didn't exist. Hell, Hamish already knew blasphemy numbered among his employer's sins. Kidnapping was just one more peccadillo.

Still, Kylemore, ruthless, heartless knave that he was, couldn't quite summon the courage to confess why he skulked in this remote corner of Scotland with one of the world's most beautiful women in tow.

"Look after the horses," he snapped, tired of the censure

that underlay Hamish's manner in spite of all the reawakened camaraderie.

Perhaps because of the reawakened camaraderie.

He was tired too of battling inconvenient scruples over his captive. Everything had seemed so clear when he'd searched for her. Soraya had duped him into giving her a fortune. She'd betrayed him by running away without a word. She deserved to be punished.

And by God, he'd enjoy punishing her.

But that was before he'd witnessed her uncomplaining bravery on the long and difficult journey when she'd been so scared of where she'd been going. Of horses. Of him.

That was before he'd seen her vulnerability when exhaustion had forced her to the edge of her endurance. When she'd still summoned the strength to defy him. Even while she must have known that defiance was useless.

Now he was going to take her.

The outcome had never been in doubt. What he hadn't expected when he'd plotted his revenge was that his body and his heart would be so divided about his intentions.

Damn her.

"Goodnight, Your Grace," Hamish said to Kylemore's retreating back as he unsaddled the big gray horse.

The duke slammed open the door to Verity's room with such force that the curtains billowed and the fire flickered wildly in the grate. It was late and she lay awake and afraid in the large bed. She knew there was no escape.

There had never been any escape.

How right she'd been to feel wary of the Duke of Kylemore from the moment they'd met. She'd been tragically wrong thinking she could manage him. Now she faced the consequences of that calamitous error of judgment.

Still, she refused to shrink before him like a cringing

coward. She raised herself on her elbows against the pillows and tilted her chin.

"Good evening, Your Grace," she said coolly.

Never let him guess how hard she fought to keep her voice steady, she prayed silently. Her heart thundered with fear, and only the outer limits of her will kept her from raising the sheet against her chest like a shield.

He stared across the room at her as if he hated her. She suspected he did.

"Good evening, Your Grace," he mimicked cruelly. "By all means, let us preserve the formalities, madam."

She couldn't entirely read his mood. She was familiar with how he looked when intent on sex. As the object of his desire for more than a year, she ought to.

That wasn't how he looked tonight.

He supported one arm high against the doorframe, a picture of male power and beauty in his loose white shirt and tight dark breeches.

She'd always recognized the Duke of Kylemore as an unusually handsome man, but for many reasons, she'd never allowed herself to dwell on his attractions. Tonight, his physical splendor struck her with the force of a blow. She worried at her bottom lip before she realized it was a fatal admission of nervousness.

He straightened his lean body and sauntered toward her, kicking the door closed behind him. She flinched as it crashed shut.

"Don't bother asking for mercy. You've had a week to prepare for this."

She'd had a week to recall her loss of control the last time he'd kissed her. Which was just what the monster had intended. Whatever happened tonight, she swore she wouldn't surrender to him as she had that stormy afternoon in Yorkshire.

He loomed above her at the side of the bed. The strongly marked black eyebrows lowered over his dark blue eyes.

"Where the hell did you get this?" He extended one long-fingered hand and flicked contemptuously at the neckline of her plain white nightdress. "I'm sure I never ordered such a rag from Madame Yvette."

"One of the maids lent it to me," she said sullenly.

She'd been surprised to find ready for her an armoire full of clothes from Soraya's favorite modiste. Yet again she'd reflected on the planning the duke had put into bringing her here. She hadn't stood a chance.

Included in the luxurious wardrobe were nightdresses so filmy as hardly to justify the name of clothing. She'd needed a flurry of sign language to convince the maids she much preferred to borrow something less revealing. She'd needed a good five minutes to divert the girls' horrified attention from the diaphanous garments in the first place.

"Take it off," he said, still frowning. "This game has gone on long enough. I'm your lover, madam. You've never evinced distaste for me before."

He was right. And he was utterly wrong.

Kylemore might think he had her where he wanted her. Kylemore *did* have her where he wanted her, but she wasn't going to deliver herself gift-wrapped for his delectation.

No, he'd find little enjoyment in her bed tonight. Or not if she could help it.

She looked away to where the fire blazed in the grate. "Things have changed. I've changed," she whispered.

She heard the rustle of linen and turned her head to see him tugging off his shirt. The smooth skin of arms and shoulders gleamed golden as he dropped the garment carelessly to the floor.

"No one changes that much," he said with such confidence

that she curled her fingers into her palms to stop herself from attacking him.

Her one goal had been the chance to abandon her detestable career, yet here she was about to lie beneath a man in another loveless coupling.

She had a terrifying glimpse of a future where she'd never be free and she must play Soraya forever. Abruptly, unable to bear another moment of this torment, she flung the sheet aside and lay back.

"Go on," she said stiffly, closing her eyes. She wouldn't add to his triumph by begging for mercy. "Take me."

Damn him, she should have known she couldn't rattle him with such theatrics. His response was a softly derisive laugh.

"Oh, no, madam. That's too easy."

She clenched her fists at her sides and told herself she'd endure this, as she'd always endured before.

But the words had lost their power. She listened to the slide of fabric on skin as he shucked the rest of his clothing.

She didn't look at him. She didn't need to. She already knew what he looked like naked.

Tall. Slender, with the long, powerful muscles of a born swordsman. A light scattering of black hair on his chest. And the heavy, erect penis he'd soon thrust inside her.

For such a lean man, the duke was remarkably well endowed—yet another indication of how laughably inaccurate his cold nickname was. Kylemore's body spoke of driven, even uncontrollable, passions. Although he'd never before lost control with her.

Until tonight.

What was about to happen carried no deceiving gloss of courtesy or civilization. This man wanted to brand her as his in the most primitive way. She felt the mattress sag as he knelt on the bed, then the heat of his body, shocking in spite of the familiarity, when he straddled her.

"You keep up the pretense of reluctance," he said drily.

"It's no pretense." She still refused to look at him. If she couldn't see him, perhaps she could hide from what he did.

"Yes, it is," he insisted.

The sudden shift of air should have warned her. With one powerful tug, he ripped the nightdress from neck to hem, leaving her exposed to his gaze as she'd been exposed so many times before. She fought the urge to cover herself with the tattered shreds of the gown, with her hands, with the sheet.

His face was strained and determined in the candlelight. She'd never seen him like this. He'd always approached her with eager anticipation, but there was no joy in him now. The odd thought crossed her mind that he fought his own deepest nature when he came to her in anger.

Then she looked down at his sex, hard and avid and seeking, and she dismissed her naïveté with the scorn it deserved. His nature was clear. It was to conquer and subdue. That was all there was in him.

"Anything you take, you take as a thief," she said bitterly.

Her insult angered him, she saw, as the blue eyes narrowed. But it was too late to reconsider the wisdom of taunting a man who held her at such a disadvantage.

"I'm no thief, madam," he said harshly. Then fleeting, turbulent emotion darkened his intent gaze and his tone softened into velvety enticement. "Verity, think what you do. It doesn't have to be like this. The pleasure we shared was a miracle."

Pleasure. The word slashed at her like a sword, while deep within, a tangled knot loosened as the inevitable, unwelcome memory awoke of his body moving in hers with delight. So many familiar elements here conspired to vanquish her. His clean scent, his alluring heat, his cursed, lost beauty.

"That implies something freely bestowed," she said through taut lips. "You know that was never true."

"I know that was *always* true." The danger in his soft voice sent a shiver, not entirely of revulsion, through her. Oh, how she wished her response was as simple as revulsion.

"Never." God help her, she lied.

His brows contracted, and fool that she was, she read sorrow rather than fury in his face. "Well, if I must take you as a thief, then I shall be a thief."

He pushed her legs apart, moved between them and thrust inside her.

There had been no preliminaries. Verity tensed, but her betraying body had already prepared for his possession.

He rammed into her hard and gave a groan that echoed the defeat in her heart. For a long, dark moment, she lay pinioned under him. The world had shrunk to the man above her. It felt of him. It smelled of him. His weight held her motionless.

He withdrew and plunged back into her once, twice. Then he jerked convulsively as his control broke and his essence spurted into her. He seemed to shudder over her forever before he groaned once more, then rolled away.

It was over. He'd taken her quickly, carelessly, irrevocably. She was once again the Duke of Kylemore's lover and she wished she were dead.

She took her first full breath for what felt like an eternity. The air still smelled like Kylemore. Like Kylemore and sex. She needed to wash. Slowly, as if she were an old woman, she got out of the bed.

Her movement roused him enough to reach over and grab her arm. "Where are you going?" He lifted himself up on one elbow to look at her. "If you run away from the glen, you'll die in the mountains. It's hard country out there, and people unfamiliar with it don't survive."

She thought now that he'd taken her, he'd sound victorious, gloating. After all, he'd gone to a world of trouble to get her on her back in this bed. But his voice was flat and devoid of emotion.

"I'm not running away," she said dully, despite herself clutching the remnants of her nightdress around her as if she'd been a violated virgin.

A laughable notion, she thought sourly. But she didn't feel like laughing. She felt like crying, as she'd cried when she'd first sold herself.

She lit a candle with shaking hands and left the room. Only later did she think how strange it was that he didn't try to stop her.

Chapter 10

On unsteady legs, Verity found her way downstairs to the kitchen. The banked range shed enough light for her to fill a kettle and heat some water. Her ruined nightgown provided little protection against the night air, but she was so numb that she hardly noticed the cold. Between her legs, she was sticky and wet with Kylemore's seed.

The sensation was unusual. The duke had never spent himself inside her. In London, they'd used sheaths, or she'd satisfied him some other way. An old courtesan she'd known in Paris had taught her the tricks of a whore's trade. Verity had learned, even while her heart had despaired, because she'd had to.

But tonight Kylemore hadn't cared about planting a bastard in her womb. Perhaps he meant that to be part of her punishment. He wanted to give her a permanent reminder of him. She could have told him that was one revenge he'd never have.

Like an automaton, she poured warm water into a bowl

and began to wash. The sheer banality of her actions gradually coaxed her soul back from the shivering hell where it had retreated. But still, she couldn't bear to contemplate that moment when he'd invaded her body.

With trembling hands, she wiped herself with the ragged remains of her nightdress, then pitched it into the fire. To cover her nakedness, she tugged a man's shirt, probably Hamish's, from a pile of fresh laundry. She threw the dirty water in the drain and lit a candle, then went in search of somewhere to sleep. That morning, she'd noticed a chamber on the upper floor that contained a roughly made up cot.

Slowly—she ached all over, even though he hadn't hurt her—she mounted the stairs in quest of a place that didn't contain the Duke of Kylemore. She was frightened, but the fear was strangely distant, as all her emotions had been strangely distant since she'd left him. Perhaps he waited at the top of the stairs to force her back into his bed. But mercifully she made it into the humble room without encountering anyone.

She crept between the sheets and pulled the blanket high around her shaking body. Only then, in the spurious security of this narrow cot, did she begin to cry, great, gulping sobs that scraped her throat as they emerged. Sobs too loud and too heartbroken to muffle in the pillows, much as she tried.

He'd used her coldly, without care or feeling. He'd rammed into her as if he owned her. When she'd been his mistress, he'd never treated her with such callousness. Then, he'd wanted her to share the pleasure, to become his willing partner as they'd explored the world of sensuality.

But he'd used her tonight as if he loathed her.

As he must loathe her.

And the worst betrayal of all?

She'd recognized the contempt he'd expressed with each action. Even so, her traitorous body had fluttered with the beginning of response, a response owing nothing to Soraya's practiced wiles and everything to Verity's lonely soul.

Kylemore stirred with a startled grunt from the deathlike sleep into which he'd plunged after sex. He was alone in Verity's bed, and the smell of their coupling surrounded him.

This was, of course, familiar.

Less familiar were the guilt and regret that lurked in the sordid vacuum within him where most men had a heart.

Tumbling his mistress had always left him with an inner peace nothing else in life offered. When she'd gone, she had snatched away his only source of happiness. He'd been desperate to get it back, like a child who had lost his favorite toy and cried until it was restored.

Well, he had his favorite toy back and he still felt like crying.

His rage at her disappearance. Three months of miserable celibacy. Her insults. All these might explain what he'd just done to her.

Nothing could excuse it.

Groaning, he sat up. He'd pounded into her like a wild animal. He'd simply lost control. Never had he treated a woman so.

With a shudder, he remembered pouring himself into her. At that moment, he'd wanted to drown her in his essence, fill her utterly so no trace of anything but him remained in that slender body.

His conscience winced to recall what he'd done, but his unruly flesh rejoiced in how it had felt to take her fully, uninhibitedly, for the first time. Always, he'd been careful to spawn no bastards to suffer the cursed Kinmurrie blood. But in those frantic seconds when he'd pumped all his unhappiness into Verity—and to his shame, it had indeed only been seconds—no thought of future consequences had intruded.

The world shrank to contain just him and the woman, and his body claiming her in nature's most basic way.

It had been glorious.

But now he felt sick and sad and tired of the game.

He gave a harsh laugh. The game had only started. He couldn't give up now. His desire wouldn't permit it, whatever the better man inside him insisted he do.

Would his mad urge to possess this woman end in his destruction? Right now he hardly cared.

Kylemore found Verity easily, although he was surprised that of all sanctuaries, she'd chosen his room. But then, she probably hadn't known it was his. Her room was larger and better furnished, befitting the house's main chamber.

He raised the candle higher and studied her sleeping face against the creased pillow. Even in the uncertain light, he saw the tearstains on her cheeks. The regret and guilt inside him coalesced into one roiling black mass. She hadn't cried once during this whole ordeal, but he'd made her cry tonight.

How she must hate him. For his clumsiness. For his blind need. For the way he couldn't help wanting her. Any man worthy of the name would let her go. But the prospect of losing her made everything within him howl in anguished denial.

Let her go? As if he could. Even the thought of her leaving his bed made him want to break something.

He blew out the candle and placed it on a cabinet. Slowly, he bent to brush aside the blanket and pick her up. He thought she still wore the shabby white nightgown before he remembered he'd destroyed it in his anger. No, the rough cotton garment under his hands was a man's shirt she must have found somewhere. She whimpered, a broken, husky sound that furrowed his heart until he remembered he possessed no such organ.

Then she awoke. "No!" she cried, immediately struggling. "Let me go! Don't touch me, you devil!"

His grip tightened as he tried to ignore the slide of her barely covered skin on his and the way her scent, warm and heavy with sleep, teased him.

"Never." He knew his damnation lay in the word.

"Leave me in peace," she whispered, finally going still in his arms. "That's all I ask."

"I can't." He heard the sadness in his voice. "Hush now." Hitching her higher, he carried his prisoner back to her bed.

In the bleak hour just before dawn, Kylemore woke hard and ready.

A kind man, a *good* man, would leave his mistress in peace, let her sleep, grant her a reprieve. But she must know now she could expect neither kindness nor goodness from her cold lover.

Although *cold* was the last word he'd apply to himself at this moment.

He shifted to ease his aching erection, disturbing Verity, who stirred from her troubled doze. Neither had slept well. This house would forever put genuine rest out of his reach. And he couldn't forget the woman who lay such a careful distance away from him.

Even asleep, she didn't want to touch him. A fleeting memory arose of that strange moment when she'd woken in his arms on the journey north. For one brief instant, his world had spun smoothly on its axis before everything had gone reliably awry again. It had been awry ever since.

With a fatuous optimism he should have known better than to feel, he'd thought sex with her would bring everything back into kilter. But after what he'd done to her in this room tonight, he felt even more lost and adrift than ever.

Although that wouldn't stop him from having her now.

He flung the sheet to the base of the bed and reached out to place his hand on Verity's shoulder, feeling the delicate bones and hollows. She was naked—he'd snatched the shabby shirt from her body when he'd returned her to his bed. Now the sweet scent of her skin curled out to urge him closer.

Her skin was so white that even in the darkness, he could follow the graceful curve of her back and waist and the flaring splendor of her hips. Need ratcheted up another notch, became unbearable. His hold tightened.

"No," she said indistinctly, keeping her back to him and hunching against the edge of the mattress.

"Yes," he said firmly and rolled her onto her back, releasing another eddy of her tantalizing essence.

To him, it would always be the scent of paradise. And he could brook no delay before he achieved this particular heaven.

Surprisingly, he felt no resistance in her. He moved over her, supporting himself on his elbows. "Put your arms around me."

Her arms stayed stubbornly at her side.

Ah, he understood her game now. She meant her sullen acquiescence to shame him into leaving her alone. Foolish chit. She should know better than that.

Still, he didn't immediately thrust inside her. Although the brush of her silky thighs against his hips and the teasing heat of her sex so close to his arousal measured the remotest limits of his control.

But he refused to act the mindless savage again. He'd done that last night. And he'd made her cry.

He'd hurt her, and in spite of three months of dreaming nothing but revenge, he was piercingly sorry. The recollection of tears drying on her pale cheeks gentled the hand he cupped around her breast. The gesture became one of aching tenderness.

Her skin was cool and smooth beneath his fingers. He tested the glorious roundness of her breast, then bent his head and took her nipple into his mouth. Immediately it pebbled hard under his lips.

Triumphantly, he recognized this as familiar—it seemed Soraya wasn't totally lost to him after all. She tasted like ripe raspberries, and he gorged himself on her summer sweetness, licking and laving and sucking, listening to how her breath hitched with every marauding caress.

She didn't want to respond to him, he knew. But she couldn't help herself.

He turned his attention to her other breast. Lengthy delay was beyond his capability, after so many empty months of wanting her and last night's unsatisfactory coupling, but even so, he was desperate to erase the memory of his earlier brutality. Something in him wanted to cherish her. She was so small and brave and beautiful.

So he made himself linger over her breasts, learning again their taste and texture. And his hand made a slow, stroking journey down the slight arch of her stomach to the plumpness of her mound. As his fingers tangled in the soft hair there, she stifled a moan of pleasure and moved restlessly under him. He gave his own moan as her thigh inadvertently brushed his cock. He'd reached a stage of excitement where even the rasp of the sheet on his skin threatened to send him over the edge.

He couldn't wait much longer. He dipped his fingers lower, to the secret recesses of her body.

A carillon of victory joined the desire pounding through his veins to create a thunderous symphony of desire. She was hot and wet, ready for him. He wanted to taste her there, to see if she was as succulent and delicious as he remembered.

But his restraint was fraying. He had to take her now or

lose his mind. He withdrew his hand and poised himself to possess her.

She hadn't stopped fighting him. He knew that in his bones. But he had dominion over her body for now, and she wouldn't deny him at least her physical capitulation.

With a groan that seemed to rise from the soles of his feet, he slid into her, feeling her muscles resist, then relax to accept his entry. Her inner passage was slick and tight around him, drawing him deeper.

No other feeling in the world rivaled this. Would ever rival this. He clutched her closer, as if daring fate to take her from him.

Against his chest, her nipples formed hard little nubs. Clumsily, he grabbed her knees and bent them up around him to ease his penetration. He was deep enough inside her to touch her very heart.

He waited for her to rise to meet him. She always had. Except for last night.

But she lay still beneath him, her breath emerging in distressed little gasps. He lifted his head to try and read her expression through the darkness. He caught the silvery glint of her eyes as she stared fixedly up at the ceiling. And there was no mistaking the tension in the slender, unmoving body under his.

After a moment, he realized her will would withstand any magic he worked on her senses. How could he bear the mental barriers she raised against him at this moment of greatest intimacy? He had to destroy them or go mad.

He began to move, establishing the slow, intense rhythm that he knew drove her wild. He exerted every ounce of his skill to woo her into surrender. After a year as her paramour, he knew her and he knew what gave her pleasure.

He wanted her so desperately that holding himself back

was agony. The need to seek his own release threatened to snap his spine, incinerate his brain, tear every nerve from his body.

But still he persisted. Gritting his teeth, he harnessed every shred of control to force her to admit defeat in this, if nothing else.

But no change in angle or touch or pressure could make her participate in the journey to ecstasy. Her body recognized his mastery, but with every stroke into her hot depths, he felt her will defy him.

Damn her. She wouldn't cheat him of this. This, the only part of her that he could still reach.

Anger corroded what little command he still held over himself. His movements became more ferocious as the force inside him gathered, built, ignited. He'd meant to be gentle with her, but those intentions disintegrated under the titanic force of his passion.

Still she didn't move to join him. Still she didn't give any acknowledgment that she wanted him, wanted this, although her body was slippery with musky perspiration and every time he thrust into her, she clasped him harder.

Knowing he couldn't hold on much longer, he pounded into her. Through the inferno in his mind, he heard her moan. Whether in discomfort or pleasure, he didn't know.

Even if it killed him, he had to break her resistance.

He had to wait.

He couldn't wait.

He couldn't wait . . .

At last, at last, on the very edge of his breaking point, she began to tremble in his arms. She was almost there. He skated his hand down to touch between her legs.

With a strangled cry, she reached out to cling to his shoulders, digging her nails in hard. He ignored the stinging pain.

It meant nothing compared to the fact that she held him of her own volition.

He took a great shuddering breath as her sleek inner muscles clenched in the prelude to her climax.

She finally lost control and convulsed around him. He kept still, luxuriating in her quaking pleasure.

Even in his own extremity, he knew what this meant. She wanted him. He didn't suffer this tempest of desire alone. Burying his head in the curve of her neck, he drowned in the sensations of her shivering peak.

She was his. She'd never escape. *Never.*

But too soon, it was over, and her exhausted sighs rattled hot against the side of his face.

Then all awareness of everything except his own crisis abandoned him and he was lost. His sinews and bones tightened almost to pain as he spilled himself inside her in a blinding explosion of rapture.

For what felt like forever, he emptied the bitterness and yearning in his soul into her prone body. He shuddered over her until his limbs lost their strength and he collapsed on her, utterly spent. His heart pounded as if it wanted to break out of his chest. His head held nothing but the hot scent of her.

Slowly, reality returned. Gradually, the torrent of his blood quietened and calmed, although blinding pleasure still thrummed steadily through his veins.

His weight must have been crushing her, but she made no protest. Her hands had slid off his shoulders after her climax and now her arms extended stiffly at her sides. She was trembling.

Bitter disappointment was a rusty taste in his mouth and worried at the edges of his physical satisfaction.

He'd forced a climax from her, but in the desolate reaches of his mind, he recognized that in the end he hadn't really vanquished her. He wanted her complete surrender. He wanted her willing in his bed. He hadn't even come close to either goal.

Soraya had always sought her satisfaction with an openness he'd found bewitching. Verity had lain in contemptuous silence beneath him until he'd finished.

He rolled off her. She exhaled on a muffled sob and scrambled across the mattress to curl up as far away from him as she could.

He didn't have the strength to protest. His chest heaving as he fought for air, he stretched out next to her. His muscles still quivered from the powerful sex, and sweat chilled his bare skin. He raised an unsteady hand to brush his damp hair back from his forehead and wondered what the hell would become of the two of them. And then asked himself if he cared.

A long time afterward, he finally dredged up the energy to speak. "Your coldness won't deter me."

The sound of his own voice was almost shocking after the wordless coupling. First light seeped into the room through the drawn curtains, and he saw how she'd gone back to huddling on the edge of the bed.

"I have nothing but coldness for you," she said woodenly.

He couldn't see her face. He didn't need to. He knew the pride and suffering it would convey. "Soraya is a woman who understands pleasure."

"Soraya never existed."

Ignoring how she flinched away, he leaned over her. He'd expected her to appear composed and distant, but he read only vulnerability in her lush mouth and shadowed eyes. "You're wrong. You are Soraya."

She closed her eyes and shook her head. "No, I am Verity."

"You are Verity and Soraya."

He bent his head to kiss that soft mouth. For a moment,

her lips moved against his, and he thought he'd won. Then she jerked away.

In the growing light, she looked exhausted. A man with any compassion would leave her alone.

Hell, a man with any compassion would never bully her into his bed in the first place.

"Soraya still exists in you and I mean to find her." The words were a vow.

She merely shook her head once more. He rolled away from her in impatience and sat up. With a disgusted gesture, he flung the sheet up to cover her nakedness.

In truth, he wanted her again. After so long without her, he was still far from sated. But the compassion he denied he possessed prevented him acting totally the selfish libertine, much as he wanted her to think that was all he was.

After the long night, he sensed she was very close to shattering. Once, he'd have said nothing short of cannon fire could rattle the gorgeous Soraya. But this woman, still flinching away from him in rejection, had fewer defenses than his exotic mistress.

Of course, one day he might have to break her.

But not yet. Dear God, not yet.

Kylemore paused at the top of the waterfall that tumbled from the cliff at the end of the glen. The afternoon light was dazzling on the rushing water, but he was blind to the scene's beauties.

Instead, he brooded upon his mistress. That was nothing new. His mistress had dominated his thoughts since she'd left him. And for a considerable portion of time before that, if the truth were known.

Would he ever be free of this damned inconvenient itch for the chit? She didn't know it, but she wasn't the only one struggling against unwilling captivity.

He sat back against a rock familiar from his childhood and stretched his legs along the sun-warmed ground. It dismayed him how clearly he remembered so many things here, despite having left when he was seven years old for his unhappy sojourn at Eton. He'd thought time would have softened the painful memories. The hope had been unfulfilled.

He'd had a long walk up to this spot, and he'd need most of the rest of the day to return. Just as he'd intended when he'd set out this morning.

Although he wasn't hungry, he took some bread and cheese from his pocket and bit into it. Scotland had the ability to kill his appetite, he discovered.

Below him spread the pitched jumble of roofs that made up the hunting box and its surrounding buildings. Originally, this lonely glen had contained only a crofter's cottage. His grandfather had used the simple house while stalking the estate's abundant deer. Of course, the isolation meant this was a lunatic place to want to live. But his grandfather had been an obsessive hunter.

Not for the first time Kylemore reflected that every Kinmurrie seemed to fall victim to some particular mania. By all reports, his grandfather had spent increasingly long periods here, slaughtering the local wildlife and avoiding his fiercely Calvinist duchess.

Unhappy marriages. Another Kinmurrie specialty. At Kylemore Castle, likenesses of people who had quite clearly loathed each other lined the portrait gallery.

The hunting box had undergone extensive renovation, of course, when his father had become a permanent resident. The estate's isolation had made it the perfect location for hiding the sixth duke's unsuitable and dangerous proclivities.

Those renovations meant this was also the ideal place to

imprison Soraya. Or Verity, as Kylemore increasingly thought of her.

Damn. He was thinking about his mistress again. He flung the rest of his meal aside with a disgruntled gesture.

Discontentedly, he considered the house. What was Verity doing now? Still lying in her bed like a wounded animal, the way he'd left her?

The thought settled like a cold stone in his gut. She'd looked so broken and lost this morning. The image pained him beyond endurance, which was stupid, as he'd carted her all this way to teach her a lesson.

But how he hated to see the great Soraya brought so low.

Except somehow she was no longer his disdainful, worldly mistress. And therein lay a large part of the problem.

The woman he kept against her will wasn't the woman he'd used with such businesslike passion in London.

At first, he'd thought her recent reluctance just some trick to make him pity her, relax his guard, perhaps even let her go. But her distress last night and this morning had been real. He'd stake his dukedom on it.

Not that he'd particularly regret relinquishing that poisoned inheritance.

He realized that after all these years of studying Soraya, of hunting her as his grandfather had hunted the glen's deer, he didn't understand her at all. And until he knew what made her the way she was, he'd never completely possess her.

He had to possess her or he'd go mad.

If he wasn't mad already.

Clearly, some split existed in her mind between Soraya and Verity. Which was absurd. She was the same person. The way he ached for her attested to that. This new, more complex version of his mistress still exercised the same inconvenient fascination over him—more strongly, if anything. Two unsatisfactory couplings only spurred him to demand a greater share of her. To demand everything.

And he'd make sure that was what she gave him before he was finished. Everything.

In a state of nervous determination, Verity sat on the window seat in her room and waited for the duke. He'd been away all day. Now it was evening and she knew in her bones he'd come to her.

During the endless dreary hours since she'd woken, her only companions had been the silent and ever-watchful giants and the little maids who had helped her dress and served her dinner in the parlor. As the day had limped on toward twilight with no sign of her arrogant lover, she'd stifled her unhappiness and instead summoned righteous anger.

He had no right to treat her as he did. She couldn't allow this situation to continue. The duke wasn't a heathen savage. Surely she could dredge some chivalry from his black soul and persuade him to release her.

She wore the least provocative of the gowns Kylemore had ordered, a dashing cobalt merino with black military-style frogging—not totally inappropriate, as she intended to fight.

She resented the loss of her widow's weeds, although the dress had been ruined past repair on the rough journey to this godforsaken wilderness. At least it had been hers, paid for with her own labor, no matter if the money had originally been Kylemore's. She abominated the way every moment in this valley leeched away a little more of her independence.

As she watched the light fade over the loch and the mountains, the magnificence of the landscape struck her as ominous, hostile to humanity. No wonder so few people lived in this oppressive emptiness. She shivered and drew her cream cashmere shawl closer around her, although the evening wasn't cold and a fire burned in the grate.

Kylemore paused in the doorway, and she saw him take in the scene with one single, scowling glance.

"What is the meaning of this?" he snapped. "Take off that dress, let down your hair and get into bed now."

Clearly her defiance hadn't escaped him. She'd expected him to be annoyed; she'd even planned on it.

He moved across to lean against the dresser. She rose and linked her hands in front of her to control their trembling.

"I'm tired of being led like a lamb to the slaughter, Your Grace," she said firmly. "Your claim on my body ceased at the end of our contract in London."

"I told you what I want." He folded his arms implacably over his half-open linen shirt.

He wore country clothes. Plain shirt, buff breeches, tall boots. He looked as if he'd been outside all day, as though he still carried the freshness of the wind with him. The uncertain golden light shed by the candles and the fire glanced across his collarbone and hinted at the black hair on his chest.

She was dismayed to realize she sidled away from him like a mare scenting a stallion. This was ridiculous. She was letting his physical presence distract her from what she needed to say. For all their decadent play in London, she was more aware of him as a man here than she'd ever been before.

"You've got what you want. You've had your revenge." She forced herself to hold her ground. "Let me go. You must stop this . . . this gothic horror before it gets out of hand."

A sardonic smile twisted his lips. "Is that the best you can do?"

Startled, she met his eyes fully for the first time. She'd expected to see anger, but instead, he looked tired and terrifyingly cynical. And deeply unhappy.

As if realizing she perceived more than he wished her to, he straightened and crossed the room to stare moodily out the barred window.

"I assume you've been concocting that little speech all day." His voice dripped sarcasm. "What did you expect it to achieve? The offer of a peaceful night to yourself and a quick trip home tomorrow? For such a concession, at least conjure up a tear or two. A man would be a monster indeed to say no to beauty arrayed in weeping distress at his feet."

How she hated that superior drawl. With an effort, she kept her voice steady. "If that would work, I'm certainly willing to try it."

He turned to look at her. Cynicism had conquered whatever else he felt. "Don't waste your time. Or mine. We both already know I'm a monster." He gave her clothing a slashing wave. "Stop this nonsense. I can have you out of that fiercely elegant ensemble and under me in five minutes flat and we both know it."

His eyes were so cold that she shivered again. But she refused to let his threat, phrased in a tone of bored indolence, cow her.

"No."

"You still don't understand, do you, Verity? And I've always considered you such a clever little poppet. You have no power. You have no rights. You belong to me. This isn't London. This is a forgotten corner of a feudal domain. And I am its lord. There's nowhere to run. There's no one to help you. If I want you—and we both know I do—I take you."

She was powerless to control her rapid, shallow breathing, even though she knew it betrayed her rising fear. "You think because I'm a whore, I must accept any man with coin to pay for my services?" she asked hardily.

"No. I think because you're mine and you'll always be mine, you should surrender to the inevitable."

Still she didn't yield. "Whatever else I am, I'm a sovereign soul. I am no man's creature." She'd repeated those words over and over to herself all day in a futile effort to bolster what little courage she retained.

A derisive smile curled his expressive mouth. "You'll be my creature. You're already my creature."

Because one craven element of her feared that was true, she drew herself up and glared at him with all the contempt she could muster. "Never."

He arched one supercilious eyebrow, as if he knew how thin her veneer of recalcitrance was. He probably did.

She went on. "I will never lie down willingly with you. Surely the great Duke of Kylemore has too much pride to pursue a reluctance mistress."

She meant the words to needle, but his expression remained stony. "The great Duke of Kylemore does what he wants, madam. I've withstood three months as the laughingstock of London. I've humiliated myself scouring the kingdom for news of you. I've brawled with a common yokel. I've descended to kidnap. Don't delude yourself that pride prevents me from any action—*any action*—that achieves my ends. My pride has been in the dust since you left. You'll find no aid there."

Despite herself, she felt a flash of unwilling sympathy at the picture he painted. The man she knew in London had been the mirror of the perfect aristocrat—not, perhaps, generally liked but certainly admired, respected, feared, envied.

Losing her had cost him dearly.

Softly, she said, "Kylemore, I'm sorry I left without telling you. That was badly done of me. That last . . ." She paused. She still quailed to remember his final, furious visit to Kensington and that lunatic marriage proposal. "That last day when you came to call, I should have explained, I should have said good-bye. Then we'd at least have parted amicably."

He gave a huff of unamused laughter, and the bitter lines on his face deepened. "As if I'd have let you go. We both know I wouldn't. You knew it then—it's why you sneaked away."

She'd taken a step toward him before she realized what she did. "I'll pay back the money."

He couldn't possibly know the sacrifice she was making with the offer, a sacrifice on behalf of not just herself but her sister and brother as well. But she'd spent all day trying to devise some way to break free of this nightmare. If it cost her the fortune she still believed was legally hers, she'd gladly pay.

The Ashtons would manage, she told herself guiltily. She'd see they did.

She pressed on. "If you give me a few days to make arrangements, I'll return every penny."

Kylemore whirled on her. Because of her brainless moment of pity, she was close enough for him to clamp his fingers around her upper arms.

"Don't be a damned fool, woman! It's not the money. It never was the money, except as a symbol of what you stole." His grip dug into her arms, and Verity braced herself for a good shaking. But he just held her.

Desperately, she looked up at him, seeking some sign he might relent. But while his face conveyed anguish and turmoil, there wasn't the slightest hint of hesitation.

She took an unsteady breath. "I stole nothing."

His fingers flexed against the sleeves of her dress. "You stole yourself. Now I have stolen you back. And I'll never let you go."

She gave a broken cry and wrenched free of him. "This is impossible. You must see that."

"No. It is my will." He moved after her as though he tracked a wild animal.

She backed away, horrified by how certain he sounded. If she stayed any longer, she might start to think he made sense.

Then she noticed he'd neglected to shut the door behind him when he'd arrived. With frantic speed, she dove for the entrance. A half second too late, he leaped after her. She felt the shift in the air as he lunged to catch her.

But she reached the door first and slammed it after her. She dashed down the staircase and across the entrance hall. She had a fleeting impression of rows of dead animal eyes watching her run past. Then she was tugging at the bolt on the massive front door.

Sobbing, she struggled with the heavy iron latch. The duke was nearly upon her. She heard the approaching thud of his boot heels on the wooden steps.

The door swung open just as he jumped and hit the floor a breath away from her. She flung herself out into the darkness with no clear idea where she went apart from her overwhelming need to escape her pursuer.

Chapter 11

A tangled mass of shrubbery crowded against the side of the house and offered hope of sanctuary. Verity would have made for the woods if she thought she could outrun Kylemore over the open area she needed to cross first. But even in her panic, she knew better.

Skittering on the damp grass, she scrambled into the bushes. Twigs and thorns tore at her hair and dress as she pushed her way toward the center, only stopping when the branches became an impassable barrier.

She huddled into a ball, trying to make herself invisible, although no one outside would be able to see her through the undergrowth and the darkness. She tried without success to control her sawing breath.

He was near. She couldn't hear him or see him, but the prickling hairs on her skin told her he was watching, waiting for her to betray her position.

"Verity, come out," he eventually said. As expected, he was very close. "There's nowhere for you to go."

He sounded like a reasonable man when he used that coaxing tone. Once, she might have believed that was what he was. No longer.

The gossip was right. All the Kinmurries were mad. The duke's thirst for revenge threatened to make him the maddest of them all.

She shrank deeper into her hiding place and didn't answer. A chilly trickle of water ran down her nape, but she didn't dare move to wipe it away.

"The night will turn cold, and it's going to rain again." He hadn't shifted. Curse him, he must have seen her tunnel her way in.

As if he read her thoughts, he said, "I know just where you are. There's a hollow at the heart of the shrubbery. I grew up here. There are no secret places for me in this glen. It's useless trying to escape. There isn't a nook or cranny or bolthole for miles I haven't already found and used."

She supposed he'd played pranks like all children and found hiding places. Strange to imagine him as a little boy. She didn't think she ever had before. Her momentary distraction ended abruptly when she heard an ominous rustling.

"I'll come and get you if I have to. Or you can come out of your own volition. But you're not staying outside."

As her breathing calmed, the blind fear that had sent her on this pointless flight subsided. And it was a pointless flight, she saw now. Where could she go? It was the middle of the night. She wasn't dressed for travel. She had no provisions or money. She hadn't a clue how to get out of the valley.

Kylemore sighed. "All right. I'm coming in."

"No," she said tonelessly. "No, wait." She couldn't bear the thought of him dragging her out kicking and screaming.

Defeat replaced her earlier crazed fury and she was aware of every snag and scratch on the way out. Wet, muddy and smarting from a hundred small abrasions, she crawled into the open, but nothing smarted as much as recognizing her stupidity in running away from him like that.

She needed more than hysteria to escape the Duke of Kylemore. Hadn't she tried to leave him after a year of hard-headed planning? And that had only landed her squarely in her present predicament.

In spite of her chastened obedience to his bidding, she faced him without cowering. "I won't sleep with you."

"Yes, you will."

He reached out and took her arm. The heat of his touch burned through the damp wool of her sleeve and made the blood throb sullenly in her cold flesh. He turned her back toward the doorway and began to walk with her.

His hold was firm without bruising. Why exert his power overtly? He knew as well as she that he'd emerged the victor tonight, however staunchly she stood up to him now.

A great wave of misery swept her as Kylemore led her, outwardly submissive, inside the house and up the stairs. She'd never escape this man. She'd never escape Soraya. For thirteen years, the thought of being free one day was all that had kept her going. She hadn't foreseen the duke and his obstinate desire for her.

But surely desire died when it received no encouragement to live and thrive. When its object gave nothing, offered nothing, shared nothing. He was too proud to beat himself to destruction against the unbreakable rocks of her resistance.

Except he'd told her he had already abandoned his pride.

And even over the last few days, she hadn't always been unresponsive. Corrosive shame ate at her as she remembered moments—more than moments, if she included his kiss in the carriage or this morning's explosive climax—when her body had answered his with pleasure and not denial.

She told herself it was habit. After all, she'd been his mistress for a year.

Or it was his unquestionable skill as a lover.

Or her irredeemably sinful nature.

It certainly wasn't because his touch had the power to circumvent everything she wished for and believed in, she insisted in desperation. If she stayed strong and strove to remain like ice in his arms, he'd tire of his mad quest.

But even if he did, what then? Would he just wave her on her way and allow her to return to the life she wanted? She doubted it.

Perhaps he meant to kill her when he finished with her. In this isolated place, he could dispose of her easily enough.

However, she couldn't picture the duke murdering her, no matter how angry he was. He might dominate her sexually, he might force himself upon her, but her instincts told her he preferred her alive.

If only the thought provided the slightest comfort.

Verity stood shivering with cold and reaction in the center of her bedroom and watched Kylemore feed the fire. He must believe she was unlikely to make another dash for liberty, at least for the present. He hadn't locked the door. Now he seemed content to take his time at the grate.

For one of the nation's greatest noblemen, he showed great dexterity with kindling and bellows. Not for the first time, she reflected how she'd underestimated him in London. Then, she'd considered him just another useless aristocrat. Cleverer and perhaps more ruthless than the other men who'd vied for her favors, but basically made of the same stuff.

Since then, she'd seen him slough off the effects of hard travel. And he didn't act as if he found this humble house beneath his dignity. While it would have seemed the height of luxury to her in her rustic youth, it hardly matched the standards a duke was used to.

She looked at him now, on his knees building the fire, a task for the lowliest maid in any of his mansions. He was strong. He was intelligent. And he was alarmingly complicated.

Oh, how she wished he really was the effete wastrel she'd once judged him to be. But if this last week had demonstrated anything, it was that she didn't understand the Duke of Kylemore at all. He was darker, deeper, more dangerous than she'd ever imagined, although there had been clues in London to the truth of his nature, if she'd cared to read them.

His dogged pursuit of her. Certainly, his unquenchable passion when he came to her bed.

She remembered what a revelation that potent ardor had been. Eldreth had been a man of sedate habits, and she'd had to train James out of his inept fumblings.

How Kylemore would laugh if she admitted one of the reasons she'd misjudged him so disastrously was her own inexperience. London's most notorious courtesan as taken aback by a man's powerful virility as any green young miss? She almost laughed herself.

Part of her had always considered Kylemore a threat. Why else resist his blandishments as long as she had?

But those vague instincts had given no hint of the evil she'd courted when she'd become his mistress. What she'd thought of as her sensible self had discounted her vague feelings of mistrust and had insisted she grab the chance for financial security.

Sensible self? She should have jumped into the Thames before she'd accepted him in her bed.

All this hard-won wisdom came too late. She'd become

entangled with the wrong man and had to pay the price. That would be soon enough, if the knowing glint in his blue eyes was any indication as he rose and prowled across the room to her.

"Why keep fighting me?" he murmured, flicking open the hussar fastenings of her bodice with a deftness that rankled even in her fear.

Her trembling intensified, but she didn't move away. What was the point? He'd only catch her again.

"You know why," she said stiffly.

A strange smile drifted across his face as he pulled the gown down from her shoulders. "I think I'm beginning to."

She stood like a doll as he undressed her. Unexpectedly, he seemed in no rush to use her. She tried not to mind her nakedness, told herself she'd been naked for him so many times before. But she couldn't stem the quivering vulnerability she felt standing nude in front of him.

When he reached for her hairbrush, a horrible thought occurred to her. "You're not going to spank me?" she asked in dismay. For some reason, that would be the final humiliation in a night filled with humiliations.

His soft laugh grated on her nerves. "No, although you might enjoy it."

With sure fingers, he reached up and let down what remained of the knot she'd twisted her hair into earlier. Her dash into the bushes had tangled it into an impossible mess. Slowly, thoroughly, he began to smooth the long black strands into order.

She stood motionless under his attentions. For a long time, the room was quiet as he concentrated on his task, his face calm and serious, as if brushing her hair were the most important thing in the world.

Eventually, he put aside the brush and gently pushed her

down onto the bed. She lay staring upward and listened to him tug the clothes from his body. For all her denials and refusals, she was back where he wanted her.

She fought the urge to burst into tears.

It was like last night. Tomorrow night would be the same. And the night after that.

And every night until he tired of this cruel game.

Without extinguishing the candles, he lay down next to her. She waited for him to part her legs and claim her. But tonight he seemed determined to take his time. Perhaps because after this morning, he knew pleasure was the worst punishment he could inflict. He wanted to make her pay for her abortive attempt to escape him.

Verity turned her head and watched him raise himself up on one elbow in a characteristic pose. As he made a leisurely inspection of her prone form, the ghost of a smile curled his lips. The room was silent except for the crackle of the fire and the soft susurration of her nervous breathing.

She stiffened in silent rejection of what that smile promised. After everything that had happened, she could remain unmoved if he merely rutted over her, seeking his own release and ignoring hers. She was staunchly certain she could resist a thoughtless lover.

But now he promised to be anything but a thoughtless lover. He reached out to stroke his hand across her body, learning its shape and texture. It was as though touch were the only sense available to him.

He sighed with a pleasure she couldn't mistake as he trailed his fingers across the hollows of her collarbone and down her arms. He touched her belly and her shoulders and her legs. His hand was warm and gentle on her naked flesh.

Against her will, her pulse quickened after each seemingly casual brush of his fingers. His gaze was intent and serious as he studied the intricate, meaningless patterns he drew on her skin, patterns which made every inch of her sing.

She closed her eyes and told herself he'd done this before. On so many long, languid afternoons in Kensington.

The first time he'd shared her bed, he'd taken the trouble to arouse her. She'd been surprised at his care. Then shocked at her reaction.

With Eldreth, she'd gradually learned to tolerate sex. She'd quickly decided that if she had to earn her living on her back, she might as well make the best of the bargain. But the Duke of Kylemore had unveiled a dazzling new world of sensuality—a world which beckoned so strongly that she'd been frantic to escape its pull by the time she'd left him.

Now she fought to stay unresponsive under Kylemore's touch. Surely, she knew all the weapons in his arsenal of seduction. Familiarity must blunt their effectiveness against her.

But here, his touch seemed different. Just as Kylemore seemed a different man in many ways, some too subtle even to describe.

Gently, he shaped her thighs, her flanks, her arms. As if testing what a woman was. Her heart fluttered within her like a trapped bird. The light skimming hands were tender and astonishingly arousing.

Verity's nipples tightened. The reaction was immediate and uncontrollable, and she had no hope of hiding it from him. Her uneven breathing caught, then resumed an even more erratic rhythm as she tensed, waiting for him to touch her breasts.

But he concentrated on parts of her she'd never before considered particularly erotic. Although she knew from her year as his lover that her whole body offered him the promise of delight.

Only after long minutes of silently enduring his attentions did she realize he deliberately avoided her breasts and between her legs.

Nor had he kissed her.

He meant to demonstrate his superiority. Of course he did. She'd never fooled herself that this was anything but a quest for supremacy. That insight helped her beat back the shimmering response his fingers created wherever they glanced.

You abducted me, she chanted in her mind. *You think you own me. You want to destroy me. You're nothing but a selfish brute.*

The litany went on, eventually overcoming the spell of his caresses. Her wanton body might strain to surrender to him. The memory of the ecstasy he could call forth was imprinted on her skin. But her head and her heart were stronger, and they would prevail.

As her own arousal faded, she became more aware of Kylemore's. He breathed unsteadily, and his touch lost its effortless mastery. Next to her, he radiated heat like a great fire. His hand wandered down her stomach, tantalizingly close to her sex.

Then there was nothing.

After a moment, she opened her eyes. He still leaned on one bent arm, watching her. His face was flushed and his eyes were dark with desire. Although she'd long ago abandoned modesty as a luxury a whore couldn't afford, she fought the urge to cover herself with the sheet.

"This isn't working," he murmured, lifting his hand to brush a few stray strands of hair back from her cheeks.

How she abhorred the false tenderness of the gesture. Loathing lent her response an acid edge. "I told you I wasn't willing."

He ignored her interjection. "I'm too disturbed myself. I find the strategy I've chosen . . . distracting."

"What do you want from me? Sympathy?" she gritted out.

In the candlelight, he was almost sinfully beautiful. His narrow face was thoughtful under the wing of black hair that fell across his brow. It lent him a boyish air she knew was a lie.

His gaze dwelled on her as though she were a philosophical problem he was compelled to solve. "I'm trying to stir you into a frenzy of lust," he said consideringly.

The idea was so ridiculous that she couldn't restrain a scornful laugh. "You must know that won't happen."

"You shouldn't make challenges you can't live up to." He tugged at a lock of her hair in gentle reproof. "You're far from unaffected now. But I can't concentrate on driving you out of your mind while I'm so unsettled myself."

Part of her wished he'd just get on with it and take her. Another part dreaded his possession. Every time he gave her pleasure she didn't want, he chipped another piece of her soul away. Soon there would be nothing left.

"Perhaps you should go away and think about it," she suggested without any expectation he'd heed her.

His own huff of laughter contained a trace of genuine humor. "And perhaps not."

Strange that after all the turbulent emotion, they should speak almost like friends. This was something new. Soraya had always treated the duke with the distance due his rank, even when she'd used her mouth and hands and body to bring him to climax.

It was doubly strange when at any moment the duke would be inside her. The flickering light gilded the strong, lean lines of his body and left her in no doubt at all of his rampant readiness.

As he rose above her, she searched desperately for her hatred and anger. Both had receded further than she'd have believed possible.

He bent to kiss a long scratch a thorn had left on her neck, and they receded even further.

"You're hurt," he whispered.

Yes, she was, but not in the way he meant.

"It's nothing," she said, making her tone hostile.

The spurious intimacy of the warm bed in this candlelit room sapped her ability to resist. When she stopped resisting, he'd destroy her. His scent surrounded her, reminding her irresistibly of other occasions when she'd lain next to him willingly.

"Let me kiss it better." He lifted one of her hands and deliberately pressed his mouth to each mark. Her hands had borne the brunt of her wild flight into the shrubbery.

For a moment, she remained quiescent. Absurd, but his kisses did soothe the sting. She realized how close she came to wavering, and she snatched her hand away.

Yet again, Kylemore summoned tenderness to vanquish her. She had to conceal just how vulnerable she was to that particular ploy, although he was frighteningly perceptive and he'd probably already guessed, damn him.

"Stop it!" she snapped. "There's no need to dress up what you intend to do to me in pretty words or gestures."

He caught her hand again and gently but inexorably unfurled her fingers. He studied them for a long time.

"Soraya had perfect skin. Verity has calluses."

He swept his thumb across the rough area at the base of her palm. By now, she was so sensitized to his touch that the caress tingled right through her and down to where liquid heat pooled in her loins. She shifted uncomfortably against the cool sheets.

"I'm sorry if that offends you," she said with feeble sarcasm. "I never pretended to be anything but a peasant."

He kissed the place he'd just touched and she experienced another of those unwelcome inner tugs. Surely he couldn't seduce her with a mere kiss on the hand, could he?

"Actually, I don't think we ever discussed your background. An oversight I intend to correct very soon. I take it from your brother's execrable accent that you're originally from the north of England."

She frowned up at him, so annoyed that she didn't even try to draw away as he lowered himself between her legs. "I don't exist purely for your entertainment, Your Grace."

He braced himself on his arms and stared down at her with a breathtaking mixture of amusement and hunger. "Entertainment is a flimsy word for what we share, don't you think?"

He moved back slightly to clasp her hips and angle them up toward him. But still he didn't take her. She hated to admit the pause tantalized her. It must just be that she wanted the long torture over.

Why did he take the trouble to linger over her like this? Her availability to him couldn't be clearer.

She struggled to adopt Soraya's cool tone. Not surprisingly, given her trembling awareness of the massively aroused male poised above her, she failed. "A mistress is only a rich man's plaything."

"This particular mistress seems a considerably graver matter than that," he said gently.

He tensed and finally—*finally*—slid into her. Her gasp mingled with his deep groan of pleasure.

For a long moment, he was still. Then he began to thrust into her, deeply, fully and with a relentless drive she couldn't help but recognize. His skin against hers burned hot, belying the teasing edge to his words. As did the implacable fierceness of his possession.

Her body had only just adjusted to his size and heat when he gave another groan and lost himself inside her.

Verity lay panting beneath his weight. They were still joined. She felt uncomfortable and sticky.

And that couldn't be frustration skulking in her heart, could it? After such extended preliminaries, she'd imagined he'd make more of an effort to bring her to completion.

Hadn't he mentioned sending her mad with lust? Her obdurate soul had looked forward to denying him.

Although perhaps this businesslike coupling had been an inadvertent rescue. For a few moments before he'd taken her, her soul had been about as obdurate as blancmange.

She raised her hands from where they lay at her sides and gave him a push. His bare skin felt like warm rock under her palms. It was the first time she'd touched him of her own free will all night. "Get off me, Kylemore!"

He lifted himself on both elbows, although he didn't break the connection between their bodies. "Oh, we're not finished yet," he said softly.

He moved his hips suggestively, and she felt him swell inside her again.

"Oh, yes, we are," she insisted, squirming in protest.

"That was nice. Do it again." A wolfish smile, familiar from London days, creased his face. That particular expression had always warned her he meant to launch some inventive piece of love play.

And she'd always gone along with him. But not tonight.

She was very near the end of her resistance. She knew it. He knew it. A glance into his intense indigo eyes told her he considered victory already his.

Verity made herself remember everything she had at stake. Her self-respect. Her future. Ben and Maria's future.

She deliberately sought the cold obsidian center of herself. The obsidian center that had helped her survive as a demimondaine. The center where no one reached her. The center that was utterly Verity and which Soraya had never touched.

Closing her eyes, she waited, secure in the knowledge that her true self was safe from him.

There was a silence. Kylemore must have noted and understood how firmly she was now locked away from him. He might possess her body, but the real Verity was as inaccessible as the moons of Jupiter.

She heard him sigh. Then he began to move within her, slow strokes as powerful and endless as the tide. After a few seconds, he reached out and raised her knees so his penetration went deeper, surer.

She could have told him it didn't matter. She was isolated in her inviolable sanctum.

Except her cold black center was neither as cold nor as black as she longed for it to be. She was too aware of his scent and the evocative sounds of his body moving in hers. She closed her eyes more tightly and clutched her inner bastion.

Kylemore's heat beckoned to her. It took all her willpower to keep herself from sliding against him, answering that rhythmic rocking of his body with her own warmth.

A moan escaped her. She wanted it to be a furious protest, but it emerged as a mew of pleasure. To stop herself reaching for him, she fisted her hands into the rumpled sheet beneath her.

"Open your eyes, Verity." His low voice teased across nerves raw with sensual excitement. "Open your eyes."

"No," she said stubbornly, knowing any surrender, however

small, would lead to ultimate defeat. She turned her head away to deny the almost overwhelming temptation to obey him.

"Open your eyes." When that had no effect, he continued almost dreamily, "I can keep going all night, you know."

She whipped her head around and met his gaze. It was dark and intent and steady. She couldn't doubt he meant what he said.

Her lips parted on a wordless sob. She couldn't keep fighting him. As if to underline that thought, her inner muscles clenched to draw him deeper.

This time, he was the one to close his eyes, and his sigh was a long *aah* of appreciation. He dropped down against her and rubbed his beard-roughened cheek upon hers in a gesture almost more intimate than the sex itself.

Against her will, she arched into him, her breasts brushing the hair on his chest. He reached down to stroke between her legs. No deceiving herself this time that her cry conveyed anything but pleasure.

With a broken exhalation of defeat, she began to move with him in the heady dance of passion. As she rose to meet his next thrust, she heard him give a low growl of triumph.

And why not? What price her defiance and hatred now?

But the thought was distant, unrelated to the climbing spiral of tension inside her, tension that built higher with every thrust of his powerful body into hers. She twined trembling arms around him and threw her head back as the storm within her gathered.

By now, Kylemore's inhuman control faltered. His slow, powerful pace changed, became faster, more relentless. She hardly noticed. Her own response rose, tightening her muscles, compelling her to cling to him even as he drove into her for the last time.

She broke in his arms on a peak higher, purer, more distressing than anything she'd ever known before. Kylemore's groan of release underscored the shockingly exquisite turbulence. Her body leaped greedily to devour every second of rapture, every ravishing sensation.

He flung her up to fly free among the stars. While her heart lingered behind to grieve.

When some shred of control returned, tears dried on Verity's cheeks. She clasped Kylemore as if she'd die before she let him go. His rough breathing warmed her ear.

She had no idea what that fiery encounter had meant to him apart from providing yet more evidence that physically, she had no defenses against him.

Their lovemaking had turned her every hope to ashes.

In spite of her bravery and determination, he'd required a mere two days to have her panting and begging in his arms.

Two days.

How he must laugh. How he must gloat over his quick victory. Soraya had held her own against him for a year. But Verity, with so many more reasons to deny him, had crumbled before half a week was out.

Although she knew it was too late for any pretense of distaste or reluctance, she unwound her arms from his back.

He raised himself so he could see her.

She searched his face for triumph, but he looked as shaken as she felt. Or perhaps her own reaction was so overwhelming that she imagined she saw its reflection in him. Her body quaked with after-tremors, and the memory of mind-shattering bliss ran sluggishly in her veins.

"I hate you," she said clearly.

Something flickered in his eyes, but she was too tired and heartsick to try and read it. He lifted himself off her, then, surprisingly, left the bed.

"It doesn't matter," he said flatly, bending to pick up his scattered clothes.

He was right. It didn't. He'd already demonstrated that by proving she was as vulnerable to him as she'd ever been.

More.

She stared up at the heavy beams that crossed the white-washed ceiling and told herself she wouldn't cry. Although more tears couldn't worsen her humiliation.

The door opened, then shut behind him.

It was much, much later and she'd fallen into a disturbed sleep when the first tortured cry woke her.

Chapter 12

A t first, Verity thought that the strangled sound was part of her confused dreams, but as she raised eyelids still heavy and swollen with tears, the cry came again.

Somewhere in the house, a man called out in inconsolable agony.

One of the servants must be troubled or sick, although she'd thought that all the people in the valley, apart from Kylemore and herself, slept in the cottages.

Without consciously deciding to act, she was on her feet and pulling on the first piece of clothing her hand lighted on in the armoire—a silk robe. Habits instilled through years of looking after her brother and sister had never left her. She couldn't ignore the terrible need in those hoarse screams.

Fumbling, she lit a candle, then let herself out of the room. She paused in the hallway, unsure which direction to take.

The man cried out again, a long keen that faded away into broken sobs. It came from down the corridor. Clutching the robe around her naked body, she went toward the room where she'd sought refuge from the duke last night.

She quietly pushed open the door to the simple chamber with its narrow bed only to discover no servant broke the silence of the night.

Instead, it was the Duke of Kylemore.

She stood in the doorway as hatred rose in a black tide to choke her. Nightmares should plague a man with such evil on his soul. In any just universe, he'd never enjoy a peaceful moment. No other revenge lay open to her, but at least knowing he battled night demons was something.

The long, lean body in the bed thrashed wildly, as if he fought some invisible assailant. Twisted sheets tangled around him, mute testimony to his struggles. His chest was bare, and sweat shimmered on his white skin under the light covering of black hair.

The duke had bad dreams. What was it to her? He'd kidnapped and abused her. His conscience *should* trouble him.

She turned to go. Let him rot in his misery. Let pains in this world give him a foretaste of the pains of hell that surely awaited him.

Behind her, he gave a low moan. She paused, not wanting to hear the bone-deep grief in the sound but unable to help herself.

She straightened her spine. No, she must be ruthless, as Kylemore was ruthless. Her fear and entreaties and resistance had never kept him from taking what he wanted. So why should she care if his sins returned to haunt his sleep?

Her enemy's agony was her only vengeance.

He writhed again in the grip of his dream, so violently that the bed creaked loudly in the small room. She tried to rejoice in his anguish, but something stronger than her futile dreams of retribution prevented her leaving.

Slowly, reluctantly, she turned back.

This time, she couldn't help edging closer. He'd rolled to lie spread-eagled on his back, braced for imaginary attack. She told herself she wanted to luxuriate in his distress while he was too lost in his fantasies to threaten her.

But when the light of her candle spilled across the sleeping duke—for all his turmoil, he was still fast asleep—she didn't feel remotely like laughing.

No trace now of the supercilious aristocrat she'd known in London, or even the ruthless tyrant who had abducted her. Instead, the man stretched out before her was tormented to the edge of sanity.

He tossed his head with its sweat-dampened dark hair from side to side as if in violent denial. His breathing was loud, and his powerful chest heaved with each difficult inhalation.

In spite of everything he'd done to her, in spite of how she *wanted* to react, Verity's heart contracted with pity. She couldn't abandon any fellow creature, however despicable, to suffer as the duke so obviously suffered.

"Your Grace," she said softly, leaning over and hesitantly touching his bare shoulder.

The smooth skin was clammy beneath her hand. Some monumental crisis gripped him.

"Your Grace, you're having a bad dream. Wake up."

He jerked away as though her touch scorched him. The marks of tears on his cheeks shocked her. He was still deeply asleep, lost in his nightmare.

She curled her fingers around his shoulder and gave it a gentle shake. "Your Grace, wake up."

His hand shot out and grabbed her wrist as the gentian eyes opened wide. For one startled moment, he looked up at her through that hazy blue like a lost child. She had another sudden vision of the little boy he must once have been.

All the while, his adult strength crushed her fragile wrist.

"Who is it?" he grated out, his gaze blind.

She doubted he was actually awake. The dream still dug its claws into him.

"Kylemore, it's me." She tried to break away, cursing herself for her stupidity in venturing so close. Did she never learn?

He didn't seem to hear her as he inexorably dragged her toward him. When he forced her to bend over him, her unbound hair tumbled forward to pool on his naked chest.

"Who is it?" he asked again.

"It's Verity."

The room was silent except for his ragged breathing. Hesitantly, he brought up his free hand to tangle in her hair. The gesture was almost tender.

"Black silk," he said in husky wonder. Then more sharply, "Verity? Is that you?"

"You're hurting my hand, Kylemore," she said firmly, hoping to disperse the miasma in his mind.

His dazed glance fell to where he gripped her with such bruising force. "Your pardon."

He immediately freed her. She should seize this reprieve and flee to her room, but still she didn't go.

He pushed himself upright against the pillows and looked around as if unsure exactly where he was. "Verity," he said in a more normal tone. "What are you doing here?"

She rubbed her sore wrist. "You called out in your sleep. I came to see if you were all right."

"Just a bad dream," he said with a carelessness she knew better than to believe.

It had been more than just a bad dream. His terrifying distress still echoed in her ears. And he'd cried. She wouldn't have thought the heartless duke capable of tears, but tonight proved her wrong.

"Go back to bed." He spoke as though dismissing a servant in his grand London house. "I promise not to disturb your rest further."

She couldn't ignore this reprieve. She should be relieved he was sending her away unscathed apart from a few bruises.

With every second, he returned to his usual self. And Kylemore's usual self was dangerous, as she knew to her cost. She retrieved her candle and began to sidle out of the room. Out of the corner of her eye, she tried not to notice how his hand shook when he raised it to brush his hair back from his face.

He didn't look at her. "Good night."

"Good night, then," she said, telling herself she imagined the bereft note in his voice.

At the door, she impulsively looked back and caught the naked desolation on his fine-boned face. He sat up as if he meant to watch out the rest of the night.

For once, the shell of his self-confidence had cracked, and she saw him more clearly than ever before. Exhaustion marked his face—she suddenly wondered if he'd slept at all since they'd arrived in the valley—and the beautiful mouth was taut with anguish.

Cursing herself for being every variety of fool, she returned to stand beside the bed. "Can I get Your Grace anything? A glass of wine? Something from the kitchen?"

He focused those bleak indigo eyes on her, and she struggled not to recognize a loneliness as strong as her own.

"No," he said.

"Very well."

But as she turned once more to leave, he reached out and snatched for her hand. "Yes. Yes, stay." His voice was harsh, turning what should have been a plea into a command.

"Your Grace, I . . ." If she crawled between the sheets, she was all too aware what he'd do.

He must have read the refusal in her face, because he dropped her hand and looked past her with an attempt at his usual hauteur. "Of course you must go."

Ridiculous to be moved by his foolish pride. She reminded herself he plotted her destruction. But at the moment, it was difficult to think of him as the unrelenting, omnipotent Duke of Kylemore. If anything, he reminded her of Ben, who as a child had always been quickest to deny he wanted comfort just when he needed it most.

But he wasn't Ben. He was the man who contrived to make her his slave. He was the man who, only hours ago, had come close to achieving that end. She was mad to pretend that a troubled, grieving Kylemore wasn't as perilous to her as his daytime self ever was. Perhaps even more perilous.

His thin face indicated aristocratic disdain as he stared stoically into the distance. But shadows darkened the hollows around his eyes and a muscle jerked spasmodically in his cheek.

She'd regret relenting. Even as she placed the candle on the ugly oak side table and climbed onto the mattress, she knew she'd regret it. But common sense had lost all authority over her actions.

"Verity?"

When she didn't answer, he shifted to make room for her.

She didn't want to touch him. Although she might be a fool, she wasn't that much of a fool. But while he was a lean man, lying apart from him on the narrow cot meant she only just balanced on the edge.

She was close enough for the heat of his body to curl out and beckon her nearer. She waited for him to haul her to him and spread her legs so he could rut over her, but instead, he lay still and tense beside her. It was as if somehow the rules of engagement between them had changed.

For a long moment, neither spoke. Verity became more and more uncomfortable. His musky scent was everywhere, reminding her cruelly of how she'd responded to him earlier.

What was the duke to make of her rebuffs when she came willingly to his bed now?

This was wrong. Terribly wrong.

"I should go," she said shakily, starting to rise.

"No."

He surged up and lashed his arms around her to drag her down so she lay with her back pressed to his chest. Through the silk of her robe, she felt him tremble. It vividly brought back the memory of how she'd found him. Hesitantly, knowing she was making one of the worst mistakes in her life, she turned and very gently embraced him.

"Sleep, Your Grace," she whispered. "It's not long until morning." It was the same tone she'd used to soothe Ben and Maria when they'd woken frightened in the night.

She waited for mockery or triumph. After all, what credence would her claims that she hated him have when she lay here cradling him like the most precious thing on earth?

But for once, Kylemore's cutting tongue was silent. Instead, he pulled her fully against him and relaxed with a great sigh. His bare flesh under her hands gradually lost its worrying coldness, and his breathing became deep and even.

The Duke of Kylemore slept in her arms.

Kylemore stirred from the sweetest sleep he could remember in years. The capricious Highland sun poured through the humble chamber's uncurtained windows. It was warm. It was late. And he held a fragrant bundle of slumbering femininity within the shelter of his body.

Or actually, she held him. His head rested on Verity's breast and her arms encircled him as though she protected him from every threat. Curious and rather sad to reflect that no one had ever held him like this before.

And even more curious that he should feel so safe in the arms of someone who detested him so virulently.

Detested him with good reason.

The unwelcome thought had no power to disturb him. He'd slept deeply and well. He'd woken with the woman he wanted above all others.

Literally. He was hard and ready.

But most curious of all, he made no attempt to seek relief. Although relief, asleep and defenseless, lay at hand.

He wished he were pitiless enough to take advantage of having her in his bed. He could be inside her before she woke. Before she set up any barriers. And after last night's astounding inferno of pleasure, those barriers would be dangerously weak.

So why did he hesitate?

Perhaps because she'd conquered her fear and abhorrence to come to his aid. She'd joined him of her own free will and had offered solace where he'd deserved only loathing. She'd seen his pain and risked herself to ease it.

Altogether, last night had been a revelation.

He'd been a brute, forcing her to flee from him into the night. He'd caught her and manipulated her into surrender. He'd schemed and blustered and bullied. And his reward had been the best sexual experience of his life.

But now her gallantry had changed everything between them.

The anger driving him for the last three months was absent this morning. His craving for revenge had retreated.

But though he no longer wanted to punish her, he couldn't

let her go. She was his only hope for peace. If nothing else, last night proved that was truer than ever.

Verity was his shield against the demons that pursued him. So her fate was sealed. She must stay with him forever.

The sun was warm on the back of Verity's neck as she tugged relentlessly at the weeds infesting the flowerbeds behind the house. Kate Macleish, Hamish's wife, kept a forbiddingly neat kitchen garden to supply the household, but she had no time left over for growing flowers. Verity had noticed the untidy beds yesterday, and the Yorkshire farm lass who still lurked within her had itched to create order.

She hadn't seen Kylemore all day—he'd been mercifully absent when she'd awoken. She had no idea what she could have said to him.

Actually, she was astonished she'd remained unmolested. Good heavens, she'd slept the night cuddled up to him, for all the world as if she'd wanted to be there. A better man than the duke would have made use of the woman so conveniently at hand.

For the thousandth time, she berated herself for a fool.

What had possessed her to go to Kylemore? Her only hope of prevailing against him was continued resistance. Yet how convincing would refusals sound after she'd crept into his bed without a murmur of protest?

She'd survived and prospered as a courtesan because she'd used her head and not her heart. What if that heart she repudiated ached for his misery? The duke was nothing to her.

But if he was nothing to her, why had the sight of his tears, tears he wasn't even aware he shed, cut her so deeply?

Some old sorrow plagued him. Some old sorrow that

taught him to hide his true feelings behind a mask of ruthless autocracy and perfect control.

She growled her exasperation. With him. With the situation.
And with herself most of all. Why should she fret over him?
All she wanted was to be free of him, immediately, utterly and
forever.

She began to worry at a particularly stubborn root.

Last night, he'd given her sexual pleasure such as she'd
never known. She'd never forgive him for it.

But worse, he'd opened a chasm in her heart. She could
fight his strength and perhaps even win. But she had no defenses against his need.

She must get away before she did something really stupid.

Like fall in love with the oppressive tyrant who believed
he owned her, body and soul. Damn him.

She gave the root a vicious tug, but still it didn't budge.

"Whisht, lassie! You'll do yourself a mischief!"

She looked up from her turbulent thoughts to find Hamish
Macleish staring at her in consternation. In the outlandish
local costume, he looked large and capable, and his bare
legs under the kilt were straight and strong.

Earlier, Angus had been on guard duty. He'd tried to divert her from what he'd clearly thought was an inappropriate
activity for the lady of the house. She'd pretended not to
understand and had kept going.

She was surprised to see Hamish. He'd always studiously
avoided her—probably because he was the only servant who
spoke English. She couldn't subvert people who didn't understand a word she said.

"Good morning, Mr. Macleish."

The angels had been remarkably deaf to her pleas of late.
But perhaps they'd heard her last desperate prayer for escape.

"Good morning, my lady." He stepped closer. "It's gey stony soil for flowers. My Kate gave up."

Verity stood and wiped her hands on the faded apron that protected her skirts. "Mr. Macleish, will you help me?"

"Aye, my lady. Although ye ken it's a wee while since I've done any gardening."

She shook her head. "No, you misunderstand me." She took a deep breath and marshaled her courage. "I see you as a man of honor."

He met her eyes squarely—these Scottish rustics were remarkably free of their southern counterparts' sycophantic ways. "May the good Lord keep me so, my lady."

"A man who wouldn't stand by and allow a woman to be abducted and abused."

The man's expression became shuttered. "Ye ask me tae help ye get away," he said flatly.

She took a step closer and injected a pleading note into her voice. "The Duke of Kylemore stole me from my family. I'm here against my will. My heart is set on a virtuous life, yet he forces me to play his mistress. You must believe me. As a man of honor, you must assist me."

He shook his head. "No, my lady."

"But you must help me!" she cried desperately, reaching for his arm. Surely he couldn't just abandon her to her fate now that he knew what the duke had done to her.

"I serve His Grace tae the last breath in my body." He sounded regretful but immovable as he shook himself free of her clinging grip. "I feel for your troubles. But I cannae help ye. I gave my oath of obedience tae the duke."

Although she knew she wasted her time, she couldn't give up. This might be her only chance to persuade Hamish to her cause. If he failed her, where else could she turn?

Her voice shook with urgency. "I'll pay you. I'll pay you

well. Take me back to my brother. I swear you'll be rewarded."

His frown indicated the offer offended him. "No, lassie, I dinna want your money."

She spread her hands in frantic appeal. "But your master commits a great wrong."

"No Macleish will gae against His Grace's word. Without the duke's favor, there wouldnae be Macleishes left in the Highlands. He saved us all from ruin and exile. So I'm sorry, my lady." His eyes sharpened on her face. "And don't ye be thinking of trying tae run off on your own. Folk die in these mountains, even folk who ken them. A wee lassie wouldnae ken what tae do when a fog came down or the rocks crumbled under her feet."

The picture was graphic enough and underlined what the duke had told her. It didn't necessarily mean it was true.

The man's weathered face grew more kindly, "Och, my lady, I've served His Grace since he was a bairn. I cannae break faith. All I can say is he'll have reasons for what he does."

Yes, lust and pique and anger, she felt like retorting.

But what would it serve? This was the second time she'd sought help from Kylemore's retainers, and she'd failed abysmally on both occasions. The selfish oaf had certainly surrounded himself with unhesitatingly loyal servants.

Hamish obviously felt he owed a debt to the duke. Feudal ties must still hold strong in this isolated corner of the kingdom, however iniquitous the particular lord of the manor.

Her shoulders slumped, and she turned away to hide a sudden rush of tears. It was starkly apparent the old man wouldn't help her. Defeated, she went back to grubbing at the weeds. If she was to escape, she was on her own.

* * *

Unexpectedly, Kylemore joined Verity for dinner in the parlor that also served as the house's dining room. When she found him waiting, it suddenly struck her how little time he spent in the house. She supposed he must pass the daylight hours revisiting childhood haunts.

Well, wherever he went and whatever he did, it didn't bring him ease. She recalled his bleak expression last night. Yet again, she wondered what torments lay beneath the duke's composure. His unnaturally self-assured facade would never deceive her again.

He turned from the window where he stood. The room faced the loch, and the evening sun glittered gold on the flat water behind him. "Verity."

"Your Grace."

Manners dictated that she curtsey. She ignored them. The small defiance bolstered her faltering confidence. A kidnapper didn't deserve observations due his rank.

She was unsure how to behave with him. Her usual sullen recalcitrance seemed misplaced after a night in his arms.

How she wished she'd never heard those terrible cries. It was impossible to treat the Duke of Kylemore as an inhuman monster when she'd glimpsed his inner agony.

He stepped forward to pull out her chair at the table where she usually ate in solitude. Although still dressed for the country, a buff coat covered his shirtsleeves and he wore a neckcloth tied in a simple knot.

"Hamish tells me you've taken up gardening."

He almost sounded conversational. She cast him a suspicious glance under her lashes. Had Mr. Macleish also told him she'd asked for help to run away? She studied his face as she sat down where he'd indicated, but she couldn't tell what he thought.

Nothing new there.

Kylemore sat opposite her and reached out to pour the

wine. The hunting box was well stocked with life's luxuries. For the first time, Verity reflected upon how such goods arrived. Surely not along that rough road over the mountains. There must be another way in. The loch perhaps.

"I find in my captivity, time hangs heavily on my hands," she said pointedly, although she'd long ago given up hope of awakening any guilt over his crimes against her.

"I've asked him to help you tomorrow." He shook his napkin out of its folds and placed it on his lap.

"Are you worried I'll dig my way out unless you place a guard over me?" she asked acidly.

Kylemore's affability made her nervous. She much preferred their unambiguously open conflict. He lifted his glass and leaned back with a negligent grace that tugged at her senses. Her determination to escape hardened. If she stayed and let her unwilling attraction have its way, she'd be lost forever.

Kate Macleish came in with a tureen of soup. When they were alone once more, Verity returned to hostilities. A sharp tongue hid the growing softness within, a softness she had every intention of stifling.

"Or perhaps you're afraid I'll come after you with a spade if you're reckless enough to put gardening tools within reach."

He put down his spoon. "Verity, you have a choice," he said gently. "We eat, we talk, we pass the evening with an attempt at civility. Or we fuck. It's up to you."

Kylemore watched as her remarkable gray eyes widened. He'd have said that nothing could shock Soraya. But Verity was much less hardened by the life she'd led.

Hell, now even he was doing it. He had to stop thinking of her as two different people. He'd quickly guessed on the journey to the glen that in her mind she divided herself into separate entities. Soraya, the notorious courtesan. And Verity, the woman who preserved an odd air of innocence whatever debaucheries he'd committed on her body.

Over the last few days, avoiding this cursed house had given him hours alone in the fresh air to puzzle over his captive.

He must have been out of his mind with thwarted lust when he'd found her in Whitby, or he would have realized immediately that she believed the virtuous widow was much closer to her real self than the glittering demimondaine was.

He'd abducted her to get his fascinating mistress back and to make her pay for her betrayal. Now the problem was that while he wanted to find Soraya in Verity, he also wanted to find Verity in Soraya.

God knew why. Soraya offered him all a sensible man wished for. A willing partner in bed. A sophisticated companion. No inconvenient emotional storms.

Whereas Verity . . .

Face it, Kylemore, he told himself wryly. *Verity is sweet and vulnerable in ways Soraya never was. She's gallant and honest and as luscious a peach as you could sink your teeth into. Verity banishes your nightmares. Verity gives you peace.*

He wanted them both.

Last night, she'd finally surrendered to the sensual hunger between them. Even lost in his own release, he hadn't mistaken her response. He only needed to seduce her into a malleable frame of mind once more. Then he'd convince her of the advantages of becoming the Duchess of Kylemore.

The advantages?

Sour amusement filled him. What were the advantages to marriage with him?

A troubled self-destructive husband who had spent his life in his own private hell?

Centuries of misery, madness, addiction in his blood-lines?

A future as a social pariah?

Alliance with the foul lout who bore the Kylemore title would disgrace the woman he now knew, whatever the world might think of the match.

Damn her.

Across from him, he noted the droop of her graceful neck. Against the Elizabethan collar of her crimson gown, stiffened and raised at the back to frame her upswept hair, her face was as pale and sad as an effigy on a marble tomb.

There had been a subdued air to her all evening. He was used to her bristling at everything he said. He relied upon her prickly reactions to keep his damned inconvenient urge to cherish her in check. But tonight's jibes contained a desperate edge, as if she forced herself to snipe and fight.

"Well?" he asked.

"As Your Grace wishes," she said colorlessly, picking up her spoon and beginning to eat her soup.

He resisted the impulse to whisk her upstairs and make good his crude threat—anything to rouse her from despair. Her inner fire was doused and cold tonight, and the absence of its warmth left him frozen and alone.

Kylemore waited until after dinner before he asked the questions that really interested him, none of which fell into the category of civility, despite what he'd said earlier.

He lounged beside Verity on a settle in front of the fire, and a glass of port dangled from his fingers. Her glass of wine from dinner rested untouched on the table near her elbow. She'd hardly eaten any of the elaborate food Kate had prepared.

Confound it, he worried over the chit like a damned

nursemaid. Where the hell had the wicked Duke of Kyle-more gone? He reminded himself with increasing despera-tion that his goal in this glen was revenge on a deceitful mistress.

Still, in the three months since she'd run away, it had nig-gled just how little he knew of her. He'd explored every inch of her delectable body, yet he had no idea where she'd grown up. He needed to learn what went on behind those beautiful silver eyes. That curiosity had become paramount last night.

Last night, when she'd insisted she hated him. Then held him safe against his nightmares.

"You never told me what caused you to adopt your profes-sion," he said with deliberate idleness.

A haunted expression fleetingly crossed her face. If he hadn't observed her so closely, he would have missed it.

"I'm sure every whore has a similar tale to tell," she said in a biting tone and without looking at him. "I see no need to bore Your Grace with the details."

How quick she was to refer to herself as a whore. Yet if ever a demirep held herself above the gutter, it was Soraya.

"Indulge me," he said softly, noticing the beguiling play of the firelight across the creamy skin revealed above the dress's low square neckline.

At least his question dispelled the defeat from her eyes. She raised her head and glared at him with a return of her usual blazing defiance. "Is this part of my punishment—reliving my every sin for your delectation?"

"Confession is good for the soul," he said mildly. "Why not tell me? I'll let you know if the tale becomes tedious."

She stood up, her face stiff with disdain. He should have guessed she'd never surrender her secrets just for the asking.

"No."

Soraya had never said no and Verity seemed to say nothing

else. He caught her hand to stop her leaving. "I mean to find out, Verity," he vowed.

She snatched away from him. "You bought my body, not my mind, a year ago, Your Grace."

As imperious as any duchess, she marched out.

Chapter 13

Kylemore stalked into Verity's room, intent on proving *to both of them* that he was still her heartless lover.

Abandoned to brood in the parlor, he'd decided he was heartily sick of debating the phantom essences of Soraya and Verity. In Whitby, he'd known exactly what he'd wanted of his mistress. She'd learn her place: in his bed. And after learning that, she'd stay there, willing, inventive, endlessly available.

He was desperate to regain that simplicity of purpose.

After the chit's haughty exit, he wasn't surprised to discover her perched on the window seat ready for battle. She hadn't removed the gorgeous dress she'd worn at dinner. Her beautiful face indicated stubborn resistance. She was clearly as willing to lie beneath him as she was to walk to Morocco barefoot.

Perhaps her reprieve from his attentions this morning meant she assumed she could persuade him to leave her alone.

Foolish jade to believe that could ever be true. He was hot and randy, and he thirsted for the relief only she offered him.

"Your Grace," she said without rising and without a trace of welcome.

"Take your clothes off and get on the damned bed," he snarled softly from the doorway.

Familiar annoyance submerged the momentary vulnerability he thought he'd caught in her eyes. "I see Your Grace is pressed for time," she snapped. "Why don't I just lift my skirts and lean against the wall? That way, you need only devote five minutes to the business."

"Don't push me, Verity." He ripped his neckcloth off and flung it to the floor as he stepped closer to her. "You won't like the results."

"I don't like the results now," she said coldly.

At this moment, he had no difficulty recognizing her as Soraya. Except once she'd taken him as her lover, refusal had never been part of Soraya's repertoire.

He gave her the level glare that always gained instant obedience from everyone in the world but this one slender woman. "Liar. You like the results well enough. What I can't understand is why you go through this elaborate minuet before we both get what we want."

"I don't want you," she said steadily. "You've always confused what I do out of necessity with what I'd do if free to follow my own inclination."

He tugged his shirt over his head and sent it sailing after the neckcloth. "I know you better than that. You're a sensualist at heart, my dear. It's what made you a great courtesan. You come alive to my touch. You always have."

She looked frostier by the minute. He sat down on the bed and extended one leg in her direction.

"Help me with my boots."

She stood, and her eyes sparked with fury. "Take them off yourself."

With a shrug, he tugged at his footwear. "If I must."

He looked across to where she waited, proud and stiff as a statue. Truly, she outdid any great lady he knew when it came to bearing.

Where had she learned her grand manner? One day she'd tell him, he promised himself.

"You're wasting your time, you know," he pointed out, tucking his curiosity away for later consideration. "Nothing you say will make me storm out in a temper."

Surprisingly, a disdainful smile curved that lush mouth. "I've seen Your Grace in more equable frames of mind."

"There are other ways to work off ill humor than a fit of the sullens," he pointed out silkily and was pleased to see dismay expel her brief confidence. He pursued his momentary advantage. "I requested the removal of your clothing."

"I don't believe any *request* was involved," she sniped back.

He slung his boots into the corner, where they landed with a loud thud. Generally, he was an orderly man. It was part of his carefully cultivated control. But he wanted her to recognize that everything in this house was his—including her—and he treated his possessions as he liked.

Barefoot and still wearing his breeches, he swaggered over to where she stood. She retreated a step before she gathered her courage and held her ground.

Futile courage. Much better for her if she'd taken to her heels. But of course, she'd tried that last night and had only delayed her inevitable fate.

As he'd told her, he knew every hideout on this estate. When madness gripped his father, Kylemore's very life had depended upon his ability to disappear. He'd often used the hollow in the shrubbery, if only because it was close enough to the house for a quick escape.

She raised her chin and glared at him. "Kylemore, don't do this."

He was relieved to note that her words held more demand than entreaty. He preferred her when she acted his insolent mistress. When she was sad, he felt like the meanest worm that ever crawled upon the earth.

God, he was doing it again. She was one woman, not two. Even if she gave him enough trouble for a hundred.

"Pleas are futile and you know it," he said evenly.

"Aren't you tired of forcing yourself on me? What satisfaction is there?"

He laughed derisively. "You're not so naïve. We both know satisfaction's not the problem. I might even say I find your resistance exciting. Soraya was always so . . . amenable."

Something that might have been shame welled up in her gray eyes, but to her credit, she didn't waver. "So if I spread my legs without argument, you'll give up this game?"

Was it a game? At this precise moment, it seemed like life and death.

But then, he'd always been a slave to his desire for her. Having her, incredibly, had only doubled the weight of his chains.

"Let's try it and see, shall we?" He'd take her any way he could, although he didn't pretend he'd yet gotten anything like the surrender he craved.

"Damn you," she said in a low, shaking voice, her hands fisting at her sides. She whirled away in a flurry of crimson skirts.

He grabbed her arm, feeling the willowy strength in her, and swung her back to face him. She was no weakling, his woman. But she needed to understand he'd always be stronger.

"Oh, no. I'm not chasing you through the hedgerows tonight, my dear," he drawled. "We'll save that particular amusement for some other occasion."

"I'm not some inanimate object," she protested.

"Lately when you've been under me, I've found myself wondering," he said cruelly.

Her sharp inhalation was his only warning. She lifted her hand and slapped him hard across the face.

The crack of the blow echoed in the suddenly silent room.

Then she released her breath in a sob and began to struggle in earnest. Kylemore, his face stinging, seized her roughly with both hands.

"You'll be sorry you did that," he grated out.

"I'm sorry I ever met you!" she cried wildly.

"You're not alone in that sentiment."

"Then why don't you let me go? End this evil before it ruins us both."

He felt a vulpine smile spread across his face. "You know why." He buried his fingers in the thick mass of black hair confined in its elaborate knot. "Because of this."

Ignoring her wriggling, he forced her head back and swooped down to take her mouth with his. For the space of a second, her lips were taut with rejection. Then she answered his fury with a fury of her own and kissed him back, viciously, hungrily.

Passionately.

He raked his hands through her hair until it tumbled in lavish abandon down her back, while all the time his mouth ravished hers, demanding capitulation she couldn't help but give. That desperate, unhappy kiss hinted at needs of her own swimming beneath her defiant surface. Needs not too far removed from his own.

Gasping, he raised his head, her taste sharp and rich on his tongue. He searched for some sign that her will and her desire had coalesced at last. But while her mouth was swollen and wet with his kisses, her eyes shone brilliant with rage.

"Concede, Verity," he begged hoarsely, his pride dust when it came to his overwhelming hunger.

"Never," she insisted.

Then astoundingly, she reached up to drag him down for another kiss. Their mouths dueled and parted, then met again, this time for what felt like eternity.

This was like no kiss he'd ever shared. This spoke of passion and anger and misery and an endless battle for supremacy.

And pleasure. Pleasure so intoxicating that it made his head spin.

Curling his arm around her slim waist, he bowed her back to press his mouth to her pale throat. Her pulse pounded wildly beneath his lips. The wanton blood beat a relentless rhythm of temptation that beckoned him as opium had beckoned his father to ruin.

He tasted each shuddering breath she took. The sensation was unbearably intimate, as though she lived by his kisses alone. Her hot scent swirled, luring him to further importunities. His nostrils flared as he tested her building arousal in the most primitive way.

Her fingers clutched convulsively at his flesh. Her nails scraped across the crisp hair on his chest, teased a nipple. She rubbed her lithe body in its silk dress against his bare torso as though she wanted to climb into his skin. His excitement leaped another notch to reach an unbearable pitch.

At last, he'd scratched beneath Verity's surface, perhaps even deep enough to unearth Soraya, although Soraya would never fall victim to such violent need. The woman in his arms quaked at the very edge of control.

If only he could force her over that edge.

With an unsteady laugh, he twisted her around and flung her onto the bed. She gave a strangled cry as she bounced upon the mattress. Before she could roll away, he climbed on top of her and shoved her down onto the covers.

"I hate you," she hissed.

"So you've said. The repetition risks becoming tiresome," he said in a deliberately bored tone even while the hot blood thundered through his veins.

"Repetition doesn't make it less true," she said savagely. Her eyes glittered with fury and unshed tears as she stared up into his face.

God knew what she saw. Certainly, he'd abandoned any remnant of the civilized man he'd once considered himself. He'd treated her roughly before, but this verged on something darker and they both knew it. Straddling her, he clamped his fingers around her dress's elaborately embroidered collar.

He briefly recalled his pleasure at choosing the lovely gown from the modiste. It had cost a sultan's ransom, but he hadn't cared. He'd been too captivated picturing the vivid color against his mistress's flawless skin.

"I will not bear this." Her breath emerged in panting gasps, and her mouth glistened damply from their fierce kiss.

"Oh, yes, you will," he grunted. "You will bear me."

One massive wrench. The extravagant dress and the shift underneath split to her waist. Her magnificent breasts spilled free.

Her nipples were hard and puckered, tempting as ripe berries. He bent his head and tongued one rosy peak. Her taste immediately flooded his mouth, heightening his rampant excitement. She moaned, and even through his blind arousal, he heard despair in the muffled sound.

He rolled her nipple in his lips and drew hard on it. She was exquisite. Perfect. Perfect for him. He slid his hands along her flanks and turned his attention to her other breast.

He had to take her. No delays. No hesitation. *Now.* The demon in him strained to meet its equal in the demon he knew she leashed within her.

"I don't want to hurt you," he muttered with one last drowning trace of consideration.

"You hurt me just by existing!" she cried.

In wordless denial of what she said, he claimed her lips in another urgent exploration.

Through her frenzy of rejection, her hands curved like claws around his bare shoulders. The savage who lurked within him exulted to know he'd bear her mark.

He kissed her again, using his tongue and compelling her participation.

He shoved up the skirts of what was now the expensive rag she wore and stroked between her legs. She was already wet. Soon he felt the rush of her response against his probing fingers.

She groaned into his mouth and at last kissed him back. He ripped at his breeches to free himself and thrust into her full length.

She gasped and lay still. Her life-giving heat surrounded him. The muscles in her sleek inner passage tightened as if she meant to keep him inside her forever.

He'd meant to brand her as his in the most basic way. He'd meant to show her he really was the heartless beast she believed him to be. But as she lifted her hips to accommodate him, the radiant sweetness of the moment defeated him. The old hankering to possess and pleasure seeped through his frenzy and tempered his rapacious lust.

His touch automatically gentled, and instead of ravaging her like a conqueror, he held himself above her, basking in the exquisite moment.

She was everything he'd ever wanted. This, this was what

he lived for. This was worth the eternal damnation he courted with his sins against her. He'd fight through hellfire itself if this ineffable joining was his eventual prize.

He clung to the glorious stasis as long as he could. Then he began to move, each stroke deep and deliberate to emphasize his mastery. She sighed and released her death grip on his shoulders, sliding her arms around his back.

Ridiculous to find that reluctant embrace so affecting. But it did affect him. More than her practiced caresses in London ever had. Her hands began to stroke him in time with his thrusts, tracing his straining spine, going lower to knead the tense muscles of his buttocks. He knew she was so lost to the sensual pull and release between them that she had no idea she was touching him.

The incendiary heat in his loins threatened to explode, but he battled to contain himself. He needed her to cede her ecstasy to him almost more than he needed his own release, even if delaying his own satisfaction damn near killed him.

He pushed the pace. And this time, she matched him. She moaned again, the sound sweet in his ears, and wrapped her legs around his hips, urging him closer. Then he became blind and deaf to everything except the delicious friction of moving in and out of her body.

Soon, he felt her quiver with the onset of her crisis. He tried desperately to harness the instant when she gave in to him, when he at last held sway over her.

But it was impossible. The familiar whirlwind snatched him up and swirled him to the skies.

And as ever in the conflagration of desire, questions of ownership and domination dissolved to ashes.

Kylemore gradually returned to awareness to find Verity lying silent and unresisting beneath him. Tears marked silvery trails across her ivory cheeks and clumped her thick black lashes together around her dazed gray eyes. She didn't need to tell him she despised herself for what had just happened.

If his goal had been to return their interactions to their simplest level, he'd failed utterly. She still held him in thrall. Every time he took her, hard, fast, or slowly, tenderly, the bonds uniting them twisted tighter.

He was a barbarian, but he'd willingly go through all the turmoil and trouble again just for these precious moments in her arms.

He hadn't found Soraya in the end. He hadn't reawakened the daring, uninhibited lover she kept locked within her, the lover he remembered from London.

Yet when he made love to this woman, who opposed him with every ounce of her soul, he touched emotional depths he'd never sounded before.

He broke away from her slowly, reluctantly. She gave a soft grunt of discomfort.

He'd been brutal. But he hadn't missed, even in his drive to completion, that she'd reached her own peak. It hadn't been last night's dazzling explosion, but at the height of the tempest, she'd embraced him. He'd made her confront the truth that she could no more deny him than he could deny her.

Her body had opened to his. While she'd kept her mind and heart closed.

He told himself her body was all he wanted.

The declaration sounded laughably hollow. The feverish encounter had bitten more deeply than the fleeting demands of flesh alone ever could, however much he wished it otherwise.

She took a shuddering breath as he settled at her side. He fought the urge to stroke the damp black hair back from her brow. She wouldn't welcome his tenderness, he knew with piercing regret.

They lay in tense silence for a long moment. Then, without glancing in his direction, she rose from the tumbled bed, gathering her ruined dress around her.

She looked sad, crushed, used. She looked beautiful and as necessary to him as breathing.

Exhausted as he was, he reached out and caught at her crushed skirts. "Where are you going?"

"To wash," she said desolately.

"Stay with me."

"Yes."

He frowned. Such easy agreement seemed unlikely. "Yes?"

She looked at him fully. Her eyes were flat and lifeless as he'd never seen them before.

He'd summoned passion from her. But at what cost?

"If I run, you'll only find me. So I will stay."

"Good." He let her go, hating himself as she hated him, however tightly she'd clung to him as she'd ridden out her climax.

When she raised her hand to brush back the heavy fall of hair, he noticed a ring of bruises circling one slim wrist.

"I've hurt you," he said, loathing himself even more.

She glanced at the marks without interest. "They're from last night. They don't matter." She turned away, her head bowed under the tumbled mass of hair. "Nothing matters."

He'd fought like a madman to crush her defiance. Why, now that he'd succeeded, did such grief slice into the heart he denied he possessed?

Chapter 14

⟨ ∼∼∽◯◯∽∼∼ ⟩

Kylemore crawled into the dark hollow in the bushes where he'd always been safe. Outside, the monster rampaged closer and closer, then it began tearing at the protective wall of branches and brambles.

When it found him, it would kill him.

He shrank into the darkness, trying not to breathe. The monster already knew where he was, but maybe in the blackness, he could disappear.

But of course, he couldn't disappear. The monster reached out its terrifying white hands and twisted them into the front of his torn and soiled shirt.

Kylemore whimpered with horror. Thorns at his back dug at his flesh, preventing escape, even if the impossible happened and the monster let him go. He whimpered again, despising his weakness, despising his stupidity in getting caught.

The monster gave its mad laugh and tugged him forward.

More pain awaited, he knew. The monster would cut him into pieces and feed him to the dogs, just as it had promised so many times before. Before, when he'd managed to escape.

But this time, he hadn't been so lucky.

"No! No, Papa! No, please! I promise I'll be good. Just don't hurt me! Papa, no!"

But the long white hands that were larger, crueler versions of his own dragged him onward.

"No!" he sobbed. "Please."

The long white hands shook him.

But they no longer bit like talons into his flesh. Instead they were cool and gentle. He opened his eyes to find Verity leaning over him in the darkness. For a moment, he was too disoriented to be ashamed of his trembling and his tears.

"Kylemore, wake up. You're having another nightmare," a soothing voice said.

No monster then. He was safe.

This particular monster had died twenty years ago. Coming back to reality, he blinked and took a deep breath. His chest hurt, as if he'd been running for hours.

"A nightmare," he repeated and abominated the croak in his voice.

He'd suffered bad dreams right through Eton. His hardier schoolfellows had tormented him endlessly about his sobbing and moaning in the night. Those bad dreams had continued into early manhood. He thought he'd trained himself out of them. The memories hadn't overtaken him for years. Cold Kylemore, the magnificent duke, permitted no vulnerability to rattle his sangfroid.

It was this glen. He should never have returned. Coming back to this house had been the final test to see if he'd become as impervious as he so desperately wanted to be.

A test he spectacularly failed.

His body was slick with sweat, and he shivered. He felt so alone that he thought he'd die.

With a wordless groan, he wrapped his arms around the woman who hated him and buried his head in the softness of her breasts. Immediately, her haunting scent filled his senses, and his racing heart calmed.

How did she imagine he could ever let her go? She was the only being in creation who gave him this peace. Verity was all that stood between him and madness. It was the intolerable and eternal burden fate placed upon them both.

For a long moment, they lay entwined in silence. He anticipated her rebuff. What a pathetic admission that in his whole life no one had given him kindness or comfort he hadn't bought. Until she'd come to his room yesterday. When she'd offered up her strength and warmth as lights against the dark.

He didn't deserve her generosity. Even in his overwhelming need, he recognized that. He tightened his grip on her slender body, braced for mockery and rejection.

"Shh, Kylemore," the woman in his arms murmured. "You're safe here." She shifted up toward the headboard so he lay more comfortably against her.

Astonishment clawed at him, banished his ability to speak. She abhorred him, wished him dead.

So why was her voice so soft? Why was her touch so gentle?

"Shh." She smoothed the hair away from his damp brow with a tenderness that cut him to the bone. "It was only a dream."

Such consolation was sweet indeed from the woman he wanted above all others. But for once, his craving for simple human warmth exceeded his craving for sex.

His own mother had never held him like this. His own mother had never touched him in affection as far as he could remember.

He lay motionless while Verity's cool hand brushed across

his hair. Each slow stroke drew out a little more of the dream's lingering dread.

She smelled like everything good in the world. Baking bread and mown grass and the countryside after rain and the clean air above the waterfall at the top of the glen.

Yet she smelled like none of these, but purely herself.

If she sent him away now, he thought he'd scream like the terrified boy who had fled in fear of his life from his own father. But she didn't send him away. Instead, she curved around him to shield him from the house's dark shadows.

She crooned soft nonsense in his ear. It was the most enchanting sound he'd ever heard. He pressed up against her, his fingers tangling in the nightdress she'd put on before sleeping. Gradually the nightmare receded.

Still he didn't move away. He listened to the even tenor of her breathing, while her warmth slowly seeped through his cold, cold soul.

What was she thinking? He sensed no condemnation or scorn, although he deserved both after the wild, destructive passion he'd conjured between them earlier.

"I was born on a farm in Yorkshire," she began quietly after a long silence. "My father was a tenant to Sir Charles Norton."

She paused, as if waiting for some reaction, but Kylemore didn't speak, afraid that if he did, she might stop.

Astounding to think that she finally offered him a clue to her mystery. Astounding she offered her secrets when he least deserved such a gift.

"My brother, Benjamin, is five years younger than I, and I have a sister, Maria, five years younger again. My mother's health wasn't strong, and I cared for the little ones."

She would have been good at that, he thought. At her most basic level was a nurturing instinct. Witness how she succored him now, even after everything he'd done to her.

Her voice was calm and level, as if she read a fairy tale to a child. The night crowded in, inviting confidences.

"My father wasn't much of a farmer, but we managed well enough until I was fifteen and fever swept the moors." Here the calmness faltered slightly, but after a longer hesitation, she went on. "Both my parents died within a week of each other. There was no money, and I was too young to take over the farm, even if Sir Charles would have rented it to a female. We had no family to turn to for help. So I found Ben and Maria a place with a woman in the village and I became a maid up at the big house. I didn't earn much, but it was enough to keep the children from going hungry."

And it had been unending drudgery, Kylemore knew.

Perhaps because the only people who had shown him any kindness as a boy had been servants, he was unusually aware of conditions below stairs. A fifteen-year-old rustic would have obtained only the most junior post in a great household. And junior maids did the roughest, hardest, most unpleasant work.

"I wasn't happy, but I was determined to endure." Another hesitation, one fraught with emotion. She stopped stroking him. "Until . . ."

Kylemore raised his head from where it rested on her breasts. In the gloom, he just discerned the perfect line of her cheek and jaw above him. The candles had long ago burned down to unlit stubs. The lack of light emphasized other senses. Touch, smell, hearing.

"What is it, Verity?" he coaxed. "Until what?" He shifted up so she lay in his embrace now. She hardly seemed to notice.

Her body was tense, where before there had only been supple ease. She shook her head.

"This is stupid," she said in a voice that grated. "I don't know why I'm telling you. What interest can a man like you have in the life of a whore?"

"Don't call yourself that!" he snapped, then he forced himself to speak more temperately before he aroused the self-protective caution she usually hid behind. "Tell me what happened, Verity." He no longer clung to her as his only refuge but held her fast to give her the strength to go on.

"Sir Charles was old. A widower. Kind enough in his own way. Life was bearable. Until that summer." Her short, choppy sentences revealed her agitation. "His son John came down from Cambridge. By rights, he shouldn't have known I existed."

"But he wanted you." *The old story,* Kylemore thought bitterly, but that didn't make it any more palatable.

He could imagine Verity at fifteen. Good Lord, she must be nearing thirty now and she still took his breath away. Just emerging from girlhood, she'd have been exquisite.

Exquisite and utterly defenseless.

She nodded, her silky, unbound hair sliding pleasurably against the bare skin of his sheltering arms. "Yes." She took a shuddering breath. "I tried to stay out of John's way once I understood what he wanted. I begged him to leave me alone. I asked the other servants for help. They did what they could. But—"

"But he was the son and heir and you were a penniless nothing."

Kylemore wished the unknown John Norton was here so he could have claimed the privilege of beating him senseless. Ironic, considering his own behavior toward Verity.

"Yes. I was such a bumpkin then. My parents were strict Methodists, and I was as naïve a country mushroom as you could meet." She gave a humorless laugh. "I had a foolish trust in the goodness of humanity I can't believe possible now."

"The bastard tricked you," Kylemore said flatly. What she said hurt him, cast cruel reflection on his own behavior.

"He . . . he sent a note telling me he wanted to apologize.

As if that cod-faced ninny ever lowered himself to such a thing. I was so stupid, I asked for what happened."

Kylemore's hold tightened around her. "No," he said hollowly. "You didn't ask for it."

He meant every evil that had befallen her, not just rape from a thoughtless young scion of the gentry. Shame flowed black and acrid in his veins, and his belly churned with contrition and regret.

"He asked me to meet him one afternoon in the music room. And he . . . and he . . ."

She buried her head against him as if to hide from the old memories. Did she even realize the man who tormented her in the present held her safe against old ghosts? Did she guess how his heart contracted with pity and wonder when she turned to him in her extremity?

"He attacked you," Kylemore said, sickened.

"Yes. I couldn't fight him off." Her husky voice was muffled in his chest. "I screamed for help, but no one came. He ripped at my clothes and he punched me. I fought, but he was bigger and stronger. He knocked me to the floor. As I fell, I hit my head. When I could see again, he was . . . he was on top of me and he was trying . . . he was trying—"

"He raped you." How could he bear to hear any more?

"No," she said unsteadily, raising her head and looking up at him. Her eyes shimmered in her pale face. "No, he didn't rape me. Sir Eldreth Morse was a guest in the house. He heard the screaming and he came in before . . ."

She sucked in a shaky breath before she went on. "He pulled John away from me and refused to listen when the cur tried to blame me for what happened. It must have been clear he'd forced me—I was bleeding where he'd hit me."

"So Eldreth rescued you only to debauch you himself," Kylemore said austerely.

Why the hell was he so angry? He hadn't behaved any

better when faced with the temptation this one woman presented. The brutal reality was that he and John Norton were brothers under the skin. Kylemore might never have forced himself on the servants—he'd never had to—but his treatment of his mistress shone in no kindlier light.

"No, you misunderstand. Sir Eldreth helped me," she said vehemently. "He was kind. He told Sir Charles about John. It wasn't his fault I lost my position."

"They dismissed you for the crime of attracting their son's notice."

"They believed John rather than Eldreth. They shouldn't have. I wasn't the first servant girl who took his fancy, and I certainly wasn't the last—or the most unfortunate. I realize now he was a man who liked to hurt women. Sir Eldreth saved me from all that."

"Christ," Kylemore muttered under his breath.

Roughly, he tore himself from her arms and left the bed. The violence in his soul threatened to erupt. He needed to regain control before he shattered under the storm of emotions buffeting him. Guilt. Sorrow. Anger. Unwilling empathy for someone who had a past as tortured as his own.

Continuing to swear, he strode across the room and flung the curtains wide with a loud rattle. It was still dark outside. But not nearly so dark as the raging tumult within him.

With shaking fingers, he fastened the breeches he hadn't even bothered to remove before he'd taken her. The air was cold on his bare shoulders as he glared out the window.

"Kylemore?" she asked in bewilderment from the bed.

"Eldreth saved you for a life of vice and degradation," he said with difficulty, scowling through the bars at the mountains outlined against the night sky.

"It was better than going on the streets," she returned with equal heat. "Which is where I'd have ended up. And what would have happened to Ben and Maria then?"

God help her, God help him, she was right. His hands crushed the rich brocade of the drapes. She'd begun her story to divert him from his nightmare. Little did she know that what she described created its own nightmares.

This was a confession, but a confession made to a priest cast into hell for his own vile sins.

"Sir Eldreth found me in the village. When he saw my destitution and that I had the little ones to look after, he asked me to be his mistress."

"And you said yes," Kylemore said bitterly.

Mixed in with his other corrosive reactions, jealousy gnawed like acid in his gut. Jealousy over the elderly baronet's physical possession of her, but even more over the affection in her voice when she spoke of him. She still admired, respected, liked Sir Eldreth.

Had she loved him?

Why did the question even arise? Love wasn't part of any bargain he'd ever made with Soraya. Or Verity.

"It wasn't what I wanted," she retorted, clearly stung, although he hadn't implied she'd sold herself gladly. "He said he'd support Maria and Ben. He told me I could use my advantages. Or else allow myself to become their victim."

Kylemore turned away from the view to light a candle, and only then did he look at her. She braced herself high against the pillows, and her eyes were cloudy with turmoil.

"He told you men would always want you." He heard the cynicism in his voice.

"That's a crude approximation," she snapped. "He offered me shelter and security. Luxury. A world I'd never known. A chance to learn and experience and develop."

"In return for which he took your innocence."

Verity bestowed a worldly smile upon him that was a brief reminder that she'd once had all London at her feet.

"Kylemore, you more than anyone know men don't take care of women without asking something in return."

He wished he could deny it. He wished he could claim he was different, but they would both recognize the lie. It was too late for him to become Verity's white knight even if a vile miscreant like him could play that role with any conviction.

With piercing sadness, he mourned all the lost innocence, his own as much as hers. Unlucky circumstances and human evil had forced them both into adulthood long before they'd been ready.

When he didn't speak, she shrugged and went on. The gesture was so much the notorious Soraya's that the breath caught in his throat. "At least Eldreth kept his side of the arrangement faithfully. With exceptional generosity, in fact. He took me to Paris, he hired tutors, he created the famous courtesan. Believe me, a grand personage such as the Duke of Kylemore wouldn't have spared the Yorkshire farm lass a moment's notice."

Except he would have noticed her.

Yes, she now had the gloss of sophistication. But what drew him, what had always drawn him, was some indefinable essence that was purely her. What she told him might answer his abiding curiosity, but nothing tempered his fascination. He was coming to accept nothing ever would.

He didn't tell her this. Instead, he asked something that had always intrigued him. "Where did the name Soraya come from?"

Then he was sorry he'd voiced the question. A fond smile crossed her face, and his doubt hardened into certainty. She'd loved Morse.

It made him yearn to smash something. Violence might ease the tempest in his soul, a tempest he had no right to feel.

"You must know about Eldreth's collection of naughty books. It was famous."

"Yes."

During his investigations into Soraya's background, he'd ended up learning as much about her rich protector as he had about her. More, in fact. The celebrated collection of obscure erotica had befitted a man with a beautiful young mistress, a great fortune and no troublesome responsibilities to home and hearth.

"Soraya was the heroine of one of his favorite stories. He used to read it to me—she was a young captive in the sera-glio who restored an aging sultan's vitality. Eldreth started calling me Soraya as a joke shortly after we arrived in Paris, and the name persisted."

This recollection of laughing intimacy provoked another surge of churning envy. It hinted at a relationship richer than anything Kylemore had ever achieved with her.

What did he and Verity really share? Sex, which he now had to exact from her. Suspicion. Dislike.

He stared sightlessly out the window and tried to stifle his turbulent emotions. He had so many reasons to thank her dead protector. Morse had saved her from assault and pov-erty. He'd recognized her qualities and fostered them. Few men would have done so much.

A vivid memory arose in his mind of the moment he'd first met Soraya.

When Sir Eldreth Morse had presented his mistress to that crowded room, Kylemore had read only gloating own-ership in the baronet's face. Now he looked back with the eyes of experience, of six years desiring that same woman. And he saw something else.

Pride. Morse had been openly proud of the perfect jewel he'd produced to dazzle society.

Without the old man's intervention, this incomparable woman would never have moved into Kylemore's orbit. Any sensible man would curse Morse to hell for that fact alone.

Without Morse, he would never have endured years of frustration and misery. Soraya was the only thing that had ever come close to destroying him. She was his torment and his peril.

She was his only hope of salvation.

The predawn light let him make out the bruised fullness of her lips and the wary expression in her beautiful gray eyes. Surely, she couldn't fear he'd condemn her for what she'd done. Her dilemma had been impossible, with other people's survival hinging on her actions. She'd had the courage to use the beauty and wit God had given her to forge a future. A brilliant future, at that.

"Where's John Norton now?" He focused on her story's least ambiguous element.

"Kylemore, it's too late to call him out for what he did to a servant girl over ten years ago," she said quietly, her gray eyes not wavering from his face.

He knew she was clever and perceptive. But even so, it surprised him she saw so much. He'd tried to hide the full extent of his reaction to what she'd told him.

"It's never too late," he said grimly.

He broke the wordless connection between them and turned back to the window. Without pleasure, he watched the pale light gleam on the loch. The bars had been on the window so long that he hardly noticed them.

He heard the rustle of bedclothes as she rose, then the soft pad of her feet as she came toward him. She stopped behind him and her scent drifted around him, urging him, as always, to sin.

But for once, he found the will to resist temptation.

"It's too late for John," she said, still in that soft voice. "He was killed in a tavern brawl in York. He fought over a wench. He hadn't changed."

So the bastard burned in hell and was eternally out of his

reach. Kylemore tamped down his rage. Then unbelievably, he felt two slender arms encircle his waist and a sweet pressure as she leaned into his back.

Soraya had never touched him in affection, until that last betraying kiss. And Verity never wanted to touch him at all. Yet here she embraced him without coercion. He felt lost, as though he'd been snatched into some alternative world while he'd slept. How had they moved from the bruising, turbulent passions of their last coupling to this strange truce?

"You can't defend my honor," she murmured into his left shoulder. Her breath brushed warm upon his skin, a sensual contrast to the cool air of the new day. "Anyway, we both know I've had no honor to defend since I was fifteen."

Perhaps because he meant what he said so intensely, he didn't look at her. Instead, he fixed his gaze on the shining surface of the loch. "Verity, you have more honor than anyone I know."

She made a stifled, unhappy sound and tried to pull away, but he caught her hands and drew her around so she faced him. "You gave up everything you believed in for the sake of the people you love. Then you were brave enough to seize the opportunities your new life offered."

The eyes she lifted to his were bleak with self-hatred. "You haven't always thought so highly of me."

"Hell, Verity, I wanted you and you ran away. I was angry. I always admired you. Now I realize your true quality."

She flinched and tried to withdraw. "Stop it."

He kept hold of her. "I never despised you—although I tried my damnedest when you left me. You sacrificed yourself to keep your family safe, yet you can't forgive yourself for what you did."

This time when she pulled free, he let her go.

Chapter 15

Panting as if she'd just climbed a mountain rather than walked down one floor to the kitchen, Verity leaned both hands on the scarred old table and bent her head. For a long moment, she stood there, hunched and shaking. Her body still ached from the vigorous sex hours before, and she was light-headed with fear, fatigue and too much emotion.

Reliving her past had hurt, but it was Kylemore himself who had cut through her every defense and harrowed her heart.

She muffled a sob. She had to get away from here. She had to get away even if it killed her.

If she didn't, she was lost.

The handsome nobleman who dispensed rubies as though they were apples was no threat. The seductive rake who drew shuddering pleasure from her body touched her senses but not her heart.

But she couldn't fight the man who cried out in the night and clung to her as if she was his only hope.

Nor could she fight the revelation that she and the duke weren't so very different after all. A sneaking empathy for him had always undermined the emotional distance she struggled to maintain. Now to her wrenching sorrow, she knew why.

When faced with an impossible choice, she'd created Soraya. In a similar fashion and for similar reasons, the terrors of the duke's childhood had forced him to become Cold Kylemore. The hairs rose on the back of her neck when she recalled how his long-dead father revisited his dreams.

Soraya and Cold Kylemore. Both necessary masquerades. Both requiring deception and lies. Both requiring a desperate, silent courage to keep the curious, spiteful world at bay.

His soul was dark and twisted and tormented.

His soul was full of evil and pain and regret.

His soul was twin to hers.

No, she wouldn't let it be so. She was a common strumpet. He counted among the kingdom's most powerful men. Nothing linked them other than a past liaison and his endless thirst for revenge.

The light brightened as day advanced. She lifted her head and wildly looked around the empty room. This cursed place made her doubt herself. If ever—please, God, let it be so!—she made it back to Ben, she'd forget this insanity. The isolation made her question what she'd always known was true.

The Duke of Kylemore was a self-centered autocrat. Shallow, cruel, thoughtless.

She was a whore who raised her skirts for any man who paid her. Her heart was ice.

Her hand bunched into a fist and she pounded the table, beating those harsh facts into her brain. Pain throbbed up her arm and dragged her back to the present.

She sucked in a deep breath and looked up. Summer dawn

filtered through the high windows to reveal the astonishing truth that she was completely alone.

No Hamish Macleish. No giants. Not even the little giggling maids, Morag and Kirsty, who, she'd worked out, were Hamish's nieces. The duke was in bed upstairs, almost certainly sleeping after his long, disturbed night.

This empty kitchen presented a chance to escape. If she ran away, no one would seek her for hours. Her heart started to gallop with nervous excitement and fear.

She didn't have long. The servants started work early. With full day, the walls of her captivity would close around her.

Meanwhile, she stood in the nightdress she'd borrowed from Morag. She was desperate, but she wasn't a fool—she needed clothing and supplies if she hoped to survive the mountains.

A quick search of the kitchen unearthed a basket of clean laundry and her half boots, polished and ready. Swiftly, she flung off her nightrail and tugged on one of Kate Macleish's kirtles. It was worn and far too large, but it was warm.

Thick stockings. And a coat—Hamish's, she suspected—hanging from a hook by the door. She plaited her heavy hair into a long braid and tied it with a scrap of rag.

A check of the pantry turned up a loaf of bread, some cheese and a few late apricots, a fruit for which the duke had a particular fondness. She filled a flask with water and tied her bounty in a cloth.

If heaven had been kind, a couple of coins would have been scattered on the bench, but thrifty Highland servants didn't leave money lying about.

Oh, what she'd give for just one of the gorgeous baubles Soraya had amassed in her long and scandalous career. But she'd sold her jewelry when she'd left Kensington and used the money to fund her futile dreams of freedom.

Perhaps not so futile after all, she thought on a rising tide of optimism.

Her plan was shaky. She recognized this even as she let herself out of the house. The weather could turn, she could get lost, aid mightn't materialize.

But anything was better than waiting here for her inevitable destruction.

If she succumbed to what lurked unspoken in her heart, Kylemore would leave her devastated and alone when everything between them was over. As it must inevitably one day be over. She faced less danger from the looming ranges than she did from one tall tormented man.

If she succeeded in getting away, she'd never see the duke again. This time when she left him, she'd make sure not even the recording angel could trace her.

She blinked away a rush of tears as she dashed across the grass to the shelter of the trees.

Three days ago, she'd have scoffed if anyone had suggested she'd regret leaving Kylemore. Her defenses had taken a woefully short time to crumble.

How had she come to this? She fought to awaken the anger and loathing that had sustained her from the beginning of her ordeal.

But all she found within herself was her cowering, lonely heart, a heart crammed with pain and longing.

Such weak emotions when she had to be strong. She took a deep breath, hitched up her bundle and began to walk fast down the valley in the direction of the coast.

When Kylemore awoke, the sun blazed from a clear sky. He was alone in the wreck of the bed.

Idly, he wondered where Verity was. After she'd left him last night, the new peace between them had sent him into a catatonic sleep.

The raw emotion they'd shared should have left him feeling vulnerable.

But instead he felt . . . *safe*.

He'd been too distraught to hide his shameful nighttime terrors; she'd trusted him with her sad history. The bond that united them was now indestructible.

Her habits of self-concealment were familiar. He shared them. He knew what it had cost her to reveal so much. And to someone she considered an enemy.

Someone she no longer considered an enemy.

Surely she couldn't offer such sweet comfort to a man she hated. Surely she wouldn't divulge her tragic past to someone she despised.

Now he wanted to know everything about her. Last night's difficult confession had only whetted his curiosity to find out more.

And he wanted to make love to her.

Of course, he always wanted to make love to her. But this time, perhaps, she'd offer him the privilege of her consent.

The shadows that dogged his life had retreated. Verity had banished them.

He sat up, determined to find her. She must like him a little, trust him a little, to act as she had.

What a pathetic reflection on the great Duke of Kylemore that he placed such importance on this small concession.

Hope had been excised from his life since earliest childhood. But as he dressed in that quiet room, hope was the only cause he could find for the sudden lightness in his soul.

Kylemore entered the small chamber he'd chosen as his own, but she wasn't there, nor had the narrow bed been used.

Perhaps reliving her unhappy story meant sleep had eluded her and she'd sat out the dawn downstairs. He was desperate to see her, to test if their strange intimacy survived the daylight.

He was desperate to see her because away from her, he felt incomplete.

But the gloomy parlor was empty as well. Foreboding began to beat a doom-laden chant in his heart.

Where was she? She couldn't have left him. Not after last night. Devil take it, she'd trusted him, cared for him, confided in him.

But before that, he'd forced her into his bed.

Of course, she'd eventually succumbed to desire, as she always did. A desire of the body, not the mind. Her mind had resisted him right to the end.

Then she'd held him through his terrors. Which meant they had at last moved beyond compulsion and misery, hadn't they?

His answer to that question grew more hesitant as he searched the grounds. Heartsick and uneasy, he returned to the house. In the kitchen, Morag and Kirsty harangued Hamish in shrill Gaelic. Apparently, food and clothing were missing.

In an instant, Kylemore's fragile hopes crumbled to ash.

"Has anyone seen *madame* this morning?" He cut through the argument, although he already knew what response he'd receive.

With a frown, Hamish looked past his voluble nieces. "The lassie isnae with Your Grace? She hasnae been down yet."

Kylemore's fears coalesced into bleak certainty.

She'd gone. She'd lulled him into relaxing his vigilance, then seized her opportunity to escape. Bloody fool he was, he'd forgotten that she was never less than clever, whether she was Verity or Soraya.

"Get Angus and Andy," he said sharply, cursing her, cursing himself. "We'll organize a search."

If she'd gone as soon as she'd left him—and he had no reason to assume otherwise—she had several hours start. He had to find her before she left the glen. The dangers this harsh environment presented were hellishly real.

A quick trip to the stables assured him she hadn't taken a horse. Given her fear of the animals, that was no surprise.

For the first time since he'd realized she'd abandoned him again, he felt faint optimism. If she was on foot, riders would have less difficulty overtaking her.

"Angus and Andy, you take the road over the range." He didn't modify the harshness of his tone. "Hamish and I will follow the loch."

Only two routes led out of the glen—the mountain road and the path along the lochside to the coast. Verity already knew how difficult travel was over land. The loch presented an easier prospect until she reached the narrow passage between the mountains, where she'd need a boat. With any luck, he'd trap her there.

"Kate, Morag and Kirsty, check if she's anywhere near the house. Perhaps she's merely taking the air." He already knew she'd run away. It was what he'd have done.

Curse him for a blockhead. Ever since he'd kidnapped her, he'd made sure she was watched. But last night had made him stupid. Now she could pay with her life for his stupidity.

Christ, he couldn't bear to think she might die. Better he'd left her in Whitby than that. His gut clenched with guilt and despair.

He and Hamish rode westward. The day was fine and still, but such warmth often portended storms later.

For God's sake, had she dismissed his warnings? Even men born here lost their lives in these mountains when the weather turned sour—as it did with alarming regularity.

Hamish caught up to him as he reined in near a stand of rowans. Kylemore saw his own fears reflected in the older man's eyes.

"If the lassie came this way, she'll be safe until she reaches the cliffs, laddie," Hamish said reassuringly.

"Unless she slips into the water," Kylemore said, narrowing his eyes against the dazzling sunlight as he checked along the steep bank.

In spite of the loch's apparent placidity, it was deep and full of treacherous currents. A ghillie had drowned in its waters when he was six. Kylemore remembered the men carrying the pale, sodden body back to the house and the women wailing in grief. There had been more servants then, of course, to care for his father.

"Och, she's a canny lassie. I doubt she'll go so close tae the water. She'll use the trees instead."

Something in Hamish's tone caught Kylemore's attention. "You don't sound surprised she's run off."

The older man shrugged. "She asked me tae help her, but I couldnae break loyalty with ye. I warned her of the dangers. But she's a willful wee thing."

The patent admiration in Hamish's voice when he spoke of Verity nettled Kylemore. "You've never approved of me bringing her here," he snapped. "But you don't know the full story."

He should have guessed his display of ducal temper wouldn't cow Hamish. "No, I dinna approve. But ye know weel ye have my obedience." His voice hardened noticeably. "But I've kept a close watch on her since she came tae the glen. And she's a braw kindhearted lassie. I canna imagine what she's done tae deserve being kept prisoner."

Stung at the criticism, fair as it was, Kylemore retorted, "She's no blushing virgin, man. She's been my mistress for the past year."

The moment the words left his mouth, he wanted to snatch them back. They made him feel small and shabby, especially after what Verity had told him last night.

Hamish's eyes expressed equal disappointment. "Whisht, laddie. No need tae blacken her name. If she wants tae bring herself back tae virtue's path, she's tae be commended. If Your Grace's lust stops her, ye bear the shame, no her." The old Highlander kicked his pony into a trot and rode ahead as if he could no longer tolerate his employer's presence.

Kylemore hardly blamed him. He could hardly tolerate his own company either.

He slumped in the saddle. If any shred of goodness clung to Kylemore's black soul, it was thanks to the man who had just left him. The man who plainly now believed he'd wasted his regard on Kylemore.

Hamish had every reason to be disgusted at his protégé's behavior. More than he knew.

But it was too late for second thoughts. Or second chances.

Verity sighed in frustration as she surveyed the smooth cliff face before her. She wiped palms clammy with nerves on Kate's worn brown kirtle.

She'd walked for hours to reach the end of the valley. Now she was tired and sticky and stinging, courtesy of a nettle patch she'd unwittingly stumbled into. She took a deep breath of the humid air and tried to whip up her courage, but it had shrunk into a cold, hard kernel inside her.

With every step, she'd feared the duke would catch her. The morning was well advanced, and he must know by now she'd gone. Nausea rose in her throat as she imagined his anger at what he'd consider yet another betrayal.

One thing was sure—he'd pursue her on horseback. She'd briefly considered taking a pony, but horses still scared her silly, not to mention she risked waking the giants who slept above the stables.

If luck was with her, Kylemore would concentrate his

search on the road over the mountains. But then, luck had been notably absent from her life lately, and her lover was clever enough to guess she'd make for the coast, a coast she now realized lay on the other side of this monolith.

Her heart sank with defeat. The rocks before her were unscalable. She'd already tried and failed to find a way up several times. Swimming across the loch was too risky, given the speed and depth of the current through the defile. And what would be the use? A second steep cliff loomed on the other side.

Now her only hope was to follow the base of the ridge south until she found somewhere to climb up. The scheme was uncertain but the best she could devise.

She took a mouthful of water from her flask, told herself to be brave—an admonition losing its power through sheer repetition—and trudged on.

When Verity heard the horses approach, it was past midday and she still hadn't found a way out of the valley.

Immediately, she crouched low. Sheer exhaustion had dulled her constant dread. Now it welled up sharp as ever, making her head spin. Awkwardly, she edged into the thick undergrowth and fought to control her ragged breathing.

Kylemore and Hamish Macleish rode into view. The duke wore his rough country clothes. She had a sudden sharp recollection of his perfectly turned out London self. His immaculate tailoring had been famous, yet here he seemed content to dress not much better than his henchmen. Although nobody would mistake the tall, handsome man with the commanding bearing for anything other than the aristocrat he was.

He turned his head to speak to Hamish. Hungrily, she stared at the clear profile, with its high forehead, long haughty nose and strong jaw. The older man bowed briefly and rode back the way they had come.

The duke wheeled his great gray horse in the direction she'd intended to go. Before he cantered away, she had a brief glimpse of flashing eyes and a mouth set in a determined line. He looked resolute and angry.

Her stomach clenched with renewed terror, filling her mouth with a bitter taste. But beneath the terror lurked other emotions, emotions a woman such as she could never acknowledge.

This was probably—*hopefully*—the last time she'd see the Duke of Kylemore. While escaping him had never been so necessary, the thought made her want to keen in sorrow.

She was going mad. She had to be. During the year Kylemore had been her lover, they had enjoyed untold sexual adventures. And her deeper self had remained completely untouched. When he'd stolen her away from her home a matter of days ago, she'd hated and feared him.

So when had that lean face with its controlled, passionate mouth become so precious?

He'd snatched her from her home. Forced himself on her. Ignored everything she wanted. Wrung a response from her she'd been determined not to give.

She had cause to loathe him—as she'd unequivocally loathed him on the journey from Whitby. He was a selfish brute who deserved to hang for his crimes.

He was a lonely man tormented by harrowing memories she couldn't begin to imagine.

And last night, he'd listened to her sordid history and told her she was magnificent.

"I will not countenance this," she whispered aloud as she crawled stealthily from her hiding place. "I will not."

Muscles held tense too long protested as she stood upright. She placed a trembling hand on her lower back as she stretched. All the while, her eyes strained after the direction the duke had taken.

Dear Lord, how could she feel this way? And about that ruthless devil Kylemore, of all men.

Pray heaven all this uncomfortable soul-searching ended when she was free. She'd resume the life she'd planned, and this fraught interlude would fade into just an unpleasant memory.

Revealing her past had been a huge mistake. She and Kylemore now shared an emotional link that might prove hard to break although in time, she would break it.

She must break it.

She collected her bundle of food from behind the bushes. Her empty stomach growled, but she ignored it, determined to conserve her meager rations.

For a long while, she stared blankly at the cliff, trying to reawaken her enthusiasm for a life devoted to good works and independence. But her mind filled instead with images of the duke's courageous battle against his demons and how that courage melted into sweet need when he rested in her arms.

For God's sake, leave me in peace, Kylemore.

She inhaled deeply to banish her lover's persistent ghost, and her eyes sharpened on the mountainside. If she took her chances scrambling over some steep rocks, she might find a way up. The cliff offered nothing so friendly as a path, but perhaps she could use the jagged ledges.

She had to try. With the duke ahead and Hamish behind, this was her only chance to leave this cursed valley and with it, her agonizing confusion.

She began to climb, using her hands on the rough stones.

Midafternoon, the rain set in, as Kylemore had known it would. Cold, miserable Scottish rain that seeped into his bones. Chilly, soaking rain that suited his all-encompassing despair.

Somehow she'd escaped him. His damned complacency might have signed her death warrant.

No, he had to keep believing she was alive. *He willed her to stay alive.*

"She hasnae turned back tae the house," Hamish said, riding up. He passed Kylemore a thick coat and a hat similar to the ones he now wore. "I circled through the forest on the way here. There's nae sign of her. The lassie couldnae grow wings and fly away, could she?"

Kylemore tugged on the welcome dry clothing. "I'd not put anything past her."

He looked around in helpless rage. Didn't the girl realize the danger? The temperature was dropping. If she was still out after dark, who knew what state she'd be in by morning?

"Where the hell can she be?" he growled. "She can't have got this far on foot."

Hamish's voice remained calm, as it had throughout the day's frantic searching. "Angus and Andy are at Kilorton Pass. If the lassie takes tae the hill road, they'll catch her."

"We've missed something," Kylemore said grimly. Tannasg shifted restlessly as his master's hands clenched hard on the reins. "She's no soft city puss. She grew up on a farm. Perhaps she's managed to climb out of the glen. I've been caught out underestimating her before."

Hamish frowned. "These ranges are a maze for anyone who doesnae ken them. She could fall off a cliff and we wouldnae find her before next summer."

The horrifying possibility of Verity tumbling to a lonely death had haunted Kylemore's thoughts since he'd discovered her gone. "I can ride up onto the ridge if I continue another mile. You go through the woods again."

Hamish nodded. "Aye. Be careful up there, laddie. It's treacherous gaeing. I dinna want tae be out looking for ye as weel." He wheeled his horse around and rode away.

* * *

Gasping for breath, Verity heaved herself over the ledge and collapsed facedown. For a long moment, she lay on the ground, panting. Cold rain drizzled upon her, but she didn't have the breath to get up.

The ascent had taken hours. Her hands were scraped and dirty. But thank God, she'd reached the top. She'd lost her footing twice and slithered to the bottom, and once, the rocks themselves had disintegrated beneath her. For one sickening moment before she'd landed hard on a ledge, she'd thought her luck—and her life—had ended. But while she might be alive now, she was bruised and shaken, and she'd lost her provisions.

The rain had started by then, and her ascent had turned into slippery misery. Only the memory of how her heart had leaped at the sight of Kylemore kept her going. If she returned to him, he'd destroy her more thoroughly than mere inhospitable crags could.

He'd destroy her, then walk away without a word.

Stiffly, painfully, she lifted herself to her knees. Her shredded palms were stinging, and every muscle ached. Still, she'd done it. At last freedom beckoned.

She lifted her head, hoping she'd reached the coast.

But there were only more mountains. Lines and lines of them as far as she could see.

With a groan, she slumped back, ignoring the rain. She could be lost in this wilderness forever. It was worse than the desolate track she'd followed into the valley. She had no food, no map and no clothes, apart from what she wore.

"Oh, God," she whimpered. "Oh, God, help me."

For a long while, she lay unmoving while weak, defeated tears trickled down her dirty face and mingled with the rain-drops. Behind her, the duke waited to ensnare her with his tortured soul and sensual magic. Ahead lay an unforgiving wilderness where she could perish without trace.

But eventually, she struggled to her feet. She couldn't stay on this open ridge until winter froze her into an ice statue. There must be a way through the mountains. After she found it, she'd have everything she wanted. An independent life. A future for Ben and Maria. Hope. Purpose. Liberty.

She ripped a strip off her petticoat, sobbing softly at the pain, and bound her torn and bloody hands. If she needed to climb on hands and knees again, she'd be in trouble. The wind had sharpened and she shivered, clutching her coarse coat more tightly about her. It was summer still, but in this cruel and terrible place, that word had no power.

Had she made a dreadful mistake by running away? Both the duke and Hamish had warned her that people died in these ranges. Only now, when it was too late, did she believe them.

With a shaking hand, she wiped the moisture from her face. She had to remember what rewards awaited her. She had to remember that the man she'd abandoned promised her nothing but humiliation and degradation.

Summoning what little courage she retained, she took a deep breath. She couldn't go back, and this open hillside offered no shelter. So she must go forward and pray she found some path out of this desolation. She put her head down and trudged through the thickening rain.

Hamish rode up at sunset. Kylemore immediately noticed the filthy bundle tied to the Highlander's saddle.

"What's that?" He failed to keep the dull hopelessness from his voice. All day, they'd searched without finding any trace of Verity. The image of her sliding helplessly into the loch had become more vivid with every weary mile he'd traveled.

Hamish passed the bundle across to Kylemore. "I think the lassie dropped it as she climbed up the hillside."

This was the first genuine indication Verity was alive. Kylemore bent his head and tore at the bundle, but the humble contents told him nothing except that she'd now lost what few provisions she'd carried.

Hamish was still speaking. "She must have had a difficult time of it. There were fresh rockfalls at the base. I'd no have thought a female could do it—it's a climb most men would baulk at."

"Oh, I've never doubted her nerve," Kylemore said on a surge of hope.

She was brave, clever and determined. Perhaps she'd survive this unforgiving landscape until he found her.

Hamish studied him. "She must be gey eager tae get away from ye, laddie." The steady blue eyes sharpened on the duke's face. "What in God's name did ye do tae her?"

Unseeingly, Kylemore gazed ahead, knowing he deserved every ounce of his companion's condemnation. "I tried to break her," he said grimly.

Only now did he acknowledge he'd failed. As he'd deserved to fail. He shook himself out of his abstraction. Self-pity was an indulgence he couldn't afford. With desperate eyes, he surveyed the rain-swept landscape. He'd get her back. Then he'd worry about the amends he needed to make. The amends he was capable of making.

Hamish reached out to touch his arm. It was an act of terrible presumption that offered a brief reassurance which, in his distress, the duke noticed and appreciated.

"Dinna fash yourself, laddie. We'll find her." He looked around. "But not tonight."

Kylemore became aware that the day waned. "Go back to the house and bring Angus and Andy here at first light. She obviously came this way."

"And what about ye? In the dark, you'll tumble off a cliff yourself."

"I'll be safe enough." Verity faced the elements. It was only right he shared her discomfort and peril.

The morning brought no letup in the cold drizzle.

Kylemore jerked out of a restless doze. He straightened against the damp rock that had kept him from the worst of the rain, aware he deserved every stiff muscle.

Where had Verity slept? Had she slept? He prayed she'd found shelter somewhere.

Oh, dear God, let her be alive.

The words beat an ominous tattoo in his heart as he rose. In the predawn half light, he saddled Tannasg, who hadn't fared much better than his master. The horse had a longer line of aristocratic antecedents than he did and wasn't used to roughing it through a wet Highland night.

Scotland could be a damned awful place, he thought, stretching to ease his aching body. He must be getting soft. He'd often spent a night in the open when he'd been a boy. Once, when he hadn't managed to reach his usual hiding places, he'd run off into midwinter snow to escape his father's uncontrollable rage. On that occasion, he'd been gone three days before Hamish had found him, starving and blue with cold.

Not that he'd emerged unscathed from that particular escapade. His raging fever had come near to killing him.

Kate had nursed him back to health, he remembered. The Macleishes spoke of what they owed him. He wondered if they realized what he owed them in return.

The rain eased as the morning progressed. With every hour, Kylemore's hopes waned of finding Verity unhurt. Even if alive, she must be cold, tired, hungry, confused.

Why the hell hadn't she listened to him and stayed safe in the glen?

He knew why. She was afraid he meant to force her into his bed again. They both knew he couldn't keep his hands off her, damn it all to hell.

As he followed the jagged ridge, he wished it had been otherwise. He wished he'd been another man, one worthy of the woman he pursued. But he was the same wretched miscreant he'd always been. Redemption, expiation and absolution were utterly beyond his reach.

But, God be his witness, if he found her in one piece, he was at least willing to try to reform.

He was fording a stream at the top of a waterfall when he looked ahead to see her picking her way through scree on the other side. For one brilliant moment, blazing relief transfixed him, and he just stared speechlessly at her.

She had her back to him as she threaded her way through the field of rocks. The falling torrent muffled the sound of his approach as he spurred Tannasg toward her. When she finally turned, he was close enough to see her gray eyes darken in shock, then terror.

When had he come to this? When had a matter of simple physical desire degenerate into this nightmare of fear and coercion?

"No!" She flung herself into an awkward run across the rough gravel.

He chased her, ignoring the dangers of the uneven surface. Tannasg snorted in protest at such cavalier treatment, but his loyal heart responded and he bounded forward gallantly.

No power on earth could keep Kylemore from catching her now. She was his. He'd die before he let her go.

"Verity!" he shouted after her retreating figure.

She only tried more frantically to get away.

"Verity, you'll hurt yourself! Stop!"

She was now trapped on a jutting point with a sheer drop

on either side. Kylemore's massive gray horse blocked her exit. There was nowhere for her to go.

"Leave me alone!" she panted, backing away. The fear and hatred he heard in her voice cut him to the heart.

"I can't," he said with perfect honesty and piercing regret.

"I'm not coming with you," she said bravely, although she must have known her bid for freedom was over. She raised her chin and glared at him as she'd once glared at him across Sir Eldreth's drawing room.

He almost laughed, in spite of the moment's gravity. Break her? He might just as well try to catch the moon and bring it down to earth.

Even if he managed such an unlikely feat, he'd merely set the moon before her for her delight. His passion for this one woman was his eternal fate.

He dismounted swiftly and took a stride toward her. Tannasg was perfectly trained and stayed where he was.

"Verity, it's over. Give up. You'll never find your way through these mountains." Trying to sound unthreatening, he stretched his hand out. "Come to me."

She shook her tousled, dark head. She looked tired, dirty, wet, bedraggled. And heart-stoppingly beautiful. The bizarre assortment of clothes she'd stolen from the house hung too large on her and added to her air of fragility.

"No." She was frighteningly near the edge, and he didn't want to startle her into any sudden move.

He made his voice soft and coaxing. "Come to me, Verity."

"I haven't gone through all this for nothing," she said bitterly.

"I promise I won't hurt you." He risked another step. She was almost within reach.

She laughed scornfully. "I know what your promises are worth."

"Verity," he said and lunged across the last distance to grab her.

She jerked away, and his hand slid uselessly on the smooth skin of her arm. She screamed as she toppled over the edge.

Chapter 16

~~~⌒⌒⌒~~~

"*Jesus, no!*"

Was it a prayer or a curse? Kylemore didn't know. Verity's scream rang in his ears as he flung himself to his knees and crawled to the edge of the cliff. Every second seemed to stretch into an hour. Every falling stone echoed like a thunderclap.

"Thank God," he whispered as he peered over the ledge.

She clung to the precarious slope about a dozen feet down. The cliff didn't fall away in a sheer drop, but the stony surface was unstable and she could slide to the base of the ravine any time in a deadly tumble of rocks.

"Hold on." He looked directly into her terrified eyes, desperate to instill what strength he could.

"Of course I'll hold on!" she snapped back.

This reaction was so purely her, so utterly true to the woman he'd come to know, that he almost smiled. She fought her fear the only way she could. With anger. He understood the response. But unspoken terror flattened her lush lips, and her arms strained against the rocks. His own terror coiled like a cobra in his belly. If she let go, nothing would save her.

He fought to keep his voice steady. "I haven't got a rope. But if I throw you my coat, you can use it to climb up."

He lifted himself up far enough to strip off his coat with trembling hands. All the time, he held her gaze, as if he kept her on that rockface through sheer mental power alone.

"Hurry, Kylemore." This time her voice held no bravado.

"Don't look down," he said urgently. "Look at me."

She closed her eyes, as if gathering her will. When she opened them again, they focused unwaveringly on him.

"Trust me. I'll get you out of this," he told her.

Let it be true, oh, let it be true, his heart pleaded.

He reached out as far as he could and threw the long coat, holding tightly to one sleeve. Even with his arm fully extended, the garment still landed a good four feet above Verity. He swore under his breath and cast again.

It was no good. The coat was too short.

"Verity, Hamish should be here soon. Can you hold on? If I climb down to you, the whole hill will likely go flying." A small rockfall near her left hand confirmed what he said.

"I can't be sure."

Her reply was a thread of sound. He saw in her face that she didn't expect to survive.

If sheer determination alone could get her out of this, by God and all His angels, he'd get her out of it. He studied the uneven rocks between the coat and her. "Wait."

He surged to his feet and ran back to Tannasg.

"Steady, boy," he whispered.

The thoroughbred sensed his desperation and sidled nervously under his hands as he removed the saddle. With deftness born of necessity, Kylemore dismantled the saddle and swiftly buckled the straps together.

The task still took too long. With every second's delay, the possibility of her tumbling to her death increased.

"Verity?" he called.

Was she still there?

"Yes. Hurry!" He could tell she was near the end of her endurance. Few would have contained their panic so long.

With a yank, he tested the makeshift length. He desperately hoped it would reach her. And that his improvised rope held. And that she'd have the strength to grasp it when he threw it.

Desperate hope was all he had. How would he survive if he didn't bring her safely through this?

He couldn't dwell on failure. He *would* rescue her.

Breathing hoarsely, he dashed back to the edge and collapsed to his knees. God be praised, she was still there.

But she was tiring. Her hands, in their filthy ragged bandages, had clenched into claws, and even at that distance, he heard her rapid and uneven breathing.

Verity looked up when he appeared above her and managed a shaky smile. Not for the first time, her courage humbled him.

"Did you have a sudden inspiration?" She still strove to sound composed, but the words emerged on a gasp.

"I hope so," he said fervently. "Hell, I hope so."

Fumbling with the weight and length, he swung the awkward combination of leathers down. It landed just above her.

The slap of leather on the rough surface created another rockfall. Kylemore's belly knotted in dread as he realized the hillside was about to subside.

"Reach for it, Verity," he begged. Then an entreaty that came from the depths of his being. "Reach, my love."

Live, my love.

Her silver eyes, glittering with fear and despair, widened at the unprecedented endearment. Then he saw her realize that to grab the straps, she had to let go of the hollow in the rock face that supported her.

"Come on, Verity. You'll be all right." He hoped to the bottom of his worthless soul that he was right. Asking her to chance her safety was the greatest risk he'd ever taken in his misbegotten life. "It isn't far."

Her beautiful face, streaked with dirt and tearstains, turned up toward him, and he saw her swallow. Her expression was rigid with fear. "I can't do it."

"Yes, you can." He injected certainty into his voice. "Don't fail me now. You've never given up before." He tried to tell her with his eyes how he believed in her.

She bit her lip and nodded. He held his breath as she let go and stretched upward. The shift in weight sent rivers of stones slithering past her.

"Only a little further," he urged. His knuckles whitened on the leathers as he prepared to take her weight.

She grunted with effort and pushed herself up. With a sharp cry he felt to his boots, she lurched up and snatched the line.

Not a moment too soon. The cliff around her collapsed in a deafening roar.

"Kylemore!" she screamed while the world around her turned to chaos. "Kylemore, help me!"

"I've got you." He leaned back as her full weight dragged painfully on his arms. For a long moment, she swung free. Then she fell back against the rock face.

"Hold on. I'll pull you," he said after the worst of his paralyzing horror had passed. His muscles strained to support her and the leather creaked in protest.

Slowly, unsteadily but, thank God, surely, he hauled her upward inch by inch. A few times, ledges or hollows disintegrated under the weight of a hand or a foot, but having brought her so far, he wasn't letting her fall now.

Finally, he hauled her over the rim. His arms and legs felt like they were on fire. He was too damned relieved to care.

With a groan, he crumpled to his knees and wrenched her into his arms.

"Never do that to me again," he gritted out and pressed her face into his chest with hands that shook uncontrollably.

Dear heaven, he smelled good. Warm. Alive. The special scent of Kylemore. Sobbing, Verity buried her nose in his filthy shirt and closed her eyes while reality slowly returned.

She wasn't lying crushed and broken at the foot of the ravine. Instead, she was with Kylemore.

She tried to regret the failure of her desperate escape attempt, but all she felt was overwhelming gratitude that she hadn't plunged to her death. Overwhelming gratitude and shaming joy to be with him. She'd thought never to see him again. The pain of leaving him had weighted every step out of the valley.

Curling her arms around him, she burrowed into his embrace. Her heart pounded with the remnants of terror, and she couldn't dam her weak tears.

She cried in reaction to her ordeal. She also cried because she'd fought so hard and long against this surrender. Her hands clenched in the linen covering his powerful back.

In spite of all her efforts, every trial she'd endured, she was still Kylemore's captive. As the heat of his shuddering body surrounded her, she realized she'd never be free. Even if he let her go, she was his forever.

"Shh, *mo cridhe*. Shh. It's all right," he murmured. He stroked her tangled hair, soothing her convulsive sobs. "You're safe now. I've got you. Nothing's going to hurt you."

Except you, she whispered silently.

But even that insight couldn't make her pull away.

She'd expected him to be furious with her, as he'd been

furious in Whitby. Instead, he just offered endless comfort. She told herself his fleeting kindness meant nothing, but she couldn't stop her aching heart opening to his every word.

She didn't know how long they stayed like that, kneeling on the stony ground like survivors of a shipwreck. With her face pressed against his chest, she listened as gradually his heartbeat slowed.

He'd been so calm, so sure when he'd hauled her up that hillside. But now she knew he'd been terrified too.

"Your Grace?" Hamish's question sliced into their silent communion, a communion full of gratitude and relief and emotions she'd never dare to name.

With surprise, she raised her head. She'd been so lost in Kylemore's embrace that she hadn't even heard the horse approach.

The older man had dismounted and stood several feet away, watching them. She couldn't mistake the relief in his lined face.

"Och, thanks be tae the Lord. You've found her."

"Yes, Hamish."

She waited for Kylemore to say more, perhaps boast of his heroics. Only his valor, strength and cleverness had saved her.

But he merely said, "Find the others. I'll bring *madame*. We can all go home."

Home, yes. The isolated house did feel like home now. How easy everything became once she ceased to struggle against the inevitable. She could float calmly and joyfully to her doom.

Gently, Kylemore untangled himself from her and stood up. It was just another sign of her ruin that she missed his warmth the moment he left her. The world seemed a cold place when she didn't rest in his arms.

He spoke softly from his great height down to where she

knelt before him like a supplicant. "I know you're frightened of horses, Verity. But if I take you up before me, I promise no harm will come to you."

Oh, if only it were true, she thought painfully.

She accepted his hand and rose stiffly to her feet. Her body hurt in a thousand places, and she couldn't suppress a deep groan. She was battered and bruised and still humiliatingly teary.

Her silent docility must have worried him, because he looked at her searchingly. "Are you injured, Verity?"

"No."

She was shaking and felt alarmingly light-headed. She began to sway.

Stupid, really. She had more self-control than this. But she couldn't stop the way everything around her approached, then receded, in bleary waves.

From far away, she heard Kylemore swear softly and savagely. Then he snatched her up in his arms and carried her across to the huge thoroughbred he always rode. She was too distraught even to protest at getting on the beast. In a daze, she felt Kylemore pass her across to Hamish.

"Whisht, lassie. We'll soon have ye home."

She suddenly welcomed Hamish's lilting Scottish burr. She'd always found it dauntingly alien before.

Vaguely, she was aware that the duke reassembled the saddle and placed it on Tannasg's back. Then, very carefully, Hamish handed her up to Kylemore. Tenderly he tucked her in front of him on the massive horse. His arms encircled her with a confidence that promised to keep all hazards at bay.

Poor, foolish Verity to credit such sentimental pap, she thought without any great emotion.

Silently, they made their way back to the house she thought she'd left behind forever.

* * *

Verity propped herself up against the pillows in the large bed where she'd fought so many skirmishes with the Duke of Kylemore. Skirmishes she'd invariably lost. A fire blazed in the grate, banishing any chill from the room.

Everyone had treated her with exaggerated care since their return. A long, hot bath perfumed with rose oil had eased her strained muscles. Then Morag and Kirsty had helped her change into a plain white nightgown; the scandalous creations Kylemore had ordered still lay unworn in the armoire against the wall. Exclaiming their sympathy in musical Gaelic, the maids had salved her scratches and bandaged her torn hands before leaving her to sleep off her ordeal.

What Verity would have liked most of all was one of Kylemore's massages, but she hadn't seen him since he'd carried her up the stairs and set her on the bed so gently that she'd felt like a fragile princess.

Now, and with a heart lighter than she'd ever expected, she admitted defeat. When the duke came to her tonight, he wouldn't find her defiant or unwilling. The woman who had fought his every caress was lost somewhere in the mountains.

Verity had changed. She was no longer Kylemore's intransigent captive. Or even the complacent mistress he'd kept in such style in London.

She wished she knew what was left.

Was anything left?

Her nervous fingers pleated the sheet over her knees. Kylemore had been concerned and considerate after he saved her life. But now he'd had time to remember that she'd run away yet again.

Was his temper seething? Heaven help her, the last time she'd deserted him, he'd kidnapped her, brought her to this hideaway and forced his way into her bed.

Oh, Verity, that can't be a tiny thrill at the idea of him forcing his way into your bed once again, can it?

The door opened, saving her from examining this unwelcome thought too closely. Kylemore stood in the entrance, wearing his customary wardrobe of white shirt and breeches.

He paused, studying her. Trying to contain his rage, she supposed. Her gaze fluttered downward, then some force stronger than her apprehension made her raise her eyes.

It was as if she'd never really seen him before.

Hungrily, she traced the straight shoulders. The lean, beautiful body. The narrow hips. The long, powerful legs.

He was truly a man to take a woman's breath away.

Her gaze moved across his chest and up the strong neck to his face. Shadows still lingered there. Her attention sharpened on the strikingly autocratic features.

Tonight, perhaps because her own barriers were so perilously low, she saw more than just the endless drive to dominate and possess.

She read the signs of old wretchedness. He might hide his torments from the daytime world, but they emerged in the screaming nightmares that shattered his sleep. She read pride and intelligence. She read the passion that made him, as much as her, its victim.

Strangely, she could find no anger in his face. She wondered why.

He sighed heavily and came into the room. "Are you all right?" His dark blue eyes searched her face. "Kate tells me there's no fever."

"I'm fine. I'm never sick." Her sturdy Yorkshire forebears had gifted her with an iron constitution. Her eyes sharpened on the duke. He looked strained and unhappy. "How are you?"

"Me?" He was clearly surprised at her inquiry.

It struck her he was a man who never expected anything as commonplace as kindness.

"Yes," she said steadily. "You were out in the elements too."

The wry smile that somewhere in the last days she'd learned to treasure flickered and died. "The recollection of my sins kept me warm."

With apparent reluctance, he stepped forward to the bedside and ran his hand down the shining braid of hair that fell over her shoulder and across her breast. The gesture conveyed a rare tenderness. Even so, her heart began to race with excitement and her nipples tightened under their chaste cotton covering. He was close enough for her to hear his breath catch at the swift response.

He stepped away, and the warmth of his touch went with him. "Sleep now."

Shock silenced her for the few seconds it took him to reach the door. "Your Grace?"

He didn't turn. "Good night."

Good night?

Clumsily, she scrambled out of the bed, ignoring the screaming protest of her aching muscles. "Wait, Your Grace."

He looked back at her, his eyes opaque.

"Yes, what is it?" He sounded calm, uninvolved, neutral.

What was happening? She'd braced herself to meet rage, disdain, insult, vengeance. But this indifference bewildered her.

In her head, she'd played out many scenes of what might happen tonight. None had included having to coax him into her bed. Good Lord, hadn't she spent the last days battling without surcease to keep him out of it?

"Aren't you . . . aren't you going to stay?" she asked awkwardly.

Soraya would have come up with something alluring to say. Verity, however, was at a loss.

He shook his head, although at least he didn't leave. "No."

No?

She must be going mad. Did her insatiable lover deny her?

On trembling legs, she went after him and put her hand on his arm. She had a moment to register the tension in his muscles before he shook himself free.

"Your Grace?" she asked softly.

"Madam, I am weary," he said in a cold voice. Still he didn't look at her.

Unbelievably, he rejected her. And it hurt. How it hurt.

Had she hurt him like this each time she'd denied him? No, of course not. He wasn't vulnerable to her the way she was vulnerable to him. How could he be? She'd merely been a challenge to his pride. Now she wasn't even that much.

"I see," she said slowly, fighting desperately to conceal her pain. "I ask your pardon for detaining you, then."

"Christ give me strength!" he bit out under his breath. "You'll catch pneumonia, woman!"

He swept her up into his arms and strode back to the bed. She had a moment to register his heat and scent before he tucked her safely under the covers and returned to the door.

"I'll see you tomorrow," he said without looking at her.

"I don't understand," she whispered, pushing herself up into a sitting position.

"Devil take this," he muttered under his breath as he whirled around to face her. "What the hell do you want, Verity?"

She didn't know. She hadn't thought that what she wanted mattered to him. It certainly hadn't up until now.

"I imagined you'd be angry with me for leaving you again," she said uncertainly.

"I know why you ran away," he said flatly. "It was my fault, not yours. Hell, this entire damnable mess is my fault."

None of this made sense. "So you're not angry with me?"

240   ANNA CAMPBELL

"No, I'm not angry with you. We'll talk in the morning."

She didn't want to talk in the morning. She didn't want to talk at all.

Dredging up the right words to seduce her previously demanding paramour shouldn't have been so difficult. Hadn't she shared her body with this man for over a year?

But her voice cracked as she spoke. "Your Grace, it's all right if you . . . I mean, I . . . I won't object if you want to—"

"No." He spoke firmly, as though argument would never change his mind.

The pillar supporting the structure of her life collapsed into rubble with a mighty crash. Ruins lay all around her.

Of course, she'd known this day would come. No man made a lifetime commitment to his mistress, after all.

Yesterday, he'd wanted her. Today, he didn't.

The transition was too abrupt. She hadn't prepared herself to meet her dismissal with pride-salving coolness or self-possession.

"Is it over, then?" she asked starkly.

A muscle jerked in his cheek. He sounded so certain when he repudiated her, but that tiny, betraying movement told a different story. "Isn't that what you'd prefer?"

A fraught question she had no intention of answering. "So you no longer desire me?"

His short laugh was bitter. "Madam, there hasn't been a second since the day I met you when I haven't desired you."

She tried to interpret his expression. The only word that came to mind was *hunted*.

Continuing this inquisition took every shred of her courage. With her bandaged hands, she clutched at the blanket he'd pulled over her with such care.

"But that's changed?"

A spasm of strong emotion crossed his face and made

him look almost savage. "For God's sake, woman, of course that hasn't changed."

"But I'm inviting you into my bed," she said helplessly, wondering why she wasn't dancing around the room in relief.

He bowed in her direction, momentarily reminding her of the formality that had prevailed between them in London. "I thank you for the offer, but regretfully, I must decline."

She spoke after him as he started to go. "Are you releasing me, then, Your Grace?"

The hand he'd placed on the door bunched into a fist against the wooden frame. "I don't know. I should. I will." She watched his shoulders tense as if he braced himself to meet a powerful foe. "*I will.* Just not tonight."

She frowned at the stiff line of his back.

More was happening here than the careless discarding of a mistress who had outstayed her welcome. She could smell the lust on him. That at least hadn't changed.

So why didn't he tumble her without delay in the bed that had been their battleground?

"Please tell me what this is about, Your Grace," she said calmly.

"Jesus, Verity!" He whipped around to confront her again, and she saw she'd finally awakened the anger she'd feared earlier. "My name is Justin. Kylemore, if you must. Stop bloody *Your Gracing* me into the ground. You don't need to hammer the message home."

"What message?" she asked, confused but strangely undaunted.

His long mouth flattened in self-derision. "I want you. You don't want me. But you've accepted that escape is impossible so you're making the best of a bad situation by humoring me. I can't blame you. It's the sensible choice. Perhaps if I were a sensible man, it would be enough for me too."

"You think I'm being pragmatic?"

"Aren't you?" His remarkable eyes were haunted as they settled on her.

At last she thought she understood. "You want Soraya back. I'm not enough for you," she said sadly.

He inhaled deeply, audibly. "Yes, I want Soraya back. But I also want Verity. They're both the same person, you bloody little fool."

Suddenly under attack from an unexpected quarter, she flinched back against the pillows. "No, they're not," she said sharply.

His eyes burned into hers. "Yes, they are. You created Soraya because you wanted someone to blame for everything you've done, everything pious little Verity can't countenance in herself. Soraya sold her body. Soraya enjoyed sex. Soraya wasn't afraid."

He took another deep breath, and his gaze didn't waver from hers. "Well, here's a revelation, Verity Ashton. Soraya is you. Soraya's innate sensuality and sense of adventure are also yours. Verity is sweet and virtuous and Soraya is a woman who goes after what she wants without regret or fear. Those two women unite in you. Until you recognize that, you're no use to me or to yourself." He turned once more to go.

"What do you want, Kylemore?" she asked unsteadily to his back. His accusations charred a path through her mind. Was he right? And if he was right, what could she do about it?

He didn't look at her as he spoke very slowly and clearly. "I want you to want me the way I want you. I want you to come to me and tell me that. Then I want you to show me it's true."

She'd been prepared to surrender so much tonight, but

never had she thought she risked this final bastion of her soul. He was too demanding, too greedy.

"You ask too much," she whispered, shocked.

"Yes, I do," he said, and the sorrow in his voice lingered in her ears as he left her alone in the firelit room.

Chapter 17

V erity still pondered the duke's extraordinary parting
lines—how could she not?—the next afternoon as she
sat in the sunlit garden. The rain that had made her escape so
wretched had relented for the moment. She ached all over
from her ordeal in the mountains, and she was tired after a
troubled night.

Kylemore had been gone all day. Which, she told herself,
was a blessing.

What could she say to him? Especially now, when he
wanted more than her simple physical surrender. Instead, he
wanted everything—her heart, her soul, her body. More than
Verity had ever been capable of giving.

He saw too clearly, damn him. Somehow, he comprehended the games she'd played for her sanity's sake.

At fifteen, she'd created a being called Soraya who could
commit any sin, break any rule. Verity, the core of who she
was, remained as pure and untouched as she'd been when
she'd sat in chapel with her Methodist parents.

The fiction was fragile. But it had helped her survive.

Now Kylemore wanted to meld the two halves of her nature into one. More, he wanted her to present that unified whole unconditionally to him.

Was all this just one more twist to his revenge?

If she gave him everything he wanted and he spurned her, he'd destroy her. She knew that in her bones.

His rejection would cut to her soul because she no longer had Soraya to hide behind. She risked her real, vulnerable self.

Her hatred had retreated impossibly far, considering how she'd raged when he'd kidnapped her, dragged her to Scotland, forced himself upon her.

She'd lost Soraya. She'd lost her sustaining resentment against him. She'd lost her longing for freedom.

What was left? She hardly dared to find out.

Somewhere in the last days she'd forgiven him. Perhaps when he'd wept in her arms. Or when he'd listened to her sorry history without judging her.

Or perhaps she'd finally forgiven him during that desolate moment in the kitchen before she'd escaped. The moment she'd admitted he and she shared much more than just carnal passion.

Certainly, by the time he'd been so furiously intent on saving her life yesterday, she hadn't hated him.

How could she hate a man who acted as though, without her, he lost every hope of happiness? For one strange second on that cliff face, she'd recognized that he would have gladly changed places with her if it meant she stayed safe.

Oh, why did she even think about this? Hadn't she wanted him to keep away from her? And at last she'd managed to coax him into a halfhearted agreement to let her go.

But she couldn't forget how he'd looked as he'd left last night.

He'd been a man at the limits of his endurance. She'd seen him in the grip of physical desire, but this was something else, something infinitely more powerful.

Not for the first time, she wondered if they'd end up annihilating each other before this contest played out.

"Och, lassie, it's too bright a day tae look so fashed." Hamish came around the corner of the house.

The giants were nowhere to be seen. Clearly, Kylemore thought he'd vanquished her impulse to run off. Why not? He had.

She managed a smile for the older man. Chasing her fears and doubts around her head was driving her mad. At least company promised distraction.

"It's a strange place, this valley. Yesterday, it was utter misery. Today, it's the Garden of Eden."

Hamish stopped in front of her, his bright eyes considering as they rested on her. She wondered what he saw. Nothing of Soraya, that was sure. His manner was unguarded, and for the first time, he sounded genuinely friendly.

"Aye, it's a country of extremes," he said. "Much like the people born here."

Verity's curiosity got the better of her now that the normally taciturn Scotsman seemed in a mood to chat. "Does that include the Duke of Kylemore?"

Hamish shook his grizzled head. "No, my lady. The heir is always born at the castle further down the coast. Young Kylemore grew up in this glen, though. At least until he was seven and they sent him away tae some Sassenach school tae learn tae be a wee gentleman." Hamish's sarcastic tone indicated what he thought of that plan.

Verity glanced around at the isolated valley. It was an unlikely location to raise one of the kingdom's greatest land-owners.

"And you were here then?"

"Aye, I worked for his father, the sixth duke. The Macleishes have always been in service tae the Kinmurries."

"I understand your loyalty to the duke," she said softly.

Hamish looked at her sharply. "I doubt ye do, lassie. I doubt ye do. Justin Kinmurrie is a better man than he lets ye or anybody see."

Once she'd have laughed such a statement to scorn. But recently, the duke hadn't behaved like the unredeemed villain she'd believed him on the road north. And even on that onerous journey, he hadn't been as cruel to her as she was sure he'd intended.

Light and dark battled for supremacy in Kylemore's soul. Occasionally, she was lunatic enough to imagine light might emerge victorious.

Oh, you're a willfully blind fool, she chastised herself. *He kidnapped and abused you. Never forget that. Don't make the mistake of imagining just because he saved your life, he's some sort of hero.*

She bit her lip. Did she really want to learn more about Kylemore? She was too confused already. Right now, she needed a clear head and a cold heart. A devoted servant's reminiscences about the duke's childhood would only cloud her thinking, remind her that Kylemore was human and not the monster she so desperately wanted him to be.

But Hamish's teasing offer of information lured her. This might be her only chance to answer her questions.

She met the old Scotsman's steady gaze with equally unwavering eyes. "You know him so well," she said.

Was that approval she read in his face? Surely not. A woman who had led the life she had would be anathema to this stern man.

"Aye, that I do. Ever since he was a wee bairn." He gestured to her bench. "May I join ye, my lady?"

She nodded. "Of course."

"Thank you." He took the space next to her and stretched his bare legs under the kilt out to the sun. "I'm not as young as I used tae be."

She didn't say anything, afraid she might discourage confidences. Because confidences were about to flow, she knew.

After a pause, he went on. "I was gey lucky—I've always had work on the estate. Most other crofters werenae so fortunate. They were all tossed off their land when the duke's mother decided more gold lay in sheep than in folk. Families who had served the Kinmurries for centuries were cast away like so much rubbish tae starve or emigrate or find what work they could far from all they knew and loved."

Verity was appalled. "Surely you exaggerate."

"No, lassie," he said sadly. "I wish I did. It's a common story since the lairds started tae cut a dash down south. The clearances were late coming tae Kinmurrie holdings. But when she decided tae act, the duchess was ruthless. Folk tried tae resist but there wasnae anything they could do. And when the troopers shot John Macleish, my nephew, most of us went quietly enough. We couldnae fight the law."

It was a terrible story, more terrible for what Verity suspected Hamish left out—the destruction of a whole way of life. "On the way here, I thought it was odd that we saw no people, just ruined cottages."

"Aye. This happened all over the Highlands," he said with a bitterness he didn't hide.

"Yet you don't blame the duke?" Surely this tragic tale provided her with another sin to heap on Kylemore's head.

"Och, he was but a bairn. He might have inherited the title, but he had nae real power until he reached his majority. The duchess had all the say, and she's no a woman tae put anything ahead of her own selfish wishes."

"But Kylemore continued to profit from what she did."

Hamish stared straight ahead into the misty hills. His expression was distant, as though he relived those tragic events.

"No, he did his best tae make amends. When His Grace took over, he set out tae find everyone he could. But by then, fourteen hard years had passed. Folk died or were lost. Many went across the water tae Nova Scotia. Still, he tracked down those he could and invited them back. Those with new lives, he gave them money tae make up for their trouble."

"Fergus and his family," she said, remembering their fervent and, at the time, inexplicable devotion to Kylemore.

"Aye. Fergus is my brother. Search as ye will, my lady, ye won't find a soul on any Kinmurrie estate tae say a word against His Grace."

Once she mightn't have believed Hamish. But while the last days had revealed a darker, more complex Kylemore, they had also shown her the honorable man hidden inside him too. She had no trouble imagining that honorable man moving heaven and earth to make recompense for the pain his mother had caused.

The duke would abhor them discussing him like this. He wanted her to view him as the impossibly self-assured Cold Kylemore.

But she'd held him in her arms too often. Held him when he'd shuddered with sexual release. Held him when he'd sobbed with misery.

He'd never be that impervious aristocrat to her again. Hamish's revelations only moved that false perfection further out of reach.

"Why are you telling me this?" she asked.

He turned his head and looked at her squarely. "I've watched ye, lassie. I've watched the laddie with ye. I know he's done wrong by ye. I think in his soul, he admits that. But there's good in him, if ye look. And for all his privileges, he's no had an easy life."

"He's rich and handsome enough," Verity said, echoing her brother's dismissive reply when she'd falteringly tried to describe the tormented depths she'd sensed in her lover's soul even then.

"Aye, weel, neither make ye happy. Ask him about his father some time."

She already knew Kylemore had feared his father. She shivered as she recalled him begging his papa to leave him alone. A child's cry in a sleeping man's voice.

"Can't you tell me?"

The older man smiled ruefully down at her. "Och, I've gossiped enough for one day. Too much, folk might think."

Kylemore would certainly agree, but Hamish had only whetted her curiosity.

"The duke has bad dreams," she said abruptly.

Hamish looked unsurprised. "Aye. He's had them since he was a ween." He gave her another of those straight looks, as though he sought some commitment from her. "But ye can help him. If ye feel braw enough tae take the task. And the lassie who climbed Ben Tassoch yesterday is as braw a lassie as any I've ever met." He stood up and stared down at her.

"I was so frightened," she admitted, remembering the raw panic that had threatened to paralyze her throughout her misguided attempt to flee. She hadn't been brave. She'd been utterly terrified.

Hamish's smile didn't fade. "Aye, but ye still did it, my lady." He bowed his head to her, one of the few times she'd seen him show anything like conventional respect for anyone, even the duke. "Good day tae you."

Clearly, he'd tell her nothing more. Troubled, she watched him walk away toward the stables.

Was he right? Did she have the heart to take on Kylemore and the demons that pursued him?

Did she have a heart left at all?

Kylemore's ultimatum last night had demanded a surrender that was already so precariously close.

Her abject surrender had been his goal from the start. She wasn't fool enough to imagine anything else.

Oh, why couldn't she have fallen in love with someone simple and straightforward? Someone who at least promised her a tiny hope of happiness.

She'd never asked much from life. Experience had taught her to make do with what was within reach and never to howl after the moon. She'd be content with kindness and a few shared interests. Companionship. Consideration.

She didn't want a difficult, brilliant, mercurial, tormented man like the Duke of Kylemore.

But she did.

A horrified gasp escaped her, and she staggered to her feet in denial. The devastating truth hammered at her with the grim inevitability of the cold Scottish rain she'd endured in the mountains yesterday.

She'd struggled against this fate since she'd seen a gloriously handsome young man across a London drawing room. Something within her had immediately warned her of danger. But she'd kept her head over the years, difficult as that had sometimes proven.

Until he'd radically altered the game between them.

In London, she'd been able to maintain the detachment that kept her safe. Here in this small house, where Kylemore refused to countenance barriers between them, she couldn't pretend she felt nothing for her lover.

Was this the revenge he'd planned all along? Had he fought to stay in her bed because he'd known that eventually she'd fall victim to love?

Love.

Such a small word for what she felt.

Yet what other word could there be?

She loved the Duke of Kylemore. And that love could only lead to disaster.

Chapter 18

Kylemore lay awake in the barren little room he'd claimed for himself in this hated house. It wasn't the room he'd used as a boy. Neither pride nor will could make him sleep in that particular chamber: It remained empty and abandoned at the end of the corridor.

Empty, that is, of everything except the screaming ghosts that returned to rupture his slumber.

He'd dream again tonight. He knew it. And in his extremity, he'd find no soft comfort, no warm arms to embrace him, no whispered words of reassurance.

Verity wouldn't come to him. Why would she?

He hadn't seen her since he'd left her to sleep on her own last night. Perhaps it was best if he never saw her again.

Hamish could take her by boat along the loch and down to Oban, where she could arrange passage to Whitby. Hamish would undertake the task with alacrity. His old mentor had always disapproved of Kylemore's treatment of his mistress.

With good reason.

He shifted restlessly. Physically, he was exhausted. He'd set off on Tannasg just after dawn and stayed out until nightfall with precisely that aim. But his mind refused to settle. It felt so wrong to be in here alone when the woman he wanted slept just down the hallway.

The woman who had nearly died because of his transgressions.

No matter how hard or how far he rode, he couldn't outrun his guilt-plagued memories. His black despair when Verity had fallen. The unalloyed terror in her eyes as she'd clung to the mountainside. Her collapse into unconsciousness after he'd rescued her.

He'd told Hamish he wanted to break her. Damn it, that had been the point of this entire misguided exercise.

But contrary to every expectation, he'd found no satisfaction in seeing her humbled last night.

When she'd made it clear she would endure his presence in her bed because she had no alternative.

Once, a willing and cooperative mistress was all he'd sought. Once, he wouldn't have hesitated to take what she'd offered. But that was when he'd only known Soraya.

Soraya would tolerate his attentions.

Verity, the Verity he'd come to know in the last days, would suffer as she lay beneath him. As she'd suffered since he'd brought her to the glen.

He was tired of self-deception. He could no longer pretend she masked her desire for him with false reluctance.

No, she'd told him repeatedly she despised him. It was time he had the courage to accept that as the truth.

Oh, yes, he gave her pleasure, but that pleasure wounded her like a knife. She hated him for seducing her. Worse, she hated herself for being weak enough to respond.

He'd always feared his passion would lead to devastation. It was too late for him. It had been too late the moment he'd seen her six years ago. He should never have pursued her when she'd left Kensington. But if he let her go now, surely she'd be able to escape his catastrophic obsession.

He must let her go.

Releasing her would be the most difficult thing he'd ever do. But if keeping her meant risk to her life and sanity, he had to set her free.

Her scream as she'd fallen down the cliff still echoed in his mind and made his gut clench with horror. He'd come so close to losing her. And now it seemed he was to lose her indeed.

Yesterday, he'd learned a number of salutary lessons. None welcome. All well overdue. Among them, that he'd leap over that cliff himself before he caused her one iota more of pain.

Unseeingly, he stared out into the darkness and swore he'd do the right thing. For once.

He had no choice, damn it all to hell.

The harrowing decision made, he tried for the thousandth time that night to sleep. But wisdom in hindsight proved an unsettling companion. Especially when the woman he wanted was forever out of reach.

Forever.

What a bleak word.

Christ, if only he could sleep. Even bad dreams would be an improvement on lying here contemplating life without her.

He stifled a groan. The pain was too sharp.

He couldn't bear it.

I can bear it. For her sake.

He rolled over with another groan. The sheets chafed his naked skin. His muscles were sore from yesterday's exertions and today's long ride. He needed rest, but the endless night extended ahead of him as a desolate watch.

The first of many. His only consolation was that finally,

too late and after the damage was done, he'd found the will to act like a man.

If only dawn would come.

But when dawn came, he must say good-bye to Verity.

God, let the night never end.

It was well past midnight when Kylemore heard the latch rattle. He rolled over and watched as slowly the door swung open.

Flickering, golden light illuminated the darkness. Dazzled, disbelieving, he looked up to see Verity on the threshold. Her candle made her eyes glow dark and mysterious in her pale face. A silk robe was loosely belted at her slender waist, and her glorious hair tumbled loose around her.

Being strong was difficult enough when he had only his regrets for company. With the focus of his every desire hovering so close, resolution was well nigh impossible.

Then he realized only an emergency would force her to seek him out. In an instant, concern had him shoving himself up against the headboard.

"Verity, are you all right?" he asked, his voice edged with urgency. Had she taken a fever?

"Perfectly, thank you."

He couldn't doubt she meant it. Her voice was calm, even carried a hint of amusement, and her face was grave but strangely untroubled. She held the candle so steadily that the flame hardly wavered in the still air.

His astonishment mounted. If she wasn't ill, what in the Devil's name was she up to?

Surprise and confusion pinned him to the bed as the door clicked shut behind her. She set the candle on the plain deal dresser. When she moved, he caught the shadowy outline of breast and thigh through her thin robe. His ferocious need ratcheted higher.

His conscience insisted he had no right to touch her. His body most emphatically disagreed. To confirm this, his cock rose, eager, ready, unruly. Thank God the bedclothes hid his arousal. He was more than a brute animal, he told himself without conviction.

She drifted toward him in a rustle of silk. The uncertain light revealed a smile that was pure Soraya. Seductive. Knowing. Confident. In another woman, he'd have interpreted the gleam in her eyes as desire.

But this was Verity, and he knew better.

"What the hell do you want?" he asked sharply, summoning anger as his only defense.

Had she come here to make him suffer? If so, she succeeded, damn her.

"I want you," she said huskily.

He closed his eyes in anguish. How he'd longed to hear her say those words. But circumstances had changed—*he had changed*—in the last few days.

"I don't believe you," he snapped, resentful because he wished so desperately that what she said was true.

"You will."

Her voice rang with sincerity as she padded nearer. Her slim, elegant feet brushed across the floorboards. The night wasn't cold, but still he fought the impulse to pick her up and carry her back to her bed. His control was so frail that if he touched her, he was lost.

"You don't have to do this," he bit out while his wanton blood beat out the command to take her, take her, take her.

"Yes, I do," she said without a hint of faltering.

God, why did she stand so close? Her damned evocative scent wrapped around him and lured him to sin.

God, why didn't she stand closer still so he could tear off that concealing robe and tug her under him?

"You owe me nothing. You were right to call me a thief."

His tone grated as he made the difficult confession. He looked away into the shadowy corner and spoke in a voice that was dull with hard-held self-restraint. "I've given up revenge. I've given up forcing you. I've given up asking anything of you at all."

She leaned over him, releasing another tantalizing eddy of scent, subtle rose soap and woman. "You talk too much," she whispered. "Where's my ferocious lover gone? Where's the demon Duke of Kylemore?"

What?

He whipped his head around. Unbelievably, she still smiled. His hands fisted in the sheets as he battled the urge to grab her.

She was so close that he felt her warmth. But his sins against her exiled him forever to an icy hell.

"Stop it," he snarled. "Listen to me! I've set you free."

Her presence was sheerest torment.

He thought he'd die if she left him alone.

He spoke on a surge of self-hatred. "I should never have started this cruel nonsense in the first place."

"It's too late for regrets," she said softly.

"Yes."

Too late to redeem himself and become worthy of her, certainly. There was a universe of sorrow in the thought.

His mind rehearsed the endless litany. He should never have hunted her down at Whitby. He should never have forced her into his carriage—at gunpoint, he recalled with corrosive shame. He should never have bullied her into his bed.

Although without the abduction, he'd never have really known her. He'd go through hellfire itself before he forsook that privilege.

But she, not you, went through hellfire. She almost lost her life yesterday.

"I'm letting you go." His voice shook with desperation.

"Are you?" she asked idly.

After her long struggle to escape him, he'd have expected her to sound more than merely interested when he granted her freedom. Baffled, he stared into the exquisite face that had haunted him for so many years.

"Don't torment me."

"You deserve it," she said without heat.

And without moving away, damn her.

"Yes, I do. But the Devil if I'll lie here and let you sink your damned claws into me, little cat."

Her luscious mouth curled upward. "I think you might."

His screaming tension tightened to breaking point as he strove to banish the sensual images her words sent rocketing through his mind. She played a dangerous game to tease him like this. He shifted higher up against the pillows until his eyes were level with hers.

"Go away, Verity," he said with difficulty.

Stay, Verity, his heart pleaded.

"That's not what you want," she whispered.

He couldn't take much more of this. "It's what you want that matters."

She bent closer, and he heard her shaky inhalation before she spoke. "I think . . ." She hesitated, then continued in a rush. "I think that's why I can be here with you now."

Then impossibly, she kissed him.

It was a kiss unlike anything he'd ever known. Her mouth was soft, coaxing, inviting. She summoned the arts Soraya had so carefully cultivated, yet beneath hovered the poignant innocence he'd always recognize as Verity's.

He was helpless to stop himself from kissing her back with all the fiery yearning in his heart. He plunged his hand into her silky mass of hair. It slid cool and fragrant against his fingers as her mouth branded his with heat. She slid down so she lay across his bare chest, and she twined her arms around his neck, bringing him closer.

Before he drowned in dark ravishment, he tore his mouth from hers.

"For God's sake, I'm trying to do what's right," he panted, staring down into her flushed face. He clung to his scruples by only the thinnest thread.

"Oh, Kylemore." Her smoky laugh brushed like exquisite torture across every nerve.

Despairingly, he thought he'd give her everything he owned if she'd only once call him Justin.

"Why are you doing this?" he grated out even while his arms tensed to keep her in his embrace. "Why, Verity?"

Her fingers tangled in the hair at his nape. "Don't you know? Can't you see?" Her eyes were clear as they met his. "The war is over. I've laid down my weapons. The victory is yours."

"So easily?" He didn't trust her capitulation. In spite of the kiss. In spite of the fact that she offered this sinner a paradise he thought he'd never attain. "You told me you hated me. You *should* hate me for what I've done to you."

Her expression darkened at the reminder. "Yes, I did hate you. But I can't hate you any more. I nearly died yesterday. And I don't want to die before I give myself unreservedly to the man I want. You're the man I want, Kylemore."

He was speechless with wonder. She was brave, braver by far than he. She was beautiful. And despite his crimes against her, she committed herself to his keeping.

His heart contracted within him. After all the misery and violence and pain and anger, he could hardly believe safe harbor beckoned. Safe harbor where the woman he yearned for wanted him in return.

The concession seemed so simple. The concession changed his life.

She gazed into his face. Tears glittered in her eyes, and her expression was stark with need. "Do you want me to beg, Kylemore? I will if that's what it takes." Her voice cracked.

"For pity's sake, no!"

How could she doubt him after his years of ceaseless hunger? He clutched her to him, so close her tears flowed damp against his shoulder.

His voice shook with turbulent emotion. "Don't cry, *mo leannan.* I'm yours for the asking. I've always been yours. You could give me no more precious gift than yourself."

She drew away and wiped a shaking hand across her face before, surprisingly, she gave a broken laugh. "What are you waiting for, then?"

She'd told him she wanted him, and he most definitely wanted her. What, indeed, was he waiting for? He reached out to untie her robe and slide it from her shoulders.

"My God," he breathed. "What have you got on?"

She glanced down at her sheer ice-blue silk negligee. The intensity seeped from her expression, and she smiled with sudden humor.

"Don't you recognize it? I suspect it cost you a fortune at Madame Yvette's."

"It was worth every penny," he said hoarsely.

In the candlelight, the slippery material hid, then revealed, the curve of a hip, the jut of a breast, the shadowy apex of her thighs. She moved, and silk jagged on one puckered nipple. His breath caught in his throat at the sight.

He hauled her down and kissed her again.

He'd never been a man who'd taken much interest in kissing. He'd always considered it a distraction from earthier satisfactions. Now he couldn't get enough of the taste of her, the succulent lushness of her mouth.

When he rolled her beneath him, heat flared along his body. He lay between her legs, poised for joining. His arousal clamored for him to take her, but he prolonged the moment. He intended to savor his happiness before a malign fate snatched it away.

"We should adjourn to your room if you're feeling particularly adventurous, *mo cridhe*." He laughed softly. "This cot won't allow much more than the traditional relief."

He thrust his aching sex against her belly. He fervently hoped she didn't plan an elaborate seduction, or he'd never last the distance.

"Mo cridhe?" he prompted.

"What?" she asked in a dazed voice.

"Your room. Shall we go?"

She looked around, and he saw her take in the cramped space.

"One of us will end up on the floor if we stay here."

She gave an enchanting gurgle of amusement. "That wouldn't sit well with the ducal dignity."

"That wouldn't sit well with the ducal rump."

This laughter was a heady new experience. He and Soraya had shared pleasure but never joy. And his passion for Verity had been dark and driven by destruction.

What a marvelous discovery that after over a year with this woman, he still had untold new worlds to seek.

He lifted himself off her and stood up, offering his hand. Not long ago, she'd have treated the gesture with suspicion. Tonight, she took his hand willingly and rose in a billow of transparent blue silk.

"Let me have my wicked way with you," she whispered, releasing him to collect the candle and move toward the door.

He followed and swung her around to face him. The man he'd once been would have accepted this bounty without question. The man he'd become needed final confirmation of consent.

Startled silver eyes flashed up to his. The candle's flame wavered wildly. "Your Grace?"

His hold firmed. "Kylemore. Or Justin. I prefer Justin."

The smile she gave him was pure temptation. "Perhaps when I know you better."

He left that argument for another day. Instead, he spoke somberly. "Are you sure, Verity?"

"Yes, I'm sure." She raised her hand to cup the side of his face with a tender gesture, then she took his hand once more. The warmth of her touch flowed along his veins like brandy. "Come with me. I promise to chase the bad dreams away."

Chapter 19

As she made her way along the hallway, Verity was dauntingly conscious that more than six feet of lean, strong male followed only a breath behind.

Lean, strong, *aroused* male. He was naked, and his interest in her was blatantly clear.

It was unnerving.

It was exciting.

A thrill shivered through her to have that leashed potency utterly focused on her. As recently as a mere two days ago, that potency had terrified her. Now she luxuriated in its power.

She was no longer the reluctant demimondaine who shared her bed in return for a livelihood. She was no longer poor lost Verity, afraid that if she surrendered to her deepest impulses, she'd forfeit her eternal soul.

But still when they reached her room, she hesitated at the edge of the bed.

This suddenly seemed such an irrevocable step.

Kylemore stepped behind her and encircled her with his arms. Immediate heat surrounded her. "What is it?" he murmured.

Was this new, the way he was in tune with her merest thought?

No. For how else had he managed to lure her along the difficult but inexorable path to surrender?

She laughed softly, nervously. "Would you believe I feel shy? You'll think I'm ridiculous."

"I think you're perfect." He released her and moved across to stretch out on the bed. His erection jutted out, giving the lie to his outward patience. "I'm all yours."

Tonight, she knew, that was true. She'd already accepted it wouldn't be true forever. A woman like her could never have forever.

Still, tonight was enough for now.

With one smooth movement, she tugged the filmy negligee over her head and let it float to the floor. His sex twitched, and his mouth took on a strained line.

"I'm not sure that was a good idea," he said huskily. "Not if you want me to keep my hands to myself."

She gave Soraya's laugh, except this time it emerged perfectly spontaneously. "I'll tie you up if I have to. It has to be your turn."

How could she jest about her abduction? But somehow, when she'd recognized that she loved the Duke of Kylemore, all earlier pain and rancor had faded.

If he hadn't kidnapped her, she'd still be a crippled creature willing to settle for a half life. Good works, independent celibacy, family duty couldn't compete with the abundant wealth of emotion that swirled around them tonight.

The possibility of heartbreak hovered too, but she faced it down. She meant to grab joy and hang on as firmly as she could. No matter how long it lasted. No matter what pain awaited in the future.

She climbed onto the bed and knelt above him. Her knees pressed into his lean flanks, and her hair flowed down around them. She smiled slowly, lasciviously, when he curled his strong hands around her waist as if he'd never let her go.

Soraya had been powerful, but Soraya had been a lie. What she felt now came from her very core. The core that was heavy and molten with desire for this one difficult, beloved man.

His indigo eyes darkened to black as he read her expression. Mutual arousal was familiar. This incendiary level of excitement wasn't, whatever stellar heights they'd scaled in the past.

She bent to run her mouth down the center of his chest, lingering, tasting, enjoying. His musky scent intoxicated her as no wine ever could. Gradually, inevitably, she traced the arrow of silky hair that led to the base of his belly.

With great satisfaction, she felt him struggle to draw breath. She'd meant her leisurely exploration to splinter her lover's vaunted self-control. Apparently, she succeeded.

She dipped her tongue in his navel and placed her hand very deliberately on his sex. He shuddered as she stroked him, testing his heat and vigor.

Oh, she had chosen a wonderfully virile man for herself. And all that robust masculinity was hers, all hers, lucky girl that she was.

Soon, so soon, she'd taste him there. With a sigh, she slid lower to where he rose in proud glory under her exploring fingers. He groaned, and his hands tangled in her hair.

Slowly, she licked his length, feeling the tension build in the muscles of his thigh, where she'd moved her hand to balance herself. Then, with a concentration that she knew tortured him, she flicked her tongue across the head, savoring his arousal. Beneath her other hand, his belly clenched hard. When he groaned once more, she felt the sound well out from the deepest part of him.

Of course, she'd pleasured him with her mouth before. Often. But tonight, the act held a joyous freedom she'd never experienced during all those torrid afternoons in London.

She tried to prolong this teasing overture. The sight of him stretched on a sensual rack satisfied some innately feminine element in her. He jerked under her tantalizing kisses, silently begging for more.

And she wanted to give him more. Need tugged insistently in her blood, dictating an end to delay. Almost greedily, she took him in her mouth.

He was hot, so hot. When she began to suck, he trembled beneath her as if he suffered a fever. How intoxicating to have him at her mercy like this. She increased the pressure, initiating a rhythm that echoed the act of love.

"Mo cridhe . . ." he grated out, tilting his hips up toward her.

She leaned closer to take more of him, and his fingers clenched convulsively against her scalp. He was very close to breaking, she knew. Her own excitement sparked like lightning as she sensed his futile but frantic struggle to harness his desire.

She wanted him to lose control. *She wanted him to lose control for her.*

But before she achieved her goal, he dragged her upward with shaking hands. She gave a frustrated whimper as he deftly rolled her beneath him. His weight pressed her down into the mattress, and the thought of all that lean strength above her made her shiver with anticipation.

"I want to give you pleasure," she protested in a voice she hardly recognized as her own. She licked her lips and tasted his skin. She wanted to taste *more*.

He raised his head, and for once, his smile held no darkness. Even piqued of her objective, she couldn't help thinking with a stab of longing how beautiful he was.

"This time is for you," he said softly.

The wild desperation to snatch this moment and guard it as a miser guarded his gold seeped out of her even while her desire blazed higher, more brightly.

"Yes," she whispered. And watched the final shadow slip away from his face as she at last gave him her consent.

Kylemore shifted over her very gently. Her hips cradled him, and his cock nudged eagerly at the softness of her belly. After their decadent past, this should be so familiar.

But he couldn't dismiss the extraordinary idea that he made love to a virgin. In spite of all the pleasure they'd shared. In spite of what he'd done to her in this house. In spite of the frenzy her clever mouth and hands drove him into.

Softly, as though touching her for the first time, he explored her body. The unsteady pattern of her breathing guided him to where her pleasure lay.

He took his time, struggling against the need that seethed like a whirlpool within him. His heart beat such a mad tattoo in his chest that he thought it might burst. But he clamped down on his hunger and concentrated on her. After all his transgressions against her, he owed her this.

He caressed and kissed her breasts until she gasped and shook in his arms. Her nipples were so sensitive that he knew he could bring her to climax like this.

But still it wasn't enough. He'd promised her pleasure and, by God, he meant to give her pleasure such as she'd never known before. The ache in his loins clenched into agony, but somehow he contained the urge to enter and possess.

He touched her dewy center and smiled his satisfaction

when she bucked and moaned under his hand. He'd always loved her responsiveness. The redolent scent of her arousal invaded his senses as he stroked the plump, damp folds until they were swollen and wet beneath his fingers.

He pushed two fingers into her and bent his head to sink his teeth into the curve where her neck met her shoulder. She cried out and shuddered, rewarding him with a hot flow of moisture against his seeking hand.

Immediately, he gentled, nuzzling the fragrant hollows of her neck as he began to work his fingers in and out of her. She shivered and wound her arms around his naked back. Soon she trembled like a sapling in a high wind, and her breath emerged in panting moans.

But his ruthlessness hadn't altogether vanished. He continued until she broke and clung to him, sobbing. She was still shaking when he positioned himself between her thighs.

He fought for breath and for the willpower to make this good for her. Carefully, with a restraint that almost killed him, he slid into her. Her sigh as he penetrated fully was the sweetest sound he'd ever heard.

He'd been a power in the great world. He'd commanded the destinies of multitudes. Yet, despite that, he knew this private, silent moment was the most important of his life.

For a long moment, he remained motionless, suspended in perfect connection.

They were one.

He'd always dismissed that idea as sentimental claptrap. But for a few transcendent seconds, he didn't know where he ended and she began.

But he was, after all, merely human. The urge to move became irresistible. He withdrew and thrust once more.

Immediately he felt again that sense of ultimate homecoming.

She sighed with delight and lifted herself to him. The

graceful arch of her body told him all he needed to know about what she wanted.

His famous control shattered into a thousand glittering shards. Wildly, he plunged into her over and over, riding out the volcanic force of one climax and another even more turbulent. Then, while the tremors still shook her, he thrust hard for the last time. With a mighty groan, he unleashed his passion into the welcoming darkness of her womb.

Verity drifted back from the dazzling realms of ultimate pleasure to find Kylemore slumped over her, his head buried in her shoulder. He was heavy and hot, pressing her into the mattress, but she couldn't bear him to move away yet. Her arms tightened around his back as his ragged breathing gradually slowed.

Hard to believe she, the great expert on carnality, had known nothing at all. What she'd just experienced revealed her previous encounters as pale imitations of something rare and real.

She felt like laughing with joy. She felt like crying her heart out over what she'd missed. What she hadn't even guessed existed.

She closed her eyes, remembering her stunned flash of recognition when his body had finally joined hers.

For the first time in her life, she'd felt complete. The ignorant country girl. Ben and Maria's careful provider. The frightened servant. Eldreth's mistress, as much daughter as lover, especially after the onset of his illness. James's worldly tutor. Kylemore's obsession. Then his angry resentful captive.

Daughter. Sister. Mistress. Prisoner. Lover. United in the woman who loved Kylemore. In the wake of all the painful storms, she basked now in a peace unlike anything she'd ever known.

The words *I love you* trembled on her lips.

But she could never tell him. Not for her sake—she'd never stop loving him. But for his.

The last few days had revealed he was far from the unfeeling monolith he strove so diligently to present. He already carried so much pain. She wouldn't allow herself to add to it.

Kylemore stirred. His breathing was steadier, and his heart no longer thundered against her.

As he raised his head and looked down into her eyes, she saw he too had changed. His gaze was clear and sure. The cynicism that had always veiled his features had vanished. For the first time, he truly looked like a man a year younger than she.

Her heart was so full, she reached up to touch his cheek. His shadow beard bristled beneath her fingers.

"I've got a bear in my bed." She sought relief in lightness.

Under her fingers, she felt his cheek crease into a smile. "I should have shaved."

"Mmm."

"I'm too heavy for you."

"Maybe a little."

She trailed her fingers upward and brushed his tangled, dark hair back from his temple. She'd never before permitted herself the tentative explorations of a new lover. She knew his body so well, yet these simple gestures of affection were utterly unfamiliar.

He pushed into her touch, reminding her of a kitten she'd had as a child. The memory was innocent, harking back to a time she'd almost forgotten.

She laughed softly. "You'll start purring soon."

"Ah, *mo cridhe.* I'm already purring. Surely you hear me." His voice even sounded different, softer, hinting at a Highland lilt.

She could fall in love with a man with a voice like that.

"What do you call me?" she asked idly, continuing to stroke the lean planes of his face, his arrogant nose, his ears, his eyebrows.

Even more catlike under her ministrations, he closed his eyes. "Oh, it's only a local term for a woman."

When he raised his eyelids and glanced at her, she caught the blue glitter of amusement. Plainly, there was more to the soft endearment than he meant to tell her.

What did it matter in such a perfect moment? Her hands slid down to his back, tracing muscle and bone.

She could touch him like this forever. And still ask for more.

Who knew a man's body offered such delights? Certainly not London's most infamous courtesan.

He bent his head to kiss her—short, playful nips and pecks that soon had her giggling and wrestling with him in an ecstatic tangle of naked limbs.

She felt like a child again. A child with her very best friend in the world.

A child soon engulfed in distinctly adult desire when the game became more purposeful. His mouth touched her everywhere, her neck, her back, her buttocks, her breasts, between her legs. It was as if he staked his possession with kisses. Kisses that built heat a degree at a time until she burned with need.

This time, the climax was cataclysmic. Her world fragmented in a burst of molten white. Gasping, she clung to Kylemore as the only solid object in her fracturing universe. But a more lasting radiance lingered beneath the violent explosion of pleasure. And when she floated back to reality, it was the radiance she remembered.

Afterward, they slept briefly.

She woke to find Kylemore raised on one elbow, watching

her with a slumberous expression in his indigo eyes. Indigo eyes that for the first time since she'd known him were tranquil, like a calm sea at sunset. He must have gotten up while she'd dozed, because a forest of candles lit the room to gold.

His expression was tender as he shaped her breast. He brushed his thumb against the plump nipple, and it hardened in immediate response.

"This is what I wanted in London," he murmured, bending to place a kiss where his thumb teased. His lips were hot on her tender skin, and she shifted under a renewed surge of desire.

"Why did you make me wait so long, Verity?"

She didn't pretend to misunderstand. "You seemed . . . you seemed more than I could handle. I preferred easier men." How did he expect her to concentrate on his questions when he touched her?

"So you took Mallory as your lover."

Her last protector's name crashed into the harmony between them with the force of a knife thrown at a door. Her pleasurable stirrings of arousal vanished in an instant.

"I can't help what I was," she snapped. She tried to draw away, but he caught her shoulder and stopped her.

"I'm just trying to understand. I know why you owed Eldreth loyalty. But Mallory was a joke."

"He was sweet. I thought I could help him." She smiled, then wished she hadn't as a frown darkened Kylemore's face.

"You loved him," he growled.

She bit back a vehement denial as she looked more closely at Kylemore. He wasn't furious. Instead, he appeared uncomfortable, shamefaced, annoyed.

Jealous.

Heavens, how marvelous. He was jealous. Because of her! His liaison with her wasn't at all the unequal match she'd always believed it. When he mentioned James, he didn't taunt her about her wicked past. He sought reassurance that she wanted no one but him.

Her resistance seeped away. She lay back beside him.

"No. I wasn't capable of loving anybody then."

With horror, she realized just what she'd said. Dear heaven, don't let her astute lover pick up on the telling use of the past tense.

But he still fretted about the man who had occupied her bed so briefly. "He loved you. He must have."

He seemed unduly concerned with the notion of love.

She'd have thought love an alien concept to the Duke of Kylemore. Clearly, she was mistaken.

"Very flattering, Your Grace," she said dryly. "But in truth, he didn't know what to do with me once he'd won me. He was a home-and-hearth sort. I taught him social polish, gave him advice about wooing his Sarah and waved him good-bye happily enough when it ended. He's a kind, dear man who married his sweetheart. He's not worth your hatred."

"Except he had you when you should have been mine." His powerful arm tightened around her. "You've driven me mad for years, you know. Tell me about the others."

"What others?"

He tugged a long strand of her hair in gentle rebuke. "Don't play me for a fool, Verity. You were the most notorious woman in London. You've had more paramours than just an elderly baronet and a parvenu milksop."

"Yes," she said on a growl, trying once more to free herself from his embrace. "There was a presumptuous Scotsman who should have had his ears boxed."

Kylemore lifted himself above her, his face white with shock. "Three lovers?" he asked in patent disbelief.

"There's no need to sound so smug," she said with genuine displeasure.

"Shh," he whispered and began to kiss her. She wanted to resist, but as always, it was impossible.

When he'd subdued her into a bundle of quivering pleasure, he laughed wryly. "You've led us on, *mo cridhe*. The kingdom's most scandalous woman is pure as the driven snow."

"Don't mock me, Kylemore," she protested, nettled anew.

"I'm not. But you need to reconsider your role as a scarlet woman. You'd put most ladies of the ton to the blush."

"You forget I drove all those men to suicide with my wiles when I first came to London," she said bitterly. The old wound still festered.

"Their deaths weren't your fault, Verity," he said softly. She searched his face for censure, anger or disgust, but the deep blue eyes were grave and held no condemnation.

He sounded so sure. But her regret had bitten too deeply for mere words to offer absolution. She dragged in a sobbing breath. "On my soul, I didn't encourage them. Yet they blew their brains out because of me. Why?"

Ignoring her quivering stiffness, Kylemore settled himself higher until she lay across his bare chest. Her naked skin slid against his as he tucked her head under his chin.

He understood futile guilt better than most. He knew how it ate at the soul. Hadn't he suffered because he couldn't stop his mother gutting the estates to fund her political ambitions?

Verity had endured years of hatred and sly talk over her supposedly fatal charms. Gossip had condemned her coldness and accused her of luxuriating in her power over the unsuspecting and gullible male sex.

The ton had known nothing about the real woman.

"They suffered a kind of madness. You were only the excuse," he said slowly, searching for the right words to soothe her pain. "There was something feverish in the air that season. I remember the wildness, the ever more profligate gambling, the unfettered womanizing, the duels to the death. Soraya, with her beauty and her mystery, formed part of it. But nothing she did drove those men to take their lives."

"They died because of me," she whispered, hiding her face in his shoulder. "Because of what I was and what I did."

Kylemore's covetous soul exulted that he was the one she turned to for comfort.

Then he felt her hot tears against his throat. His greed to be the eternal center of her world faded as bone-deep pity overwhelmed him.

His hold on her tightened. "It's time to forgive yourself as I'm sure the ghosts of those troubled young men have long ago forgiven you. The suicides were a tragedy and a cruel waste, but they were never your fault."

"Do you really mean that?" Her hesitant question was a murmur against his chest.

"More than I can say."

She lay calm and exhausted upon him, fragile in his arms, yet stronger than anyone he knew. He yearned to make extravagant promises, swear eternal fealty, go on his knees and offer her the world on a gold platter.

But he settled for a simple, "Sleep now, *mo cridhe*. I'll keep you safe."

Chapter 20

$\sim$

Verity was still wallowing in a daze of bliss and newly awakened love the next afternoon when she and Kylemore ate a belated meal in the parlor. Giving herself—all of herself—to him had been extraordinarily liberating.

Beneath the lethargy lingering after a night of passion, new self-confidence flowered. For the moment, this extraordinary man's ardor, intelligence, courage, beauty were utterly hers.

Whatever the future held, nothing could alter what had happened between them. She'd never be the same. Nor would Kylemore.

Eventually, he'd leave to take his rightful place in the great world. But he'd never be free of her.

Never.

The day had started with rain, providing the ideal excuse to detain the duke in bed. Now she contemplated the outrages she meant to perpetrate upon his body when they returned to her room. Which would be soon, she hoped.

She was definitely hungry, but not necessarily for food.

"What is it?" He lifted his hand from where it lay near his plate and reached over the table to play with her fingers.

All morning, he'd touched her like this. The tiny gestures of connection surprised her. He'd always been a vigorous lover, but she'd never otherwise regarded him as a demonstrative man.

He looked across the remains of their luncheon at her. "You're blushing," he said smugly.

Smugness was one of his abiding characteristics today. She must be in a bad way indeed to find it charming rather than irritating.

But he wasn't having everything his own way. "I was thinking how it felt to take you in my mouth this morning," she said lightly, glancing at him under her lashes. She smiled her own satisfaction as he choked on a mouthful of claret.

Soraya retained her uses, not the least of which was keeping her temperamental lover from complacency.

Still smiling, she took a sip of her own wine and studied the room. A particularly fierce stag glaring at her from the wall captured her attention. "You know," she said absently, "these decorations always seem out of character. I never pictured you as quite such the swaggering huntsman."

Although he'd hunted her effectively enough, she admitted, for once without a trace of resentment.

He set his glass down, brought his napkin to his lips and glanced at the funereal décor without interest. "The trophies were my grandfather's."

"Don't you find them oppressive when you visit?"

"I don't visit. I lived here with my father until I was seven. I haven't been back since. Unless I'd needed to stash a troublesome mistress, I wouldn't have returned now." His expression was guarded as usual when she probed his past.

"It's certainly inconvenient." She used a neutral voice.

"It's a hellhole," he said flatly. "And no," he continued when she opened her mouth, "I don't want to discuss it. Let's go back to bed."

Startled to hear him echo her own wanton thoughts, she put down her glass. "We only came downstairs an hour ago."

His black brows lowered in a frown. "Is that a no?"

"No." Then, when the frown darkened, "That's not a no."

He laughed softly, and the deep sound skittered up her spine like hot lightning. He quickly rounded the table to pull out her chair.

"I don't know what I've done to deserve you," he said fervently.

She sent him a level look. "Neither do I. And don't think you can always use sex to distract me."

"Why not? It works."

Smug again, damn him. He was so beguilingly pleased with himself.

But if he thought she'd abandoned her curiosity, he was wrong. Last night, he'd forced her to come to terms with who she was and what she'd done. Her love made her determined to help him conquer his demons in return. If this determination abetted her purely feminine need to learn about the man she loved, so be it.

Something terrible lay buried in his past. He'd never be free until he confronted it.

She was thoughtful as she left the parlor on his arm.

Kylemore crossed his arms behind his head and relaxed against the pillows while he studied Verity. To his drowsy chagrin, she'd just tugged a green day gown over her delicately embroidered chemise. The shift had done nothing to hide the splendors of her body. The dress required him to use a little more imagination.

She sat down at the dressing table and began to brush her

long, shining hair. The regular pull and release of the silver brush was sensuously soporific.

His body ached pleasurably in passion's aftermath, and unfamiliar contentment lulled his mind. The afternoon edged toward evening. Outside, rain fell, filling the room with cold, gray light.

He'd always watched her. From the first, when he'd been desperate to have her and her elusiveness had proven so frustrating. But after last night, it was as if she was giving him permission to stare. The pastime would never pall.

A feline smile curved her lush mouth as she caught his eye in the mirror. She knew he couldn't get enough of her, the witch.

She was the most intriguing mixture of sophistication and innocence. Over the last hours, the sophisticate had dominated. But at the height of their pleasure, he'd caught a flash in her eyes that had pierced straight to the soul he'd sworn he didn't possess.

Until now.

In the mirror, she regarded him with the thoughtful expression she'd worn downstairs.

Hell, he should have known she wouldn't forget her damnable questions. Perhaps he should have tried harder to divert her. Unbelievably, given what had just taken place, his body expressed its enthusiasm for the idea.

"Mr. Macleish said I should ask you about your father," she said evenly.

Blazing anger banished his sleepy well-being. He thrust himself up against the bedhead and glared at her with all the hauteur a duke could muster. "Did he, by God?"

"Yes," she said with remarkable calmness, considering his growl. "He wants me to cultivate a better opinion of you."

"I'll have his head on a plate," he muttered.

Hell, he wasn't just furious; he felt betrayed.

Hamish Macleish had witnessed every humiliating moment in a boyhood crammed with shame and pain. Someone bruiting those tribulations as idle gossip wounded him to the marrow.

"He presumes too much on old obligations." He used Cold Kylemore's voice, clipped, frigid, cutting. "As, madam, do you."

In the mirror, he watched the light fade from her shimmering gray eyes. "Yes, Your Grace," she said listlessly and returned to fiddling with her hair.

The formal address stung. It always had. But it smarted more today. He sighed and rose from the bed. Her expression indicated that he was unlikely to coax her back into it any time soon.

"Verity, allow me my secrets. This isn't a matter for frivolous chatter," he said heavily, drawing on his breeches. Obscurely, clothing felt like armor against her attack.

She set her brush down on the table with a sharp click. "I wasn't making frivolous chatter. Your precious secrets give you nightmares. When you scream, you call out for your father."

With jerky movements that indicated temper, she began to wind the thick black hair into a knot. He strode forward and took her busy hands in his. Bending down, he stared at her in the mirror. The slippery strands tumbled into disarray around her shoulders.

"Stop this, Verity."

"I'm trying to do my hair," she said crossly.

"It will wait. Or don't do it at all. I prefer it loose." He released her hands and stroked his palms down the side of her head until he held her face looking straight ahead into the glass. Defiant silver eyes met his.

"Can't we just enjoy what we have?" It was a plea. "We've only just found one another. Don't spoil it."

Her fine dark brows contracted in displeasure. "Soraya was paid to do what she was told, Your Grace. I'm afraid your next mistress is a woman of more independent character."

He laughed. He couldn't help it. "Soraya was no wilting violet either. Your memory plays you false, *mo leannan*."

"Stop using those outlandish foreign words to me," she snapped, irritated even further by his humor.

"It's English that's foreign here, *mo cridhe*." He bent to kiss her glossy crown.

"As you wish, Your Grace," she said woodenly.

She shook her head, dislodging his grip. He stayed behind her for another moment, then swung away to pace the room.

"Devil take you, you won't play me. Sulk as much as you like, but you won't make me your toy." He wouldn't accept this. His whole life, he'd fought his mother's self-serving machinations. He'd be damned before he accepted similar manipulation from his lover.

"As you wish, Your Grace."

Calmly, she returned to doing her hair. She ignored his request to leave it down. Pleasing him plainly wasn't her priority. The more agitated he became, the more composed she appeared.

The chit meant to provoke. And, damn her, she definitely provoked.

Looking cool and remote, she turned on the stool and faced him when she'd finished pinning up that luxuriant mass. "What is Your Grace's pleasure now?"

It was Soraya's voice and he hated it. He bit back a blistering setdown.

Because he read what she hid beneath her tranquility. And what he saw made his barren heart ache.

God, he'd hurt her. He couldn't bear it.

He'd sworn nothing would hurt her again. He'd sworn that

on his life when he'd brought her home from the mountains.

This moment revealed the value of his oath.

To save her from hurt, he'd injure himself, he'd injure others. He'd fight, lie, steal, kill. He'd do anything.

Anything except reveal his shame.

Hell, this wasn't worth it.

She wasn't worth it.

He snatched up his shirt and tugged it over his head. Then he turned on his heel and marched to the door. Let the baggage pout at not getting her own way. When they were back in London, he'd buy some pretty bauble to soothe the sting.

He stopped on the threshold. Oh, Lord, how he deceived himself.

Soraya would be content with such sops. He could only satisfy Verity with tribute more costly than even the most precious diamond.

Verity wanted his quivering, inadequate, vulnerable soul. And she wanted him on his knees when he offered it.

Damn her. Damn her to hell. He couldn't do this.

But what did his pride matter when he'd made her unhappy?

Nothing. Less than a single speck of dust.

Still, he couldn't bring himself to watch her face while he told her. Once, she'd loathed and despised him. With good reason.

After the miracle that had flowered between them since last night, his courage failed at the prospect of reviving her contempt. Slowly, he moved across to the window and looked through the bars onto the rain-swept glen.

"Madam, I will speak of this once and once only."

His voice was low with the control he exerted. The

humiliations he'd endured since his mistress ran away last spring paled in comparison to this bitter moment.

He waited for her to say something, perhaps encourage him to go on. If she called him Your Grace again, he honestly thought he might strike her. But she remained silent, though he felt her gaze trained steadily on his back.

He curled one hand hard against the window frame. "My father, the sixth duke, was a debaucher, a drunkard and an opium addict. The poisons he'd taken since his schooldays gradually but inexorably sent him mad. My mother had him confined in this glen to avoid the scandal of committing him to a lunatic asylum."

He paused for her to make some conventional expression of surprise or dismay or even denial.

She said nothing. Perhaps he'd already shocked her into speechlessness. Worse was to come, he grimly and silently told her.

He wished he didn't need to say more.

He steeled himself to continue. "My father's retinue included Hamish and a twelve-year-old mistress called Lucy. And my infant self. He had some idea snatching the heir would spite my mother." He used the same flat voice. "He never understood his wife. He hated her, but he certainly never understood her."

As though appearance of distance made it so in fact, he spoke quickly, unemotionally. Because, of course, the pain and fear still fed on him. They were close as his own skin.

Closer.

He no longer saw the rain-sodden view outside the window.

Instead, his head filled with the long, dark nights of debasement and imprisonment in this house. Long, dark nights that insidious memory melted into one endless night. He took a deep, shuddering breath, bracing himself to reveal the rest.

"When the mania was upon him—and it grew increasingly more severe—he became violent. Everyone within reach was at risk, but he took a particularly virulent hatred to me. Perhaps because I look so much like my mother. At his worst, he tried to kill me. Several times, he tried to kill himself."

He paused, the memories rising as poisonous as any adder. His voice was bitter as he continued. "He died in Lucy's arms when I was seven. The poor little bitch didn't know that his foul diseases would finish her a year later. After my father's death, my mother sent me to Eton while she evicted most of the tenants to starve or emigrate."

He paused again. Surely, Verity would say something now. Protest, express sympathy. Scoff, even. But the taut silence extended.

And extended.

Perhaps she gloated to see him brought so low. His mother would have relished the moment. She'd made it her lifetime's work to crush his pride and turn him into one of her creatures.

She'd never succeeded. But Verity could destroy him with one word.

Christ, he was so very tired of pretending to be the great Duke of Kylemore. He found a bleak freedom in owning to the truth behind his sham magnificence.

The silence continued.

Christ, what was wrong with her? Why the hell didn't she speak? Surely his pathetic confession deserved some response.

A gust of wind spattered cold rain against the windowpane.

What was the use of hiding? He had to face her. He was no

longer the frightened child he'd once been in this glen. Even so, making himself turn tested the limits of his courage.

As he moved, he hardly dared to look at her. What would he find in her face? Contempt? Pity? Triumph?

Or worse, indifference?

Slowly, his eyes traveled up from the trailing green hem of her dress. She hadn't shifted from her dressing stool, and her heavy hairbrush dangled in her lap. Reluctantly, he met her gaze.

And finally, finally, understood her silence.

Disbelievingly, he searched her beautiful face. Her eyes were stark with sorrow, and tears glittered on her cheeks.

"Oh, my dear," she said brokenly. She smiled shakily and held out one trembling hand in his direction.

His lonely, doubting heart opened to the beckoning gesture. He crossed the room in a couple of steps and stumbled to his knees at her side.

"Verity . . ." he whispered and buried his head in her lap, his arms lashing around her waist. The brush slid to the floor as she bent over him and surrounded him with warmth.

"It's over. It's over. I'm so sorry for what you went through. I'm so sorry." Her voice was husky with crying. "But you must have been such a brave little boy."

She kept murmuring over him, stroking his hair with a tenderness that made him want to weep.

But he didn't weep. Instead, he clung to her as the only good thing in his life. He stopped listening to her words and just let her endless compassion flow through him and melt the frozen emptiness at his center.

Closing his eyes, he surrendered to the welcoming blackness. A blackness full of sweet Verity.

And in that blackness, the truth that had skulked in his heart right from the beginning finally made itself heard.

He'd fled what he felt for so long that even now he resisted the inevitable moment.

But it was too late. The truth clawed into the light. He could do nothing to silence its clamoring insistence.

He'd had such a hunger for this woman's body because he had an even greater need of her soul.

She fulfilled him in ways he only started to understand, although his heart had always recognized her as his other half.

He'd committed crimes against her, used her, wanted her, hated her, mistreated her.

All the while, she'd been his only hope of redemption.

He knelt beside her, clutching at her like a man lost on a stormy sea. She'd faced hardship, loss and violence. She'd confronted them all with courage and an endless willingness to sacrifice herself for those she loved. She hadn't resorted, as he had, to the easy defenses of cynicism and indifference.

He loved her with every fiber of his being.

He loved her.

The oppressive weights of his solitude and anguish fell away. It wasn't even important that she didn't love him. Instead, he just felt the joyous relief of trusting himself to her and knowing she wouldn't betray him.

She'd seen the worst of him. Yet she accepted him.

One day, he'd tell her of the long, difficult years at Eton, where he'd arrived as a barely literate savage after inheriting the title. He'd been mocked, beaten and bullied by other boys only too quick to sense his essential isolation.

Thank God he'd inherited a good brain from his harpy of a mother. By the time he'd left for Oxford, his academic brilliance and cool noninvolvement had been the envy of his classmates. They'd never guessed the years of lonely training that had created Cold Kylemore out of the frightened barbarian dragged kicking and screaming from the only home he'd known.

He'd tell her about the ruin the shallow, self-obsessed creature who'd borne him had perpetrated in his name on the tenants while he'd stood by, powerless to stop the devastation she'd wreaked.

He'd threatened to grow into an equally shallow, self-obsessed creature.

What would have become of him if he hadn't surrendered to his curiosity about the woman who'd set tongues wagging the year he'd come into his inheritance? If he hadn't met a pair of wary silver eyes across a crowded London salon?

His need for Soraya—*Verity*—had always been his one weakness. He'd spent years struggling to break free of her.

Thank the Lord he hadn't.

Yes, one day, he'd tell her all of this.

Or maybe he no longer needed to. He had her understanding and forgiveness already. He felt it in her touch, in her soft voice as she whispered tender comfort over him.

And he had the privilege of loving her.

Chapter 21

~~~OC~~~

Verity noticed the change in the duke immediately. Her ruthless lover didn't exactly turn into an ordinary man, but his manner took on a new ease and lightness.

Nightmares no longer broke his sleep.

If the horrors of his childhood haunted her instead, that was the price of love. She should have immediately guessed monstrous deeds had occurred in this place, but she'd been too wrapped up in her own tribulations to notice the signs.

The bars on the windows, obviously installed years before her arrival. The duke's noticeable skittishness and reluctance to spend time inside. The house's air of long neglect and unspoken misery.

His dreams.

Oh, yes, his dreams should have alerted her. Even in London, she should have suspected anyone who maintained such inhuman control must hide suppurating wounds deep within.

She didn't gull herself into believing those wounds were

near to healed. But she prayed this new gentler, more open man had a chance to become whole at last.

The new Kylemore was inclined to play the slugabed. She didn't mind. Reward enough to watch the exhaustion and tension fade from his fine-boned face. Every night, he slumbered with perfect trust in her arms while she wept over the agonies he'd born so bravely and in such isolation. Wept in heartbroken silence. If he caught her crying, those preternaturally perceptive eyes would divine her secret love.

A week after the duke's devastating revelations about his childhood, Verity came downstairs one morning to discover him in the hallway. He balanced a stag head under each powerful arm.

"What are you doing?" she asked in astonishment.

"Making a pyre from our stern chaperons." He dropped his burdens without ceremony and came over to take her in his embrace. "Unless you'd like to keep them," he murmured into her hair.

"Heaven forbid." He was in his shirtsleeves, and the long muscles of his back flexed under her stroking hands.

Andy tramped in from outside and grabbed a pine marten and a particularly lugubrious badger from a pile she now noticed near the door. He hardly glanced at the entwined couple. She supposed he, like everyone else in the valley, was inured to the sight of her in Kylemore's arms.

Still, she blushed. It was absurd. She'd been a courtesan for thirteen years, yet during these last days, in spite of the wildest debaucheries of her life, part of her felt pure and reborn. Almost virgin.

A virgin with her first love.

Well, she thought with another concealed smile, while she was woefully far from a virgin, he was most definitely her first love.

"Can I help?" Ever since Kylemore's confession, she'd itched to strip the wretched memories from the house. Perhaps then he'd find peace.

Reluctantly, she drew away from him to watch Andy sling his load into a handcart at the door. "Kylemore?" she prompted softly.

He'd asked her to use his Christian name, but she didn't feel comfortable with the intimacy. It was nonsensical, when he treated her body as his private pleasure ground.

"You don't have to work as my skivvy, *mo leannan*."

"I'm sure if a duke of the realm can get his hands dirty, a peasant like me can too," she said dryly.

Without waiting for his agreement, she went into the parlor and gasped at the chaos. Hamish and Angus stood on stools in front of adjoining walls, wrenching the parade of animal heads down with crowbars and brute strength. They greeted her, then went back to their task.

"Your grandfather clearly wanted his trophies to hang until the crack of doom," she said and promptly sneezed as the largest of the heads crashed to the floor in a cloud of dust.

"Here." Kylemore passed her a handkerchief that cost more than she'd have earned in a year as a servant. "I wasn't joking about the dirt."

"Apparently not," she said after blowing her nose. "I'll look after the smaller things."

She turned to the massive glass-and-mahogany specimen cases, which displayed examples of the valley's wildlife. She'd hated these poor, stiff, dead animals from the moment she'd seen them. She reached in with great satisfaction and tugged out a stuffed weasel.

Clearing the room took most of the day. Once, she'd never have believed the magnificent Duke of Kylemore would lower himself to such menial work. At the very least, he wouldn't have subjected his perfect tailoring to such despoliation. But now, she wasn't surprised to see him work diligently and un-complainingly beside his servants.

How she'd misunderstood him in London. And she'd al-ways considered herself a clever woman!

As Hamish, Angus and Andy carried out stag's head after stag's head, something new seeped into the atmosphere. Something that felt like happiness.

But for her, it was a happiness tinged with regret. It was a happiness that couldn't endure.

Verity carefully straightened from the bottom shelf of the last case. She put a hand behind her aching back. To think she'd once worked like this every day as a maid in Sir Charles Norton's manor. She must be getting old.

She turned her head and caught Kylemore studying her from the corner. His dark blue eyes held a familiar glint that sent blood pounding low and heavy in her belly.

Perhaps she wasn't that old after all.

They were alone for the first time that afternoon. After a murmured discussion with the duke, the others had disap-peared to consign the last gruesome decorations to the bonfire.

He stepped over the only remaining detritus, a quartet of remarkably bloodthirsty hunting scenes, and crossed to her side. With one elegant hand, he tilted her chin toward the light flooding through the large windows on her left.

"You have dirt on your cheek, *mo cridhe*." A gentle smile flickered across his face. "Soraya would be ashamed of you."

Once, the reference to Soraya would have stung. Once, he would have intended it to sting. They'd moved far beyond those days, but even so, she suffered a twinge of insecurity.

She looked searchingly into his face. "Do you miss her?"

He raised his other hand and smoothed the tendrils of

hair that escaped the braids twined around her head. "Why would I? She's here. She's Verity." A very male satisfaction deepened his smile. "And she's mine."

Verity didn't bother arguing. They both knew it was true. As they both knew that while this idyll lasted, he was hers.

When surrender was so equal, what shame was there in defeat? She cast him a searing glance under her lashes. She'd quickly learned that particular look drove him wild with desire.

Predictably, the fingers on her chin tightened and his voice roughened into urgency. "I want you now."

Not the most subtle seduction, but the heat of his body and the intent glow in his eyes were enough for her. Sometimes, he wooed with sweet words and extravagant compliments. Sometimes, he swept her off her feet with a forceful passion that made her heart race.

Right now, she read the sapphire blaze in his eyes and saw he was too impatient to devote time to preliminaries. She didn't mind. "Let's go upstairs."

He shook his head and his smile took on a devilish edge. "No, I mean *now*."

She felt her eyes widen. "But anyone could come in."

"They won't. I've dismissed them for the day." He let her go and strode across to lock the door. "Take off your drawers and lie down on the rug." His voice was uncompromising.

Verity gave a shiver of anticipation at the brazen demand but didn't immediately obey. "Just my drawers, Your Grace?"

"For now." He turned to face her and tapped the room key on his palm, all aristocratic impatience. Only the hard bulge that pressed against his breeches belied his aura of control.

She bent her head to conceal her gathering excitement. "As you wish."

She heard his breath catch as she raised her skirts to reach the strings. A few quick tugs and her underwear sagged to lie at her feet. She stepped out of it and draped it with deliberate provocation over the massive oak chair she'd noticed on her first day here.

The cream silk, with its elaborate embroidery of violets and lilies, looked incongruous against the heavily carved wood. Like a banner of challenge. Which, of course, it was.

His eyes were avid as he watched her every movement from where he stood near the door. She felt like a rabbit in a fox's sights. But in this case, the rabbit was more than happy to be devoured. Her pulse skittered when she saw his gaze dwell on her drawers, shamelessly displayed for his delectation.

"The rug," he said hoarsely.

She hid a gloating smile. His autocratic manner had cracked already. It hadn't taken much effort on her part.

Without a word, she crossed the room and reclined on the red-and-blue Persian carpet in front of the unlit fire. She bent one knee in his direction and parted her legs slightly. He wouldn't be able to resist the bold invitation.

Oh, what a wicked, wicked woman she was to taunt him. He really ought to punish her.

She closed her eyes and waited on a thrilling edge of suspense for him to come to her.

She didn't have to wait long. The key clattered onto the table, and suddenly he was on his knees between her legs. He'd moved so fast that she hadn't even heard him cross the room.

"You think I'm putty in your hands, don't you?" he growled. He wasn't touching her. But he would soon, she knew.

Verity pretended a yawn, knowing it would push him to the bounds of his control. How she loved teasing him like this. "Yes."

He gave a rueful laugh. "And you're right, damn you."

Over his uneven breathing, she listened to the faint rustle of his clothing as he released the front of his breeches. She couldn't mistake his eagerness. Her heart moved from a restless trot to a careening gallop that surely he must hear. She raised her other leg a fraction just so he knew she hadn't finished tormenting him yet.

He roughly bunched her skirts and petticoats at her waist. Her excitement rose as the air flowed cool across her bare skin. She must look utterly depraved, lying before him in such abandonment. But she didn't feel depraved, she felt free.

She let her legs fall open a little more. Even without opening her eyes, she felt the heated inspection he made of her. The room was silent, apart from the accelerating scratch of his breath.

He placed his hands on her knees and ruthlessly drew them wide apart. The heat of his palms through the thin silk of her stockings made her tremble with excitement.

With her eyes shut, all her other senses became more acute. She could smell his arousal and hear the unsteady rattle of his inhalations as he fought to contain himself. She shifted sinuously against the thick rug and waited for him to thrust into her. He must know she was ripe for his possession.

But he didn't immediately take her as she'd expected him to do. Instead, his head nudged between her legs and his silky hair brushed against the sensitive skin of her thighs. She gave a start of surprise as the warmth of his breath touched her damp center. Then his mouth took her and she gave a low moan of rapture. He sucked and licked at her until she quivered beneath him.

He was a devil. He was *her* devil.

Her spine arched into a rigid curve as the tension inside her built to an unbearable pitch. He took a firm grip on her hips and shifted her so he could taste her more fully. As his tongue penetrated her, she shuddered in primitive response. But she wanted more.

"Please," she begged raggedly, her fingers clenching and unclenching in his thick hair. She pressed herself closer, hovering on the brink. But still he played with her, forcing her higher and higher.

Then he drew hard on the source of her pleasure, and she screamed as a hundred suns exploded behind her eyes. Fire cascaded along her veins, and every muscle in her body spasmed with blinding delight.

The blazing peak seemed to last forever. She hung suspended in the splendor only he could create in her. He made her dance among the stars. How she adored him.

When the fiery joy had subsided into rippling aftershocks, she opened her eyes to find him watching her from between her splayed legs. She lay exposed, and enough of her girlhood self remained for her to slide one hand down to fiddle her skirts into modesty. Even that simple action tested her strength. She felt as though her bones had turned into wet muslin.

"We're not finished yet," he murmured, stopping her before she could cover herself.

"I don't think I could move a muscle," she protested.

It wasn't true. Already, her interest stirred. Just because he looked at her as if she were a miracle sent down to him from heaven. Sometimes his sway over her frightened her.

"I think you could." His lips curled in a smile of promise.

He hooked his arms around her and drew her upright so she knelt facing him when he sat back on his heels. She rested one hand on his chest. Her fingers tightened in his shirt as she felt his furious heartbeat beneath the fine white lawn. Then he lifted her over him until her dark green skirts settled around them, lending a spurious decorum to their profligacy.

But beneath that concealing material, she straddled him, open and ready for his entry. His erection pressed imperiously against the damp curls at the base of her belly, making her womb clench with a pang of desire.

She wanted all that heat and power. She wanted him inside her.

She grasped his sinewy shoulders with both hands and raised herself up and forward. His hold on her back tightened convulsively and she watched his eyes go opaque as she slowly slid down upon him. Even wet as she was, there was a moment's delicious resistance before she took all of him. His breath escaped in a rasping sigh when she settled around him. She gave a mew of pleasure as she stretched to accommodate his size.

Their gazes met, meshed, held. She read in his eyes that for now, he was willing to let her set the pace. A knowledge of her own power thrilled her as she established an undulating rhythm on him, almost withdrawing, then descending to accept him fully. Every thrust probed deep.

At times like this, the bond between them seemed unbreakable, although she knew that could never be true. She loved him slowly, thoroughly, intently, giving him all of herself with each rise and fall of her body.

He dragged her up for a long, passionate kiss. He used his tongue and teeth on her mouth as he'd used his tongue and teeth on her core. She tasted her juices in his kiss.

The idea was astonishingly arousing. Her interior muscles contracted to grip him, and she moved more quickly.

Her peak was so close. So close. She clenched her hands in the front of his shirt as she hurtled toward the abyss.

He tore his mouth from hers and flung his head back as he strained into her. All vestige of control disintegrated in the frenzy. She bit and scratched at him like an animal and reveled in her wildness.

Her climax hit with blinding force just as he wrenched upward and erupted into her. Even through her crisis, she felt the scalding heat of his seed flood her. For an eon of flame, she clung to him while her world reeled around her.

When it was over, they collapsed upon the rug. Verity sprawled across Kylemore's heaving chest and listened as his heart gradually calmed. Her body ached with glorious exhaustion. She wasn't convinced she'd ever have the energy to move again.

Surely one day she would die of this pleasure. But not yet.

After a long, emotion-filled silence, he raised a shaking hand to touch her hair. She felt the tenderness in the caress right to her toes.

"Now there are no more ghosts," he said softly.

Following the destruction of his grandfather's grisly trophies, Verity thought that Kylemore had finally sloughed off the miseries of his past. As each day passed in a haze of joy, she began to nurture fragile hope that he'd vanquished his demons.

Unfortunately, her own demons clamored closer and closer.

And they wanted blood.

In this secret valley, the world didn't intrude. It hardly mattered that Kylemore was one of the kingdom's greatest noblemen or she was a harlot with a name bandied about in every tavern from John O'Groats to Land's End.

But she couldn't forget the duke had responsibilities he ignored. He must wed and beget an heir. And it was brutally apparent he couldn't marry his mistress, in spite of his insane proposal in Kensington. She guessed now that he'd intended his marriage as an attack against his family. Thank God that confused, angry man no longer existed.

Every moment with Kylemore, every time they made love so sweetly, every time they laughed or argued or spoke quietly by the fire after a long, fulfilled day, she knew that as long as she stayed, he'd never seek a wife.

He hadn't said he loved her, just as she hadn't said she loved him. But each look, each gesture, each word announced that his attachment to her was the kind that shook kingdoms.

And a fallen woman like her wasn't worthy.

Loving her would destroy him. She couldn't bear to see him debased, mocked and derided because he was brave and good enough to see past her notoriety to the real woman. She had to make him release her.

But as every new day dawned and she woke in his arms, drowsy, happy, replete, she promised herself she'd leave him tomorrow.

When the time came, it struck her with the force of a physical blow.

At this latitude, autumn set in quickly and the night air carried a chill even while the hillsides were still hazy purple with heather. Kylemore came into the parlor carrying the fresh scent of the late afternoon with him.

Verity had difficulty remembering her elegant protector. After a month in Scotland, his hair had grown and he looked tanned and relaxed. In his rough clothes, one could easily mistake him for a well-to-do farmer. Until one noted the effortless command in his stance.

"What?" he asked as he caught her watching him from where she stood at the window.

"I was just thinking what a handsome lover I've got," she said with perfect honesty.

It never failed to surprise her how patently unused he was to compliments. He gave her an embarrassed half smile.

"Och, but you're a foolish wee lassie."

She laughed at the theatrically broad brogue. "Well, if you doubt me, ask Morag and Kirsty. I swear those girls go red as rowan berries just at the sound of your voice."

It was true. The duke's improved temper had percolated

through the whole household so even the maids, once utterly in awe of him, had taken to mooning after him like lost lambs.

Not that he noticed. Once she'd thought him puffed up with conceit, but personal vanity had been only another element in the complex disguise he'd cultivated in London.

"They're as foolish as you are, *mo cridhe*."

Hamish had told her *mo cridhe* meant "my heart" and *mo leannan* meant "my beloved." She knew she shouldn't quiver with delight every time Kylemore used the endearments, but she couldn't help it.

He was right. She was most definitely a foolish lassie.

Kylemore crossed to take her hand and lead her toward the couch in front of the grate. A fire was a constant feature now the year drew in.

"I want to talk to you."

He didn't sound as if he had anything serious on his mind. He lounged against the cushions like a young sultan contemplating his favorite concubine.

"For the last time, I don't want to learn to ride." She sat next to him.

"No, it's something else." He raised the hand he held and placed a kiss on her palm. "I've missed you," he murmured.

She gave a husky laugh and leaned forward to press her mouth briefly to his. How she loved this physical ease. It bubbled under the surface of her new life as an ever-flowing source of joy.

"You've only been away for the afternoon."

"I know, but I still missed you." Gently, he folded her fingers closed as if to keep his kiss safe.

"Now who's foolish?" She reached up to stroke the silky dark hair back from his face. "Shall I cut your hair tonight? You're turning into a shaggy Highlander. I find myself quite terrified of you."

"My valet at Kylemore Castle sees to such tasks."

"Yes, but . . ." Then, as though she staggered under a punch, she understood the significance of what he'd just said. "Kylemore Castle," she repeated, although she'd heard him perfectly clearly.

"Autumn's closing in, Verity. We can't stay over winter. The place is uninhabitable and totally inaccessible. Not to mention colder than an ice cave in Hades."

He spoke as if what he said was reasonable, while in reality, it rang the death knell to all her happiness.

"I . . . I see," she said shakily.

And of course, she did.

Their idyll had lasted a little over three weeks. Twenty-two short days. Such a paltry reward for her lonely years of struggle.

It wasn't fair, she wanted to rage although she'd come to terms with life's essential unfairness at fifteen.

Just another week. Another day.

I'm not ready to give you up yet.

And all the while, she knew no reprieve would ever be enough unless it promised forever. And forever couldn't be.

"So can you be ready to leave tomorrow?" Still that calm voice went on as if he didn't crush her with every measured word. "Angus and Andy have left to sail the boat in from the coast. They and Hamish travel with us. The others will pack up the house and follow when the boat returns to collect them."

"So soon?" she whispered. Once she'd loathed every blade of grass in this valley. Now it broke her heart to leave.

Oh, Verity, a voice inside her whispered. *It's not leaving the valley that breaks your heart and you know it.*

"This far north, the weather can turn in an instant. I want to be sure I get you out safely."

"Yes," she said dully. "Of course I'll be ready."

At her side, hidden from his eyes, her free hand clenched into a fist as she battled for control.

He frowned, and she saw he finally registered her distress. He was usually so quick to pick up on her slightest reaction, but practical matters distracted him this afternoon.

"What's wrong?" He pressed another kiss to her tense fingers. "Don't worry, *mo gradh*. You'll like the castle. It looks out to sea and has acres of gardens for you to devastate."

She couldn't summon a smile. Not when her world crumbled around her. "Yes," she said blankly.

He paused, studying her with a puzzled expression. She couldn't doubt she had his complete attention now.

"And the castle is closer to medical attention if you need it," he said slowly.

That startled her out of her dazed misery. "I'm not sick. I'm never sick."

He smiled as if he were the happiest man in the world. "No, but you may already carry my child."

Wrenching her hand from his, she struggled to her feet. She spun around to face him with her back to the fireplace. She shivered with such cold that she hardly noticed the warmth of the flames.

"No. No, that's not possible."

His dark blue eyes remained steady. "I'd say it's more than possible."

She sucked in a deep breath to calm her agitation. "You don't understand. I'm barren."

It was foolish to be ashamed to admit something she'd accepted for so long, yet ashamed she was.

"You can't know that," he said evenly.

She curled her hands at her sides so hard that the nails bit into her palms. "Yes, I can. Even when they use preventatives, women get caught. I've slept with men since I was fifteen. I'm twenty-eight and I've never conceived." At first, her infertility had seemed a blessing, but as the years had passed, she'd come to abhor her unnatural state. "I . . . I still took precautions, but more from habit than necessity."

"You're guessing," he said firmly.

"It's fairly certain," she returned with equal firmness.

He rose to stand in front of her. Thank God, he didn't touch her. She couldn't bear it if he touched her now. Her determination to leave him was shaky enough as it was.

"Verity, Sir Eldreth was well past his first vigor. Mallory, from what I gather, wasn't ardent in his attentions. You and I were always careful in London. We've been both passionate and careless in this house." His eyes were alight with joy. "A happy arrival next spring is indeed likely."

Was it true? Could Kylemore's child already grow inside her?

She hadn't had her monthly flow in weeks. But then, her cycle had always been erratic.

Oh, let it be so! She'd give anything to feel his child move within her. She'd lavish on his son or daughter all the love that his own childhood had so cruelly lacked.

He went on as if he hadn't just shattered one of the certainties she'd based her life upon. "I don't want you trapped here in the middle of winter if something goes wrong."

The heart that had surged with hope sank back to misery.

If by some miracle she had his baby, she'd have to raise the infant without him, because the possibility of pregnancy did nothing to change their essential dilemma. It merely added cruel spice to her anguish.

She struggled to hide the extent of her devastation. Once she might have succeeded. Now, she doubted she'd fool him.

But she had to try. For his sake, she had to try.

She took another deep breath. "I'm not coming to Kylemore Castle."

He didn't immediately understand. Why should he?

"Would you rather go somewhere else? I have other houses. Or we could travel. Or return to London, if you like."

Heavens, this was difficult. She moistened dry lips. "No, I'll return to my brother at Whitby. For the moment, at least."

"Whitby?" he echoed, and she witnessed the exact moment he comprehended. His face stiffened in shock. "You want to leave me." The words emerged so starkly that she almost relented.

Seeing how grievously this sudden rejection wounded him made her want to die. Then she reminded herself she did this for his sake. Somewhere in the bleak years that stretched ahead, she might find succor in that thought.

"Yes." Pray God he didn't hear the ocean of despair beneath her lie.

She braced herself for temper. Once, she'd angered him into committing a capital crime. This, she knew, was a worse betrayal than deserting him in London. She'd spoken no promises in these weeks, but each moment had been proof of her faith.

Just as, heaven help her, each moment had been proof of his.

He remained calm, although his face had paled to a stony bleakness. "Do you intend to tell me why?"

How she hurt him. She knew and hated it. But she had to do this. A duke and a whore could have no future. Or no future where they could live in honor. Each day they spent together only made the inevitable parting more painful and delayed him from doing what he must.

Or so her mind told her.

Her heart insisted no pain could be worse than what she suffered now.

She gathered her courage into a tight knot. Now she must

become all Soraya. Proud, determined, cold. Verity's yearning heart mustn't deflect her from what she must do. "In London, we had an agreement. If either partner wanted to end the liaison, it was over. Well, I want to end it, Your Grace."

He winced at her use of his title as if she struck him. "Is that the best you can do? Good-bye and good luck and we go our separate ways?" he said sharply. "Damn you, I think you owe me more than that. What the hell is going on, Verity? Why did everything change when I mentioned leaving the glen?"

She should have known he wouldn't just accept her decision to abandon him without question or argument. She couldn't tell him the truth; he'd never accept her reasons for going. He believed he warranted nothing better than a strumpet for a duchess.

But she knew differently. She came to him with a ruined soul, when he needed someone good and pure and whole.

Someone who was everything Soraya was not.

She turned her head away, unwilling to watch his pain and bewilderment. "I've known I had to leave for a long time." She fought to maintain her controlled tone. "It's time for you to take up your life and for me to take up mine."

"You are my life! I won't allow you to go," he said wildly, tugging her around to him. "Don't do this, *mo cridhe!*"

She stood unmoving in his bruising grasp and gazed up into his tormented face. "In honor, you can demand nothing of me. You said you'd never force me again. Is your word worth nothing? If you truly have changed from the man who abducted me, you won't prolong this discussion."

She was cruel to use his sins as leverage to gain her freedom, just as she was cruel to remind him of that magical night when she'd finally given herself with her whole heart.

His face was ashen as he released her. "So yet again, you

desert me with no explanation? At least this time I suppose I'm grateful you told me you're going."

"Oh, try and find it in you to forgive me!" she cried, her resolution failing as she reached out to touch his arm.

He flinched away before she made contact. She mourned the spontaneous caresses of only minutes ago.

"Madam, it's your prerogative to leave. It's mine to feel what rancor I wish."

"So . . . so you won't compel me to stay with you?" she asked unsteadily. Had she been wicked enough to hope he would?

He shook his head. "My crimes against you are unforgivable. Because of what I did, I endangered your life. I acknowledge I have no right to keep you. I'd . . ." Her heart contracted in misery as his flat voice broke briefly, revealing the blistering agony beneath his calm facade. "I'd hoped you'd stay of your own will. But clearly that is impossible after all I've done."

His formality reminded her of the self-contained lover in Kensington. The contrast with the man she'd come to know made her want to scream. He'd had a lifetime of stifling his real emotions. She felt like the worst sort of traitor for forcing him back into his frozen insulation.

"I'm sorry, Kylemore," she said unhappily, loving him, hating herself.

A quickly masked anger darkened his eyes before they took on the hooded expression she'd wanted never to see again.

"So am I, madam." He stalked toward the door. "We shall leave tomorrow as planned. From Kylemore Castle, I'll escort you to Whitby."

A drawn-out farewell would exceed her frail limits. "You don't have to do that."

"Yes, I do," he snapped with a resurgence of anger. "I removed you from your home by force. I am obliged to see you return safely." He bowed coldly in her direction and left the room before she could muster an argument.

Verity's hand curled over the back of the settle to stop herself from running after him. She didn't think she'd ever loved him so much.

Chapter 22

T he glen had never looked as beautiful as it did the next morning. The trees had just begun to change color, and on the open hillside, heather glowed rich purple. The breeze blew fresh and strong as the boat slid smoothly through the clear waters of the loch.

Kylemore looked around at the splendor and wished it all to hell.

A few feet away, Verity stood at the rail. She was pale and silent, and she appeared not to have managed much more sleep than he had.

Last night, for the first time since she'd come to him and offered herself so sweetly . . .

He wrenched the thought to a screaming halt.

Remembering the transcendent splendors of that night only made him want to smash something.

Last night, they had slept separately.

Or, to be more accurate, he'd stretched out on his mean little cot and stared into space, cursing her, loving her, yearning for her. And knowing he couldn't do one damned thing about any of it.

No persuasion he could muster canceled her right to freedom. So he'd suffered alone and silent as he'd suffered so many times before.

He should be conditioned to lonely torment. Except this time, he'd been raised from hell to paradise, then just as abruptly flung back into hell.

He'd endure. He always had.

Although right now, the point of it all escaped him.

He reached up to soothe a restless Tannasg, who had never liked water travel. While he rubbed the huge gray's nose, his eyes sharpened on Verity. For a woman who had done everything in her power to leave this glen, she didn't look happy.

In fact, she looked downright tragic.

It didn't make sense. None of this made sense.

Yesterday, they'd been together. Today, quite clearly, they weren't. And he had no idea why.

The last three weeks had been the happiest of his life. He'd even begun, unwisely, to make plans.

Because of that asinine proposal in London—no wonder she'd sent him away with a flea in his ear; he'd been an overweening blockhead—he'd been loath to speak of marriage. His scheme had been to integrate her into his life, accustom her to the idea of staying with him, and coax her into accepting him as her husband.

It was too late for him to change the past, much as he longed to. After the way he'd treated her, he could never hope she'd love him as he loved her. But they shared desire and friendship. He could be satisfied with that. If he must.

A child would be a blessed addition to the life he planned.

A child born legitimately, of course.

He had no great wish to perpetuate the poisoned blood of

the Kinmurries, but a miniature Verity—now, that would be a glorious gift to the world.

How proud he'd be to know she nurtured his seed within her. If she didn't, it wasn't for want of trying on his part. His pleasure at the thought of her bearing his child evaporated when he realized he'd never make love to her again.

His pointless dream of a life with her faded like the morning fog that had shrouded their departure. The brutal fact was she didn't love him.

He could survive on the sops of desire and friendship if he had to. Clearly and rightly, she wasn't prepared to settle for such a paltry bargain.

His fist bunched against Tannasg's glossy hide and the horse whickered softly, as if sensing his distress and anger.

By God, he wouldn't let this happen. He'd bloody well make her stay. When they reached Kylemore, he'd lock her up in the highest tower until she saw sense. Until she promised to marry him and be his duchess and keep the ghosts away forever.

Just as he'd locked her up at the hunting box.

His sigh was heavy. He couldn't imprison her. He'd already used physical force to keep her with him. He couldn't do it again.

Honor had never been a particularly hardy plant in the fetid garden of his soul, but somewhere in the last weeks, it had set roots he couldn't eradicate. After what he'd done to Verity, after what she'd endured before becoming his mistress, he had no right to deny her what she wanted.

But it hurt. It hurt like hell.

Before noon on the second day, they reached Kylemore's ancestral home. Grimly, he watched the fairy-tale jumble of towers and turrets come into view along the coast.

This was where he'd planned to establish a life with Verity as his unconventional duchess. But all his hopes had since disintegrated to dust.

The wind had blown fair and they'd made good time down to Inverathie, the village that clustered around the castle. Even so, he'd wished the boat could have grown wings and flown. Anything to save him from Verity's silent, unhappy presence.

Then he'd realized that with every mile they traveled, they were a mile closer to parting. And he'd wished the voyage would never end.

Hamish stepped up to where Kylemore stood at the rail. Behind them, Angus and Andy took the ship into port with the skill of long practice.

"Am I still tae return tae the glen tomorrow, Your Grace?" Hamish asked.

Even his old mentor had gone back to addressing him formally. He'd only been allowed to feel part of humanity for a fleeting moment.

"Yes," he said. "Take Angus with you. Andy comes with me when I escort *madame* back to Whitby."

"Whitby?" Hamish frowned in confusion. "The lassie doesnae stay on at Inverathie?"

"Hasn't she told you?" There was a bite to the question. "You've been clucking around her like a mother hen long enough on this voyage to exchange a parcel of confidences."

He sounded jealous, he knew. But Verity had so carefully avoided him—a difficult feat on this small boat—while she'd readily accepted Hamish's company.

Hamish eyed him with a disapproval familiar since they'd left the glen. "The lassie hasnae told me anything. Even when I've caught her crying."

Kylemore's gut twisted with anguish. He couldn't take much more of this. Yet he must. He still had the long journey overland to Whitby ahead of him. He owed it to her to return her safely to her brother.

"I'm sure the lady's tears are her own concern," he said through gritted teeth.

"Hers and yours, Your Grace."

"You presume too much," he said coldly.

Hamish's weathered features expressed a disappointment equal to his disapproval. "Aye, weel, I presume you're a young fool who doesnae appreciate the bonny treasure he's about tae lose. And, aye, Your Grace, there's no need tae put me in my place. I'll go away now before I presume you right intae the seas for a good dunking."

Kylemore didn't bother rebuking the older man for his insolence. Of course he knew the value of what he lost. The painful knowledge threatened to shatter him. But for all his cleverness, he couldn't work out how to lure Verity back.

As Kylemore escorted Verity down the gangway to the small wharf, he noted a disturbance among the crowd milling around the dock. He paid little heed and concentrated instead on the woman who lightly held his arm.

This was the first time she'd touched him since she'd ended their affair. He resisted the urge to grab those fragile fingers and bundle her away to some place where she'd never escape him. To have her so close yet so unreachable was a punishment harsher than anything he could have devised even at the peak of his vengeful rage.

The hubbub below grew more insistent. The duke's presence at his family seat was a rare enough occurrence to warrant curiosity from the locals, he supposed. He looked past the curtseying and bowing villagers in his immediate vicinity to see what caused the commotion.

"Are we to set out for Whitby immediately, Your Grace?" Verity asked in a husky voice.

They were the first words she'd addressed to him all day. She sounded as if she'd been crying. Hamish said she had been. The knot of pain in Kylemore's belly tightened to agony.

Immediately he forgot the noise on the dock and focused on her. She looked pale and tired and sad, but determined.

He wondered what went on in her head. For a cruelly short interval, they'd been so close that he'd have known immediately.

"Wouldn't you rather rest here today?"

They were on the quay now. He waited for her to move away. When she didn't, he couldn't suppress his relief. She'd kept herself so separate during the last days that even this small concession seemed important.

"I still don't think it's necessary for you to accompany me," she said in a stronger voice.

"Well, I do."

Once that arrogant assertion would have roused an argument. Now she merely bent her head in silent acquiescence. The hand she'd placed on his sleeve trembled.

All the fight had been knocked out of her. He couldn't understand it. She'd gotten what she wanted—the chance to leave him. She should be joyfully anticipating a new life. A new life, damn it, free from his interference.

Perhaps she was ill after all. Concern made him frown as he tried to see her face under the brim of her smart chip bonnet. As he bent over her with a protectiveness he knew to his chagrin she didn't want, he was vaguely aware of someone looming up behind him.

"You bastard!"

A powerful hand grabbed him by the shoulder and swung him around. Kylemore had a moment to register a pair of furious black eyes before a huge fist powered into his face.

"Jesus!" He released Verity and staggered back.

"Better call to Satan, your master!"

Benjamin Ashton punched him in the face again, and this

time he went down against the cobbles in an ungainly stumble. Uproar shook the crowd, but nobody stepped forward to manhandle his assailant or to help him to his feet.

"Ashton . . ." Kylemore said, trying to sit up. He shook his head to clear it and raised a shaking hand to his bruised jaw to check if it was broken.

Apparently not, although it hurt like the very devil.

"Ben, stop!" Verity screamed from somewhere in the crowd.

"I'll stop when he's a dead man," Ashton snarled. "Get up, you whoreson. Damned if I'll kick you when you're down."

"Ben!" Through the ringing in his ears, Kylemore heard Verity defend him. "Ben, he's bringing me back to you."

Unsteadily, Kylemore struggled to his feet and brushed himself off. "Get out of the way, Verity."

"Aye, get out of the way, Verity," Ashton said grimly. "I need to teach His Grace a lesson."

He bunched his fists for another assault. Although Kylemore prepared to defend himself, his heart wasn't in it. Ashton had every right to pound him to a pulp.

Hell, he hoped the brute killed him.

He shook his head again to bring the world back into kilter. He had trouble focusing his eyes, and his ears buzzed like a thousand angry bees.

In a whirl of claret merino, Verity threw herself in front of him. "Ben, if you want to hurt him, you'll have to go through me first," she snapped.

"So he's hiding behind a lass's skirts now," Ben sneered.

"You heard me, Benjamin Ashton," she said firmly.

"Verity, stand aside," Kylemore said wearily. The hum in his head gradually subsided, but the side of his face stung like merry hell. "He won't hurt me."

"Yes, he will," she said stubbornly and without moving. "He'll kill you. You heard him."

"Verity, there must be a hundred people watching us. Someone will stop him before he does too much damage."

Now that he was capable of thought, he was actually surprised that no one had stepped in to restrain his assailant before now.

Ah, yes. Relief was on the way.

His bailiff raced up with a couple of estate workers in tow just as Angus and Andy leaped onto the dock. Hamish had observed the whole scene imperviously from the boat.

Kylemore supposed that all that angry Yorkshire muscle intimidated the villagers. A justified reaction, he admitted, blearily eyeing his assailant's brawny form.

Ashton's rage remained banked behind his black eyes, but at last he glanced at his sister, who stood as a barrier between him and her kidnapper. "Are you all right, lass? By God, if he's hurt you, I'll kill him in truth."

"Your Grace!" The bailiff arrived, panting in his heavy black coat and old-fashioned knee breeches. "This villain's rampaging around the estate accusing you of terrible crimes. I've warned him you'll have him in the stocks for slander."

"Aye, and I'll see this overbred wastrel hang for rape and kidnap," Ashton growled. "Verity lass, tell them what he did to you."

"Ben . . ." she said unsteadily.

"Go on, tell them. Tell them how he set those great bully boys on me and abducted you at the point of a gun. I've had no rest for weeks imagining what you've suffered."

Kylemore braced himself for the scalding condemnation he deserved. If she chose to denounce him, he had no defense.

She lifted her chin in a gesture he found heartbreakingly familiar. Her face was pale and set with proud determination.

"I am the Duke of Kylemore's mistress and I am with him of my own free will," she said loudly enough for all around them to hear. Then softly and in a broken voice, she added, "I'm sorry, Ben."

Kylemore was moved beyond words to hear her claim him so unequivocally as her lover. How he loved her. He'd do anything for her. Anything. Including let her go if that was what she really wanted. In spite of their estrangement, he took her in his arms. Without hesitation, she leaned into him.

Bewilderment replaced the violence in Ashton's expression. "Verity lass?"

Kylemore found it in himself to pity the man's confusion. Benjamin Ashton wasn't the villain here. He merely protected his sister. It wasn't his fault the game had become considerably more complicated since that stormy day in Whitby.

Kylemore spoke over the top of Verity's head, which rested with a trust he couldn't help but cherish on his chest. "Come up to the house, man. It does your sister's honor no credit to stand around brawling in the public street."

Ashton's "You give nowt for my sister's honor," clashed with his bailiff's protests. "Your Grace, this lout is a public menace. Surely you want him in custody."

Kylemore quelled his bailiff's objections with a glare. "No, I think not." He looked around and found what he wanted. "We'll take your carriage. I'll send it back for you."

The bailiff wrung his hands in nervousness. "Your Grace, there's something else I have to tell you."

The man was thorough but inclined to fuss. Details of estate management could wait.

"Later, McNab," Kylemore snapped.

"But, Your Grace . . ." The man all but clucked with anxiety.

"I said later, man. Andy will drive. Ashton, if you'll ride with us?"

The tone of ducal authority had the required effect on everyone, including the fractious Mr. Ashton and the fluttering Mr. McNab. The mob dispersed as Kylemore lifted Verity very gently up into his arms. Immediately, her lush scent filled his senses, reminding him piercingly of other times they had been as close as this, times when they'd been even closer and he thought he'd die with pure rapture.

"I can walk," she protested.

"I know, *mo cridhe*." The endearment slipped out although he knew he no longer had any right to use it. "But allow me to do you this service."

She nodded and curled her arms around his neck as he limped across the flagstones to McNab's carriage. His body ached after his pounding at Ashton's hands, but there was no way in heaven or hell he was putting her down. Having Verity in his arms was too sweet.

He'd never hold her like this again.

What she'd said to her brother still echoed in his mind—would always echo in his mind.

He glanced back at Ashton to see if he meant to cooperate. The fellow hesitated, then followed, his face stiff with barely controlled anger.

Verity still trembled with reaction as she sat next to Kylemore and opposite Ben in the carriage. The rig wasn't designed to hold two such large men at one time, and space was cramped. It seemed more restricted because of the hostility smoldering between her companions.

"Stop it, both of you! You're acting like schoolboys!" she snapped when the door closed on them. "Kylemore, he had every right to hit you. Ben, if I've forgiven him for abducting me, you can too."

"I've run myself ragged all over the country seeking you, lass," Ben returned with equal ill humor. "I've been to London and to at least a dozen of this bastard's estates. The bugger's got his mucky paws on half the kingdom."

"Mind your language, sirrah!" Kylemore growled. "You're in the presence of a lady."

"I know that. But you've treated her nowt better than some trull you picked up at Covent Garden for a shilling."

"Shut your mouth, man, or I'll shut it for you."

"The lass has been in my charge for the last four years. There's nowt you can teach me about how to look after her," Ben sneered.

"Yes, I know all about Ben Ahbood, the famous Arabian eunuch," Kylemore said with equal snideness.

"I was there to keep her safe from self-serving pretty boys like you, Your Grace." Ben made the formal address sound more of an insult than the unflattering description.

"Well, you did a remarkably poor job, then, didn't you?" Kylemore said coolly.

"Oh, stop it! Please, stop it!" Verity cried in distress. The possibility of violence simmered closer to the surface. She decided to cut in before it exploded into another fight. The memory of her brother attacking her lover still plagued her. "Ben, I'm fine. Aren't you glad to see me?"

The question summoned her brother's familiar smile, perhaps a little reluctant but indubitably there. "Aye, lass. I am that. It's grand."

"And is that all the welcome I get?" she asked and laughed brokenly as he leaned across the carriage to crush her in a long embrace.

Verity closed her eyes and basked in her brother's familiar presence. For so long, he'd been her only bastion against the world, the one person who had known the truth behind Soraya. She'd missed him so much, and now he was here. She stifled a grateful sob against his dark coat.

Eventually, Ben pulled away and gazed at her, his black eyes bright with unshed tears. "I didn't know if you were alive or dead. What did he do to you, lass? Where have you been? I've heard nowt from you. Couldn't you have got word to me somehow? I've been that worried about you."

"Oh, Ben, it's a long story." Most of it, she was aware, unfit for a brother's ears. "But the main thing is we can leave and forget this ever happened."

Kylemore shifted next to her in silent protest, but what else could she say? That he'd kidnapped her, forced himself on her and now she loved him so much that she thought she'd die of it? Even to her, it hardly made sense.

They rolled through an ornate gateway and into a spacious courtyard. What seemed an army of servants flooded out of the massive arched entrance to hold the horses, open the coach's doors and line the steps to greet their master.

The castle's gray stone walls glistened in the sunlight. When Verity stepped out of the carriage, they towered above her, mocking her presumption to love so great a personage as their master.

Kylemore stood at her side, seemingly oblivious to the magnificence. Even with his bruised face and dirty clothes, he was still the most beautiful man she had ever seen.

She thought she'd inured herself to leaving him. After all, she'd learned to endure her life as a whore when every shred of her had revolted at the idea. But each time she looked at him, the pain of parting sliced deeper.

Blind with tears she struggled not to shed, she accepted Kylemore's arm. She dashed her gloved hand across her eyes to clear her vision and looked up past the serried ranks lining the sweeping stone staircase. At the top, imposing double doors stood open to admit Kylemore Castle's long-absent lord.

An exquisite woman glided across the entrance. She was slender and uncommonly tall and wore a dizzyingly expensive gown cut to emphasize her height and fine figure.

Even at the distance, one couldn't mistake her air of

confident possession. Or her incandescent outrage as she glared down at the newcomers.

"Justin, good God! Are you so utterly lost to propriety that you bring your doxy here? Send the slut away at once!"

Verity was close enough to Kylemore to feel him stiffen in reaction.

"Mother," he said flatly.

Chapter 23

Although Verity had never seen her in the flesh, she immediately recognized the warrior queen who faced them down as the Duchess of Kylemore.

Even if a thousand sketches and portraits hadn't immortalized her famous beauty, she bore a notable resemblance to the duke. Strange to see Kylemore's uncompromisingly masculine features mirrored in his mother's delicate face. And the chilly arrogance of expression was familiar after years' acquaintance with the son.

"Your Grace," she said shakily as Ben emerged from the carriage behind her. Kylemore's uncompromising grip on her arm made escape impossible, so she sank into a deep curtsey.

The duchess didn't even glance her way. Perfectly properly. Great ladies didn't acknowledge demireps.

Kylemore hauled Verity upright and dragged her up the stairs, leaving Ben in their wake. For a moment, she thought he meant to bundle her across the threshold without addressing his mother, but he paused as he reached the older woman.

This close, Verity saw that age had marked the Duchess of Kylemore's face. Skillfully applied paint couldn't hide the lines of temper around her mouth, and the gentian eyes were less lovely when one saw the hardness shining in their depths.

"What are you doing here?" Kylemore asked in his coldest manner.

His lack of welcome didn't cow the duchess. Her winged brows lowered in a frown the image of his. "I am the Duchess of Kylemore. I may visit the family estates as I please."

He laughed humorlessly. "You haven't been to Scotland for twenty years, madam. Last time you left, you swore you'd never set foot in this barbarous land again."

"Send your whore away and I'll tell you why I've come," she said with the unmistakable voice of command. Behind her, the magnificent edifice rose to the sky, declaring that the duchess had every right to be here and Verity had none.

"I should go," she murmured to Kylemore.

"No, you're staying," he said stubbornly.

"Ben and I will return to the village. Squabbling openly like this with your mother does no good." Then, on a note of entreaty because she couldn't take many more emotional storms. "Please, I beg you!"

She should have known he'd respond no better to her pleading than he did to his mother's orders. The unyielding hand around her arm didn't relax. "You're going nowhere."

The duchess stared at her son with palpable dislike. "I've arrived just in time. It's as I feared. Your father's madness didn't die with him. You're the rotten branch from the rotten tree."

Shock rippled through the lines of servants at this attack on their master. Verity couldn't let this public fracas continue.

"I'll wait for you in the village," she whispered urgently. "You can't want the household to witness this quarrel, Kylemore."

The duchess's mouth tightened in aristocratic disdain. "You permit this common harlot to use your familiar name?"

Beside her, Verity felt him draw himself up to his full impressive height. The duchess was tall for a woman, but he loomed over her. "I do. I would be the most fortunate man on earth if this *lady* were to call me husband, madam."

This was too much for Her Grace. The perfect complexion whitened and the delicate jaw dropped in astonishment.

But she could hardly be more startled by the declaration than Verity was. He hadn't mentioned marriage since Kensington. The concept of her as a duchess was still nonsensical, but nothing could dam the traitorous warmth his words poured into her grieving heart.

"This lady adorns any abode she cares to enter," Kylemore said in a low voice that still managed to cut. "You, however, have long been a disgrace to your exalted name and rank. Kylemore Castle belongs to me. You are not welcome here."

The duchess staggered back. For one awful moment, Verity thought she might collapse. "Justin! I am your mother!"

"To my eternal regret," he said softly.

"Kylemore, you can't throw your mother out," Verity gasped. He had every right to hate the duchess, but an open break would only bring further scandal down on their heads.

She turned to the duchess and tried to keep a reasonable tone. "Your Grace, my brother and I leave today. My arrangement with your son has ended. I won't embarrass you further."

The duchess's expression became more forbidding. Verity forgot the legendary beauty and saw only the obdurate, destructive will.

What could it have been like to call this woman mother?

She was astonished Kylemore had emerged from childhood with even a shred of humanity intact.

As she'd expected, the duchess still refused to address her directly. "Justin, your behavior is unacceptable," she said in an autocratic voice. "I am here to insist you act in a manner appropriate to your position. Dismiss this slut at once and return to London to select a bride. Pray, boy, recall who you are."

He remained unmoved. "I am the Duke of Kylemore. These are my domains. If you aren't off my lands by this evening, Mother, my servants will escort you to the boundary."

He turned to face the staff with all the authority at his disposal. "The duchess will ride in Mr. McNab's vehicle to Inverathie, where she will wait at the inn. Pack her trunks and send them down with her carriage, which she will then use for her immediate departure."

"Justin, you cannot be serious!" his mother protested, clutching at his sleeve.

"I've never been more serious in my life, madam." He shook her free as if she were an unwelcome petitioner. "Good day to you."

He turned to glance at Ben, who stood aghast at the base of the staircase. Verity realized Kylemore's mention of marriage must have astonished her brother. She'd never confided in him about what had happened that last afternoon in London.

Kylemore's voice was peremptory. "Ashton, if you care to join us?"

He dismissed his mother with a spin on his heel and strode inside. Perforce, Verity followed into an impressive hall decorated with displays of spears and swords arranged in complicated geometric patterns. Behind her, she was aware of Ben mounting the steps and the servants preventing the vociferously protesting duchess from pursuing them.

She was still in a daze. How she'd treasure that moment when he'd announced that she was the wife he'd choose.

But the duchess's disbelieving response only echoed the world's derisive reaction if he actually went ahead and wed his mistress.

Her reasons for leaving him were as urgent as ever.

Kylemore didn't wait to see what happened to his mother. His staff had their orders, and he knew they'd obey unquestioningly. Instead, he drew Verity into a salon on the ground floor.

He turned to his two unwilling guests. Ashton remained mercifully silent, but Kylemore read displeasure and shock in the square-jawed face. Verity was exhausted, and strain left dark shadows under her beautiful eyes. He didn't care about the brother, but he most definitely cared about her. He gently took her hand.

"I'm sorry I couldn't save you from that," he said softly. "I had no idea my mother was in residence."

"I shouldn't be here," Verity said unsteadily.

"Yes, you should." His statement brooked no argument.

If I had my way, you'd be here always, my soul's darling.

He handed her carefully into a chair and crossed to the sideboard to pour three glasses of local whisky. After what they'd been through, they all needed it, he thought grimly.

"Here, drink this," he said, handing one to Ashton. He couldn't say he was any fonder of the fellow, but for Verity's sake, he was willing to make an effort.

"What is it?" Suspicion laced the man's question.

"Hemlock, of course." Without pausing to see what Ashton did with the drink, he went back to Verity.

"This will make you feel better," he said in a totally different tone as he crouched down on his haunches before her.

"I don't drink spirits," she said shakily.

"Just this once, *mo cridhe*. It will help."

She nodded, and he pressed the crystal glass into her chilled fingers. He stood up and downed his own drink. The liquor soothed the physical aches lingering from his scuffle with Ashton. Unfortunately, nothing short of a bullet could cure the pain in his heart.

Ashton returned the empty glass to the sideboard with a click. The whisky had revived his usual combative self. Perhaps hemlock would have been a better choice.

"You heard what the lass said. I'm taking her home with me this afternoon," he said with familiar belligerence.

"Surely that's her decision," Kylemore said neutrally.

Down on the dock, she'd all but announced that he had her full allegiance. How could she leave him now? Or was it that while she might want him, she wanted freedom more? Anguish clenched hard fingers into his heart at the thought.

Verity raised her head. He waited in desperate hope for her to tell her brother that she'd changed her mind, that she meant to stay.

But she looked over to Ashton and spoke in a firm voice. "Yes, Ben, I'll come with you."

No!

Ashton looked relieved, damn him. "That's grand, lass. I've got a hired carriage ready. We'll go when you say the word."

Kylemore swung around toward the tall windows open to the garden outside. He couldn't let her go. Not now. Not when he knew she cared, even if she didn't care *enough*. One hand lifted to the curtains and crushed the silk so tightly that his knuckles shone white.

Even with his back to her, he felt her eyes upon him.

He'd sworn when she'd nearly perished that he'd never compel her to anything again. But this was impossible.

"Stay and eat something, at least," he said to the gardens, although he hardly saw the sun shining on the perfectly maintained grounds. How absurd he could still sound like a civilized man when ravening demons clawed at his soul. "And use my traveling coach. It will be more comfortable."

"We want nowt of yours," Ashton snapped. "Throwing your brass around won't make up for what you've done. Any road, I'd prefer to get my sister well away from your bully boys before you change your mind and decide to keep her."

Kylemore didn't bother to defend himself. What was the point? Ben Ashton would find out soon enough that he meant to abide by Verity's wishes, no matter what it cost him.

Perhaps one day she'd remember this moment and know she left him a better man than she'd found him.

What a pathetic epitaph to his great love.

"Ben," Verity said quietly. "I'd like you to go to the village and arrange our departure. I want to talk to His Grace."

"I'm not leaving you on your ane with this sodding bastard. He'll spirit you away before I get back."

Kylemore could hardly blame the fellow for mistrusting him. At their last encounter, he'd left the younger man to shiver naked in a cold ruin while his sister had disappeared to face who knew what violence and abuse.

"He won't." Unmistakable certainty rang in Verity's low voice.

Thank you, mo cridhe, he whispered silently, before he spoke to Ashton. "The servants can collect your carriage and belongings while you wait in the hall."

"You could still bundle her off without me knowing owt," the bumpkin insisted with a stubborn set to his jaw.

"Ben, there's nothing stopping him having you constrained now while he abducts me," Verity pointed out gently. "Please leave us. There are things I need to say to His Grace."

Kylemore turned around to see Ashton glaring at his sister in indecision. Then he nodded abruptly. "If this villain makes the slightest false move, scream."

She tried to smile. Kylemore couldn't say she made a success of it. "If he so much as touches my hand."

Kylemore didn't pause for further objections. He led Ashton outside and gave the appropriate orders to his butler.

He would have insisted they use his coach, but he saw that the disharmony between Ashton and himself upset Verity. And she, in spite of the fact that she'd gotten exactly what she wanted, had clearly reached the end of her strength.

He left Ashton to kick his heels in the hall and returned to Verity. She'd risen and stood staring down into the flickering fire. Her profile was perfect and unutterably sad against the mythical revels carved on the marble fireplace. When she looked up, her silver eyes were dark with a misery equal to his own.

How could he bear this? He leaned against the closed doors behind him and braced himself for what was to come.

Verity knew this was the last time she'd be alone with the man she loved. Hungrily, her eyes traced his face and body. He looked the worst kind of ruffian, with his ruffled hair and rumpled clothes and the darkening bruises on his face.

"I'm sorry he hit you," she said softly without moving from the grate.

"I deserved it." Kylemore straightened and gingerly touched his cheek. "If your brother ever finds himself short of the ready, he'd make quite a career as a boxer, I warrant."

Automatically, she took a step toward him and her hand rose to soothe his injuries. Then she remembered she'd forbidden herself such tender gestures.

"At least he's saved you a journey to Whitby," she said, unable to hide her regret. She hadn't wanted to prolong the pain of parting, but now that the final moment had arrived, she resented every second's passing.

"It would have been a privilege." His expression was somber. "Verity, what you told everyone down at the dock, you didn't have to say it." He paused, obviously at a loss, then finished gruffly, "Thank you."

This time, she couldn't keep herself from reaching for him. "Well, I couldn't let him hurt you."

He took her hand in a rough grip. "Verity, don't go. For God's sake, don't go."

She closed her eyes, fighting tears. Her own unhappiness was devastating enough. But the agony he no longer troubled to hide made her want to die.

"I must." She spoke as much to herself as to him.

"Oh, Christ, I can't stomach this! Why do you have to go? Why, *mo gradh?*"

He flung himself away from her and prowled restlessly around the room as if he couldn't contain his frustration when he remained still. "Hell, I thought it was clear enough. You were happy to be my lover for a few weeks in the glen, but you always meant to seek your independence." Angrily, he ran his hand through his hair. "I'd even accepted it. God knows, after what I've done, you'd be deranged to stay with me."

He came to a furious halt in front of her. "But I was wrong, wasn't I? You're not leaving because you want to. It's what you'd like me to believe, but it's not the truth, is it?"

"Kylemore, don't," she pleaded, vulnerable to this sudden attack.

He ignored her entreaty. "Tell me, Verity—back at the glen, you said you wanted me. Was that true?" His eyes burned in his pale face and a muscle jerked in his cheek.

"There's no point in this."

"Was that true?"

"Yes, it was true. You know it was," she said wearily, unable to lie, although it would have been better for both of them if she had.

"You still want me. Tell me I'm mistaken, Verity."

She bent her head, unable to bear the stormy torment in his eyes. Why was it so hard to do what was right?

"No, you're not mistaken," she whispered and lifted a hand to ward him off as he made a convulsive move in her direction. "But it's more complicated than what we feel. You're a duke. I'm a whore."

"For God's sake! You've had three lovers. My mother goes through more men in a week. And she's received everywhere."

Regretfully, Verity shook her head. "My protectors paid to use my body. The whole world knows it and condemns me."

"I don't," he said steadily.

"Perhaps not. But that doesn't mean there's any future for us. You must marry and have an heir, Kylemore."

"You're the only woman I want to marry," he said gravely. "Verity Ashton, will you grant me the unparalleled joy of consenting to become my wife?"

She fought back another searing flood of tears. "You do me too much honor."

He stood straight and oddly still as if any untoward movement might startle her into running away. "If your fear is I'll tire of you and abandon you in favor of another, it's misplaced." Then on a burst of feeling, "By my soul, *mo cridhe*, I have wanted you without ceasing from the first moment I saw you. Surely you cannot doubt my steadfastness."

The strange thing was, she didn't.

In spite of the dissolute habits of the society he moved in. In spite of his charm and manifold attractions.

She'd accepted that what he felt for her went far beyond physical desire, powerful as that physical desire was.

But still, it wasn't enough.

She shook her head. "I cannot marry you, Kylemore. Our children would be outcasts. You'd be a pariah."

"Society can go to hell," he said shortly.

"You say that now. But you'll repent giving your name to a woman like me. I couldn't bear to cause you harm. It's better we separate now." Her voice broke on a sob, although she'd promised herself she wouldn't cry. "Don't press me, I beg of you. I've told myself a thousand times we can defy the world and live for ourselves alone. But we can't! We can't, Kylemore. All I ask is that you don't make this any harder than it already is."

He finally came to rest near the windows. He looked strong, controlled, arrogant. Infinitely dear.

How can I bear to leave him?

Because it's what I must do for his sake.

"I'll give you the world if you stay." His voice was low and laced with deep feeling. "My God, woman. Don't you know I'd lie down and die for you if you asked?"

Yes, she knew now that he cared for her. She found it in herself to wish he didn't care quite so much, even while her heart opened to every ardent declaration.

"I don't want anything from you," she said sadly.

"Except your freedom."

"Yes," she said, drawing on the core of steel that had helped her survive as Soraya.

"I can say nothing to change your mind?" he whispered despairingly.

"Nothing," she confirmed in a husky voice. Then, summoning every shred of her courage, she looked directly at him. "Don't bid me a decorous farewell outside. I . . . I couldn't bear it. Let's finish everything here. Good-bye, Your Grace."

His eyes darkened to navy as he registered her use of his title. But she was determined to remind him of the gulf that gaped between them, a gulf nothing as fragile as love could ever cross.

She watched acceptance seep into his features, along with a deathly bleakness that made her stomach cramp with wretchedness. He bowed his head in her direction but mercifully didn't touch her.

She'd been brave enough to kiss him farewell back in Kensington. She couldn't kiss him now. If she did, she'd shatter beyond repair.

She took one last, longing look at him. *Good-bye, my love.*

"Good-bye, Verity," he said softly, then turned back to the window as if he couldn't bear to watch her walk away.

Chapter 24

"**V**erity lass, will you tell me what happened?" Ben asked softly from beside her on the curricle's padded bench.

What had happened? Nothing out of the ordinary. She'd fallen in love, that was all.

Hardly worth the fuss she made, she thought, staring dry-eyed into the woods they passed in their hired carriage.

"Verity?" her brother prompted. They'd traveled for several hours, and he hadn't pressed her for details. She appreciated his consideration, but even Ben's patient silence couldn't last forever.

"I . . . I promise I'll tell you everything." A lie. She could never tell him everything that had happened in Kylemore's hidden Highland valley. But she could say enough to make Ben understand, she hoped. She turned to face the brother who'd endured so much for her sake. "Just not now."

They were the first words she'd spoken in over an hour, since Ben had leaned down to broach the basket the butler at

Kylemore Castle had pressed upon them. She'd refused to share the lavish provisions.

The idea of food still sent nausea coiling through the leaden sorrow in her belly. A logical part of her mind knew that one day she'd talk and laugh and eat and sleep and act like a real person again, but her grieving core as yet couldn't believe it.

"Just tell me one thing." Ben's massive hands were white-knuckled on the reins, and he stared with a rigid jaw at their horses. "Did he hurt you?"

"Yes," she whispered.

She fumbled desperately for the gray mist of apathy that had gripped her since she'd left her lover, but its protective edges became more ragged with every moment that passed.

"Lord in heaven!" Ben wrenched their vehicle to a shuddering halt and whirled to face her. "I'll lay charges against him at the first town we come to. I care nowt that he's a sodding duke. If he hurt you, he'll pay for it, lass."

His rage scorched away the last of her numbness. A massive wave of agony rushed into her soul. She dragged in an unsteady breath.

"No, you don't understand, Ben." Then she spoke aloud the truth she'd repudiated for so long. "I love him."

"Love? What damned twaddle is . . ."

Even in her misery, she saw Ben's fury fade into angry bewilderment, into denial. Then his expression became ineffably sad. He knew her so well, this brother who had given up his own hopes and ambitions—and, yes, pride in his manhood—to watch over her.

He knew just what this unwelcome love would cost her. Had already cost her.

"Oh, lass, I'm that sorry."

Yes, he knew indeed. She managed a shaky smile. "I am

too." She reached out and took his hand where it held the reins across his knees. "But least said, soonest mended."

One of their mother's favorite sayings. She saw the last of the tension drain from his face, leaving only compassion.

"Aye, lass, that's true. I'll get you back to Whitby and you'll forget what you've been through right soon enough."

He was wrong, but she honored his attempt to cheer her. "We can't stay in Whitby, Ben. The scandal of the false Mrs. Symonds will still be the talk of the town."

He urged the horses to walk on. "Then we'll buy a sheep farm where no one's any the wiser about who you are. We'll get Maria out of that school and have her live with us. Don't you fret owt, lass. Good Yorkshire air will bring the roses back into your cheeks. This won't seem so bad when your family's around you."

"Yes, Ben," she said, although she didn't believe it.

She stared over the horses' flickering ears and told herself the pain would pass. One day. When she was very old.

When she was dead.

They drove on in silence, while Verity tried not to remember. Remembering hurt too much.

But she couldn't help it. And her starkest memory was of Kylemore's face when he'd asked her to marry him today. He'd looked as though her refusal had crushed his last hope.

Ben intruded into her private hell when he shoved a crumpled white handkerchief in her direction.

"What's this for?" she asked unsteadily.

"You're crying, lass," he said in a gentle voice.

"Am I?" She raised a shaking hand to her face and found it soaked with tears she hadn't known she'd shed.

No, she'd never forget. Not even when age turned her hair gray and lined her face. She didn't want to forget, however much remembering tortured her.

Silently, she wiped her face and stared ahead. She gave up

her futile battle with herself and began to revisit each precious moment of the last weeks.

The cruelty, the violence, the sadness, the sweetness.

The overwhelming love.

Beside her, Ben clicked his tongue to encourage the horses to a faster pace.

"What the Devil?"

Ben's muttered imprecation stirred Verity from her stupor of exhausted misery.

"Oh!" The curricle lurched to an ungainly halt and threw her hard against her brother's side. She clutched at his shoulder as the horses neighed and plunged in their traces.

"Someone's blocked the road, Verity lass," Ben said, peering ahead.

"Blocked the road?" she repeated dazedly.

Before she could gather her thoughts, rough hands grabbed her and hauled her from the carriage. Surprise more than terror made her scream for her brother as her assailant hurled her to the road. She landed painfully on one knee and threw out her hands to save herself from sprawling flat.

"Verity!" Ben shouted as two men dragged him from his seat and flung him to the ground beside her. She struggled to rise, ignoring the way her grazed and bleeding palms smarted.

"Don't hurt him. I'll come willingly," she said sharply.

In spite of the harsh treatment, joy flooded her heart. This wasn't some random robbery. Kylemore must have come to get her and take her back to the valley.

She didn't care if they couldn't be together forever. She didn't care that what they did was wrong. She'd be with him now. That was all that mattered.

She looked up at the brawny men in nondescript clothing

who surrounded her, expecting to recognize a Macleish or two.

But the men who encircled her in the late afternoon light were strangers. Desperately, she tried to see past them to where Kylemore must wait for her.

"I'll kill the bastard!" Ben staggered upright. "I told you not to trust him, lass!"

"Get down!" The largest of their captors aimed a kick at Ben's legs. Her brother collapsed with a groan. "Tie him up."

Verity was confused. The orders were delivered in an English accent. In Scotland, the duke always relied on local retainers.

"Kylemore?" she called in a puzzled voice. "I won't fight you. You must know that."

The man who had spoken reached down to grab her arm in a bruising grip. "Shut your gob," he growled, wrenching her to her feet.

"I told you I won't resist."

She stumbled before she regained her balance. Surely, her lover knew he had no need to force her to go with him. They'd moved on so far since Whitby.

Hadn't they?

Foolish to be frightened. He'd never hurt her. He'd sworn that, and she believed him. But chillingly, she remembered his anger when she'd refused his proposal then abandoned him in London.

Hadn't she done exactly the same this afternoon?

Her heart thundered with wild apprehension. Trembling and at last completely alert, her eyes raked the deserted stretch of road. Deserted except for four men, the hired vehicle, a makeshift barricade of rocks and branches, and an elaborate closed carriage a few yards away.

Ben still fought to break free, but, as at Whitby, sheer

numbers made it impossible. He swore savagely, but the devils restraining him paid no attention while they trussed him and left him prone under the trees that crowded the roadside.

One of the men left Ben and hurried to open the coach's door, which was painted with the familiar golden eagle of the Kinmurries. By the time the occupant emerged, Verity's wits had returned and she experienced no jolt of surprise.

"Well done, Smithson." The Duchess of Kylemore sent a heartbreakingly lovely smile to the huge brute who loomed beside Verity.

"My pleasure, Your Grace." The man bowed briefly. "Shall we dispose of them? It will look like an attack by footpads."

"No!" Verity gasped, beginning to struggle in earnest. This couldn't be happening. Not now, when she'd relinquished her powerful lover so he could follow the dictates of duty. "Ben's done nothing to deserve this!"

"Quiet, bitch." Smithson slammed his free arm across her throat and yanked her back against his coarse linen shirt. Her head swam with the stench of stale sweat, and she gave an involuntary moan that squeaked into silence as his arm tightened.

The duchess's cold, cold eyes settled on her. Verity shivered at the absolute hatred in those indigo depths.

"You've been a thorn in my side since my son first saw you," the duchess said, her tone as pitiless as her gaze.

"But I'm leaving him. You know I'm leaving him," Verity gasped, fighting for breath.

She squirmed to loosen Smithson's hold, but to no avail. She raised her hand to claw at his hand. He gave a satisfying grunt of pain, then jerked hard against her throat, making her gag.

"Stop that, you poxy trull," he muttered. "Stay still or I'll hurt you in earnest."

He released the punishing pressure on her airway and the blackness gradually receded from her vision. As the pounding blood rushed back into her bruised flesh, it throbbed painfully.

She dragged reviving air into her lungs and focused on the duchess. Smithson was merely a bully. The real danger stood before her in the person of this beautiful, perfectly dressed woman with frozen eyes. Fear made Verity's head spin, but she fought to hide her spiraling terror.

"I'm never going to see His Grace again," Verity rasped out. Talking scraped painfully at her abused throat.

The duchess's eyebrows arched with patent disbelief. "I know my son. Justin won't accept his dismissal so easily. I shudder to recall the laughingstock he made of himself when you left London. I could hardly hold my head up in society." Her voice rang with self-righteous outrage. "I'm afraid you've aroused my displeasure, Soraya. And you must pay."

Verity stood perfectly still in Smithson's hold and raised her chin.

"Kill me if you must," she said in a low, shaking voice. There would be no escape. She could see that the duchess's calcified soul held no mercy for a recalcitrant harlot. Still, she had to try and save Ben. "But my brother has done you no ill. Please let him go, Your Grace."

The duchess's stained lips curved in a disdainful smile. "Oh, very moving, my dear. I should have guessed that more than just your pretty face drew my son to his downfall. He's always had such pathetic admiration for courage."

"There's nothing pathetic about the duke," Verity snapped unwisely.

The duchess stepped forward and slapped Verity hard across the face. "You will address me with respect, slut."

Verity would have crumpled under the blow if Smithson hadn't gripped her arms so tightly. As it was, the left side of her face felt like it was on fire. She lifted a shaking hand to her cheek and adopted a more conciliatory tone in spite of how it galled her.

"I'm sorry, Your Grace," she said, while every particle of her wanted to spit disgust into the woman's exquisite face.

"That's better." The duchess's expression changed from displeasure to gloating expectancy. "And you mistake me. I have no intention of killing you or your pimp. I want you to remember the day you crossed Margaret Kinmurrie. And live to rue it."

"Let her go, you bloody witch!" Ben rolled in the dirt, kicking and pulling as his powerful muscles strained against the ropes.

"Silence the fellow," the duchess said negligently to her henchmen. Her glittering gaze didn't shift from Verity. She looked ruthless. She looked excited. The violence had triggered something primitive and uncontrollable in her.

Sickened, Verity closed her eyes.

The duchess continued in the same idle tone. "But don't make him insensible. I want him to witness the consequences of presuming above one's station."

A scream tightened Verity's throat, but she fought to contain it.

Screaming would do her no good. There was nobody to help her, just as there was nobody to help Ben.

The men clustered around Ben hid the beating from her, but his grunts of agony rose above the sickening thud of fists on vulnerable flesh.

She craned and twisted against Smithson's imprisoning grasp to see what they did to her brother. Nausea rose as she instinctively but uselessly tried to wrest herself free and dash to his aid.

Eventually, she gave up in panting exhaustion and sagged

in her captor's grip. Her puny strength was no match for the duchess's thug.

"No, please. Your Grace, Ben's done nothing to harm you," she pleaded, her throat still raw. Then, even though her pride revolted at the words, "I beg of you, Your Grace. Let your anger fall on me, not on my brother."

Amazingly, the duchess smiled, even while her bullies kicked and punched an innocent man toward unconsciousness. "I have anger to spare for both of you, whore."

Ben's groans became softer and more intermittent. Again, the duchess spoke without looking in his direction. "Don't forget, I want him aware. He must see every detail of his sister's punishment."

Thank God the beating was over. It had seemed to last an eon. Verity forced herself to take an unsteady breath. Agonizing certainty grew within her about the duchess's intentions.

"You mean these villains to rape me," she whispered.

Horror swelled up to choke her. She needed Smithson's cruel hands to keep her from collapsing as images of unbearable pain and shame flooded her mind.

"Yes. Eventually. An extra lover or four to a trollop like you makes no matter," the duchess said lightly, then her voice hardened. "But before that, I'll make sure you never bewitch my son—or any man—again."

"I've renounced my life as a courtesan," Verity said, although she saw that nothing would sway the duchess's purpose.

"Oh, I can guarantee that." Finally, the duchess looked across to where Ben lay in shuddering pain. "One of you, prop him up so he can watch. The rest, I need you here."

Verity gave a broken cry as the brutes moved away from her brother and she finally saw what they'd done. His face was bloody and swollen, and his clothes were torn and filthy.

What further injuries did the fading light hide? The damage she could see now made her want to vomit.

"Oh, Ben," she cried, hoping desperately he'd lost consciousness, despite the duchess's orders. But his head jerked unsteadily in her direction as she spoke his name.

Her distress meant she hardly noticed when the duchess directed Smithson to hand her over to two of the men who had beaten Ben. They stood on either side of her and grabbed her arms while the loathsome Smithson stepped forward to stand beside his employer. "What are your wishes, Your Grace?"

The woman's eyes were bright with almost sexual arousal as she drew a small silver knife from her reticule. "Cut her face. Scar her so no man can look at her without revulsion." Her voice quivered with eagerness.

"No! You can't do this!" Verity cried, struggling futilely. Pride had fled and she could no longer conceal her terror. "It's barbaric."

"Your Grace . . ." Smithson fell back from the blade the duchess extended. Even through her panic, Verity was astonished to see his impassive face crease into repugnance.

"You were happy enough to kill her," the duchess said derisively, as if she criticized a dandy on the fall of his cravat. "Be a man, for God's sake."

Smithson shook his head. "Killing is quick. But to slice a wench's pretty face open just for spite? No, Your Grace, I'm sorry, but I can't do it."

"You are dismissed from my service," she said in a frigid voice that contrasted grotesquely with the elation in her face. Her eyes fixed avidly on the villains who constrained Verity. "This woman is a harlot and a thief. She should be whipped at the cart tail, then hanged. Is anyone man enough to do my bidding?"

Verity waited in strained and panting silence to see if anyone took up the challenge.

Her beauty had always been more of a curse than a blessing, but she abhorred the prospect of becoming an object of
pity. And her courage failed as she imagined that glittering
little blade piercing her flesh.

She sucked in a ragged breath, fighting hysteria. Rape
would follow quickly upon disfigurement. How could she
endure what was about to happen?

"A hundred guineas to the man who takes the knife," the
duchess said clearly when no one moved to obey her.

Her irritation with her cohorts was written in austere lines
on the face Verity had once thought beautiful. Now all she
could see was obsessive hatred and salacious cruelty.

Verity's dread rose, threatening to suffocate her, as she
studied the circle of faces around her. A hundred guineas
was a fortune, more money than these men would see in their
lifetimes. It made no sense that they'd smash her brother to a
pulp, yet turn squeamish at the idea of scarring her for life.

Would they also balk at raping her?

"I'll do it, Your Grace." The man on her right released her
and stepped forward to take the silver knife from the duchess's trembling hand. The woman's unsteadiness didn't stem
from uncertainty, Verity knew, but from excitement.

"Cut her deep." The duchess's breath sawed audibly as her
monstrous revenge edged closer to fruition.

Ben made an unintelligible protest and lurched to his
knees before his guard knocked him down with a blow.

Verity managed to stand proudly until the man with the
knife stepped directly in front of her, but as she looked up
into his eyes, her nerve failed. She writhed against the merci-
less hands that held her fast.

"No! No, please. Don't do this. In the name of heaven,
please don't do this," she pleaded. She turned away as tears
poured down her cheeks.

The man took her chin in a firm hold and made her face

him. She braced herself for the knife's slash, for excruciating pain and rivers of blood.

"Please," she whispered shakily, searching for some trace of compassion in him.

He was so young. Younger than Ben. How absurd a mere boy could perpetrate this outrage.

"You can't do this and call yourself a Christian." She caught a flash of uncertainty in his eyes, and for a moment, she thought she'd won.

"Two hundred guineas!" the duchess urged from behind him.

The youth raised the knife and pressed it to Verity's cheekbone. There was a brief sting, and warm wetness trickled down her face.

"God damn you forever," she whispered and closed her eyes again. She waited for pain.

And she waited.

"Good Lord, and they call women the weaker sex!" The duchess's anger grated across nerves knotted tight to breaking point. "I should have known I'd have to do this myself."

"Yes, good servants are so hard to get these days, aren't they?" Verity said faintly. She opened her eyes to watch the duchess snatch the knife from the boy.

Kylemore had told her this woman blanched at nothing. She wouldn't flinch at the humiliation and degradation of a humble whore. Any reprieve was past.

The man she loved had called her the bravest person he knew. She refused to face her fate like a puling weakling. She'd scream and cry and beg for mercy in time. She knew that. Even the scratch on her cheek hurt like blazes, and worse was to come. But she'd hold on to her pride as long as she could.

Pride wouldn't save her from what was about to happen,

but it was all she had. She drew herself up as if she were the duchess and her lover's mother the cheap bawd.

Something that might have been admiration flickered in the woman's glassy eyes, eyes the same deep and beautiful blue as Kylemore's. "You're a worthy opponent, I'll give you that."

"This serves no purpose," Verity said as calmly as she could. Pleading could never succeed. Perhaps defiance would. She cursed the husky edge to her voice but couldn't do anything about it. "I told you—His Grace and I have parted forever. He has sworn he won't pursue me."

"Even if that's so, I deserve some recompense for the trouble you've given me." The duchess's voice was exultant.

"By consigning me to torture and rape?"

"These things are all relative." The woman stroked the edge of the blade and considered her victim in the fading light. "I rather think I'll take out an eye."

The gorge rose in Verity's throat. "You'd leave me blind?" she gasped in revulsion.

"No. Only one eye. I want you to see what I do. It's dangerous to range yourself against your betters, my girl."

"You're not my better," Verity spat. Fury clawed at her fear. Fury alone gave her the strength to stand stiffly and await the blade's descent. "You'll never get away with this. I'll bring the full force of the law against you."

Astonishingly, chillingly, the duchess laughed, the sound tinkling and sweet in the still air. "I'm the Duchess of Kylemore. You're my son's discarded, lowborn lover. The law will pay you no heed at all. Unless, that is, I decide to have you transported for prostitution."

"You're a devil from hell," Verity gasped in horror.

Let it be quick, she prayed, although she knew the duchess intended to draw out every last strand of torment. Fortitude was all Verity had left. Please let it not desert her now. She closed her eyes and waited.

The duchess was so close that Verity heard the slide of a silk sleeve against her bodice as she drew her hand back, ready to strike.

Then, in the breathless pause, a cold, commanding, *beloved* voice pierced her all-encompassing fog of dread.

"Shed one drop of her blood and I'll shoot you where you stand."

Chapter 25

Kylemore's clipped words wrenched Verity from the lightless bastion where she'd retreated.

It couldn't be true. He couldn't be here to save her. Such unlikely heroics belonged only in fairy tales. Fear and grief must have sent her mad.

But when she opened dazed eyes, he strode, arrogant as ever, out of the overhanging trees toward her. And how could she doubt he was real when the force of his rage made the very air quiver?

He was dressed completely in black, from his silk shirt to his long coat that swept the ground. Even the boots kicking up dust with every purposeful step were black.

Against the unrelieved darkness of his clothing, his face was pale and taut with barely curbed fury. One elegant hand rested negligently on the hilt of the sword that hung from his waist, and the other leveled a heavy pistol at his mother and Smithson.

With a gasp, the duchess spun around. "Justin, don't be ridiculous. You cannot threaten your own mother."

She sounded perfectly reasonable. The ecstatically vengeful harpy of a few moments ago had disappeared. Quickly, she hid the deadly silver knife in her skirts.

Savagery tinged the duke's smile as he stopped a few feet away from her. "I can and do threaten you, madam." He looked across to where his mother's servant held Verity. "Have they harmed you, *mo cridhe?*"

"No," Verity whispered. Trembling with reaction, she focused a tear-filled gaze on Kylemore.

She was safe now. He'd never let anyone hurt her. She knew that as she knew she needed breath to live.

"Your face is bleeding," he pointed out with a contained gentleness that sent a cold shiver down her spine.

"It's only a scratch," she said unsteadily.

Compared to what the duchess had planned for her, the sullenly seeping cut hardly mattered. Still, she saw anguish flare in his eyes as they rested on the injury.

"I hope so. Or someone will pay dearly." He masked the flash of emotion and returned his relentless focus to his mother.

The duchess's face tightened with scornful defiance as she met his stare. "You wouldn't harm me. You don't have the stomach for it."

Clearly, she'd decided bravado was her best strategy. Verity could have told her she was wrong. When Kylemore looked like that, nothing swayed him.

"Try me," he said in the same terrifyingly mild voice.

Still the duchess didn't take warning. A triumphant smile curled her lips. "You forget I have four men and you are alone."

Kylemore's lordly manner didn't falter. "Four men who

will soon be in custody and incriminating you with every word of their testimony."

He signaled with one hand to someone behind him. Eight armed men surged from the woods that edged the road. Verity recognized Hamish and Andy and Angus among the newcomers.

"Justin, think of the scandal!" the duchess snapped.

"Yes, think of it," he said with satisfaction.

With taciturn efficiency, Kylemore's companions took, at gunpoint, the boy who had come so close to scarring Verity and the bully who guarded Ben's ominously unmoving body.

The duke glanced at the man who still restrained Verity. "If you hope to live through the next minute, let her go."

His voice rang with absolute authority. Immediately, she was free. The abruptness of the action threw her off balance. She staggered and gasped for air to combat her sudden light-headedness.

Kylemore lunged to catch her before she fell. "Christ, *mo leannan,* what have they done to you?" he muttered under his breath.

She felt his arm snake around her waist to hold her upright. At his touch, her faintness receded. She turned toward his strength and heat as a flower opens to the sun.

He is here, he is here.

The trilling carol of relief and wonder allowed her to take her first unfettered breath in what felt like hours. It was a breath full of the haunting essence of Kylemore. She fought the impulse to bury her nose in his chest and pretend all danger had passed.

Because, of course, it hadn't.

Even while he sheltered her against his body, Kylemore kept his pistol leveled. A few feet away, Angus and Andy took charge of her former captor and herded him toward his two cohorts. The three thugs who had so terrified her were cowed and silent as they huddled together on the roadside.

She looked away from them and up at the man she'd thought never to see again. Her heart blossomed with difficult joy. How she wished she could stay in his embrace forever, but her wishes were as impossible now as they had ever been.

Reaction to what she'd been through set in, and she shook in his hold as though she had a fever. She stifled the urge to cling to Kylemore and shower him with grateful tears.

Struggling for control, she sucked in another deep breath. Right now, she needed to check on her brother. He'd been silent for too long.

"I have to see to Ben," she said urgently. "He's over there, beaten to within an inch of his life."

"Hamish, go with her," Kylemore said, releasing her.

He kept his pistol aimed at his mother while Verity hurried across to her brother. Ben lay on the ground, still tied up. He must have finally, mercifully lost consciousness before the duchess had grabbed the knife.

With a broken sob, Verity fell to her knees at his side.

Is he alive? Please, let him be so.

She hunched forward over his poor, battered body, cradling him to her breast. Even in the gloaming's forgiving light, she saw how badly hurt he was. Thank heaven, he was still breathing. This close to him, she could hear the air's uneven passage through his mashed mouth.

"Oh, Ben," she murmured, tears running unchecked down her cheeks as she rocked him the way she'd rocked him when he'd been a child in her care. "My poor darling brother."

He didn't hear her. Perhaps he'd never hear her again.

The beating had been prolonged and unconstrained. Who knew what damage he'd sustained? Very gently, she raised his torn and bruised head onto her lap while Hamish rolled him over on his side and cut his bonds with a horn-handled knife.

"They did a gey good job on him, my lady." The Scotsman ran his hands over her brother's frighteningly unresponsive body.

"It's all my fault," she whispered, fumbling in her sleeve for the handkerchief Ben had pressed upon her earlier.

Hamish looked up at her with a frown. "Och, no, dinna go blaming yourself. That wicked banshee over there brought this on ye."

It wasn't true. The knowledge lay like a stain on her soul that Ben had paid for his sister's sins today.

But repenting her misdeeds must wait. Ignoring the sting of her scraped palms, she tried to use the handkerchief to clean the dirt and blood from Ben's swollen, marked face. But the severity of his wounds defeated her and the linen square was soon soaked red.

His nose sat askew, and his mouth wasn't much more than a bloody gash. If not for his shock of white-blonde hair, even filthy and matted as it was, she'd have had trouble recognizing him.

"What do you think, Mr. Macleish?" she asked huskily.

"His nose is broken and I wouldnae be surprised if a few ribs are cracked. We'll get him back tae the castle where a proper doctor can see tae him."

Hamish's touch was sure and kind as he tested her brother's injuries, as sure and kind as it was when he tended the duke's horses. The thought was strangely reassuring. She bent her head and crooned comfort over Ben, just as she'd crooned when he'd been a child in her care.

"No, Justin! You jest!"

The duchess's emphatic denial dragged Verity's attention from her unconscious brother. Mother and son squared up a few feet away from where she knelt. The fine-boned faces that proclaimed their shared blood were stark with naked hatred.

"I am most definitely serious, madam." Kylemore's voice was more cutting than Verity had ever heard it. It was the voice of a man who exacted instant obedience to his merest command. "You will retire to the dowerhouse in Norfolk. You will take your odious ward with you. An escort will accompany you there and I'll set guards round the clock at the house. If you venture one foot beyond Norwich, I cease to be responsible for your expenses and you must rely purely on your jointure from my father's estate."

"That's barbaric! I am your mother!" The rage in the duchess's voice made Verity's hands pause in stroking the tangled hair back from Ben's forehead.

"Because you're my mother, only I can end the devastation you wreak." Kylemore's words dripped such ice that Verity shivered. "I should have curbed you long ago. Foolishly, I believed you powerless without access to the ducal purse. Today that grave error of judgment almost cost me everything I hold dear."

Verity's heart leaped with outlaw happiness. It was the nearest thing to an open declaration of love she'd ever have from him.

Kylemore raised one elegant hand to forestall any protest from his mother. "No, madam, don't waste your breath. I am determined. You are destined for a life of harmless rustication."

The older woman drew herself up to her full height. "Very impressive, Justin," she sneered. "But I still have one weapon in my arsenal."

"Yes, and what's that?" he asked as idly as if he discussed a trifling wager on a horserace or a boxing match.

"My husband was indubitably mad. To my distress, my son is highly strung and difficult." Insincere sadness infused her cruel words. "Your recent behavior indicates you've inherited your father's tragic affliction. Proceed with your vile plan to exile me and I'll have you committed as a lunatic."

"No! It's not true!" Verity cried in anguish. Her hands clenched in Ben's ripped and dirty shirt.

Kylemore glanced across at her, and astonishingly, he smiled. "Don't worry, *mo leannan*. This particular tigress no longer has teeth."

The duchess frowned at his assertion. "You think so, Justin? London is agog at the lengths you've taken to regain your tawdry mistress. The gossips always speculated about your sanity. It will need very little to fan those rumors, dear boy." She had the gall to reach up and tap his cheek as though he were indeed a troublesome child. "So let's have no more talk of the dowerhouse."

Kylemore's smile faded as he turned back to his mother. "The same gossips will relish the reports from your household servants, madam. The sordid tales of your insatiable appetite for brawny young footmen. Or for ruffians off the streets paid a guinea for the foul pleasures you exacted."

Even at a distance, Verity saw the duchess whiten. "Justin? What are you saying?" she gasped, reeling back.

Still he maintained that uncanny control. The more composed he sounded, the more dangerous he became, Verity knew.

"I possess sworn statements detailing your sexual excesses. Perhaps your endless affairs with members of the ton may be overlooked. Your taste for rougher trade won't encounter so much understanding. Smithson, your pander, stands beside you. I doubt he'll keep his mouth shut if he can save himself from the gallows. Consider carefully before you threaten me with your pathetic stratagems again."

"You've had me watched, you miserable little bastard?" she

snarled. The contemptuous tone sent a queasy aftershock of terror through Verity, and she held her brother's motionless body more tightly.

"Indeed," Kylemore said, unmoved by her insults. "I knew the day would come when you overstepped even the generous boundaries I set on your behavior."

The woman's voice shook as she spoke, and her rouge stood out unnaturally bright on her sallow cheeks. "No, Justin! This is too cruel. If you won't think of me, think of yourself. You cannot drag the Kinmurrie name through the mire!"

"I only did what I was told, Your Grace," Smithson insisted from behind the duchess. "It was more than my job was worth to gainsay the lady's demands."

"You are a thug and a bully," Kylemore said acidly. "And I'll see you and your cohorts hang for today's work."

"No, Kylemore," Verity said firmly. Slowly and with great tenderness, she laid Ben's head down on the thick grass verge.

Her intervention created a short silence. Kylemore looked at her more in surprise than anger. "No? You don't know how close I am to shooting them here and now and letting the law go to the Devil."

"Believe me, I know," she said gently, reading the vibrating tension in his lean body.

She rose and squared her shoulders before she crossed to the duke's side. Gingerly, she reached out and, after a moment's resistance from him, took the pistol. It rested cold and hard and heavy in her palm.

"Her Grace is right. A public scandal will damage you as much as those you prosecute," she said quietly, while inside her, her heart galloped with apprehension. Pray heaven she could make him bow to reason. "Let her go to Norfolk. Let her take her henchmen—the threat of arrest should keep them there safely enough."

"She tried to kill you." Kylemore's deep voice was a whiplash of fury. "And these animals who may yet have killed your brother aided her."

"I haven't forgotten Ben." She cast a glance across to where Hamish still worked methodically on Ben's injuries. "But if you put these men in the dock, the whole sorry story comes out, and that will do nobody any good."

"You're more generous than I, *mo cridhe,*" Kylemore said softly.

He reached out and took his mother's arm in a punishing grip. "So what do you say? Norfolk? Or confinement in an asylum for insatiable carnal mania? And damn the scandal."

Tears glittered in the duchess's deep blue eyes—tears of thwarted fury rather than remorse, Verity was sure.

"Justin, you're hurting me!" his mother whined.

The change from threats to abject weakness didn't sway the duke. "Hurt you? God, I'd like to dismember you."

He visibly reined in his sparking temper. "Well, madam? I await your answer."

The duchess was pale and drawn, and she at last looked her age. Only the faintest vestiges of her remarkable beauty remained as she licked nervous lips and met her son's ruthless expression. "I'll go to Norfolk."

"Good." He didn't unhand her. "Before you go, beg this lady's pardon."

The woman's face hardened in abomination while shock thundered through Verity and rendered her speechless. A great lady of the ton apologize to a whore? The idea was unthinkable.

The duchess tried to jerk free but failed. "Damn you, Justin, I will never humble myself to this harlot."

"You will, madam. Or you will face the consequences."

"This slut should be cast into the gutter, where she belongs," she snapped. Traces of her earlier confidence resurfaced. "And don't threaten me with confinement in an asylum.

That particular bird won't fly, sir. You'd no more have your own mother committed than you'd swim to Ireland. End this absurd playacting immediately and release me. I'll go to Norfolk, and you have my word as Duchess of Kylemore that your whore is safe. That is concession enough."

"Not nearly," he said in a voice that made Verity wince. He turned to his waiting men, who stood guard over the duchess's henchmen. "Duncan, is Sir John Firth still the local magistrate?"

"Aye, Your Grace," a man Verity didn't know answered.

"Then go to Claverton Hall and inform him I have prisoners for arraignment."

"Your Grace." Duncan lowered his pistol and strode toward the trees.

Verity waited in quivering silence as cold sweat slicked her hold on the pistol. Surely the duchess wouldn't permit her pride to bring disaster upon them all.

But the duchess's pride was an unpredictable and terrifying force, as Verity had discovered on this lonely road.

Only when Duncan was almost out of earshot did the older woman relent. "No! Damn you to hell, Justin. Stop. I'll do it." Her voice was low and uneven as she scowled at her son. "I curse the day my womb gave you life."

Kylemore bowed ironically toward her and with implacable strength drew her around to face Verity. "Life is full of small disappointments, madam. I assume this vituperative outburst forms an introduction to your apology." Without looking away from his mother, he called out after Duncan. "Wait a moment."

The duchess stared over Verity's head, her face masklike. Her voice was flat with abhorrence. "I ask forgiveness for the injuries I have done you and yours."

"Perhaps again with sincerity," Kylemore said silkily.

Verity had had enough. "Kylemore, you don't need to humiliate her further," she said through stiff lips. "You've won. She isn't worth your spite. Let her go. Ben needs a doctor."

Kylemore looked down at the duchess with unalloyed loathing. "I bow to this lady's wishes. Just remember when you're sulking at the dowerhouse that only my mistress's intervention saved you from the madhouse. That thought should sour your existence quite satisfactorily."

He turned to his men as he released his mother. "Disarm the duchess's servants, then take them to Oban and find a notary. I want sworn statements about what occurred today. Then escort them to Norfolk. I'll write to my factor, and he'll have a guard in place by the time you arrive."

The duchess inhaled with a long hiss. "No, I won't bear it!" She fumbled in her skirts, and suddenly, the silver knife glittered in her hand. She launched herself at Kylemore. "You have no right to do this, you misbegotten wretch!"

"Watch out, Kylemore! She's armed!" Verity cried, automatically raising the pistol.

He jerked beyond his mother's reach, then stretched out to restrain her. She swiped his hand aside with a sweep of the blade, a fraction away from drawing blood.

"Damn you, madam!" He didn't shift his gaze from her. "You've lost. It's too late. Do you want to hang indeed?"

"I won't hang. I'll go back to the life I've always led," she gasped, her eyes feverish in her pale face.

"Drop the knife, Your Grace," Verity said in a hard voice. Her earlier fear had evaporated the moment the duchess had threatened the man she loved. "Drop it. Or I swear I'll shoot. And if you think I don't know how to use this gun, you're sadly mistaken. Self-defense counts among the courtesan's arts." To prove her statement, she cocked the gun with the smooth assurance her lessons with Eldreth had lent her.

The duchess fixed a contemptuous gaze on Verity. "You won't kill me. You know what would happen to you."

"Perhaps I don't care. You threatened me with torture and rape today, Your Grace. And remember, we have a string of witnesses to swear I merely protect the Duke of Kylemore. I doubt I'll see the inside of a prison cell."

The duchess's stare glowed with malevolence as she trained it upon Verity. "How I wish I'd destroyed you."

Verity tilted her head in imitation of Kylemore's ironic salute. "I'm rather glad you didn't."

"You uppity bitch! I'll kill you before you crow over me!"

The woman flung herself toward Verity, the knife raised. Automatically, Verity's finger tightened on the trigger.

There was a deafening explosion. The acrid smell of gunpowder filled the air.

The duchess screamed and staggered back into Kylemore's hold. He held her upright with one arm around her waist while he tugged the knife from her slack fingers.

Ears ringing, Verity let the pistol drop uselessly to her side. "Did . . . did I injure her?" she asked unsteadily, feeling sick to her stomach.

She'd never before fired a gun in anger, and, however much the duchess deserved to suffer, it was hard to accept that she'd shot a bullet into another human being.

"No, she's untouched. More's the pity," Kylemore bit out after a perfunctory inspection.

"Thank God," Verity whispered, her dizziness receding.

"You shot at me, you damned guttersnipe," the duchess said in shock. "You shot at me!"

Kylemore's unearthly coldness returned as he spoke to the duchess. "Not another word, madam. Your antics are at an end. Now get out of my sight." He looked up at Duncan, who had rushed in their direction when the gun had gone off. "Escort Her Grace to her carriage and see she stays there."

Verity expected arguments, threats, protests from the duchess, but the woman remained silent. Against her son's tall and dominant leanness, she looked shrunken, as though today's defeat had leached the venom from her.

But Verity knew this particular snake would strike again if the opportunity arose.

While Duncan marched the duchess away toward the waiting vehicle, Kylemore turned to Verity with concern in his eyes. "Are you all right?" he asked gently.

"Yes," she said, although her heart still pounded with the nauseating wave of terror that had swept her when she'd thought she'd killed the duchess. She even dredged up an uncertain smile as she passed the gun across to him. "This might be safer with you."

Kylemore accepted it without comment. "Hamish and I will accompany you and your brother back to Kylemore Castle."

"Thank you," she whispered, while exhausted gratitude to the man who had saved her swelled her soul. She turned away to hide a sudden rush of tears. "I must check on my brother."

She forced herself from trembling immobility and crossed to kneel at Ben's side. He was stretched out on the luxuriant grass, and a coat was folded beneath his head.

"How is he, Mr. Macleish?" she asked in an unsteady voice. If her brother died because of what had happened today, she'd never forgive herself.

"Oh, he'll make it. But he'll be gey sore on the morrow."

The confidence in his tone reassured even more than his words. Through the gathering dusk, she saw that Hamish had done a marvelous job of bandaging Ben's wounds. She wondered where he'd found the linen, but she didn't ask.

In her brother's bruised face, one blackened eye opened and focused on her in the fading light. "Verity lass," he said indistinctly through his swollen mouth.

He was awake. She hadn't been sure he'd regain consciousness. She bent her head and started to cry out her overwhelming relief and her bitter guilt in great heaving sobs.

"Oh, lass! Don't take on so." Ben's face contracted with pain as he struggled to reach out to comfort her.

"No, don't move. I'm just so happy that you're alive," she wept, taking his hand carefully so she didn't hurt his poor, bruised knuckles. "I thought I'd lost you."

"Takes a sight more than those cream puffs to finish Benjamin Ashton. Give over, lass. There's nowt to cry for."

"I know," she said on a gusty sigh that produced more tears. "I don't know what's . . . what's wrong with me."

"Hamish, you ride with Ashton in their carriage." Without her noticing, Kylemore had come to stand beside her. "I'll take *madame* up with me on Tannasg."

Dazedly, Verity checked the rapidly darkening road and saw that only the four of them remained. The duchess and her men had gone, as had the rest of Kylemore's band.

"I'd rather stay with Ben," she said. She couldn't risk being alone with Kylemore when her resolution to leave him teetered so close to shattering.

Unresisting, she let him help her to her feet. "The hired curricle only takes two, Verity, and someone needs to handle the horses. Your brother will be better off with Hamish until he reaches the castle. I'll make sure you're never far away." His authoritative tone softened as he made the promise in the last sentence.

"As you wish," she said dully, too weary to argue.

Numbly, she watched Kylemore and Hamish lift Ben into the vehicle. They were careful with their burden, but her brother's tight expression indicated his pain. The jolting carriage would only worsen his discomfort, but they had no choice if they wished to get him to shelter.

She hurried forward and folded her brother's hand in hers again. "I'll see you at the castle," she murmured. Then she looked up at Hamish, who had climbed onto the bench beside Ben. "Look after him, Mr. Macleish."

"Aye, my lady, that I will. One of the lads has gone for the doctor. We'll have young Mr. Ashton right as rain in no time." Hamish took the reins and clicked his tongue at the horses.

"He'll be fine." Kylemore stepped up to stand at her shoulder as the carriage rolled away. "Don't worry, *mo gradh*."

His massive horse loomed behind him. The beast no longer frightened her. Compared to this afternoon's tribulations, her fear of horses seemed childish, feeble, unimportant.

She wiped her face with shaking fingers. Curse these tears. Soraya had never cried. Verity these days seemed to do little else. "How did you come to be here?"

"I pledged escort to Whitby. I'm a man of my word. I intended to follow at a discreet distance." Tension darkened his tone, and his gaze was grave and impossibly deep as he stared at her. "Thank God I did. The memory of my mother holding that knife to your lovely face will haunt me forever."

The reminder of the duchess's foul threats made her belly roil anew. "After she'd scarred me, she meant to hand me over to her henchmen for their amusement," she whispered.

Murderous anger flashed in his eyes. "I should have killed the bitch," he grated out fiercely.

She forced some strength into her tone. "Thankfully your good sense prevailed over your rage."

His lips turned down in bitter self-derision. "For once." Some of the intensity drained from his expression. "Come here, *mo leannan*. Your ordeal is over."

Weak fool that she was, she couldn't resist. She stepped into his embrace, and the world lit with warmth and safety. The empty years stretching ahead loomed cold and lonely when viewed from the circle of his arms. Because the prospect was so bleak, she forced her intentions into words yet again.

"I'm still leaving you, Kylemore," she said sadly. "You must make your own life. You must marry and have children."

"And you're going to what?" He paused thoughtfully, as if he considered the alternatives available to her. "Take a new protector and forget the wicked duke who kidnapped you?"

How could he be inhuman enough to mock? Leaving him had been the hardest thing she'd ever done, harder by far than turning her back on her upbringing and selling herself to Eldreth. Harder than facing the duchess's sickening vengeance.

"I'll never take another lover," she said brokenly, burying her face in his coat to hide fresh tears.

"No, I don't think you will," he said gently. "Hush now. You're too tired to fight. I'd win too easily. Let's go home."

She was too heartsick to protest at the word "home."

The castle would never be her home. She had no home apart from the man who gently lifted her onto Tannasg's back.

And that home was forever barred to her.

Kylemore slid into the saddle behind her and wrapped his arms securely around her waist. If only he could hold her safe like this forever. But even as they rode away toward his castle, she knew nothing had changed.

She was still a whore. He was still a duke.

And she still had to leave him.

Chapter 26

Papers littered the satinwood desk in Kylemore's beautiful library. It was very late, after midnight, and he made a desultory attempt to sift through the correspondence that had banked up in his absence.

But it was impossible to focus on petitioning letters or statements about his investments. He lifted the crystal glass of whisky he'd poured himself, then replaced it, untasted. He'd reached a pitch of bitter hopelessness far beyond the comforting warmth mere liquor could provide.

His gut clenched as he recalled the torture his mother had planned for Verity that day. The duchess had always been selfish and destructive, but her evil had festered unchecked to reach a peak of viciousness even he hadn't recognized.

Margaret Kinmurrie was lucky he hadn't shot her down like a rabid dog.

He wasn't sure why he hadn't. The rage and fear that had engulfed him on that lonely stretch of road still pounded like wild thunder through his veins.

What if he'd been too late? His hand tightened, white-knuckled, around the glass.

What if he'd acceded to Verity's wishes and not followed her at all?

No, he'd never have agreed to that. He'd sworn no harm would come to her. He'd sworn on his black soul.

Yet only hours after leaving his care, she'd faced disfigurement and rape, even death.

He'd never forgive his mother. *Or himself.*

It bedeviled him to think the duchess was retiring to the lovely dowerhouse. She'd be perfectly comfortable there, however barbarous she considered her surroundings.

He could draw some satisfaction from contemplating how she would chafe at her quarantine from the centers of power. She could fuck as many strapping footmen as she liked to while away the hours, but nothing would compensate for her loss of influence.

He sighed heavily and let yet another letter begging for his patronage drop unread to the desk. Terrible as the events of the day had been, they weren't what kept him here, sleepless and suffering.

The dumb misery that gnawed at him tonight stemmed from old heartbreak. Old heartbreak as sharp and fresh as when his mistress had abandoned him in Kensington so many months ago.

At the time, he'd blamed his mad frenzy on pride and lust.

Now he knew better. Verity had inflicted a mortal wound on him that day.

Over the last weeks, he'd foolishly believed that the wound had begun to heal. But his momentary reprieve in the glen had only sharpened his present anguish.

She'd plunged a blade into his heart, withdrawn it, then thrust it in again, deeper and harder.

Dully, he glanced up at the Roman triumph carved around the Adam mantel. Dancing maidens in swirling tunics led a garlanded bull to sacrifice at the delicate little temple in the far right-hand corner.

How keenly he envied the brute beast's ignorance. How he wished he faced his fate with similar insouciance. But he comprehended every measure of misery awaiting him.

Losing Verity was torment now, but as the long, barren years passed, the pain would weigh heavier and heavier, slowly squeezing the life from him.

She consigned him to a slow, agonizing death with her absence. A fitting punishment for what he'd done to her.

"Damn it all to hell," he groaned and buried his head in his hands.

He couldn't live without her.

He *had* to live without her. And he had no idea how he could do it.

"Damn it all to fucking hell."

In an excess of feeling, he flung his arm out and sent everything on the desk flying. The delicate whisky glass landed with a crack against the marble fireplace and shattered into tinkling shards.

"Your Grace?" Verity hovered in the doorway before him as if his imagination had invoked her.

He lunged to his feet and stared at her in helpless longing. Hungrily, he dwelled on every detail of her. He recognized her rose pink gown from the glen. She'd looped her hair back in a loose knot, revealing the perfect shape of her jaw and neck. Her hands were bandaged, and her slender throat was bruised. On her ashen face, the knife cut stood out as a stark red line. His anger and guilt surged anew at the reminder of what she'd borne because of him.

"Verity?"

Gently, she shut the elaborately carved double doors behind her, but she didn't venture further into the room. Her hands twined together nervously at her waist.

The gesture pierced him to the marrow. Surely she knew she had no reason to be afraid of him any more.

"I thought you'd be asleep. You're exhausted." The struggle for control made his voice flat.

How he sometimes missed the man he'd been. That man would have spirited her away to serve his pleasure without a thought to what was right or what she wanted. That man would take her and keep her and never let her go.

"I've been watching over Ben. The doctor says he can travel tomorrow if we go slowly and find appropriate transport."

"Stay here until he's recovered."

Stay here forever.

But she was already shaking her head. The pure lines of her face set with determination. "Kylemore, I must leave. Nothing has changed between us."

"No, nothing has changed." The saddest words in the language. He wanted to argue, object, insist she wait, but any reprieve merely postponed the inevitable. "Take one of my carriages so you travel in comfort."

She bent her head in acknowledgment. "Thank you."

Surprised at her ready agreement, he watched as she edged closer to the light. The brightness illuminated marks of weariness and unhappiness under her translucent eyes.

It slashed him to the heart to see her looking so defeated. His gaze focused on her cheek, where tendrils of hair escaped her simple hairstyle.

"Does your face hurt?" he asked in concern. "Christ! I should have been there to stop anything happening to you."

She smiled with an edge of irony. For a moment, Soraya's knowing, sophisticated ghost hovered. Then she was gone.

"Given what you prevented, I think I can manage to forgive you. It's only a scratch. It could have been much worse."

She drifted across to the wall to trail her hand along the alabaster top of a side table. When she raised her eyes, they were somber. She'd been pale when she'd entered the room; now every trace of color had drained from her face, leaving her white as new parchment.

"I've come to say good-bye," she said softly but implacably.

In a heartbeat, he circled the desk to reach for her. Then he remembered he no longer had the right to touch her.

"Oh, *mo leannan*," he said gruffly, although he knew it would achieve nothing. "Don't do this."

"I have to." Then, with visible effort, she added, "It's over and I must go. Heaven bless you, Your Grace."

His heart laden with despair, he watched her turn to leave. She straightened her back, as if she prepared to face an invincible foe.

It was an act of lonely gallantry. It was an act of breathtaking grace. As she walked away, he had no difficulty remembering that this woman had once held the glittering world in thrall.

In the flickering candlelight, he saw that her control wasn't as complete as she wanted him to think. The hand she extended to the latch shook as if she had a fever.

"Coward," he said softly but quite clearly behind her.

For a moment, he thought she hadn't heard.

Then she bent her head, revealing the vulnerable nape under the thickly piled hair. His throat closed with grief as he waited for her to push the door open and leave.

This was a last desperate gamble to keep her. He held no expectations he'd succeed.

"What did you call me?" she asked unsteadily.

He leaned back and braced himself on the desktop with his

hands. "I called you a coward," he said relentlessly. "My God, you were braver at fifteen."

"At fifteen, I had no choice," she choked out, still without facing him.

"Yes, you did. There's always a choice. And from that choice, you had the courage and the cleverness to create something marvelous. From chapel-going rustic to Europe's most famous courtesan? I'm awestruck."

Her elegant shoulders tensed under his attack, but mercifully, she didn't flee.

"I told you why I do this. It's for your sake," she said in a low voice.

"Rubbish. You're doing this because you're afraid." His tone lost some of its harshness. "Do you love me, Verity?"

She whirled around at the question. If he hadn't been fighting for his very life, he'd have relented then. Untold suffering was etched deep on her lovely face.

"That's not fair," she protested in a trembling voice.

No, it wasn't fair. But if he had to, he'd play dirty to win his prize. He'd do anything if it meant she stayed.

In truth, when he looked into her eyes, he already had the answer to his question.

But he continued remorselessly. "You've given me so much—your body, your trust, your comfort, your absolution, so many of your secrets. Yet that's something you've never said."

Arms outstretched against the inlaid marquetry, she pressed back into the door. In her flowing pink dress, she looked like a trapped butterfly. He stifled another wave of compassion.

"You've never said you love me either," she challenged.

He shrugged.

"I love you," he said.

It emerged with a naturalness even he hadn't expected.

For a moment, her gray eyes blazed with light as they

rested on him. Had so simple—and so momentous—an act as confessing his love finally won this battle for him?

But of course, it wasn't that straightforward.

She shook her head and glanced away. "Love isn't enough."

"It's a damned lot. Do you love me, Verity?"

She made a helpless gesture that tore at his heart, but he reminded himself he must be pitiless. For both their sakes.

"You must know I do," she admitted sadly.

Until a moment ago, he'd never been sure.

She loves me, she loves me, his heart chanted in a paean of elation. Surely now he couldn't lose her.

He fought to hide his burgeoning triumph. He hadn't won yet. "I know you're hellish ready to sacrifice yourself for the people you love. But in this particular case, you're misguided."

He took a deep breath and struggled to summon the words that would persuade her to stay. "And if you must sacrifice yourself, do that by marrying me. I'm not an easy man. You'll earn your martyr's crown before you're done. Don't condemn both of us to an eternity of unhappiness just because you're too stiff-necked to face society's censure."

"You make me sound so petty," she countered furiously. "But I know how highly you value your prestige. And you've always had Lucifer's own pride. You speak lightly of what you'd forfeit if you married me. But society's censure is crueler than you imagine. You've never had to suffer ostracism. I have."

"I can live with gossip and innuendo. I can't live without you," he said heavily.

What she said about his vanity and shallow worldliness was true. Or had been once.

But compared to the prospect of losing this one precious woman, nothing else mattered an ash in hell.

Her face contracted with turmoil. "You're like the Devil."

As she turned away, she sounded like she wasn't far from crying. "You speak seduction and tempt me to what I know is wrong."

He despised himself for hurting her this way, but he had to persevere in his ruthlessness or they were both lost.

"Marry me, become my duchess. What does anyone else matter? We can set up home in the Highlands far away from rumor and the world's disapproval. We'll create a life that's rich and fulfilled and useful. And based on love."

The eyes she leveled on him were dark and so tormented that his soul twisted in guilty agony. "Stop it, Kylemore. You're a duke. You owe an obligation to your title."

He frowned in sudden anger. All his life, his title had been a curse and a burden. Now it promised to deprive him of the only thing he'd ever wanted.

"What about my duty to myself? What about your duty?" he asked fiercely.

He drew himself upright and chanced a step in her direction. His voice became deep and sure as his brief rage receded in the face of her distress. "You've redeemed me, Verity. You've made me a better man, created honor where there was none."

"There was always honor," she whispered as tears flooded her beautiful eyes, making them shine dazzling silver.

"If there was, only you could have found it. You can't leave the task half done." He spread his hands in appeal. "Don't exile me to become the wicked Duke of Kylemore again. Now you've started the process, it's your Christian duty to finish dragging me into the light."

"Stop this," she protested brokenly. "It's cruel. You know only an illicit arrangement is possible between us. And I can't be your mistress after you wed, Kylemore. I've committed many sins, but I won't commit that one."

"If I don't marry you, I will never marry," he said quietly. "There are no more Kinmurries after me. The title dies when I do."

"Please don't say that," she begged, flinching away. "You must have an heir to take his rightful place in the world. Even if we wed and by a miracle I fall pregnant, our children will never be accepted."

"Our children will be beautiful, like their mother. And strong enough to fight their own way. You can't blame them for your obstinacy."

Last time he'd mentioned a baby, she'd been so certain she could never conceive. She sounded less certain now, he noted. Unconsciously, her hand drifted to her midriff, as though she already carried his child.

Perhaps she did.

He fought the primitive urges that thought aroused and strove to maintain his reasonable tone. Bullying and brute strength would never sway her. He'd only win her consent when she acknowledged that neither of them had the power or the right to deny what love demanded.

"Anyway, I'm sure I'm barren," she said bitterly.

"If that's true, then it will just be the mad duke and his exquisite wife alone in their Highland eyrie." He took another step toward her. She might run, but he doubted it. "You say society will scoff. I believe you're wrong. All the men, at least, in the ton will envy my good fortune."

He injected every ounce of grave sincerity he could muster into his voice. "Verity, be brave again. Be brave for both of us. I love you. Surely that's worth more than the world's scorn."

"Don't touch me." She recoiled, although he'd stopped several feet away. "When you touch me, I can't think."

For the first time, he smiled. "I know. You must reach this

decision on your own. See what an affliction you laid on me when you conjured honor from my soul?"

She didn't smile back. Instead, her face was drawn sharp with wretchedness.

"It would be so easy to say yes," she said bleakly.

"Then say yes," he coaxed, stealing nearer. "We have work to do to repair the damage my mother wrought on my estates. We have love to share. We have, God willing, children to raise to choose their own path. As their father chooses his own path. As their mother will do."

He paused, but she didn't speak. So he plowed on with all the desperate certainty he felt.

He was so sure. Why the Devil wasn't she? He drew in a shuddering breath. "Be brave, Verity, for their sake, for mine. Above all, for your own." Then, in a low, intense voice, "Don't leave me, *mo cridhe*. It tears the heart from my body to think of living without you."

He stretched out his hand. To his humiliation, it shook. But what did his pride matter now?

She looked away, fighting tears. Frantically, he searched his mind for something else to say, something that would finally convince her to stay.

But words proved such a frail weapon against her will. Instead, he stood grieving, in agony, struggling to accept that he'd failed.

"Oh, hell," he groaned and turned aside. He couldn't watch her walk away from him again. And this time, it would be forever.

All hope was gone. He'd lost.

Silence stretched endlessly between them.

His breath caught as he steeled himself to listen to the door open. When it closed, it would close on his every happiness. He strained to hear her soft footfall fade into the distance as she abandoned him to his desolation.

Still she didn't move.

What was she waiting for? His hands clenched into fists at his sides.

He'd kneel and beg if he thought it would do any good, but he knew in his heart that no plea could change her mind.

He didn't doubt now that she loved him. The tragedy was that she just didn't love him enough.

"No." Her voice cracked on the word.

Of course that's what she'd say. Hell, hadn't she tried to escape him ever since he'd first seen her?

She'd flung him back into his perpetual ice. He supposed he should be inured to it, but for one flaring moment, love had beckoned with false promises of life and warmth. So his fate now was impossible to bear.

With a soft crackle, a log crumbled to embers in the grate. The sound spurred him to movement, anything to break this agonizing stasis.

"Heaven keep you too," he said hoarsely, blindly trying to find his way back to the desk.

"No," she said more strongly. "Don't go."

He felt her fumble at his sleeve like an importunate creditor. He stopped in trembling bewilderment.

Her touch burned like fire through the superfine of his coat. Its heat was alien to the cold creeping death slowly moving through him.

"Do you really love me, Kylemore?" she whispered.

Why did she torture him like this? She must see his overwhelming misery.

Shamingly, his voice broke as he answered. "I die for love of you, *mo leannan*."

The hand on his arm tightened. "Then God help me. God help us both," she said huskily. "But, yes, I'll be your duchess."

What he heard made no sense.

"What did you say?" His question emerged as a bewildered croak.

He heard her inhale before she spoke. "I love you, Justin Kinmurrie, and I will marry you," she said clearly.

By God, this couldn't be true. Had he won after all?

He twisted around and grabbed her shoulders roughly, because in his extremity, gentleness was beyond him. "Say it again."

Tears glittered on her cheeks, but the gaze that met his was alight with certainty. "I will marry you."

The bruising force of his grasp eased. "And the rest."

"Justin Kinmurrie, I love you." She gave a fractured laugh that chimed oddly with her weeping. "I love you and I'll take up residence in your barbarian country, and if I can, I'll give you a pack of wild Highland brats to torment you into old age. And if that doesn't terrify you, you're brave to the point of recklessness."

She tried to make him smile. But he was beyond levity.

"Oh, Verity," he rasped as he clawed her into his arms. She gave a muffled sob against his shoulder and clung to him with the same possessiveness.

Eventually, he lifted his head and looked into her face. No trace now of the pale, unhappy woman who had come to him earlier. Color flushed her flawless skin, and her silver eyes glowed with incandescent joy, even through her tears.

Her beauty had caught and held him at first. But now he saw so much more. Strength. Honesty. Loyalty. Trust.

And love. So much love it banished the chill from his soul forever.

"I thought I'd lost you," he said in a wondering voice. "I thought you were going to leave me."

"Never," she said fervently. "Never. Never."

She dragged his head down to hers for a clumsy, passionate kiss that tasted of weeping and happiness. As she drew away, he caught her face in his hands and looked searchingly into her rain-clear eyes.

At last, no shadows lurked in those radiant depths.

Passion beckoned, as it would always beckon when he was with her. But for the moment, he resisted its urgings. "I swear to make you happy, Verity," he said gravely.

Her face filled with a love so powerful that it humbled him. "Just love me, Justin."

"Forever," he vowed.

"Yes, forever."

And he did.

AVON TRADE *Paperbacks*